B

Created & Written
by

"Frank Julius" Csenki - (Author)

www.frankjulius.com

Published by

FRANK JULIUS BOOKS

ISBN 978-0-9950178-4-9

First Edition - January 2016

BLOOD DICE

To: Rooney

Very Nice To Have Met!

Enjoy

[illegible signature]

BLOOD DICE

Prologue

Last night the moon, the stars and all the planets fell on me. If you fellows ever pray, pray for me.

Harry S. Truman
Statement to the press. April 13, 1945

The President of The United States of America, William Fenton, sat motionless in his chair behind the now famous desk in the now famous Presidential oval office. Many great men had known both the pleasure and the torment of the Presidential seat. For some the chair was a perfect fit, others found it at times politically uncomfortable and even detrimental to political longevity or ultimate legacy. History would judge individuals on how the chair fit. On this day in history, however, it belonged to William Fenton.

The President looked straight ahead at the five distinguished people, also sitting in chairs arranged in a semi-circular fashion directly in front of his desk. President Fenton was considered by many to be a very young man to hold the nation's highest office. He was a likable person with a pleasant personality and disposition. Today President Fenton was not amused. Recent events necessitated this emergency meeting of his top aides. It was a comfortable sixty-nine degrees Fahrenheit in the white house on this evening; all personnel in the oval office on this day were sweating.

President Fenton had both the natural cunning of a fox and the compassion for his fellow man that one only develops by having suffered personal losses of their own.

President Fenton looked carefully at each man individually as his eyes scanned the faces looking back at him. Facing the President from left to right in this semi-circle of power was Vic Amber; Director of The CIA and President Fenton's close friend.

Amber and The President had attended the same university overseas as classmates and had become great friends over the years. Next to Vic Amber sat Howard Rickover; The Secretary of Defense.

Next to Rickover was Mitchell Farnsworth; Secretary of State a very admirable man who was very highly regarded internationally as a man of action, persuasion, and trust but a hawk to be sure.

Cyril Burgess; The President's National Security Adviser sat next to The Secretary of State, and beside Burgess, was A.B. Kingsbury; the Director of The FBI, who was a tall man, graying black hair…one who projected authority and decisiveness.

All these fine men of valor looked upon William Fenton with anticipation.

"Gentlemen, your recommendations please," said the President forcefully. His voice, remaining calm but assertive.

President Fenton's eyes panned the five faces and came to rest on Howard Rickover's eyes; The Secretary of Defense.

Rickover began, "Mr. President, you already know my feelings on this subject. I am convinced beyond a shadow of any doubt that it is absolutely vital to our tactical defense parameters that this agreement remain in place. I cannot at this time favor an alternate site that would in my opinion even come close to the operational readiness that this site offers, not to mention the strategic advantage considering the geographic location. I strongly recommend to you Mr. President, not to deviate from the original plan."

"What about you Cyril?" The President asked of his National Security Adviser.

"Well Mr. President, I concur with Secretary Rickover. I too am convinced that the situation as it now stands will no doubt provide us with the needed upgrade in facilities on which we've been negotiating for years now and can only enhance our overall defense capability in that region of the globe. Especially when you take into consideration Sir, our domestic military base closing program.

Not only will it provide added deterrent to our number one concern but it will also give us increased strength and higher military profile in a region of the world that is fast becoming more hostile every day and geopolitically destabilized. I too recommend no deviation from the plans now in place Sir." Rickover finished saying.

He then he looked around the semi-circle of colleagues seeking eye contact with the others and agreement. He got what he was looking for; the four men all nodded in agreement expressing their silent approval to the President.

Fenton started in again, "A.B., are you convinced that the tactics you've employed with your team and organization are truly sound?"

Fenton was still uncomfortable and needed further assurance.

Kingsbury answered The President in no uncertain terms. "Mr. President, I can assure you Sir that my people will act as they have been trained to both in the field as well as here in Washington. That I have no qualms about. You can rest assured Mr. President." Kingsbury said most emphatically and directly to his boss.

The others in the room had no doubt that Kingsbury was telling it as it was, straight and narrow, to the point, no bullshit.

Fenton then wrapped things up in own special way. "Now look gentlemen, this operation must, I repeat must go smoothly. I want no glitches, nor any cause for suspicion cast upon this administration of any wrong doings. This administrative policy is in the best interest of The United States, its national security, and overall political stability not only for us but the entire free world. That is what is at stake here gentlemen. Do I make myself clear? I must have air-tight integrity and continuity. There must be no leaks. Everything will continue to unfold as normally as the sun rises each morning. Bring Mr. Davis into the sunlight and have him see things our way. You are to monitor and assist with our cooperation, but gentlemen; and how can I put this mildly? Let's not give away the store okay? I trust that we understand each other clearly."

All eyes glanced around the room at the others seated in front of President Fenton and once again like robots, all men nodded in agreement. The President stood up out of his chair and began to come around his large oval office desk. As he did so ever so smoothly and calculating, he started saying, "That will be all, for now, gentlemen, please keep me apprised."

As the President's men were in the process of departing, there came a heavy burden of desperation over William Fenton, and as he escorted the last member of his advisory committee out of his oval office he placed his palm on the back of Vic Amber's back and closed the door behind The Director of The Central Intelligence Agency.

The President turned to look out the large picture window directly behind his oval office desk, and he gazed out into oblivion. William Fenton was deep in thought.

The President thought to himself. "This is the last thing I need so early in my administration, especially with The Balkan crisis and Gulf War still fresh in American's minds not to mention the recent cruise missile launches into Iraq in response to the assassination attempt on the former President."

The thing that really got to President Fenton was the fact that he had recently been gaining in the polls on his approval rating. Sure, his commitment to Haiti and the re-establishment of democracy there had helped, but if word of this now gets out, everything will be lost.

"Damn it!" The President was thinking out loud to himself now.

He looked at his Omega Constellation wristwatch; a university graduation gift from Vic Amber, after they both graduated from Cambridge in England, it showed 5:27 PM. He was due for a nationally televised press conference in another hour. The President was mindful that there might already have been a leak to the press. Yes, knowing the grapevine in Washington he could not realistically rule out that possibility altogether. He may indeed be faced with having to dodge questions concerning "*The Caribbean Initiative, and Island Hop*."

Decisions had to be made, and President Fenton had now made one.

"Now he will have to face the music. At least this time he was familiar with the tune and with the words," he thought.

President Fenton reached for his intercom and announced to his communications director that he was now ready to receive The White House television makeup crew. As the crew came in to prepare the President for his second only televised national press conference since having taken office, William Fenton then said:

"All right people, bring on the lions, the crowd anxiously awaits."

***

CHAPTER ONE

Why then the world's mine oyster
Which I with sword will open.

William Shakespeare
The Merry Wives of Windsor

Cathy Davis was six years old today on this beautiful winter's day in sunny south Florida. Cathy was very busy explaining to her imaginary, secret *bestest* friend in the whole wide world "*Jodie*," just how much fun it will be to have a new addition to her doll collection. This new addition was being delivered by her loving Daddy today for her birthday. The new doll was the Fashion Barbie.

Cathy played in her playroom. She danced with her dolls and was filled with innocent joy, totally oblivious to the world outside. So pretty she was, with the sunlight beaming and radiating through her ebony hair. Her faced flushed with the excitement of her Daddy's arrival.

Cathy thought to herself. "Not too much longer to go now. When the big hand on the Mickey Mouse clock reached the top, to the center of Mickey's face making Mickey look cross-eyed, and Mickey's little hand reached the center of the clock right in between Mickey's feet to the tops of his black shoes, well that was when Daddy would be home!" Cathy began singing out loud now.

"London Bridge is falling down, falling down falling down,

London Bridge is falling down, my fair lady."

Jason's palms were now sweating profusely as he positioned himself just down the street from the Davis estate. He pressed down on the clutch pedal of the Astro Van and gently placed the vehicle into gear. Then he started driving slowly towards the Davis estate address; 6565 Sailfish Drive Pompano Beach Florida.

This was the home of Eldon Barnes Davis, the founder and Chief Executive Officer of Davis International, one of the most prestigious and influential investment firms in the country.

Today, Jason was to pose as a flower delivery person arriving at exactly 5:40 PM just late enough for Mrs. Davis to allow him entry through the security gate without too much of an interrogation, so he could be gone before her husband arrived home at 6:00 PM.

Jason had plans; big plans that were now in place. He believed his plans would enable him to realize his golden opportunity once and for all. Jason had been contracted for this job, a verbal contract, with clear instructions. But now being on the scene, Jason felt he had some leeway to do as he pleased.

His assignment was to pluck Eldon's daughter right from under his nose, from this little fortress on Sailfish Drive. It mattered not how he accomplished his task; the main thing was that he do it!

That part of the assignment was left up to him and him alone. Jason thought a great deal of himself. He was famous. A legend in his own mind, that is. He was most pleased with himself having established a long but not so illustrious career of crime. This upcoming act would place him into the big leagues.

His string of successful seven-eleven robberies and a few bank hits earned him enough of a reputation to alert the local authorities but only to attract vague federal level notice. Jason enjoyed taking other people's things. He had a phobia for taking things; he was a born thief. He enjoyed that sort of thing. Up until today, it had always been material things and cash. Jason had his fling in the illegal transport of aliens into The United States via The Bahamas along with smuggling and trafficking; now he was entering a new dimension; kidnapping.

Jason had promoted himself to kidnapper extraordinaire. This surely will bring national attention and he, yes; he will be the one pulling off this dandy little move. As with anything else; Jason chalked it up to experience. He figured, the more you did something, the better you became at it and that was pretty much how Jason looked at things in general.

Yes he was turning into a proper criminal willing to take the stakes higher with each new opportunity.

Jason's many casual acquaintances would have never thought him to be suspect of wrong doings. On the surface of everyday life, Jason appeared quite normal. But deep down, the truth be known, he reveled in his dark side, and now a soon to be kidnapper of little girls.

He especially found justification in America's history of the Noriega trials and Iran-Contra scandal, and don't even mention the President's misleading private affairs, what a joke, screwing the country like that!

This just added more fuel to his fired way of thinking. Jason squeezed out a personal sense of pride knowing that his government was engaged in the same type of activity as he now was. In Jason's mind, all of his actions were justified by the facts of his country's involvement with Noriega and the Iranians and the wool pulled over the American public's eyes on oil for humanity in Iraq.

Jason figured that if The US government was designed to penetrate Iran's Oil wealth, do a little skimming off the top and fund the contras in some Central American banana republic with hostage money, well hell what he was doing was just the same. Just like Robin Hood, stealing from Peter to pay Paul. Only this way Jason was always Paul and Jason loved to steal. After all, he was a thief.

Jason had always envied other people who had fancy things. Even in his teens growing up in heartland USA he yearned for fancy cars, fancy clothes, a fancy lifestyle and of course fancy girls.

Well wait no longer, now he was on his way to get himself a fancy little girl from one of those fancy Florida styled homes with the pink tile roof sitting on the Intracoastal waterway in the most exclusive neighborhood from Miami to Palm Beach and best of all, it was just down the street!

Linda Davis was, to say the least, excited. Today was her precious little girl's birthday, and nothing, nothing in the world was going to get in her way of celebrating this marvelous day. It will be just the three of them Eldon, Linda and Cathy.

A small family, but a happy family. Linda Davis herself was a beautiful woman. That being said, however; did no justice to describe her beauty. This lady commanded attention. She was incredibly attractive. Strangers would at times just plain stare at her. She carried herself as if she had just stepped from the front doors of the country's finest finishing schools in the art of glamor and beauty. Her posture was as graceful as a gazelle is swift and yet there was a sense of ease about her that invited one to enter her aura and feel completely at ease while staring into her emerald green eyes highlighted by her shoulder length jet black ebony hair.

She seemed to have a constant smile on her face. Not a put-on to be sure but more of her inner warmth planted ever so softly onto her moist lips. This was Linda Davis. Today Linda's heart was filled with joy. She had just been informed over the telephone by her family doctor that their dreams were to be finally realized; they were indeed going to have another baby.

A loving addition to the Davis family. So, in fact, there was inner warmth emanating from Linda. A genuine glow of motherly love and Linda's face was beaming with affection and content that she had for her family.

Cathy especially needed a loving sister or brother. Neither Eldon nor Linda wanted to see Cathy having to grow up on her own. They didn't want her missing the elements of sharing and learning experiences that brothers and sisters have in common. Linda was overcome with anxiety. She had only received confirmation from Doctor Perry today, just within the last hour and now she could hardly wait for her husband; Eldon to finally arrive home.

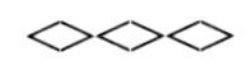

Eldon Barnes Davis was due into Ft. Lauderdale International Airport at 5:15 PM and if things went well he should be home by 6 PM as usual.

The Davis's sprawling estate was just north of Ft. Lauderdale in the affluent section of Pompano Beach, taking up a good four acres of prime

Intracoastal waterway footage. Eldon's Canadair corporate jet was usually on time. His Jaguar would be pulling up through his estate's security gate very soon now. Cathy would not have much longer to wait, only another forty minutes or so. Cathy could still be heard singing out loud...

"London Bridge is falling down, falling down, falling down, London Bridge is falling down, my fair lady."

Jason had made certain that the van he had stolen for this job was a good one. He wanted a vehicle that was reliable and therefore had to be almost new. The Wal-Mart employee arrived on time, and his vehicle fit the bill perfectly. The employee locked his van, but for Jason, it was not a challenge to steal it, it was a “piece of cake.” This too was just second nature to Jason. Stealing a van or car was something Jason became an expert at over the last few years. Jason would need the van for exactly twenty-one and a half miles.

This would be just far enough for Jason to drive north getting him to U-2 Play in Boynton Beach after having abducted the Davis girl from the Davis estate in Pompano Beach. There he would ditch the van after changing vehicles. Jason had spent the last ten weeks staking out the Davis estate. He wanted to be certain of the routine comings and goings on of the Davis family. His assignment came with plenty of time for preparation. He knew this had to be done right or not at all.

These were high stakes now. Jason was now to the point in his preparation that he knew exactly when Eldon left his home in the mornings to go to his corporate office headquarters in Ft. Lauderdale and the time that he returned home for the day.

Oddly enough Jason had determined that Eldon never came home before 6:00 PM, always just a minute or two afterward, depending upon traffic. Jason also determined that Eldon liked to drive himself to his office. Eldon apparently was someone who enjoyed driving and liked his Jaguar.

Unbeknownst to Jason, Eldon was flying in from Canada tonight just in time for Cathy's birthday celebration later this evening and would be home at the usual time just after 6:00 PM. The one lone guard at the gate house marking the entrance to the Davis estate had gone off shift at 5:30 PM and had done so every Friday; Jason had noted. That left an entire half hour with which to play and a great deal of negligence in security at the Davis estate. This would no doubt be regretted by Eldon.

Jerry the day guard, for the Davis estate had pestered Mrs. Davis long enough so that Linda had finally given in agreeing to let Jerry leave a half hour early on Fridays so that Jerry could catch the last Greyhound bus up to Altamonte Springs.

Jerry had his son living up north, and Jerry loved to visit his grandchildren spending the weekends with his son and daughter in law. If Jerry wouldn't be able to leave by 5:30 PM on Fridays, well he just wouldn't be able to make it and Mrs. Davis, well she understood.

Mrs. Davis, she was such a nice lady she was, “yessum” that she was. Jerry had been guarding the entrance to the Davis estate ever since Mr. and Mrs. Davis had moved to Florida from up north in Jersey there and that was pretty near five years ago now. That Mrs. Davis was the prettiest white woman Jerry ever did see and probably the best hearted and the kindest woman he'd ever come across in years, black or white. Mr. Davis, well now there was another story there. Smart as one of them there computers he was, had a brain like one, he heard tell, and sharp as a well-honed knife. But Jerry also heard tell that Mr. Davis was as cunning as a black swamp Florida Gator. No sir, Jerry did not want to get on the bad side of Mr. Davis. Mr. Davis was a man to be respected, he was.

Jerry left his post at exactly 5:30 PM making absolutely sure that the gate's auto locking system was engaged and the remote cameras were in the operational mode. Satisfied that all was in order, Jerry left and was on his way to see his grandchildren just outside of Orlando. Jerry was going to have a terrific weekend and leave the driving to Greyhound. Jerry's partner, Winston, wouldn't arrive for his evening shift for another half an hour. Jerry figured all was safe and sound at the Davis estate. Jerry was dead wrong.

Jason's palms were still sweating making his hands feel clammy. He was wearing a one-piece jumpsuit; rubber soled shoes, a pair of wrap around dark sunglasses, a false but well-groomed beard and most importantly he had a fake nose job that widened and lengthen his nose just enough to totally change his real appearance. Jason's disguise was crude but most effective. There was no way that anyone knowing Jason would have recognized him. Jason was a tall man, and quite heavy, sporting somewhat of a beer belly.

Jason was now ready; this was the moment in time. He pressed down on the accelerator and the van began moving down the street to the Davis estate on Sailfish Drive. He drove the van up into the driveway leading to the Davis estate and stopped in front of the automatic steel gates and flush with the intercom to the Davis house.

He reached out his driver's side window and pressed the intercom button. Instantly inside the house, Linda's attention was drawn to the sound of chimes from the front gate system, out at the front gate, Jason listened. He heard it ring once, twice, three times and then he heard Linda's voice. Linda Davis came straight away once she heard the chimes from the gate. As Linda came to answer the gate, she thought to herself "oh, well, of course, its Friday and Jerry has left early as always, I wonder who it could be out there."

Linda pressed the intercom button inside the house in the foyer and answered saying, "yes, who is it please?"

Jason was absolutely ecstatic, overwhelmed to hear her voice. Jason was terrified, and yet at the same time, he was cool as ice. This was the big one. He was about to speak to Linda Davis, wife of Eldon Barnes Davis, one of the richest men in America.

This was Jason's biggest and most dangerous prize yet. Linda had something that wasn't his but soon would be.

"Ah, Mrs. Davis, Mrs. Linda Davis please," Jason said, with a tone of uncertainty but just right.

"Yes, who is this please?" Linda asked. She was totally calm and expressed a normal tone in her voice. She had no reason for concern; not yet.

Jason continued, with control in his voice, "Ma'am this is the delivery man from Martin's flower boutique in Deerfield Beach. I have a very special delivery marked as a birthday arrangement; it's quite a large one at that. Where do you wish for me to leave this Mrs. Davis?"

Linda was not surprised at all. Floral deliveries had been coming for the past couple of days to The Davis estate.

Maria Sanchez; the housemaid would usually take care of the procedure, but Linda had given her the day off as well since it was Cathy's birthday, and Linda would tend to receiving the flowers today.

"Okay," Linda said, "you can bring the flowers to the front door. Just drive on through the gate when it opens up."

Linda hated going through these precautions, but she knew very well that Eldon had the security system installed for their own protection.

Linda continued on, "look, you'll have to first get out of your vehicle and step directly in front of the security system camera for a facial ID. After I get a printout of your face please hold up a piece of picture identification so that I can verify that you are who you say that you are. It must have a picture of you on it. Is that clear?" Linda asked.

She was somewhat embarrassed about the whole thing.

She hated doing this so. Naturally, Jason was only too happy to comply. His false picture ID was complete with beard and only made yesterday with official Martin Flower Boutique logo. Jason left nothing to chance in this respect.

And so, Jason responded, "yes, Mrs. Davis, that will be fine, I'm getting out of my van now and approaching the camera, is this okay?"

Jason asked. This was really turning Jason on, causing his heart rate to increase.

Linda waited for the camera to autofocus on the delivery man as he stood in front of the lens. She didn't pay very close attention, only impatient to get this whole process over with. She did, however, notice his sunglasses and requested that he remove them before she hit the button inside for the color

Canon laser printer to generate the image of Jason's false face.

As Jason stood there and removed his sunglasses, he said to himself under his breath "you're mine bitch, you're all mine." As Jason thought this, a smile developed over his face. The camera focused and the laser printer generated the image. Jason held up his employee identification card to the camera so it could focus on that too.

Linda compared the two and seemed satisfied. She did momentarily think to herself that this man was an unusual looking character, but then, after all, he was delivering flowers for God's sake.

Linda had always given everyone the benefit of the doubt. It was just the way she was; her nature wouldn't allow her to act any differently. That was one reason that she was so liked by all who knew her. Eldon was always on to her about how she could never be too careful. Linda continued on saying, "okay, then, please drive on up, I'll open the gates for you. Please leave the flowers outside at the front door."

No, this wasn't what Jason wanted! He had to have contact with her. He had to act fast.

Jason responded, "ah Mrs. Davis, Ma'am, this is such a large arrangement, it would be kind of you to sign for it please, plus it ought to be set upright cause it is quite heavy," Jason added that just with the right amount of urgency in his voice.

Linda thought nothing of it. She responded saying, "oh, sure, no problem, I'll take the flowers from you at the front door, come on through."

She then pushed the button opening the front gates of the Davis Estate to Jason. Jason got back into his stolen van and drove on up to the Davis estate.

Jason now felt adrenaline just pumping into his system. He could taste it in his mouth. It was now 5:35 PM. Right on time; another twenty-five seconds and Linda Davis would be his.

Jason reached over to the passenger seat to pick up the special floral arrangement. It had cost Jason a whopping hundred and eighty Dollars. It was a most fitting collection though for this occasion. Beautiful hibiscuses and oleander spotted with orchids throughout with just the right touch of birds of paradise.

No doubt would be cast on the authenticity of the good intentions this bouquet implied and surely enough to garner the attention of even the most discerning critic, if only for a few seconds; that is all that Jason needed, just a few seconds of time.

Jason was certain that this arrangement would buy him the time that he needed, just four or five seconds to catch Linda off guard and grabbing her by surprise by which time it would already be too late. Ironically the oleander's little know poisonous chemical contents provided the right touch of drama to this act, taking Jason even to higher levels of deceit.

Jason drove the van to the front door of the Davis home. Linda Davis opened the door as the van pulled up front and for the first time, Jason had a chance to lay his eyes upon Linda Davis from close range, and in real life.

The pictures he had of her did her no justice at all. In real life she was stunning. She was awesome and enchanting.

She stood approximately five feet seven inches tall, dressed in a light cotton summer dress. She wore expensive tan colored leather sandals on her feet. She was just standing there appearing to be somewhat impatient, waiting for Jason to get out of the van and bring about the delivery. Her silky shoulder length ebony hair gently lifted in the Florida trade wind's breeze, pushing through her hair and making her look like a mythical Greek Goddess. Jason paused for just a few brief moments as he too got caught up in her aura of mystique.

Then Jason came to his senses and bounced back to the task at hand. Jason picked up the arrangement of flowers from out of the van with his left hand. He climbed out of the van and came around the front and up the curb to face Linda directly. Linda's eyes locked onto the fantastic arrangement of flowers immediately and exclaimed, "Oh my, those flowers are absolutely beau..."

Before Linda knew what had happened, she realized that the delivery man had entered into her space but by that time it was already too late. The flowers of beauty had drawn out the Princess into the evil grasp of the ogre. It had worked perfectly for Jason. The arrangement had provided the momentary distraction Jason had counted upon. He was upon her like a mountain lion clawing its prey. He would not let go until his quarry was a kill.

With his right hand, Jason quickly reached out and grabbed her neck from the front, just under her chin and squeezed tightly. Ever so tightly; Jason's comparative massive weight and frame came to bear down upon Linda as she was caught by total shock, with terror filling her heart as this man of steel gripped her with the force of an industrial vice.

Linda knew immediately that resistance was futile. It would only result in further tightening of the vice on her throat, even just a half turn tighter and her windpipe would be crushed, causing her to die.

Suddenly there was a sharp pain in Linda's right side just above her hip, and at the same instance,

Linda felt that her throat was about to be ripped away from out of her neck!

Then to her amazement, as suddenly as it had come, the pain in her neck eased, but the pain in her side now became excruciating and spread clear across her back.

Linda opened her eyes and found herself facing the open the door to which she had her back towards just a moment or two ago, and now found that her attacker was repositioned behind her.

A hand with a latex surgical glove that had acted as the vice around her neck now came around quickly up under her right arm and back around her to the back of her neck, pressing her in a downward direction and forward at the same time.

Linda felt like she was going fall ahead, but her massive assailant held her body up. She was now totally in his control. If she dare yell; and she wanted to desperately, only if she could; she knew that her neck would be snapped in an instant. All Linda could do was to cry silent tears.

Jason had applied a "half nelson," a wrestler's hold, to the top half of Linda's body.

With his left hand, Jason had withdrawn a hunting knife from inside of his jumpsuit and slid the eight-inch stainless steel blade across the width of her back from Linda's right kidney to her left. Jason cut into Linda, leaving an incision in Cathy's mother's back making blood flow the entire length of the knife's path.

Linda’s breathing increased rapidly as she became fully aware of the imminent danger to her life, Cathy's life and the life of her unborn child; just weeks old.

Linda was now overcome with panic; she could not scream, nor force the slightest sound from her larynx.

Jason was forcing Linda's head straight down as far as it would bend without actually breaking it which made it virtually impossible for her to even utter the faintest of sounds.

Jason spoke, “all right there Mrs. Davis, listen carefully now… will you, hon?” Jason said those words, so sarcastically and with a matter of fact tone, then he added, “you and I are going for a little walk."

Linda knew that to struggle would be in vain. She had no choice but to be dragged by this monster to wherever he wanted to go, she would be quiet.

Just as Jason was about to drag and force her deeper into the foyer of the house, he clearly heard the high-pitched voice he was looking for.

Cathy's singing came from down the hall; just straight ahead. Yes, Cathy's singing could be heard loud and clear.

"Falling down, falling down, London Bridge is falling down, my fair lady."

Jason, of course, responded to this immediately.

"Well now, Mrs. Davis, it looks like we need go no further. Your daughter will lead me right to her. And as for you, London Bridge is coming down, right on top of your neck."

Having said that, Jason snapped Linda's neck with a loud crack of the vertebrate. He then thrust the full eight inches of the hunting knife's cold stainless steel blade into and through Linda's left kidney, thereby terminating Linda Davis's twenty-ninth year of life on this earth, and the third week of her unborn child's.

Having finished with her, Jason then released the grip he had on her body and dropped Linda's nerve quivering corpse to the marble floor with a thud. Blood spewed from the gaping wound along Linda's back and sides. Jason learned how to become a cold-blooded killer today. It came to him so easily. No hesitation, no guilt. Jason had become a very dangerous man.

***

Chapter Two

I feel when I sorrow most:
It is better to have loved and lost
Than never to have loved at all.

Alfred Lord Tennyson - In Memoriam

"This is Lauderdale Control to Canadair niner-niner, do you copy?" "Ah, Roger control, this is a niner-niner copy you and requesting vector for final approach."

"Roger Canadair, niner-niner, turn left twenty degrees, then descend to twelve hundred feet and you are cleared for landing on runway 2A."

"Roger, control, copy and cleared to land on runway 2A on final, Canadair niner-niner out."

Billy Simpson had been flying as a corporate pilot for Mr. Davis now for the better part of his civilian career. As far as Billy Simpson was concerned, there would be no need for any career changes in the foreseeable future.

Scoring this coveted corporate piloting position was about as golden of a job he could think of ever landing not to mention the additional benefits that came along with such duty. On top of all that, Billy had never been treated with more respect and regard for his professionalism as he received from Mr. Davis.

Flying for Davis Investments all over the free world definitely had its fair share of rewards. Billy had logged a good deal of hours flying to be sure, but at a hundred and sixty thousand Dollars annual salary; Billy wasn't complaining. There wasn't a place on earth that Billy hesitated flying to. When Mr. Davis called Billy, well… Billy was ready.

There had been many occasions when Mr. Davis wasn't in a position to give Billy much notice. Eldon just called, and Billy was just ready. That was the sort of relationship and understanding the two men had for each other. That perhaps was the only single drawback to this job, if there was one at all. Billy began to understand that in the world of high financial stakes, sometimes being there yesterday was already too late.

With the financial world becoming more and more a global community it seemed like Mr. Davis should be in ten places at once. With renewed unrest in the Persian Gulf and the volatile economic conditions in the far east and now globally, hard currencies the world over were bouncing up and down like rubber balls, and it took a shrewd financial manipulator to stay on top of his game.

Billy soon learned that Eldon Barnes Davis, his boss was that sort of man. But that was all Mr. Davis's area. Billy Simpson did not concern himself with Mr. Davis's business, only his travel needs and his safety when in Billy's presence. Mr. Davis was a man to be seen with and a man who garnered the attention of the international banking community, heads of states and other dignitaries. He was most of all respected and sought out for his opinion and viewpoints. Billy was grateful; this sure as hell beat flying the Greyhounds of the skies.

Billy was a Gulf War Vet. He was proud of it too. He was an ex F14 Tomcat fighter pilot. Billy had seen a great deal of action in the gulf running numerous sorties over enemy territory that finally resulted in his downing, by ground to air heat seeking missiles. His plane was hit badly, and Billy bailed out only to be captured and held as a POW in a hell hole of an Iraqi prisoner of war facility. Billy's fortitude, determination and burning desire to be free lead to a well-planned escape that proved successful.

Billy eventually earned the Congressional Medal of Honor and Purple Heart. Billy had served his country well with passion and integrity. Now Billy Simpson was doing just the same thing but this time for Mr. Davis. When he committed himself to duty, he gave his one hundred percent and then some. Billy Simpson was a proud American. Billy could be counted upon unquestionably.

Eldon could now feel the descent of his jet as they approached Ft. Lauderdale Florida. He had been airborne for exactly three hours and five minutes. There were no time zones to cross on this flight. Eldon was thankful for that. He would be saved from the jet lag that usually accompanied him on most of his flights. He was a well-traveled man.

Eldon knew and had learned from experience, when to sleep and when not to sleep on various flights. This enabled his internal body clock to adjust as smoothly as possible to time zone changes. This practice allowed him to perform at peak efficiency at all times. It no longer mattered to Eldon if his travels took him across the Pacific to Hong Kong or The Atlantic to Brussels. Eldon coped. He coped well.

Today, however, was an important day. Eldon was grateful to Billy for getting him home on time for his darling little girl's birthday. Linda too would be pleased about the good news he had concerning the financial package he had just signed and delivered with The Canadian government and Ontario Hydro the electric company for the province of Ontario.

Eldon hadn't known that the nuclear generating plant in the city of Pickering, just east of Toronto on Lake Ontario was the largest nuclear facility in the world.

Eldon was fascinated with technology, especially things on a grand scale such as nuclear power generating stations.

Eldon tried to involve his wife Linda as much as possible into his business dealings and business life. He believed in sharing as much of, his life both professionally and nonprofessionally with his wife as he could manage.

Linda welcomed this. She showed a keen interest in a variety of issues and Eldon realized that Linda often provided Eldon with confidence and support. She always offered Eldon her good sense and alternate points of view allowing Eldon to examine issues from all aspects. Eldon valued her positive sided opinions on socially impacting actions.

He would look forward to discussing his recent dealings with Linda that he had reached with The Canadian government.

Eldon thought to himself about those Canadians. "They certainly lived up to their reputation of being cautious business people." Eldon had managed to convince a group of investors based in Toronto to act in harmony with the Canadian government and the Ontario Hydro Corporation.

In accomplishing this, he secured the financing for the development of a new generation of nuclear power stations to be built in Canada and then exporting the new technology worldwide. The fact that private money had been introduced to the financing mix had supplied the equation with the added stimulus it required to ensure that it got off of the ground.

This was a ten-billion-Dollar venture in which Eldon was instrumental in making it all happen. Besides all of that, Eldon had special reasons of his own to be especially proud of this project.

Not only had he put together the greatest financing package in the history of his company. But at the same time managed to save the environment from being raped further in having to flood millions of acres of land to accommodate an equivalent sized electric dam project which would have been the alternative. This way everyone involved came out a winner.

The new technology would generate income for both the government and its private investors, and above all, Eldon felt that he had a special hand in having saved a great deal of pristine wilderness.

Eldon's next project was already taking shape in his mind. He'd harbored a great interest in energy development and intensified his research into the field of superconductivity.

Eldon envisioned a time when his company would be in a position to provide financing for the first superconductor mass transit system. That was still years off; he knew that but the thought certainly excited him.

Eldon firmly believed that the future was here today. His little girl had just become a year older, and his wife was still the most beautiful woman he had ever laid his eyes upon, even still to this day. Eldon was the epitome of the American dream." That dream, of course, was about to be turned into his most horrific nightmare.

There was no need to clear US Customs upon arrival in Ft. Lauderdale. Both Billy and Eldon had been cleared back in Toronto. Eldon was thankful for that because it was a time saver and he was in a hurry to get home today.

Billy took care of the plane after landing. He had it refueled right away and on standby at the Davis Investments corporate hangar. That hangar was on the north end of the airport. Billy taxied straight for the hangar where Eldon had his Jaguar parked. Sometimes, depending on the winds and the subsequent angle of approach for landing, the flight path corridor would take Eldon directly over his estate on Sailfish Drive.

Today had been one of those days. The flight corridor to runway 2A requires Billy to swing out wide over the Atlantic just passing over the Pompano Beach area over the Intracoastal Waterway.

Billy would place Eldon right over his house and at banking sharply to the right this time; Eldon got a good bird's eye view of his place today. Eldon could see his two boats docked down by the Intracoastal. One boat was a fifty-foot scarab, a cigarette type speed boat equipped with special electronics and the full array of conveniences. That was Eldon's little toy for weekends when he wasn't tied up with business and found himself free. The other was a fifty foot Blackfin motor yacht for entertaining business clients. Eldon employed a part-time captain for the Blackfin, but he enjoyed taking it out on his own as well, just with his family and a first mate.

Eldon could also see a brown van parked right in front of the main entrance to his house. His sharp eyes followed the driveway back from the house down the estate towards the entrance on Sailfish Drive, and he now couldn't help but see that the main gates at the guard house marking the entrance to his estate were wide open. This was never the case; it was very unusual for this to happen at best.

Eldon started to develop a very uneasy feeling in his gut. He was not alarmed, but he was very security conscious. Hopefully, it was just the anticipation he had for seeing Linda and Cathy again, and he was probably over reacting. Eldon let it go and sat back in his seat. Eldon could only let it go for about five seconds, though.

Now he leaned forward in his seat and pressed his face against the window to get another look down. The angle for viewing became less and less available as they flew further away. Eldon sat back again.

As soon as the plane touched down, and taxied to the hangar, Eldon was out. He headed for his Jaguar and immediately picked up his Panasonic cellular mobile phone. He auto-dialed Linda while pulling out of the hangar and waving a hand towards Billy to say goodbye. Eldon made his way out of the airport area and took his place in traffic on Interstate 95 heading north towards Pompano Beach. The exit to Atlantic Boulevard was only a few miles north up the highway. It wouldn't take too long to get home. He knew that Linda would be at home with Cathy.

Eldon reached over to the passenger seat and picked up one of his daughter's present. It was a Barbie doll. Eldon had a bigger surprise for Cathy, but it seemed that little girls needed very little to make them happy and this Barbie doll was all that Cathy asked from Eldon.

Eldon had his daughter's little treasure all neatly wrapped and sitting in the passenger seat. He had made certain that his private secretary Deirdre, from his office in Lauderdale went to U-2 Play and picked up the gift and set it in his car for his arrival back from Canada.

Eldon had arranged for this before his departure for Toronto. Deirdre was someone who was meticulous at ensuring Eldon's schedule was in place and in order at all times. She could be relied upon to take care of just about anything Eldon needed both personally and business wise.

The purchase of the doll was a personal task. Deirdre had placed the doll into Eldon's Jaguar just within the last hour, and now she was driving down south on I95 towards Miami, heading home and finding herself stuck in south Florida traffic gridlock. Eldon would fare no better heading north today. It was Friday. Traffic was at times the greatest drawback for deciding to live in south Florida.

Eldon listened to the cellular phone dialing his number at home and then he waited as his phone rang at home. He listened to the remote speaker. It rang nine times; he counted each ring. No answer.

Eldon thought, "why wasn't Linda answering the phone? Maybe she was getting his darling little daughter all ready for him, with a fresh new outfit, cute as can be; but still, she should have answered the phone."

Eldon was now consumed.

His imagination started taking off, full of wild and irrational thoughts. He glanced at the speedometer; he was speeding fifteen miles over the limit. He didn't need to get pulled over now and just prolong the agony of not knowing where his wife was and why she wasn't answering the phone.

He had always hated leaving her and Cathy home alone while he was on a business trip. Eldon was a realist to be sure, and he never discounted what harm can come unexpectedly to the wealthy and well known. He had always believed in tight security systems around his estate and only tolerated his wife's apathy for tight security just so that he wouldn't offend her. Eldon never really agreed to let Jerry the guard leave early on Fridays, but Linda had asked Eldon to consider Jerry's request, and he agreed reluctantly. "Winston" the late shift guard worked another job before getting to the Eldon estate, and that was just the way it was. These things all bothered Eldon.

Eldon was cautious when it came to driving, but today, especially now something deep inside was eating away at him making Eldon very nervous. Eldon had a sixth sense that was keen and it was not sending good vibes now.

Eldon maintained his speed between seventy and seventy-five miles per hour. He accelerated somewhat to eighty and speed dialed his home number once again. He noticed passing the exit to Atlantic Avenue in North Lauderdale. It was another seven miles to his exit directly north on the interstate. The phone rang and kept ringing continuously, endlessly. No one picked it up. Eldon dialed his private office number at his house.

He waited. There too the phone just rang and rang. "Where in hell was Linda? Okay, remain calm, you're just letting your mind run with this, just relax and get home fast as you can without causing an accident. Come on you know better than this, you're acting foolish."

Eldon's mind was trying to talk himself back into a state of normalcy.

"What was that truck or was it a van doing in the driveway, and why was the gate to the driveway opened like that? Jesus, what was going on?"

Now Eldon wasn't paying any attention to his driving. He had accelerated to eighty-five miles per hour almost running a car off the interstate as he pulled over to the right-hand lane for his exit off the highway.

"Okay, relax you're almost home. Another five minutes and you'll be fine holding Linda in your arms. It’s probably nothing. She may have had to do something so she just couldn't get to the phone," Eldon thought to himself trying desperately to relax.

He was now sweating bricks. He realized that he'd better get on grip on things otherwise he might look foolish in front of Linda when he got home. Then he remembered, it was Maria's day off too. Because of this being Cathy's birthday Linda had decided to give Maria the housemaid the day off so the family could be alone together.

"What was that van doing there?"

This ate away at Eldon like cancer. He had to find out. The traffic was heavy, especially on Friday at rush hour not to mention all the damn tourists. There were more cars with out of state plates on the road than local ones. Eldon could have sworn they were all deliberately getting in his way just to slow him down.

Eldon couldn't help it. He felt sick.

It was now 6:00 PM at the Davis Estate on 6565 Sailfish Drive in Pompano Beach Florida. The drawbridge over the Intracoastal had just opened up. Eldon would be stuck in traffic for another seven minutes. There was nothing he could do, absolutely nothing.

Having pushed the eight inches of stainless steel into the warm living body of Linda Davis had given Jason a big rush. Never had he known the power of life and death in his hands. This added a new dimension to the makeup of the character that was Jason Garretty. Jason realized a newfound power now, almost a sense of invulnerability overwhelmed him. He knew no fear and quite literally felt elated. He was now in full charge.

Cathy's playroom was at the end of the first-floor hallway just inside the large sunroom overlooking the back yard. Her playroom was directly down the hall across from the foyer where Jason had dropped Linda's body.

The door to Cathy's playroom was wide open, and she could be heard playing and talking with her bestest friend Jody, Cathy's imaginary playmate. Linda could often hear Cathy talking to Jody while she played and Linda was so relieved to learn that another addition was coming to the Davis family. Cathy needed a sister or brother desperately. She was such a loving child, willing to give of herself so much even now at the tender age of six.

A great deal of Linda's personality and presence was within Cathy, and she too would no doubt bloom into a most precious flower as the years would surely bless her with Linda's beauty and spirit.

Cathy's soft singing indicated that she was lost in a world of her own. She had her entire *care bear* collection spread out all around her in a circle with each one of the dolls facing inward. Behind and around the "care bears" she had the whole family of *smurf* dolls and in her lap, were two cabbage patch kids, and in her arm, she held her favorite doll of all, a cabbage patch preemie doll that she had named Dixie.

Cathy would not let go of Dixie. This was her very special and most important possession in the whole wide world. "Yes-siree," Cathy had created her own little gallery of admirers. She admired them, and she was positive they all admired her back as she explained to them that soon they'd meet the newest doll to her collection, the fashion Barbie. She was a child at play; she was six.

Jason was thirty-six, and a murderer with a mission who was now stalking a six-year-old child at play just down the hall from where he had murdered her mother in cold blood. He was about to invade this innocent child's world of "make believe."

As Jason tip-toed down the hall, he reached into the inner pocket of his jumpsuit and extracted an aluminum flask and placed it under his left armpit, then took, from his right hip pocket a thick woolen rag. Untwisting the top of the flask, he turned it upside down onto the rag. Quietly in his rubber-soled shoes, he walked down the hall towards Cathy's playroom and stopped just short of the doorway.

Cathy was chattering away to the smurf dolls with her back towards the doorway entrance as Jason peeked around into the room. Quickly like a mongoose, he leaped upon Cathy. Two steps, one second of time is all that it took. Jason snatched Cathy up from the middle of the circle of dolls and pressed the woolen cloth firmly into her face. It took but a few seconds to render Cathy unconscious. The chloroform had been absorbed into Cathy's lungs and bloodstream immediately as her young lungs fought for air against the tightly pressed blackness confronting her face.

Cathy was his. Jason had the Davis girl and was ready to make his exit when his peripheral vision caught sight of "Dixie" as it fell to the floor from out of Cathy's arms. The doll offered Jason a sudden clever idea, and he picked it up off the floor. "Okay kid, we'll take3 this along too. Two hostages are better than one anyway," Jason said to himself.

Jason ran quickly back towards the foyer passing Linda's body and holding both Cathy and "Dixie" tightly in his arms like a fullback breaking for the goal line.

Jason paused for a fraction of a moment as he came to the open front doorway. He looked around quickly outside, saw that all was clear; threw Cathy and the doll into the back seat and sped away around the circular driveway and out onto Sailfish Drive.

Jason was heading south on US federal highway one, not two minutes from the front gate of the Davis estate as he passed "Winston Clarke" the evening guard coming to work. Winston was humming an old Ray Charles tune. Fridays were always good days for work Winston thought, cause tomorrow was Saturday and Saturdays he'dah be-a-doin-no-work-fo-nobodys-a-notime.

Winston was glad this was Friday. He liked having the weekends off.

The Astro van that Jason was driving careened around the corner of Sailfish Drive and Dumont Road, no more than half a mile from the Davis House. He proceeded in a westerly direction and passed over the Intracoastal drawbridge spanning the Intracoastal Waterway.

Jason was now heading south on US Highway 1 and mixed in with major traffic. He headed straight south. Pulling away from the Davis estate he did notice a couple of joggers on the opposite side of Sailfish Drive.

Jason thought about that for a moment and considered that they might present a problem later on, but by that time he'd have the van ditched. “Still, it could be significant,” he thought.

Just five minutes after Jason left the Davis Estate, Eldon pulled up to the front of his driveway.

Ironically, Eldon and Jason had passed each other heading in opposite directions over the

Intracoastal drawbridge. If only Eldon had known, if only.

Immediately Eldon was questioning Jerry's whereabouts. He had forgotten already that it was Friday.

The gate was wide open; there was no guard on duty. Everything was wrong! "Jerry, Jerry, where the hell are you, Jerry!" Eldon was now shouting from his seat through the passenger window out towards the guard house.

Two seconds later, Eldon sped on through the gate and up the driveway to the front door of his house. Suddenly Eldon was overcome with anxiety; he saw that the front door to the house was open even before he arrived at the curb.

No sign of any security guards; the front gates were wide open, and the entire world had total access to his private domain.

Nausea set in on Eldon; his heart rate increased rapidly to over a hundred fifty beats per second; it raced on its own. He tasted an awful buildup of saliva in his mouth. His chest felt heavy. He got himself out of the car and ran through the front door of his house calling out his wife's name, "Linda, Linda, where are you?"

It was only a matter of a second once he was through the front doorway. By the time he called out his wife's name the second time; it was frozen on his lips. With a terror that unfolded like a bolt of lightning, he realized his most horrific nightmare.

It was as if Satan himself had paid a visit to his home and left his mark on the Davis family. Both terror and dread filled his heart; his mind tried to reject the horrible truth that lay in front of him but it could not. Eldon was on his way to short circuiting.

He was now running a heavy overload. His wife, his love, his world, his future, his life, his dreams were stricken down lying in a pool of blood.

"His daughter! Cathy, where is Cathy?" Eldon's darling little girl. He knew in his heart that she'd be gone. Yet, it was instinct; that drove him to search.

He yelled out her name, "Cathy, Cathy, where are you, baby? Cathy, it's daddy!" It was in vain.

Then Eldon stopped running around the house searching for his daughter. He came back to Linda's body, looked down at her and raised his head covering both his ears with the palms of his hands and let out a scream of pain and revenge at the top of his lungs that could be heard by the devil himself in is lair in hell.

Eldon had experienced tragic sorrow three years ago when his mother and father were taken from him because of an automobile accident caused by a drunken driver.

His mom and dad had just been over to visit him and Linda and Cathy. He could still recall how his mom would shower Cathy with her undivided attention for hours on end entertain his three-year-old daughter only as a grandma could, reading to her and playing dolls with her.

Cathy was what made Eldon's mother's dreams come true. She would constantly remind Eldon of how Cathy had his eyes, and it was in the eyes from where one could always tell what was truly in the heart.

Eldon's father was the driving force that pushed him through the years to forge a place for himself in the world of finance. In 1975 when Eldon first incorporated his initial business and struck out on his own with Davis International Investments, it was his father that showed him the light.

It was Eldon's father who provided him with the strength and encouragement to undertake life's challenges. Eldon remembered so clearly that autumn day down on the Jersey shore.

He and his dad had taken that long walk on the beach in Wildwood. Eldon was a young stock broker back then, not really knowing what to do with his life or what direction he should channel his energies. Len Davis; his dad, was a man not fooled easily and a man who had an ability to read people very well. When Len had opened his first motor hotel back in 1955, he already had enough savvy to know what it took to become successful in corporate America. Success Len knew, did not always come about from a methodically planned course.

Initially, it took guts, to dare to do something unusual, to recognize an opportunity at its ripest stages of potential. Yes, it took stamina to tough it out when the sharks in the ocean of business gathered. It took the foresight and most of all the courage to toss the coin and have enough balls to do some gambling.

Len had been a gambling man, and his gamble had paid off big. In a matter of ten years, Len Davis's string of small sized roadside inns sprung up all over the northeastern States. Len knew that he could be on the bandwagon if he had the guts to get on with it, and in 1955 he invested his life savings into his first motor hotel that eventually grew into a chain of accommodations whose name was now synonymous with the traveling North American public.

Holiday Jewel Hotels and Resorts; had become the most popular pit stop for the American motorist that took to the Interstate Highways as the country underwent the big-bang theory in 1955, and hadn't really eased up until the 1973 Arab oil embargo which put an abrupt end to the national driving craze.

That embargo had nearly done Len Davis in. His now famous chain of hotels had suffered terribly drastic decreasing rates in occupancy throughout the entire summer. That decrease in occupancy affected revenues to almost eliminating cash flow. This had most serious consequences; forcing Len to temporarily close some of his hotels and initiate massive employee layoffs and cutbacks throughout his hotel empire.

The properties located in major urban areas still managed to do well, holding their own and it was these properties that saved Len's overall decline.

The summer of 73 had indeed seen the oceans of American finance infested with Arabian sharks.

Len had toughed it out amongst these foreign sharks, learning to swim with them and eventually had expanded his empire right into the midst of the mid eastern countries themselves, reaping huge profits from the oil-rich sheikdoms throughout and around the Persian Gulf and Saudi Arabia, by providing lodging facilities contributing to the overall growth of the Saudi and Emirates economies.

The world changed, and Len changed with it. Eldon had owed it all really to his dad's uncanny ability to make him see things in broader ways than Eldon's tunnel vision allowed in 1975.

Eldon recalled that autumn day on the Jersey shores; it was approximately 4 PM, the wind had just started to pick up again.

He and his dad were out for a walk along the beach, just talking. Both of them had their pant legs rolled up to just below the knees, and they walked along into the wind.

The ocean surf was breaking pretty good that afternoon and Eldon remembered how the seagulls just floated in the air maintaining their altitude, playing the wind currents; not even having to flap once to stay airborne.

His dad had said to him, "so son, what have you decided, are you going to take a chance and go for the gusto this time round, or are you going to stay working for Riley Brothers for your whole life?"

Eldon had known that his dad was going to bring this up sooner or later, he was sure to bring it up on this walk.

Eldon had welcomed the subject because Eldon needed both advice and confidence building. His dad was good at those.

Eldon had been thinking of breaking out on his own recently. He certainly had enough contacts to start. Eldon had built himself a tight portfolio of clients whose trust Eldon had earned through some very shrewd portfolio management techniques that Eldon seemed to excel doing.

It just was that when it came time to looking after his own best interest, well what he really needed was a good swift kick in the behind to get him going, and Len Davis knew that.

His dad stopped walking. He turned to his son and said, "Eldon, turn around and look out to sea and tell me honestly son, what do you see?"

“Dad, are you going to get philosophical with me again?"

"Eldon, just do what I say will you?"

Eldon turned towards the ocean like his dad asked him to and said, "Okay dad, I see the Atlantic Ocean. I see that the waves are pretty high and there are a lot of seagulls in the air taking advantage of the brisk wind."

"Eldon, my dear son, God knows I love you, but you aren't looking far enough. You see only the ocean, the waves upon it and some birds in the immediate area flying around. Tell me son, is that really all you see or is that all you are willing to see. What are you afraid of son, tell me, what?"

Eldon looked at his dad standing there in front of him with a look of desperation on his father's face. His father Eldon knew was searching for a deeper response; one that Eldon knew was within himself but couldn't bring it to the surface.

Eldon's dad, Len Davis, spoke, "Eldon, I look out there far beyond the horizon, and you know what I see son? You know what I see? I see clear across to Europe. I can see the buildings; I can see the people getting in and out of their cars and I can see thousands of people checking into and out of hotels all across Europe.

Eldon, I can see guests checking into the Ritz in Paris right now and some others checking into the Savoy in London even as we speak. The best part is I can see an entire convention checking in right now to The Holiday Jewel Hotel City Center, yes Eldon, my hotel in Barcelona Spain. Eldon, do you know how I can see that my son, do you? I'll tell you how because I have vision son, not just sight and more importantly because I know it's all there; happening right now.

You can go now son, if you want and check in to your future, or you can check right out. You can check yourself right out of the future if you insist on procrastinating for much longer. Eldon, I know you have that all-important vision, you have it flowing in your blood, just like I do Eldon. Look at that ocean son and think of this."

Eldon felt his dad's arms come to rest on the back of his shoulders. His dad leaned over to speak into Eldon's right ear, and as Eldon stared at the horizon, gazing out over the ocean, his dad softly spoke these words to Eldon that would forever change his life, Len Davis said to his loving and only son,

"I do not know what I may appear to the world, but to myself I seem to have been only like a boy playing on the seashore and diverting myself in now and then finding a smoother pebble or a prettier shell than ordinary, whilst the great ocean of truth lay undiscovered before me."

Eldon looked down at the sand, and just as his father finished speaking, the sea came up to brush Eldon's feet beckoning him not to delay.

"Sir Isaac Newton said that son, he said it you, you and me son. It just took two hundred and fifty-nine years for you to hear it, and it had to come from me. The important thing is that you've now heard it." His dad finished saying.

The following morning Eldon reported in to work at Riley Brothers and finished working his last day as a stock broker for somebody else. Eldon Barnes Davis took what money he had saved and struck out on his own giving birth to Davis Investments International. After that day, he never ever did look back.

Eldon had grieved for months after his parents were killed and it was in Linda whom he found strength and comfort. That event had taken its toll on Eldon; he had retreated within himself, for Eldon was an only child, and the loss of his mother and father was indeed a major blow.

◇◇◇

Eldon dropped to his knees as they buckled beneath him. All of a sudden Eldon had no strength. Eldon felt only loss, a great sense of loss.

An emptiness of infinite magnitude. His universe at this moment was void. His family had been taken. Emptiness was replaced with anger. Immediate anger that boiled inside his heart with hatred for whoever had done this to his beloved wife and had taken his daughter.

Eldon knew immediately in the flash of the eye, at the speed of light, just what had happened. Eldon in his deepest fears had never discounted the possibility of such an evil and calculating act.

He had lived with this nightmare tucked away in the farthest reaches of his mind and prayed to God that never might it come to pass. This day it had happened. Eldon knew his wife was dead and his daughter missing from the first moment he walked through the front door and saw Linda lying in her pool of blood.

There could be no good without evil. Is that the old cliché? So too were the stakes increased exponentially as evil had more to gain from those who were forced to succumb in positions of great wealth and power.

Eldon crawled along the marble floor and lay next to his wife. He reached over and pulled her body around, still warm with life just having left her.

"My darling forgive me," he whispered under his breath.

Eldon began to sob lightly at first then uncontrollably the tears flushed from his eyes as he cried openly and freely unleashing the demons of hell within that would avenge his wife's murder and get Cathy back.

Eldon picked himself up off the floor. He too was now drenched in Linda's blood. He bent down and picked his wife up into his arms and holding her walked into Cathy's playroom.

He sat into one of Cathy's rocking chairs that was shaped like a horse and rocked with Linda hanging limply in his arms. He bent over Linda's body, pulled her close to his chest and whispered to her with a broken aching voice a pledge to his loving dead wife; "my darling sweetheart, I love you with all of my heart and soul. You shall have not died in vain. I will make them pay; Cathy will be home soon.

I love you, and I promise to get her back. We will meet again my love in another world, peace be with you, your love is in my heart, and your touch is eternally upon my soul."

Having committed himself to these words he spoke to his wife for the last time, Eldon stood up out of the chair with Linda in his arms and took her up to their bedroom placing her gently onto their large canopy bed, laying her to rest for the final time in their Florida home.

***

Chapter Three

And he "ransom" more

After Eldon had rested Linda onto their canopy brass bed he lay there beside her for a few moments and allowed his mind to run wild with memories, reflecting on the times they shared as he held her still next to himself knowing that once he let go he would never be able to dwell in the past ever again.

He recalled the time he first laid eyes upon her how he was swept away by her beauty. He remembered how nervous he had been to make the first approach introducing himself somehow breaking the ice.

Well, Eldon to his amazement was surprised at how poised she was and the ease with which he found himself addressing her all because of the atmosphere she projected, allowing him to proceed in the process of meeting his wife to be for the very first time.

There was no ice to break; her reaction was warm and friendly. She invited and encouraged his company. It was at a benefit party given by the South Jersey Chamber of Commerce for Gulf War Vets just soon after President Clinton had sent the troops into Haiti. Eldon had first seen Linda in a corner of the room by a window, flanked by a smart looking Naval Aviator.

She was sipping on a glass of pink champagne. Linda was wearing a stunning blood red full-length gown with no jewelry whatsoever on her body except for a pair of ruby studded circular platinum earrings. Her long jet black silky hair flowed down to the small of her back. She was taller than the average woman. She was in no way the average woman. Eldon was totally stunned. Eldon was certain that there was no other woman on earth like her. Eldon's heart was beating with anticipation.

The distinguished naval aviator was Officer Lieutenant Billy Simpson, her courtesy escort for the evening. Billy was a long-time friend of the family from Linda’s side. Billy being a Gulf War vet was honored by the Hughes family’s attendance this evening, and Billy watched out for Linda, like a hawk.

Billy and Linda were childhood friends, now adults in all respects, but Billy had a special eye on safety for Linda. Billy could be counted upon to shelter Linda under his wings. After all, Billy was a top gun wing commander.

Linda's warmth and inviting attitude was something unexpected by Eldon and certainly a welcomed situation. Eldon experienced no rejection nor had he sensed apprehension on her behalf. Eldon's spirits were lifted his ego never even came into play.

He had a boyish sense of shyness but an equal measure of adult passion brought on by the unknown elements of feminine allure. Eldon had learned later on that Linda had wanted to meet him all evening long and was very pleased and so very anxious when Eldon finally did come over to introduce himself.

Then his memories jumped ahead to the time when their early relationship was aflame with hot embers of lust that lead to their first time.

Their first-time experience of their unbridled passion for each other. They had decided to go on a camping trip only after their second date and that fantastic weekend was etched in stone ever so gently on Eldon's mind and forever locked into memory.

They had taken off early Friday afternoon at the start of a long weekend in summer and headed north to the Catskills. Eldon had found a perfect spot, a secluded mountain lake to make camp beside and after pitching their tent darkness had fallen.

The late evening led into midnight with a full moon. Both Linda and Eldon found it natural to take a moonlight dip. The water was clear and the moonlight reflected its silvery glow enchanting the setting even deeper off the surface of the mountain lake with the glistening pine trees all around. It truly was a magical night.

Linda had made the first advance as she swam up to him. When Linda pressed her firm body against Eldon, he discovered that she had discarded her swim suit. He could still relive that night by closing his eyes. Feeling her touch against his skin and the tenderness with which they made love in the shimmering moonlight of Osprey Lake, with the call of the loons in the background and the swish of the whispering pines; all melting together into the ripple of their passion in midnight waters.

Eldon picked himself up off the bed, then pulled the cover-up and over Linda's face. Eldon walked downstairs, picked up the telephone and proceeded to dial the Broward County sheriff's department. At the same time as Eldon picked up the telephone, "Winston Clarke" the evening security guard came through the front door.

Winston was visibly shaken to be sure when his and Eldon's eyes met.

"Mr. Davis, sir, what in heaven's name have you done to yourself? You are covered in blood, Mr. Davis."

"Winston, I know this will be difficult for you but this will undoubtedly be the most important day that you will ever work for me and today I need you to do the best job that you've ever done. I don't wish for you to do anything except return to your post at the gate and don't let anybody pass except the Police and friends of the family. Do you understand that clearly Winston?" Eldon asked.

Winston just stood in the doorway with a stunned look on his face. Then finally Eldon had to yell at him.

"Winston, do you understand?" Eldon shouted.

Immediately Winston reacted. "Yes Sir Mr. Davis, yes sir I do." “Winston!" Eldon said, don't worry about me, it’s not my blood I'll be fine now, go on back to the gate."

"It’s not Mrs. Davis is it sir. Please, Lord, tell me nothing has happened to Mrs. Davis." Winston was now terrified. Somehow, he could have dealt with Mr. Davis being injured but not Mrs. Davis.

“No, not that wonderful lady who had always wished Winston and his family well and had never forgotten his or any of his family's birthdays with a nice gift. No, not that good-hearted Mrs. Davis," Winston thought to himself.

“Winston, just go back to the gate and help me in this time will you my friend?" Eldon said with a gentle and controlled voice.

Winston turned and went back to the guard gate. Eldon had told Winston to watch out for the Police coming. Eldon didn't say what had happened, but it was obvious that someone had been killed or murdered Winston thought.

"A murder, sweet Jesus, a murder right here on the Davis Estate, Jesus sweet Jesus!" Winston was mumbling to himself all the way back to the guard house. He took up his position at the gate house thanking sweet Jesus that it hadn't all happened during his shift.

The Police arrived within minutes of Winston taking up his position at the front gate to the Davis Estate. Eldon was not about to make waves for the FBI or the local Police force investigating this incident.

He knew in his heart that both the Police department's and FBI's efforts to locate his daughter and apprehend the murderer of his wife would all be an exercise in futility. The only way to get his daughter back was through Eldon's efforts alone.

This was no ordinary criminal the envelope he had just opened and read made that very clear. Sure enough, it was a ransom note. The proverbial ransom note; God he felt like he was living through the plot of a bad "B" movie except that this was really happening and he was the main character.

Eldon had to get his wits about himself and get a grip on things. He had to comply with the requests of the kidnapper at first to gain some common ground on the situation. Eldon also knew that sooner or later, whoever left that note behind for him to read had also left a trail leading him to Cathy.

He could not see that trail yet, but he knew it was there. A good amount of digging would uncover it. Eldon had since decided to call his lifelong friend and business partner Felix Balon. Billy Simpson was next on his list of friendly recruits. Eldon was going to need some help to be sure. It was the kind of expertise that both Felix and Billy could provide. Eldon had already sent a copy of the ransom note to Felix and Felix was now on his way over to Eldon's house.

The Police had already questioned Jerry up in Altamonte Springs, but Eldon knew that would turn up nothing. Eldon had faintly recalled something about Jerry having to leave early on Fridays and how Eldon would eventually get around to talking to Linda about the lack of security during that period of time, but then Eldon had to go on this recent business trip to Toronto, and things regarding that topic just got left behind. He picked up the ransom note and read it again. It didn't say much. *"Do as you're told"* That was it, signed *"Dixie."*

Eldon placed the note back down onto the petrified wood coffee table in front of him and took another sip from the glass of scotch he had just poured for himself.

FBI Regional Director Miller had arrived a few minutes ago and was now in the process of going through his standard list of questions. Eldon tolerated the FBI man.

"Well, Mr. Davis, we have reviewed the computer generated digitized video tapes from your security camera system. We've listened to the audio portion a number of times. It would seem that Mrs. Davis provided access through the security gates for the perpetrator. We have also confirmed the brown van being here and verified it having passed Mr. Winston Clarke on his way into work. We also tracked down a couple of people who live in this area that go jogging daily around the time the murder took place, and they too have confirmed the brown van driving past them.

Unfortunately, none of these people were able to provide us with any descriptions, but you can rest assured Mr. Davis that we are doing everything we can. Time will provide further clues and lead to the arrest of this person or persons," Miller said.

Eldon could hardly control himself. He was just about ready to lay into this FBI guy.

"Agent Miller!" Eldon raised his voice and forcefully said, "my wife has just been murdered, my little girl has been kidnapped and you are talking to me like this was some sort of crime on the level of a car theft! Why don't you get your people together and get the hell out of my house!" Eldon was furious.

"This murderer comes to invade my house and kill my family; he comes to me from the bowels of the world and the gutters of hell. He violates my existence, and you have the nerve to stand there nonchalantly, talking like you had just watched a television murder mystery. Neither you nor your FBI friends are going to get my daughter back. You know that, and I know that so why don't you just make this visit your last."

Miller motioned to his team of investigators and started towards the door. Miller's team had finished working all the immediate leads.

They had checked the ID card Jason had held up to the camera. There indeed was a person by the name of "Max Schelling" as the card stated. It was Jason's disguised face, on a semi-professional looking ID card from "Martin's flower boutique." The follow up on Max Schelling proved to be a dead-end.

Indeed, Max Schelling worked at the flower boutique as a driver but had nothing to do with this afternoon's delivery and besides Max was five feet six inches tall with red hair and freckles and only nineteen years old.

Miller was gathering his team and making his exit. Before he left, Miller said, "Mr. Davis, we'll be in touch just as soon as we further analyze the videotape down at the lab."

There was a touch of compassion in Miller's voice. He walked out the door.

Eldon was relieved to see him go. This was no stupid murderer that Eldon had to deal with. Sure, he had taken a few chances, but obviously calculated risks in the beginning and now he had Cathy.

"That bastard," Eldon thought.

Eldon was relentless in everything he decided to undertake, and very methodical, as Jason Garretty was certain to find out for himself.

"This story just in; late this afternoon the Broward County Sheriff's Department received a telephone call from the home of Eldon Barnes Davis; a Pompano Beach resident and Chief executive of Davis Investments International, a multinational corporation in over a dozen countries. Murder and kidnapping victimized the Davis family earlier this evening.

Details at this time are still incomplete. As the facts come in, we will update this story with breaking developments. Stay with VNN for further coverage of this major news story. In Chechnya today Russian troops"...

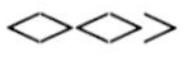

Billy Simpson couldn't believe his ears. What he had just heard on the Sony television set propped up in the corner of Hammerhead Inn and Raw Bar, on Ocean Boulevard was beyond his belief. Billy headed straight for his local watering hole just after having put the Canadair Jet away for the day after flying Mr. Davis back from Toronto not just two hours ago!

Billy sat on his bar stool, squinted his eyes, slowly turned his head to the right and then to the left looking around the entire bar to see who was in there. Billy was in a state of disbelief, denial shock and bewilderment; he said to himself under his breath, "what the hell?"

He called Ronnie the bartender and asked him to come over. "Ronnie, did you just hear what was on TV, did you see that?"

Ronnie answered Billy, "sorry Billy, that set is on all day and night I sort of tune myself out when I'm busy serving customers, why what was on there, something you found interesting?"

While Ronnie answered Billy, Billy's mind was racing on its own not paying the slightest attention to Ronnie.

Billy Simpson clicked into gear as his training sense took over. His military personality took control of all his mental thought processing. A great danger was now present that directly affected Billy's relationship with Mr. Davis. Billy was close to the Davis family on a personal level, especially to Cathy.

Billy sprang into action; storming out of the bar and running full speed to his Jeep Renegade parked along the beach side of Ocean Boulevard just next to the Pompano inlet drawbridge. Billy wasn't more than two miles from the Davis Estate.

There was no need for Eldon to call Billy; Billy was already on his way before Eldon's call. He drove straight over to the estate; the time was only 7:30 P.M. News travels fast he thought. Billy was now on a mission.

It mattered not where he found himself to be, to carry out that mission. It could have been back in the Persian Gulf, or here in Florida. Billy knew that Mr. Davis would be counting on him for his expertise; he sensed it. Mr. Davis was not one to leave matters up to others. Billy knew that Mr. Davis would want to handle this in his own special way and Billy would be there to make sure he did his part.

"Look here people; you will all have to cool your jets."

Felix Balon was now dealing with the press. He was trying to control the situation before it got out of hand. Felix was on the scene in front of the gates to Eldon's estate within minutes of receiving his call. There were reporters from all over the state already here as well as the national bureaus that had offices in Miami and Fort Lauderdale.

It was nothing short of a mob scene with all sorts of hi-tech electronic and communication devices everywhere one looked.

The street in front of Eldon's estate was jammed with mobile news vehicles. Only local traffic was being allowed access in and out of the area. As Felix drove up in his Lotus Esprit, the news media rushed him.

Damond Furst of the Miami Trumpet was on hand. Felix recognized him immediately.

Furst had been hounding Davis Investments for the last couple of years ever since the story broke in “The Times," concerning insider trading with the likes of Boesky and especially after the Milken junk bond fiasco. Furst for some reason or other was convinced that Davis Investments International also had a finger both those pies.

Furst was wrong, but he was relentless. Naturally Damond Furst of the Miami paper ran a column called “The Furst Report,” what else?

He would strive to be first with the news breaking stories. Actually Damond Furst was turning into a true pain in the ass.

Felix thought, "I'll have to deal with this dickhead while I've got everyone here together. Maybe I can turn the tide before too many vultures gather."

Furst was the reporter behind the demise of the good senator from Colorado some years ago, who eventually had to drop out as a candidate for the Presidency of the United States.

Furst could do a lot of harm if not checked in the early stages. Furst also had a low and dirty method in bringing his opponent out into the open by first laying a trap.

Felix anticipated this and was waiting. Felix understood the delicate nature of responding to questions posed by the press in a very calculated manner. The eyes and ears of everyone would be centered on his every word and reaction. Felix's number one priority was to protect Eldon and Davis Investments and Holiday Jewel Hotels, to the best of his ability.

Felix slowed down as he drove up towards the double gates leading off the driveway to Eldon's home.

There was a detachment of Police Officers present. Felix had been cleared access into the general area a block up the road. Felix stopped his car and stepped out of the vehicle.

Almost instantaneously microphones from a dozen reporters both from in front of him and on either side of him were held close to his face and mouth for recording of his comments. Felix turned an answer into a general statement in response to one of the local TV reporter's questions from eyewitness news."

"No, not at this time. We just haven't had enough of a chance to examine the circumstances, and

I can assure you all that as soon as we know more, you all will know more. We will make a statement soon."

Felix was just about to get back into his car; he was already half the way inside when he heard Damond Furst's voice. Almost shouting at him from somewhere in the midst of the crowd of reporters. Felix decided to abort his entry into the car, turned, and slammed the car door in response to Furst's accusation.

"Is it true Mr. Balon that Eldon Davis is having an affair with a local Hollywood model; is that true, can you comment on that?"

Felix was disgusted, and he felt like punching out Damond's teeth. This is a very old and dirty low-down trick. Nevertheless, it had to be answered.

To leave it just hanging there would arouse suspicion that there may indeed be more to the accusation than just a low down dirty, no good for nothing reporter's trick.

"Okay, I have no idea which one of you learned members of the press corps shouted that remark, but I'm sure most of you do know whom it came from.

Let me advise you all now and make myself crystal clear that Mr. Davis's reputation and record both within this community and on an international level are impeccable. From this point on, I would suggest that the courtesy extended to the media over the years by both Mr. Davis, his family and Davis Investments International be now recognized and reciprocated.

I can only add that any attempts at grandstanding by the use of underhanded tactics to gain yourselves sensationalized headlines will only result in major lawsuits against you and your respective employers. I don't think any of us want to waste valuable time dealing with false accusations. I trust we can now count on working together as mature professionals in which case Mr. Davis welcomes your support and information gathering abilities."

Even before Felix finished speaking, he noticed the crowd of reporters and camera crews beginning to show signs of settling down. He certainly had their attention.

There was an unmistakable air of crowd acknowledgment of the immature comment that Damond Furst had just blurted out and the crowd of reporters outwardly shunned him trying hard to disassociate themselves.

Felix was relieved to see that it had worked. Better to be honest with these people from the onset than having to fight them as well. Felix understood their ethical stance of trying to remain unbiased in reporting the news, but it certainly didn't hurt things to have them at least leaning towards his corner in a bout like the one unfolding now."

Felix continued, "so if you all be so kind as to allow Mr. Davis a little peace during these grave times, we will greatly appreciate your understanding, and as I said, there will be a more conclusive statement forthcoming shortly." Having said this, Felix noticed the throng relax. He climbed back into his Esprit and drove straight up to Eldon's front door.

Felix and Eldon were like brothers. Their relationship was rock solid.

A few minutes afterward a jeep renegade arrived at the gate. Clearance was given immediately to Billy. He drove up and parked his vehicle behind Felix's lotus esprit.

Billy was glad to see that Felix was already here to comfort Eldon. Billy's heart was pounding like a jackhammer. The need to know what had happened burned like a hearth.

The Police were still everywhere throughout the estate. Even though the FBI people had already left, the local Police were still combing the grounds. Felix, Billy, and Eldon were at the back of the house, in Eldon's den standing in front of a large window overlooking the back patio leading down to the dock on the Intracoastal.

They talked in low decibels. Eldon thanked Billy for coming over so quickly without having to be contacted. He explained what had happened as best as Eldon could fit the pieces together.

Billy then confirmed his loyalty to Eldon ensuring his total commitment in assisting Eldon in whatever Eldon had in mind to deal with this matter. Billy was in it for the duration. It mattered not what had to be done. Billy would do anything Eldon asked…anything.

"Billy, I truly welcome your friendship and your dedication. I thank you for your support. I cannot tell you how much I value your confidence and I know that your contribution will be of great importance. Your input to how our plan develops will be crucial; I have already expressed my opinion to Felix that I feel we have to do this on our own.

There is no need to go outside for assistance other than our immediate resources and trusted confidantes.

Oh, and one other thing Billy, no more "Mr. Davis" okay? I know it's in your nature to address me that way because you're my pilot, but we've been together far too long. You are my good friend Billy; you're like an uncle to my daughter, and you've known my wife for years before I ever met her."

Eldon choked up just a little when referring to his wife. His eyes started to water and a lump formed in his throat. Eldon bent his head forward as he stood in front of his two friends. He brought his right hand up grabbing the bridge of his nose and with his index finger, and thumb wiping away the forming tears. He then looked up at the two men in front of him and said in a broken voice, “that God damned bastard, he is going to pay for this with his life."

"That he will Eldon, that he will," Felix added comforting Eldon.

Felix walked over and put his arms around Eldon saying, "we'll find Cathy, Eldon. You, me and Billy, we'll find Cathy and get that bastard.”

Billy looked at Eldon and with a heavy heart and tears in his eye said, "Eldon your darling little daughter gave me some of the finest and most unforgettable times of my life. I will never forget how she comes running over to me every time I see her. She'd be calling to me with uncontrollable excitement in her voice, "Billy Bob, Billy Bob, will you take me flying up into the sky where the birds are? Billy Bob ,will you Billy Bob? Please say you will.”

As you know Eldon, I've taken her up a number of times, she loves to fly. The last time we went up in the Piper Cub out of Pompano, I had Cathy sitting on my knee. I'll never forget her joy Eldon; she showed no fear, and she loves to fly. I let her take the stick for a minute; she overflowed with excitement and happiness. You should have heard her Eldon. She was yelling at the top of her lungs, saying " look Dixie, we're flying, look we're doing it, you, me and Billy Bob, we're flying the plane, Dixie! Eldon, my heart poured out for your daughter. I just love; it the way she calls me Billy Bob. After we landed, I'll never forget it; she jumped up into my arms and hugged me around my neck still holding onto her doll and said. Oh Billy Bob we love you so much, both Dixie and me want to go flying with you again and again. She had the biggest smile on her pretty little darling face. I'll never ever as long as I live forget it. She said, we all love you so much Billy Bob. And she gave me a big kiss."

Tears kept forming in the big man's eyes as sadness overcame Billy.

He continued, "I never ever did get married but if God is willing and someday I do; why me and my wife, we're going to have a little girl just like Cathy. I tell you, Eldon, I'm in this with my life, I love your little girl, and I'll die a hundred times if need be to get her back. "Cobra One" is at your service."

That was Billy's naval aviator call sign, "Cobra One."

Billy's devotion to both Eldon and Cathy was undeniable. He was willing to and prepared to give his life for Eldon's little girl. Eldon was taken aback. He hadn't realized just how close Billy felt to his daughter.

Eldon stepped up to Billy and put his hands on his shoulders saying, "you truly are family Billy, Cathy couldn't have a better uncle than you Billy."

Eldon hugged Billy; after a moment, backed away one step. Then, automatically Eldon held out his right arm straight and true with a clenched fist. Felix reached out immediately and placed his right palm straight on top of Eldon's fist. Billy did the same, and the three men made a six-way seal of human flesh that bound them together as one entity to face the challenges that lay ahead in securing Cathy's freedom.

***

Chapter Four

Few men have virtue
to withstand the highest bidder.

George Washington

Angie Willow, President Fenton's; Press Secretary, stood behind the President's podium in the press gallery at the white house this evening and announced the President of the United States, “Ladies and gentlemen, the President of the United States; William Fenton.”

President Fenton walked out onto the press gallery stage and took his place behind the podium. This was a live ongoing nationally televised press conference, which had been on air for the past ten minutes, with Angie Willow addressing the press gallery and fielding some non-controversial questions.

The press corps seem to understand that holding back the meatier and juicier questions for President Fenton was the more prudent plan of action and their questioning was pretty light duty this evening with Angie Willow, but Angie knew that the President would not be escaping the grilling that was sure to follow.

The President spoke, “good evening fellow Americans, hello to the white house press corps and a very special greeting to our men and women stationed around the globe in ensuring America's freedom and democratic way of life. Tonight, it is with pleasure that I can announce that we have and are making significant progress in ensuring our further interests in the world; making America even more secure in the face of creeping dangers threatening our shores from abroad.

Over the past several decades, we have worked closely with our partner nations in making sure that our freedoms and ways of life are continually strengthened and enhanced. We bring aid and comfort to those nations needing American help, be that in situations of natural disasters, the relief, and aid in striving to end poverty wherever we can help and in ensuring certain nations a pathway to economic viability through joint force cooperation."

The President went on to say, "now I know that the White House press corps, is waiting with baited breath for an update concerning America's involvement in the economic and military understanding with the Caribbean island nation of Grenada.

This is the smallest independent nation in the Caribbean, with one of the greatest strategic geographical locations in terms of being situated in a natural gateway setting to the entire Caribbean, as well as being an ideal location regarding northern South America.

I want to assure Americans that our friendship and trust with the people and government of this island paradise has never been better. As a reminder, it was the United States, with the leadership of President Reagan, who liberated Grenada in 1983 from Communist domination. The US invasion of the island enabled the further liberation of the 800 American college students and eradicating the country of Communist Cuban; Soviet-supported intelligence and secret military construction projects that threatened the national security of the region and the United States.

Since having re-established a democratic government, free of communist infiltration; Grenada and its hardworking people, have enjoyed the benefits that a free island nation can realize through an atmosphere of cooperation and idealism synonymous with its immediate island neighbors.

Therefore it is with great pleasure and pride that I can report to our fellow Americans, that the Government of Grenada has today agreed to sign our joint defense treaty. This will guarantee the island's security with the strength of the United States for the next one hundred years and in turn offers the United States a strategic forward force location centered in the Caribbean allowing for greater defensive posture for America, its island neighbors and surrounding countries.

The upcoming signing of this treaty is set to take place within the next few weeks, and we are working hard at meeting the mutually beneficial terms and conditions for both our countries. Prime Minister Forbes Bishop of Grenada has given me his personal assurance that his government is on board with the Caribbean Initiative.

We both look forward to a long-lasting agreement between our two nations, with the signing of the treaty to be held in Grenada.

The United States of America welcomes the close cooperation of the nation of Grenada in the coming years and the establishment of closer economic and strategic ties in the interest of both our nations. I will be meeting with Prime Minister Bishop next week in Grenada and bringing the warmth and cooperation of the American people with the anticipation in welcoming Grenada to our North American defense alliance.

This new member alliance will ensure greater prosperity to the people of Grenada, and allow for a smoother flow of goods and material as a new gateway to South America; and with this, I am prepared to take a few questions."

Vic Amber, the President's CIA Director was listening carefully in the wings, watching President Fenton addressing the nation and the press. He was particularly pleased that his Secretary of State; Mitch Farnsworth was available this day, along with Howard Rickover; the Secretary of Defense. The presence of these two individuals sent a strong signal to the international community that this new directive, partnership, and American foreign policy was of a very serious nature and an alliance that was to produce major policy shifts and overall approach in the way American influence was to be projected throughout the region. There was to be no mistake in the clarity and determination of future intentions to be realized in the region through the development of American economic and military power.

Vic Amber had been very busy over that past six months running operation "island hop" code name for the new Grenada Caribbean Initiative undertaking. Plans were well in place to facilitate the construction of America's' new forward location Trident Missile Submarine base already under construction on the south shore of Grenada. This forward base location would ensure the strategic and tactical domination of the entire Caribbean as well as a huge portion of South America.

Guantanamo Bay in Cuba was under the threat of closure, and the US needed an alternative option for the coming century. Puerto Rico was not a viable option at this stage because of growing opposition to continued military expansion, and the negative press coming out of Puerto Rico over the naval bombing exercises carried on in Vieques had soured the Puerto Rican people and its government to further US involvement. Especially after several civilians had been killed during the US Navy bombing exercises.

Grenada was an excellent choice; small enough government to deal with, and if required even to be bought and paid for. It is a long-standing tradition in Caribbean culture that political virtue is easily trumped by the highest bidder, and the Pentagon has the deepest of all pockets. Most importantly, the island nation was a large enough island to meet the American Navy's submarine base footprint and construction requirements.

Another vital factor in the selection of Grenada was the proximity of the island to Venezuela. That had put the US Virgin Islands out of contention, since it was deemed to be too far from the South American mainland, primarily Venezuela.

Recently there had been indications and very strong indications that the stability of the country was in question. Of major concern was the deterioration of the political climate in Venezuela, that led to the Caracazo riots of 1989 that further lead to the CIA playing out a scenario of further destabilization of the current democratic government giving way to rumblings of growing socialism and the potential birth of a coming dictatorship.

President Fenton and his close team of advisers were making plans to circumvent these looming changes in the geopolitics of the Caribbean basin, heading off certain eventualities that could dramatically affect the national security of the United States. Yes indeed, these were forward-looking days, and the President's crystal ball was indeed glowing bright this evening.

Vic Amber listened as the President wrapped up his presentation and update. Vic was very satisfied and knew how adept President Fenton was at handling questions from the press corp. Vic knew very well that President Fenton was at the top of his game. "Bring on the questions, bring on the lions, the crowd anxiously awaits."

President Fenton devoured them all.

Cyril Burgess; National Security Advisor, stood beside Vic Amber in the wings. As the President was about to take the first question from a White House press reporter, Cyril leaned in towards Vic Amber and whispered, asking, "what's going on with *Island-Hop* and Holiday Jewel Hotels and Casinos; that whole Davis International ball of wax, has Eldon Davis caught wind of this yet?"

Vic Amber turned to Cyril, and said, looking directly at him, "this part he most likely already knows about" the rest well, he will just have to find out for himself."

Cyril replied, "yes, that is exactly what worries me." The two men then continued listening to President Fenton take more questions and answer the press corps.

The wheels were turning, Vic Amber couldn't help thinking, "these wheels will need some special greasing."

***

Chapter Five

Everyone is as God has made him
and often times a great deal worse.
Miguel De Cervantes, Don Quixote

It had been a whole lot easier than Jason thought it would be. He was especially pleased with himself that he had the foresight to add that little irony to the end of his ransom note, Dixie. "That ought to get Davis right where it hurt the most." Cathy's favorite doll was wearing a jumpsuit with the name "Dixie" written right across the front of it.

Jason figured it would be good to use that as his code name and added it to the note just before he left the Davis house. It was a chance to take, but Jason just couldn't resist. So far so good, he'd gotten away clean as a whistle.

Cathy was out cold on the passenger seat, and he had already dumped the van at the huge public parking lot at U-2 Play in Boynton. It was imperative that he make a transfer into another vehicle and naturally while doing so wanted to attract no attention to the transfer. Jason could think of no better place to seen with a small child than a place like U-2 Play; the place was crawling with kids and tourists.

Jason had prepared well. He had rented a late model SUV and parked it next to a no parking zone where he could pull in with the stolen van for a moment right next to his rental and make a smooth, easy transfer. Jason pulled his stolen van right up next to his rental and made a smooth, clean transfer. Jason knew very well that the Police would not be looking in the parking lot for a stolen van. That's the last place they'd be searching, U-2 Play. They'd find the van after the store had closed and the lot vacant. Jason was right.

Everything was moving along well up to this point. Jason remained clean, left no fingerprints anywhere; the latex gloves made sure of that. He had already peeled off his false face and was now sporting a blonde crew cut, wearing a very colorful Ocean Pacific flowery loose shirt that he matched with white Bermuda shorts and a pair of docksiders. Cathy, of course, was still out cold. Jason was certain that the law would be on lookout for him everywhere, but for someone; who looked completely different.

There was a new sense of confidence now overcoming Jason. Adrenaline flowed freely giving him that extra energy that seemed to compress time. The events that led to his present position had zipped by so quickly that for a while time stood still. He was now looking at just before 7 PM and act two of his plan was now coming to a close, without a hitch.

Act three was waiting to unfold as Jason's face found an ear-to-ear grin growing upon it as he looked over to the Davis girl curled up in a fetal position on the seat beside him saying to her, "you're going to be famous kid, real famous, you probably already are. Anyway your old man and me will make sure that you are."

He kept glancing over at her as he continued driving north this time right along US Highway 1 through the center of West Palm Beach, driving clean on through, continuing north to Riviera Beach and on to Palm Beach Gardens, Jason headed north.

Weariness overcame him and certain heaviness built in his eyes. Jason then remembered; his colored contact lenses were still in. He pulled his rental car over off the road and into small parking lot along the Intracoastal. He extracted the contacts and felt immediately refreshed. He pulled back onto the road and continued north.

"Christ, what a relief that is," he said to himself under his breath.

"That's it kid, just keep nice and still, another few minutes and you and me will be home free."

Jason's destination was outside of Jupiter in the Juno Beach area; only a few miles up the road. He had his prized possession at Gulliver's marina. Gulliver's had enough space to hold approximately fifty boats. Jason's boat was in slip number four.

Jason had rented the slip on a regular basis for the last few years. He was well known in the area and not suspect of any suspicious activities. Jason had a way of living two lives and managed to keep them both very separate. He would set sail tonight at midnight in a direction due east heading for Bahamian waters and then turning southeast making way for Abaco Island.

First things first, however. Jason drove the Nissan SUV up to the front of the dock and parked it close by, under a section of banyan trees with far reaching overhanging limbs offering good shelter and cover.

He moved to the back of the SUV and lifted the lid off a large five-foot ice cooler used exclusively for fishing.

Usually, it held a great deal of ice. This time however it was empty except for the two pillows already inside the cooler. He earlier drilled air holes high up along the cooler's sides before loading it into the rented SUV. He then moved Cathy from the rear seat and placed her gently into the cooler. He then topped her up with another dose of chloroform, breathing the drug into her lungs, absorbing it into her bloodstream, assuring that she remained unconscious like a dead fish. He then replaced the lid and locked it up.

He would only have her in there for a few hours; she'd have plenty of air for the time. Afterward, he would remove the top lid.

Next, Jason walked over to the Dockmaster's quarters and asked one of the marina jocks for the hand dolly.

"Good evening Captain Garretty, how are you tonight sir?" the lad said greeting Jason.

"Howdy, Jonesy, doing just fine. Fixing on taking a trip down to Key Biscayne, picking up some nice folks in the morning, then heading over to the Bahamas; gonna do some fishing over there.

Jonesy, I need to borrow the hand dolly, I have a cooler full of ice, I need to load onto The Sharker."

"Oh, no problem, Mr. Garretty, the dolly is being used, but I can give you a hand."

Jonesy was attending to straightening up some of the stock on the shelves. The Dockmaster's shop sold odds and ends. Things like sun hats, sun block, and some marine related items usually picked up as last minute items by boat owners, just before casting off for a day of fishing.

Jonesy was a twenty-one-year-old jock who loved working at the marina. It was a great place to meet rich, good looking girls. Jonesy knew it helped to rub shoulders with well to do people.

The town of Jupiter and Juno Beach was a very high-class community with its fair share of famous people. Jonesy was a courteous kid with a year-round tan and still held on to a carefree surfer-dude lifestyle.

Jonesy helped Jason move the cooler unit out of Jason's SUV. It was heavy no doubt, but Jonesy had moved lots of these; even heavier ones. Cathy was now on board Jason's boat; The Sharker.

If Jonesy had only known… if only.

Darkness had fallen over south Florida but the moon was full and its reflected sunlight shimmered over the Atlantic. The palm trees along the Intracoastal swayed in the night trade winds, fanning the marina with its cool breezes gently rocking the boats at Gulliver's marine.

The night was gentle. Jonesy had mounted a Jimmy Buffet compact disc onto the player, and the music was piped throughout the marina at a low decibel but definitely loud enough to be heard and soft enough to have a calming effect on the scene.

"Please don't say *manjana* if you don't mean it."....... and Jimmy kept singing in the late evening.

It was most idyllic, such a tranquil setting and yet such a deceitful situation with precious little Cathy Davis lying in the bottom of a fishing cooler locked away with only a few air holes just to keep her alive.

Jason had removed Cathy during the evening from out of the cooler to make a short videotape recording.

He was very careful to make certain that the videotaping of Cathy revealed nothing noteworthy. The video of Cathy lasted approximately five minutes, short but long enough to show that Cathy was breathing on her own, was unmarked in any way and was holding onto her doll "Dixie" but sound asleep; in reality, unconscious from the chloroform.

Jason made sure the video only showed Cathy laying on the bed, just plain white bed sheets, nothing notable regarding the inside of The Sharker, he had hung white bed sheets all around the immediate videotaping area and was quite satisfied as to the pristine, sanitary environment, essentially rendering a blank background, only to highlight Cathy.

He finished with the video, and now Cathy was laying back inside the cooler and looking quite comfortable, but out cold.

Jason's camouflaging techniques had proved to be very thorough. He had managed to play the parts and roles to the tee in order to blend into the environment and situation at hand to carry out his evil plans and deeds. Jason was a ruthless, cold-blooded killer; no mistake was to be made about that. Underneath that surface of *everyday boating Joe,* he was as evil as the devil wanted him to be.

Jason's arms didn't need much twisting when there was a buck to be made. Yes, to be sure, there was certain tranquility even in this ironic situation.

Cathy was out cold, and yet somehow tucked out of the way in the arms of destiny this quiet evening until her ordeal came to full realization the next day, under The Bahamian sun.

All, was indeed quiet on the eastern front. With Cathy, having been drugged enough to keep her out of the way for at least another fifteen hours, Jason had decided to go above deck.

He had already returned the Nissan SUV rental and dropped the video addressed to 6565 Sailfish Drive into the US Mailbox just down the street, and thereby was cleared of all onshore duties and responsibilities, at this time.

He didn't think twice about having the video postmarked from his nearby marina location. The origin may as well have been a diversion or decoy; the proximity didn’t configure into his risk management factors, and he may have had a point.

He had rented the SUV in his own name and drew no attention. He had no unusual behavioral traits.

Jason checked on Cathy making sure she was all right; she was.

The time was now approaching midnight,and Jason decided to cast off.

He had purchased his boat some years back in Nag's Head North Carolina. It was a nice thirty-eight foot Bertram. It was perfect for fishing, with a wide beam making it stable in rough waves. Jason was up on the fly bridge, leaning back in his Captain's chair, as he sailed the boat out into the middle of the Intracoastal and headed for the Jupiter Inlet.

This evening luck was with him again. The Jupiter Inlet is known for very fast currents especially during tidal changes, and many a boat has had trouble clearing the inlet. This night, however, all was quiet, and all was calm. It was going to be a very smooth exit from the inlet past the breakers and out into open water directly out to sea into the Gulf Stream.

Jason popped open a can of beer and found the station for the all-news broadcast channel. He listened to the newscaster report on Jason's success thus far.

“Further breaking developments in the gruesome murder of Mrs. Linda Davis this afternoon and the subsequent kidnapping of the Cathy Davis, the six-year-old daughter of Mr. and Mrs. Eldon Barnes Davis, south Florida residents were shocked today to learn of the slaying late this afternoon.

Police rushed to the posh Davis home having received a call from Mr. Davis upon discovering his slain wife and disappearance of his daughter. Mr. Davis had just returned from a business trip to Canada.

Apparently, the security procedures in place at the Davis estate had been compromised leading to this sad story.

Police are asking south Florida residents who may have eye witnessed a late model brown van in the Sailfish Drive area at approximately 5:30 to 7:30 PM this evening to please assist.

All calls will be strictly confidential and callers may remain anonymous. In addition Police are presently combing the area south of West Palm to Ft. Lauderdale and have advised motorists to be prepared for roadblocks.

Police, at this time, are unable to provide an accurate description of the assailant, but a projected image of a likely appearance will be forthcoming in due course. Eldon Barnes Davis is the Chief Executive Officer of Davis Investments International, and Holiday Jewel Hotels and Casinos, a multinational financial empire.

This has been a *WQWS* news exclusive, stay with us…as the newscaster went on, Jason was feeling very proud of himself.

The US Mail was right on time. Smitty; the Mailman upon whose route the Davis estate fell was really looking forward to getting on down to Sailfish Drive today. He was a lucky man. He did carry with him today mail for the Davis home. It was a rare Saturday there wouldn't be any mail for the Davis family and today was not a rare day.

This would give Smitty the opportunity to stop and chat a while with "Luther" the weekend guard up at the Davis estate.

As Smitty reached the Davis Estate, his spirits were somewhat dampened, when he realized that The Davis Estate was still being monitored by the local Police department.

Two Police cruisers were parked out front just either side of the driveway leading up to the main entrance gate, not to mention two more unmarked Police cars, across the street. "This was going to take some doing," Smitty said to himself.

He did want very much to speak with Luther. Smitty had a certain persistence about him. He made his way up the street driving his US Mail Jeep slowly towards two Officers leaning against the first cruiser. The Officers motioned towards Smitty to continue driving up to the mailbox located just on the far side of the gate guardhouse.

Smitty was going to get his chance after all. It was looking like the cops were going to let him get by. He'd be able to talk with Luther and perhaps get an inside scoop on this caper. However, as Smitty was to find soon out; he'd be having no such luck today.

"Good day to you sir," said one of the cops. "I'm afraid you'll have to move right along, we'll just escort you to the gate if you don't mind."

Smitty went along with the request and slowly drove his US Mail Jeep up to the gate where Luther was standing with a long face, looking very disparaging and authoritative in his freshly pressed guard uniform. Luther tried to ignore Smitty and put on a real serious face, not even flinching the slightest bit as Smitty approached.

"Luther old buddy!" Smitty called over as he came flush with the guard house. "What's the latest on this here caper, huh? Why don't you spill me a couple of beans? The boys down at the plant would love to hear from you. You know what's going on here, don't you? I just know you do.

Tell me old buddy, whatcha got?" Smitty tried desperately to get some information from Luther, but Luther just looked on past Smitty towards the two Police Officers.

Luther had worked with Smitty down at the same plant for the US Postal Service, but when Luther reached retirement age shortly afterward, he obtained this job guarding the Davis estate on weekends.

Luther and Smitty were old chums from way back, but one thing they enjoyed doing was being able to give each other the "one-upmanship" now and then.

This was an opportunity for Luther today to do just that to Smitty. Luther wasn't saying anything; he was going to remain tight lipped.

All of a sudden, Luther surprised the hell out of Smitty. Luther blurted out, addressing the Police Officers. "Officers, Officers! Look here I say! Make sure this driveway is kept clear at all times like you were asked to do."

Smitty couldn't believe his ears, here was his old buddy Luther ordering the Police around giving out commands. Smitty smiled to himself. In this instant, the Police Officers had no alternative but to comply with Luther's request. Smitty was indeed wasting time and blocking the driveway. It wasn't that the Police paid any attention to Luther, normally they'd have retaliated and reprimanded Luther, not to get involved with Police matters but in this case they just let it go. Smitty fell into Luther's trap as bait for the cops in succumbing to Luther's false authority.

Luther was pretty proud of himself as he put on his best effort in his serious make-believe look. It was a show for Smitty, and Smitty knew it.

Luther was having fun, poking around with the Police making himself seem important ordering both them and Smitty around like as if Luther was some kind of big cheese. Luther would be getting together with Smitty later on down at the greyhound races in Hollywood.

The two of them would have a beer over this one for sure. Luther loved being able to act important. Smitty was sent on his way by the Police as he handed the mail over to one of the Officers. The Police would personally handle the delivery of the mail from the postman to the Davis house.

All packages and letters were initially scanned for signs of tampering, or for trigger devices slipped inside of envelopes; that may have been modified into letter-bombs.

Once the Police examined each article by x-rays and atmospheric particle detectors for traces of chemicals consistent with explosives, only then would delivery be approved to Mr. Davis.

Today, two days after the kidnapping, Jason posted the videotape recording to Eldon Davis, which he would receive the day after Linda's funeral.

***

Chapter Six

Attempt the end, and never stand to doubt:
Nothing's so hard but search will find it out.

Richard Lovelace - Seek and Find

The night had been robbed of its ability to calm Eldon with sleep, restful sleep. As much as Eldon had tried and as weary as he was, sleep would not come. Eldon regained some strength as the sun broke the horizon spearing its rays of light in through Eldon's den window looking out onto the Intracoastal Waterway bringing Eldon finally to grips with the reality of this day.

The cold hard facts as indeed they were. Felix and Billy had been up most of the night too. In some ways, each of them individually came together as one. The three of them had not left Eldon's den all night. It had been a night of sorrow, a night of fear, a night full of desperation and longing. Each man reached out in his own way for answers to questions they knew not.

There had been the onset of lethargy creeping into the feelings floating about the room. It had been brought about no doubt by the seemingly insurmountable and immediate obstacles at hand.

Eldon was about to break that state of mind and get things rolling. He sipped on a cup of freshly brewed coffee that Maria; the housemaid had prepared. The aroma of the fresh brew permeated the den causing both Billy and Felix to awaken. It was already 6:15 AM.

Eldon poured both his friends cups of coffee, and while setting the pot back onto the tray, Eldon said, "you fellows know that it’s going to be some time before our lives get back to normal. My life will never be normal again as I have known it to be. Our number one priority is Cathy's return. I will not stop until that has happened."

Billy had been working through most of the night getting Eldon's speed boat ready. He had tended to the fueling and supplying the craft with all necessities. Eldon had suggested to Billy that it may be a good idea to ready The Stinger in case they needed it.

Once Billy had finished with the boat, he looked after the chopper; Eldon's helicopter sitting on the pad in back of the house just a half acre to the left of the dock where Eldon kept his boat.

All was made ready for immediate use no matter what mode of transportation may be required.

Felix had further lent his expertise working the various news media that had been calling in all night long and handled the press releases keeping the news hounds off of Eldon's back.

As the morning wore on Eldon, Felix and Billy understood their individual responsibilities instinctively.

Naturally, Eldon dealt with the Police and FBI. Billy looked after the equipment that may be required to mount a chase or track a fugitive, in this case, a kidnapper.

Felix was the point man. Felix or "Licks" as Eldon affectionately referred to his good friend was essential in keeping the media and Eldon's personal life in check and balance.

Felix was a psychologist, advisor, and friend all rolled into one. He was an important filter and screening Agent. Without Felix, Eldon's ability to manage would have been seriously curtailed.

Events were moving along. Television camera crews were on a constant vigil outside the gates to

Eldon's estate. Eldon now had separately secured telephone lines coming into his house that the FBI had just finished installing.

Eldon was instructed to use only this line when communicating with law enforcement officials. Eldon had been on the phone most of the morning. Billy was in and out.

The media was trying very hard to keep abreast of the events.

Billy was busy, keeping track of him was next to impossible. The press tried following Billy, but they had trouble keeping up with him especially when Billy did most of his moving about by helicopter and The Stinger Scarab.

Billy had arranged to meet contacts that were supplying him with various essentials. These contacts would meet Billy at specified times in specified places such as Davis Investment's private corporate jet hangar which was sealed off to the public. Access was granted by airport security only to personnel authorized by Mr. Davis and his associates.

Billy had been flying around most of the morning obtaining specialized equipment that Eldon had asked for during their discussion the previous night.

Time had passed without notice. It was now noon. Officer Grant brought the mail up to the house and was shown into Eldon's den by Maria.

Maria announced Officer Grant. "Mr. Davis, the good Policeman is here to deliver your mail. Should he bring it in to you or should I take it and sort it like I usually do for Mrs. Davis?"

Having just said the words “Mrs. Davis”; Maria started crying. She couldn't hold her tears back. Maria stood in the doorway to Eldon's Den sobbing as

Officer Grant stood next to her holding the canvas bag.

Eldon walked over to Maria immediately and tried to calm Maria wrapping Maria in his arms. Maria had been with Eldon and Linda ever since they moved to Florida. Maria had become part of the family. She was a sweet Cuban-American. She became a landed immigrant having arrived in Florida during the Mariel Boat Lift; when thousands of Cubans fled Castro's dictatorship. Maria loved The Davis family as she loved her own.

This tragedy had devastated Maria, but she wasn't about to desert Mr. Davis now. She knew he needed her to take care of the house while Mr. Davis was trying to get his life in order.

Maria sobbed as Eldon held her and escorted her gently over to the couch helping her sit down beside him. Eldon continued to hold Maria and kissed the top of her forehead gently.

She sat there in his arms for a few more moments holding onto a napkin wiping her endless tears saying, "oh, Mr. Davis, I loved Mrs. Davis so very much and Cathy, well Cathy, oh my God where can Cathy be Mr. Davis, where can she be?"

Eldon motioned for Officer Grant to come on over to the couch. Felix took the mailbag from Officer Grant and laid it to the side of the coffee table.

Eldon released Maria, stood up and called Officer Grant over towards the corner of his den.

He said, "Officer Grant as you can see Maria is pretty shaken up. Why don't you take her outside and give her a ride back to her house where she can be with her family for the rest of the day."

"I'd be happy to give her a ride home Mr. Davis." Eldon further comforted Maria, and suggested she go back home to her family and rest for a couple of days.

Maria left with Officer Grant.

Felix had been sifting through the mail sorting the pieces into what obviously was business mail and another pile for personal type of mail. There was one letter that looked very unusual to Felix. It was a letter to Cathy postmarked with yesterday's date mailed from Pompano Beach with the return address same as the envelope address. This, he placed aside.

“Eldon there's a letter here addressed to Cathy which looks strange,” Felix said to Eldon. Eldon reached out and took the letter from Felix as he handed it to Eldon.

Eldon examined the letter and realized that it was weird. He carefully opened the letter and saw immediately that it was composed in the same manner as the original ransom note. This time the letter was signed “Captain Video.” Eldon read the communiqué to himself first then he took a deep breath looked both Billy and Felix in the eye then started reading out loud.

Your daughter is fine, video to prove, soon.
Do as you're told

“I hope to God Cathy's okay," Eldon said.

Felix had a look of disgust on his face.

"Billy, hand me that phone will you, Eldon said.

“I'm going to give Agent Miller from the FBI a call. I better let him know we received this communiqué; he'll want to know that there's been another contact made. You know guys, even though I detest Miller and his people, I can't help it. I have to let them know. Otherwise they'll claim that we're interfering and hampering their Police work.

We must cooperate with Miller to a certain extent. Hell, who knows, their government shrinks might even come up with some mental profile from the last two messages that this menace from hell has left for me." Eldon's voice carried an element of loathing.

His eyes squinted, and his face contorted slightly to reveal a feeling of intolerance and revolt.

Eldon dialed Agent Miller's number and relayed the new developments. Miller told Eldon that he'd be over in a few minutes. "Jesus, time is passing by so damn fast that I'm having difficulty keeping track of events."

Eldon's comment showed signs of strain.

"The first thing I need to get done before anything else gets into the way is to have Linda's funeral finalized, and her body laid to rest. That's going to take place tomorrow. I want her resting in peace as soon as possible. Then I can get on managing and focus on what we all will need to do."

Eldon took a moment to reflect in his own way pausing a moment then looked at his two friends and continued saying. "Miller better get his ass over here fast because I've got no time to waste. Felix, get a hold of the funeral director and confirm the times and arrangements…would you my friend? I'm about to drop from exhaustion. I'm going to grab a quick shower; maybe that will liven me up a bit. I know I'm going to have to get some sleep pretty soon, but first I'll want to deal with Miller. Then determine what they intend to do about this communiqué."

Eldon went to grab his shower. Shortly afterward Agent Miller from the FBI arrived and was now sitting on the couch in Eldon's Den.

Miller was actually the Regional Director of the FBI for the southeast region.

Miller had been instructed to drop all his current interests and give his full attention and time to this Davis case, the minute that it had happened, and that directive was issued by the FBI director himself; A.B. Kingsbury. Miller understood this case was of paramount importance.

Miller had been around the block himself a number of times and was a seasoned veteran in the bureau. Miller's attitude today seemed a notch or two above his condescending behavior from the day before.

Eldon sat back in his designer black leather easy chair. He was feeling invigorated after having freshened up and was now ready to take on the world. His observance was now acute. Eldon sipped on a glass of orange juice regarding Miller just off slightly to his left. They hadn't said a whole lot to each other since Miller's arrival. Miller stopped looking through his notes, folded his notebook and placed it back into his jacket's inside pocket.

Having done that he then pulled himself up to the edge of the couch and leaned forward resting his elbows on the tops of his knees and addressed Eldon. "So, Mr. Davis, you've been contacted by the kidnapper. May I see the note please?” Eldon stayed in the same position in his chair and indicated to Miller with his left hand pointing to an envelope on the coffee table directly in front of Agent Miller. Then Eldon said, "Yeah you sure can, that's why I called. It's right in front of you, go ahead have a good look. Agent Miller reached out and picked the envelope up off the petrified wood coffee table.

He examined the envelope first without extracting its contents. "Mr. Davis," Miller said. "Do you realize this is postmarked the day before yesterday?" This man we are dealing with has demonstrated a high-risk factor and yet an obvious penchant for premeditation."

"Yeah, it would seem that way, I'm glad you're on top of things Miller," Eldon said in a very condescending manner.

"Now, look here Mr. Davis, I didn't come over here to get into a verbal "fisticuffs" with you."

Eldon was quick to respond. "Then I suggest to you sir, that you enlighten me with things that I do not already know and stop wasting my time."

"All right Mr. Davis lets continue." Miller finished saying.

Eldon still sat in his chair not having moved from his original position. He was tolerant of Miller. Eldon, in fact, had Miller's role figured out in this situation. Eldon had already decided that Miller would be a pawn.

Miller continued. "Mr. Davis, this guy has got to have a plan."

Eldon then interrupted Miller before he could go on. Eldon cut him off abruptly.

"Do you have a picture of this person? Have you obtained any sort of evidence as to positively identifying the gender of this person?" Eldon asked politely.

"Well, no we haven't Mr. Davis," Miller replied.

"Then how in the hell do you know the kidnapper is male? Look Agent Miller; get your facts straight before you start shooting off at the mouth…all right?" Eldon was a bit unhinged, to say the least.

Eldon knew very well that Miller had only been using a figure of speech when referring to the kidnapper as being "a guy, " but Eldon wanted to establish his ground with Miller.

Eldon wanted to give notice now in no uncertain terms that he wanted facts and the facts given to Eldon better be correct. Eldon was not yet finished, as Miller was soon to find out. "Look, Mr. Davis, you're right, we don't know who this person is and no we haven't established whether the kidnapper is male or female." Miller paused for a second.

"So, go on Agent Miller, I'm listening."

Miller opened up the envelope and took out the note inside and read it to himself. "Well, this should give our people something to go on. We'll get this bastard sooner or later Mr. Davis; I can promise you that."

After having said that Miller felt he had made another error with Davis by having made a promise that he might not be able to keep. Miller now anticipated Eldon's response but kept on talking evading Eldon.

"Well, it's not a whole lot of information, but because he has demonstrated an ability to lay plans and work that plan, I would preliminarily say; that that is a good thing. Dealing with someone whom we can track and analyze gives us the edge over someone who otherwise may act irrationally and in random moves. Eventually, I'd say he'll slip up, breaking his pattern and that's when his tracks will be uncovered."

Eldon responded, “Agent Miller, you don't seem to appreciate the urgency of this matter to the same degree that I do. You're willing to wait for a break in his plan so that you can follow his tracks. Well look here my friend, my daughter doesn't have the luxury of time that you seem to have. I'm fully aware of the fact that my wife's murderer is not some amateur. My time frame is not one of unlimited duration. Agent Miller if your people can unravel some clues from these two notes that we now have in our possession, well then that'll be greatly appreciated. But I don't want unfounded hopeful implications from you. I want just the facts if you don't mind, is that okay with you sir? I do expect your full cooperation, but I do not appreciate your overconfidence concerning your success. For God's sakes man, my daughter's life is at stake, and I'm about to bury my wife tomorrow!"

Eldon was a little hard on Miller. But Eldon did want to establish his territory and have Miller understand just exactly who was working for whom. Eldon didn't want to give Miller the slightest indication that Eldon's intelligence or trust could in any ways shape or form be compromised. The more Eldon kept his distance from Miller, the cleaner the Police investigation would remain. Besides, Eldon needed some leeway and elbow room to establish his freedom and thereby allow Felix and Billy to maneuver without interference from the authorities.

Eldon continued. "Agent Miller if that is all, I have some private matters to attend to, so if you'll excuse me."

Eldon didn't have time to finish his sentence. He knew Miller would want to ask some more questions and he was waiting for Miller's response.

"Ah, Mr. Davis, I know you're swamped with things to do now, but this will only take a moment or two longer, and then I'll be on my way. I would like to ask you just a few more questions if you don't mind.

Eldon was now about to blow Miller's mind. "Well, sure Agent Miller, no problem, but if you don't mind why don't we go to my office where I can address your concerns, and I can get started on a few of the things I need to get done as well; okay Inspector?"

Miller had no objections. He followed Eldon up the stairs leading to Eldon's private inner sanctum. Miller walked up behind Eldon following him closely. As Eldon reached the top of his stairway, he motioned to Agent Miller to follow him down to the right. Miller had been up here the day before but had not really noticed the plaques, pictures, and accolades hung on the walls of the hallway.

There were plenty of artful photographs of Eldon and Linda. Of Eldon, Linda, and Cathy.

Then there were the photographs of Eldon with members of Congress and Senators not to mention three past Presidents of The United States.

There was one of Eldon with the Secretary of the Treasury and the President of the World Bank. Eldon no doubt had the respect of the international financial community. Eldon was a powerful man.

Eldon stopped in front of an oak French door at the end of the hall. He lifted his hand to slide a panel beside the door frame which was approximately eye height. As Eldon slid the panel exposing a viewfinder, a glass door closed behind them, creating a hermetically sealed environment. Two seconds afterward, there was a soft beeping sound that signaled testing being conducted, and the following result then displayed on a readout just above the oak French doors. It read:

ENTRY DENIED.MOLECULAR SCANNING: POSITIVE

As the readout sped across the monitor, a buzzer sounded. It was loud. Eldon stood behind Miller. He watched for the reaction on Miller's face; it was there just as Eldon thought it would be.

Miller turned back to Eldon with objection and said, "what the hell is this Davis, what are you trying to do here? I've had enough of your games."

Eldon punched some codes into his handheld remote unit silencing the warning buzzer.

"Can't be too careful nowadays now can we Sam? You don't mind if I call you Sam, do you?"

The buzzer sounded due to detection of microscopic particulates found within the sensing area of the sealed compartment formed by the closing doors behind Miller and Eldon.

Eldon then turned to Miller and said, “you see, no need for a “pat down.” I know you are carrying a gun; this is just to verify it. So if you want my further cooperation, please place your piece into this tray.. there are to be no weapons from this point on.”

Miller complied, he placed his 38 into the tray on the table and stood beside Eldon watching. “I'm trying to show you that you're not dealing with some amateur here Sam. I want to cooperate with you. Didn't you say you had some questions for me? Just one more step and we're good.”

After Eldon had slid the panel beside the door, it exposed the viewfinder coupler, with a red blinking LED directly underneath the viewfinder. Eldon leaned in towards the coupler and looked into the viewfinder. Within one 10th of a second the red blinking LED switched over to a constant green LED; this was Eldon's retina scan security system.

Nobody was getting in here without having retina verification. Eldon then reached for the door handle on the French doors which then exposed a steel door, not unlike a bank vault. He then pushed a sequence of buttons on the exposed keypad and the massive doors opened sliding into the wall horizontally giving access to Eldon's inner sanctum.

Eldon had made certain that his office contained the latest technology available when it came to security entry systems. He now regretted not having addressed security to the property and protocol in access requirements to the main house, but that was now too late, Linda was gone.

As a backup, an invalid or non-authorized viewing into the scanner would generate an automated alert at Davis International Headquarters, notifying himself and Felix Balon in real time, which would then activate the dispatching of security Agents to the Davis estate. Only Linda and Eldon had scanner clearance, and even Linda had to clear it with Eldon before she attempted scanning, this was solely for security purposes, forcing Linda to view the scanner without notification to Eldon first would have triggered an automated security response. Security was tight, in this area, it should have been equally as tight at the entrance gate to his estate, but Eldon knew that would have been impractical in practice. Eldon was hoping that this little exercise would have the desired effect on Miller. It seemed to be working.

One thing about cops Eldon knew, no matter what position or rank they happened to hold; cops had a built in overzealous sense of curiosity especially for things that were unfamiliar to them; most of all for security procedures.

Miller fit this profile to a tee. Miller was starting to unravel. This being Eldon's domain, Agent Miller knew that once he crossed the threshold into Davis's private world of security, he would be at Davis' mercy.

“Fine,” Eldon thought. “If Miller wanted to play this game about asking more questions, then Eldon was going to maintain control and the upper hand. He felt it important for Miller to understand that Eldon's resources were virtually unlimited.

Whatever the FBI had in its arsenal, Eldon could match and most likely surpass." Eldon's contacts were endless. Since this incident had happened, already Eldon's information gathering and intelligence network had already been hard at work.

Those various sources were feeding this information into one of Davis Investments' specially secured mainframe computers that Eldon had programmed for sensitive matters.

The encryption software had very sophisticated algorithms, running concurrently accessing various other networks of government and private data banks throughout the United States and overseas.

Eldon was about to provide the good FBI man with a little demonstration. Eldon was not about to be upstaged. If Agent Miller was to serve a positive purpose in this case, he had better be on his toes and operate at the highest levels of efficiency.

In some ways, he wanted Miller to become an opponent, more of a competitor on the same team to be sure but ensuring and bringing to the surface every iota of Miller's professional knowledge and expertise.

Eldon asked Sam Miller to have a seat in one of the chairs facing a large mahogany desk. This private confine was Eldon's workplace. From this desk and immediate surroundings, Eldon directed the business and welfare of his global empire. Eldon conducted most of his work, thinking and managing right from this spot. Rarely did he spend time at his office headquarters in Ft. Lauderdale.

"Mr. Davis, if you don't mind humoring me for a minute or two I do need to ask you a few basic questions just so that I have a solid baseline from which to proceed. These lines of questions may be beneficial to both you and me seeing that we might uncover key aspects inadvertently all because of some basic questions and concepts."

"Sure Sam, go ahead I have no problem with that, but you know you are going to have to make it quick," Eldon said in a disarming manner.

"Mr. Davis, your company is a multinational corporation and is privately held, is that correct?"

"Yes, Sam I believe the bureau knows all about that, but yes."

"And Mr. Davis, you have some interests internationally, from Monte Carlo, to Macau, to Singapore and throughout the Caribbean isn't that right?"

"Yes Sam, you are referring to my holdings in the resort hotel and casino industry, we have currently one hundred thirty-two properties of which twenty-nine are combined luxury resort and casino operations, some small, some big.

We employ close to a hundred thousand people in the resort hotel and casino business alone throughout the world. My father as your research might provide, opened his first roadside inn, Holiday Jewel Hotel back in the early fifties, and I don't have to tell you how successful he became.

Of course, when my father passed on, I took over the company and with my close associates and the help of my wonderful wife, we built this company into what it is today.

You know Sam, the hotel and casino business is a huge part of Davis International, but the greater bulk of my operations now concentrate on shipping and transportation, and high-tech in the Aerospace sector, mainly sensitive instrumentation research and development; in cooperation with NASA and the European Space Agency.

We develop instrumentation mainly for use in satellite technology. And as you know Sam, we do a great deal of work with DND; The Pentagon, being a major customer.
My company is one of the major suppliers of high-tech components, and my association with the Federal Government is on a first name basis with key individuals, Senators and White House personnel. I need not go further; I am sure you get the picture, Sam. We are very diversified, with any luck, we will be the first company with a hotel in space. That is what I am personally aiming for, maybe even a casino up there.

But I believe there is already enough gambling going on with the entire space program. That is the one element we are trying our utmost to eliminate, being unexpected and unwanted variables. But Sam, I am now getting away from the subject at hand, so what else is it you wish to know because what I've just told you pretty much covers it all. We have offices throughout the globe with Ft. Lauderdale being my anchor."

"Mr. Davis, I am satisfied at this point. Those will be all the questions I need to ask you at this point. I believe I have what I need." Sam said in a very smug way.

Eldon thought for a moment, "I believe I have what I need." Was there something Eldon had just said that was so revealing? Or was it a ploy by Sam to make it seem like Eldon had just blinked.

Whatever Miller's game was, Eldon was a bit surprised that these low-level questions somehow seem to satisfy the Inspector's appetite for curiosity; Eldon let it go.

He was glad to be done with Miller for today which allowed Eldon to get on with his day and do what was needed, and what was needed right now was to show Miller out.

“Director Miller,” Eldon stood and motioned for Miller to stand and come with him. Eldon walked Miller out saying, “I will contact you should something else come about and Eldon watched him get into his FBI SUV and drive off.

By day’s end, all his executives and global managers would have heard about this tragedy. Eldon prepared for Linda's funeral. He would need to be at the church in Lauderdale to receive people from all over flying in for the funeral proceedings.

The next day, Eldon, Billy and Felix were ready. Billy would drive Eldon to the funeral from where Eldon would accompany Linda's casket to The Gardens of Palm Memorial Cemetery in Pompano Beach, and see his wife buried this afternoon, three days after her death, and he did.

***

Chapter Seven

By the pricking of my thumbs
Something wicked this way comes.

William Shakespeare - Macbeth

The Prime Minister; Forbes Bishop of Grenada was in charge of a very small country, but with a huge appetite for prosperity. Bishop was willing to do anything for his people to make absolutely certain that Grenadians would have the quality of life in the Caribbean second to none and for that matter not just the Caribbean but the western hemisphere. He had seen enough poverty in his day and was witness personally to the deprivation of a crumbling society and its government that was evidenced in Haiti over the years and it was Bishop's sworn duty never to let that happen to his country and his people. Bishop was willing to do whatever and indeed it was "whatever it took" to ensure prosperity for his populace.

"Another espresso Domingo?" "No, no Mr. Prime Minister and I thank you for your time this morning. I know you have made these past few minutes a priority in your day, to meet with me and it is with great pleasure I am able to make this donation to your party and government." With that, Domingo handed over a cashier's cheque in the amount of five hundred thousand Dollars US to Forbes Bishop. Forbes was very happy to take the cheque from Domingo Alvarez.

"Ziggy," as he was known in his circles was the current president of the Caribbean Hotel and Casino Workers Union. A very powerful Union that had spread its tentacles throughout the Caribbean resort and hotel industry from small hotels to large mega resorts with casino operations.

In all, Ziggy and his empire had a Union strong membership of over 45 thousand, with affiliations and divisions to other international Unions thereby making his organization a virtual global entity. With the strong Caribbean Union membership…working in hotels, resorts, and casinos, the amount of annual Union dues collected by the Union ran into tens of millions of Dollars, and once invested, the Union's bank accounts were overflowing, not to mention its director's and Union president's well doings.

Domingo Alvarez headed the Caribbean sector of an Unionized dynasty, although a single entity; his ties with other international Unions was strong. It was unwritten with cooperation and rules of engagement, forming a Caribbean-wide Labor Union web of power.

The CHCW Union controlled a very powerful politically influential position throughout the islands by systematically dishing out Union strength; strong-arming and making their presence known.

Alvarez; "Ziggy" often brought fruits bearing blemishes, with this one current donation of a half a million Dollars not unlike many other donations in the past, Alvarez further secured his organization's foothold on the island of Grenada, where the "CHCW" Caribbean Hotel Casino Workers Union was headquartered.

This location offered a sterile perception in regards to the Union's reputation and standing. The fact that Grenada, was a non-gambling resort environment, a country supposedly free from the corruption and vice, associated with casinos, that spurred on prostitution and corruption; Ziggy and

CHCW was centered in the clean, pristine nation of Grenada. Not to mention of course the recent American invasion to weed out corruption and graft also helped in countless ways regarding Grenada's public image, but in reality, nothing could be further from the truth, be it told.

This meeting between Bishop and Ziggy had come to an end. Bishop was glad for the money. In fact, Bishop was going to use these new funds to finance the purchase of an MRI machine for the Health Sciences Center in Grenada. His country had the only accredited medical college in the Caribbean, and Bishop was proud of it and meant to keep it that way. Bishop had the best interest at heart for his people and his country. Bishop stood up from behind his desk and escorted Alvarez out of the PM's office.

With that, he welcomed his 11 AM reserved appointment visitor: Howard Rickover, United States Secretary of Defense.

After his meeting with Rickover and a further receipt of a five million Dollar cheque from The Secretary, Bishop reached into his drawer for his, Prime Minister's; "seal for deposit only."

Not really watching what he was doing, Bishop caught his thumb on the sharp tip of the letter opener. He thought nothing of it, but then picking up Alvarez's cheque, noted a drop of blood that seeped into the edges of both cheques and thought to himself, "how ironic," as he recalled a line from Shakespeare's Macbeth.

"Something wicked this way comes."

He stamped the cheques with his Prime Minister's seal and forwarded both for deposit.

***

Chapter Eight

Tracks be obscured
save for the brilliance of light

Eldon held the video tape cassette in his hand. It was high definition DVC pro cassette tape. He had now viewed the tape for the fifth time after having received it yesterday.

Today, he buried his wife, to rest in the arms of eternity. Again he had Billy and Felix by his side, and they sat in Eldon's den, discussing the situation at hand.

"Guys, I don't mind telling you, that as much as I am determined to find and get Cathy, I was a little bit frightened to view this tape, my mind ran wild with the worst of all outcomes, not knowing what was on this tape."

After having viewed the tape a number of times now…there was nothing else, just this video, and the note addressed to Cathy for some odd reason.

Eldon asked Billy to mount the video again. Billy handed the remote to Eldon; Eldon pressed play. The video started with text…

"Do as you're told."

Eldon sat on the edge of his seat, his hands clasping his face on both sides, covering his mouth as he teared up, while holding back his emotions.

He swallowed hard as Cathy's image appeared. She was his tiny Angel; she was Linda, and she was Cathy combined into one.

Eldon sobbed just for a few seconds as the images of Cathy continued on the video, showing various angles.

The video was of high quality. Eldon, along with Billy and Felix clearly saw that Cathy did not appear to be outwardly harmed; she was, however, no doubt drugged.

She appeared like a soft flower at the mercy of this kidnapper. She lay so quietly with Dixie in her sleeping grasp. Eldon feared for his daughter's life, and Billy and Felix knew it.

The written message was clear, was very "matter of fact," conveying no emotion or intent; just follow the instructions, which apparently were still to follow. Had no choice; it was a waiting game.

The video ended four minutes and fifty-one seconds after it had started. Felix told Billy to rewind and replay, Eldon nodded in agreement and the three men watched again.

This time, the three men watched for some possible clue; anything that might show a light through a crack to break this darkness, but no matter how many times they viewed the tape, nothing significant showed. The environment was white and pristine. There was nothing else on the video at all, just whiteness and Cathy lying upon a white bed sheet, apparently on a bed. The videotape went blank after reaching the four minute, fifty-one-second mark.

This time Eldon said: "no don't shut it off, let it run to the end; there may be something else on there. Billy let it run to the end. The three men sat there in silence, watching the blank screen for another fifteen minutes and nine seconds. The videotape ended… nothing.

"Billy, make a copy of it, make two copies of it," Eldon said to Billy.

Billy did so and later that day gave the original recording back to Eldon.

Eldon's brain was working overtime, all circuits were firing, he was intelligent beyond most people's understanding. Eldon's intelligence and ability to calculate, anticipate, and predict with probability was a gift that was sharpened each and every day having to run his company and sprawling empire. Eldon in fact did rely on trusted individuals and utilized the best people in the business, giving them the credibility and recognition they deserved.

This trait alone, served Eldon well allowing him to gain respect and trust from those he held in high places. He was about to call on one of his associates and friends.

Eldon had a feeling that Nick Kovacs was going to work some magic for him. Nick was someone who used to work for Eldon in his R&D labs that dealt with satellite surveillance technology. Eldon had hired Nick straight out of M.I.T. after personally having interviewed Nick himself. Nick gained his Ph.D. in molecular science and laser light innovative applications; Eldon knew Nick was going to be a huge asset to his tech division.

After six years with Eldon, NASA came calling, and Nick decided to make the switch to NASA, but always maintained contact with Eldon.

As a matter of fact, Eldon had lunch last month with Nick and his wonderful two kids, up in Cocoa Beach. Nick was an expert in laser and light technology; he was the Chief scientist and engineer in laser applications for the National Aeronautics and Space Administration.

If anyone knew anything about videotape, light, and spectrum, it would be Nick.

Eldon dialed Nick's number, being Saturday, Nick was sure to be home but shortly heading to the golf course…when his phone rang. He answered, "Nick Kovacs."

"Nick; Eldon. I wanted to thank you for coming to the funeral Nick and how much it meant to me. Thankyou Nick."

"Eldon, I am so very much sorry about what happened, is there anything I can do?" Nick asked in a very endearing offering manner.

"Nick, yes there is. I received a videotape recording of Cathy from the kidnapper. Nick I don't know what you can do, there doesn't seem to be anything significant about the tape, it seems to be professional recording quality, but I thought of calling you to have a look at it. Maybe there is something on there I am not seeing. Maybe whoever made this tape, had taped over top of something already taped before hand and there is something underlying with a clue or two. I really need your help and expertise in having a look at it, analyze it, see if it gives up something, anything at all."

"Eldon, it will be my pleasure. I can do that as soon as you get the tape into my hand. I'll go to my lab and see what I can find."

Eldon replied, "Nick I wish you would never have left Davis International, but you have found a new pathway to what you enjoy doing, and I wish you the best at NASA; maybe you will have a chance to visit the ISS, I hope you do. I know that's the reason you are there. I will have Billy fly the tape up to your place by chopper right away. He should be there within the next ninety minutes."

"Eldon, I will be here waiting for him, he knows where I live, and I have plenty of room for him to land, there is a large clearing on my property. I will be expecting Billy soon then.

Once again, Eldon, my heart goes out to you and Cathy, I will let you know as soon as I have finished with the analysis."

Eldon replied. "Thank you, my friend. Billy will be on his way in a few minutes."

Eldon handed Billy the cassette tape. Billy had been standing beside Eldon the whole time, and Billy didn't need any further information from Eldon, he knew what to do. Billy was in the sky within minutes and on his way to deliver the tape to Nick Kovacs.

Eldon let out a sigh, "okay, a stab in the dark, but a stab nevertheless."

As Eldon was about to walk down to his dock, and check to see the condition of his Scarab, the phone rang.

Eldon answered it, "Eldon Davis."

"Mr. Davis, good afternoon to you, this is Prime Minister Forbes Bishop from Grenada," the voice on the other end said.

***

Chapter Nine

Your hostage I shall deliver, he said.
His bones soon to rest, among the dead.

The voyage across the Atlantic to Abaco Bahamas from Jupiter Inlet takes approximately ten to thirteen hours of sailing time. With Jason's thirty-eight foot Bertram, that should be more than doable. This late-night departure at midnight found Jason out in the Atlantic's blue waters on calming seas.

The Bertram yacht planed out beautifully, and her strong engines hummed in tune pushing her through the waters at a comfortable 16 knots per hour. Jason high up on the flybridge, sat back in his captain's chair and sipped from a can of Michelob.

Cathy; just to the left of Jason's Captain's chair, still lying on the soft blanket lined fisherman's cooler, seemed comfortable for now, still out cold of course. His instructions were to take good care of the child and not to harm her in any way.

"With some luck, the kid would not awaken until he was rid of her and handed over to his contact at Sandy Point on Abaco Island in the Bahamas."

Jason had experience and know-how in this sort of thing, having already been involved in human trafficking.

He gained the trust and the confidence of fellow his criminals in the Bahamas, that being The Chief of Police on Abaco Island; Manko Butterfield of the Queens Police Force, on Abaco had been in the human trafficking business for a few years now, smuggling Haitians and Cubans through the Bahamas into the US.

Jason was Manko's contact and partner in this activity, and for the past four years, they had built a relationship that enabled one another in making a nice sum of cash. For each person, Jason was able to smuggle into the US Jason received five thousand Dollars; that was the going rate. Manko was Chief of Police on the island, so he was free to do as he wished.

The nature of the island integrity was at best in question at all times as it was on almost every Caribbean Island. First in the 70's and 80's the out-islands of the Bahamas were used as drop-off points for illegal drugs coming into the US. But over the years the American DEA put a stop to that, and now of late, things had switched over to smuggling people.

This seemed to work for Jason, he was a risk taker anyways and so far, things were working in his favor. Jason became so proficient at what he did with and for Manko that Manko had decided to bring him in on this latest and most significant money making venture.

About eight months back, Manko visited Jason on his Bertram yacht docked at Sandy Point, putting together this caper and contract.

Jason docked his boat at the Sandy Point Marina for most of the year, and Gulliver's whenever he was stateside. This early morning having left Gulliver's behind and now being well out in the Atlantic, past the twelve-mile limit, he was in international waters, safe and good to go all the way to Sandy Point on Abaco Island.

He took in the warm Gulf Stream breezes.

Florida's coastline lights had long disappeared off the horizon. He was in night darkness, save for the moon's beam, shimmering upon the ocean waters.

He reflected, back on the time when Manko had approached him about this job. It was eight or so months ago.

Manko Butterfield, a Bahamian with roots going back to the Lucayan-Arawak Indians; the first tribe encountered by Christopher Columbus upon his landing in the Bahamas, in an area now known as Rum Cay.

Manko had spoken very proudly about his heritage to Jason, emphasizing that his roots were well anchored in the islands, and his authority was to be unquestioned.

Manko's influence and family ran through various businesses and levels of Government in the Bahamas from Grand Bahama Island to Cat Cay, Andros, and Crooked Island.

One of his two sisters was well located serving big game fishermen in Bimini from her raw bar on the ocean, and his other sister "Violet," here on Abaco served as a babysitter to most of Marsh Harbour's residents.

His family was well connected even having a cousin on the Bahamas Supreme Court. Having several relatives in high places granted him no immunity from corruption, no; he was as corrupt and as ruthless as they come.

Jason knew this, and this, was why he trusted Manko.

Understanding that Manko had the connections he needed in case, Jason ran into trouble.

Their illicit relationship began with smuggling dope in the beginning and recently transitioning to smuggling people.

Jason, now thinking about that afternoon, how Manko approached him about this caper. Having just returned from a morning Charter booking; it was 12:30 in the afternoon as Jason's Sharker pulled into Sandy Point marina and his two charter guests had disembarked when he heard Manko calling out his name from the Dock master's area.

"*Jason mon..Jason..how ya doing mon, I need to come see you bout sumptin.*"

As Manko was walking down the dock towards Jason's slip, he kept saying his name; "Jason mon..Jason, have sumptin for you mon, now listen up!" Manko made his way on board The Sharker and proceeded in making himself at home. Naturally, Manko could make himself at home any place he pleased to on Abaco; he was the Chief of Police, and he ran the island, the show, the whole shooting match. He ran it all and nobody was about to question his motives. That was how things were, and the locals were very happy about it all.

Manko made himself comfortable by occupying one of the deep-sea fishing tackle chairs bolted to the back deck, sat back and swiveled around to face Jason, with a big smile on his face, sporting two golden incisors, and wearing aviator mirrored sunglasses.

"Jason mon, I just had the best conch on the island, you should hurry down to Mildred's before it is all gone, local boys just brought some in… the best, the best in the Bahamas mon, go get yourself some!"

He remembered Manko going on and on about fresh conch, but knew that that was not the reason Manko had come to see him that day, six months ago.

Manko laid it out. He wanted Jason to grab a young girl from a Florida home, a well-secured home, a very risky business, but with a huge payoff. Manko and Jason were in the people smuggling business, and this was the same thing, but from the other direction; coming to the Bahamas from the US mainland, not going from the Bahamas to the US mainland. A total reversal of both direction and reason but the outcome; well worth the risk.

After talking more about conch, and getting the terms straight, Jason had accepted the assignment and accepted an initial cash payment of thirty thousand Dollars six months ago, with another fifty thousand to be paid upon delivery of the girl into Manko's arms. That was the deal.

Once Jason had accepted the down payment of thirty thousand Dollars, there would be no going back, no pulling out, no reeling in an empty line and no giving back the money.

If Jason were even to suggest that, it would mean the end of Jason's charter fishing days and end of his evil life. Jason was a risk taker, and he took the bait. The thirty-thousand-Dollar bait was much too juicy to refuse.

He was already thirty thousand tax-free Dollars richer, and it was just a matter of time and planning to get the rest, and that would be a nice eighty-thousand-Dollar payoff.

Jason was good with it all. Jason was a very bad and evil person, but Manko, of course, was no better.

Both Jason and Manko knew very well, that if Jason was fortunate enough to make it back to Abaco with the kid, across the gulf stream and not be detained or boarded by the US Coast Guard or the American Police or even the FBI, then he would have gotten away clean.

There was no way; that authorities would allow Jason to cross into Bahamian waters if they knew Cathy was captive aboard Jason's boat; they would apprehend Jason at sea and ensure Cathy's safety at the earliest possible time.

If Jason were to make it to Sandy Point Abaco with Cathy, then all would be in order, a clean getaway.

Once Manko was in control of Cathy, the game was far too advanced for any worries. American authority did not extend into the Bahamas. Manko was in charge here, not the Americans; Jason knew this very well, and so did Manko. The plan was sound.

The Sharker was making good time, the weather was cooperating, light had broken six hours ago. The ocean was as breathtaking as ever. Cathy was still out like a light even at 11 AM with the sun beating down. The sea began to take on a roll which seemed to rock Cathy in its arms of confidence and waves of future outcome to be decided in the next few hours.

The sun had broken over the horizon six hours ago, like a giant wagon wheel of rays shooting over the ocean, Jason was heading due east, and now he could see signs of Abaco on the horizon. He was only 45 minutes out from Sandy Point, and his part was coming to an end soon and would be free to go.

Suddenly off starboard, Jason was caught off guard as he daydreamed; a forty-foot Fountain Ocean Racer blew by at high speed. The passengers waved with big smiles, as they blew by The Sharker bouncing over the waves, the klaxons blaring loud, sending a greeting, Jason waved back, relieved it was just some locals out for a joy ride. In fact, it was a scout boat sent out by Manko.

Manko was anticipating Jason's arrival into Sandy Point, and Manko needed Jason's ETA. Manko needed to be ready for Jason, so Manko sent out his scouting party, coming off as a party boat. Certain things and situations were afoot this day, and those certain things and situations needed to be dealt with once and for all.

Manko's bosses were not happy, and Manko was not happy. Jason had left loose ends, leading to a situation, not in the plan. Manko was not happy, no he was not.

Manko's favorite lunch was conch; cracked conch to be specific. He had that every day, but today was different. Manko did not have any conch to eat today, not one bite.

***

Chapter Ten

How far that little candle
throws his beams.

Shakespeare - Merchant of Venice

“Prime Minister, how are you?” Eldon replied. Eldon was very surprised, as he replied back to Bishop he looked over to Felix, raising his eyebrows, widening his eyes in a look of surprise and slight bewilderment. He saw Felix react, Eldon responded loudly, enough to make sure that Felix heard him say Prime Minister. Eldon could see Felix's “WTF” reaction as well.

It’s not that Eldon did not know Prime Minister Bishop, it was that Eldon was not that close to The Right Honourable Forbes Bishop. They had in fact met on three prior occasions. Felix was with Eldon on one of those occasions being the Caribbean Hotel Association Awards Gala held in Fajardo Puerto Rico at the El Cortez Resort. That event Gala had taken place just two months ago, and the Prime Minister's face was still clearly etched in Eldon's mind. Prime Minister Bishop was Eldon's special table guest at the Gala for the evening and they had gotten along quite well.

One of Eldon's most exclusive luxury resort operations was just a mile outside of Grenada’s capital city; St. George’s.

It was very intimate and very exclusive. Eldon's firm “Davis International” operated the Caribbean group of hotels and resorts under the Holiday Jewel Hotels and Resorts banner, and make no mistake about it, the property in Grenada was, in fact, a jewel in Grenada's crown.

Recognized year after year as being among the top five luxury resort getaways in the Caribbean. It catered exclusively to adults only, and was a favorite destination for the rich and famous, being only 45 Villas set in the mountainside with breathtaking views of the Caribbean turquoise sea. Each villa came with its own dedicated 24-hour Butler service. Pickup at the airport was by hotel provided luxurious private Jaguar XJ automobiles. Rates, of course, were in the thousands per night, but when you have your very own infinity pool right off your bedroom and living room, well…it really doesn't get any better.

The resort in Grenada happened to be one of Eldon's favorite locations. It was Prime Minister Bishop who arranged the ribbon cutting ceremonies on the opening of the resort almost five years ago and the one other time their paths had crossed was when Eldon had to step in, to vouch and arrange for his selected General Manager to be the Chief Executive for the property.

For some unknown reason, the culture in Grenada at the time had not caught up with the lowered glass ceiling for female executives as it was in the US and Canada. Resistance to women in positions of power was very much alive and well, causing friction with Bishop's Home Affairs Minister, who was not cooperative in granting Olivia Sutton the work permit she needed to manage the property. Eldon stepped in and spoke with Bishop. The next day all was good with Ms. Sutton's work permit approval.

Eldon had come across these types of irritations throughout the Caribbean, having learned after several years that in special cases, "greasing of the palms" was required to get things done and to get things done with urgency.

Urgency was just not a commodity that existed in the islands; it was something that had to be imported in most cases.

"Mr. Davis, Eldon," Prime Minister Bishop continued. "It is with deep sadness I learned of your loss this past week, and I am shaken by the news of your missing daughter. I must tell you of my sense of loss that tears me to the bone for the loss of your wife and my sincere condolences. I know in my heart that God's angels are watching over your daughter for her safety and quick return." Eldon sensed a deep emotional connection and felt Bishop's words to hold truth and sincerity.

"Mr. Prime Minister, thank you for your kind words, we are working on all fronts to secure Cathy's return as soon as humanly possible, thank you for your call, Your Honour."

Eldon was at this point thinking the call was to be over, but Bishop continued on.

"Eldon, it is with regret that I need to call you at this time especially inopportune as it is. But as circumstances dictate, I thought it best to make you aware of a very urgent situation we are facing on the island as well as the overall status of your hotel and casino operations throughout our Caribbean community."

Eldon listened, his business sense had taken over and was now tuned in clearly to what was being said by Prime Minister Bishop. With Grenada being one of the smaller islands in the Caribbean, the Prime Minister of the island was in the very unusual position of being involved personally in a great deal of the business dealings, closely tied into the island's commerce.

The island's two major industries that kept it alive were tourism and banking, with banking being a far second. It was not surprising that Bishop himself would be involved in such comings and goings. With an island population of only fifty thousand, in terms of the USA, it was a small city.

Bishop in fact was nothing more than a glorified Mayor. But in this case, he was The Prime Minister of a nation, the small but strategically located and the very important Caribbean nation of Grenada, as the United States Secretary of Defense; Rickover had confirmed just today, with his five million Dollar installment to Bishop.

Grenada had attained full nationhood and was a member of the United Nations, yes, Eldon was dealing with a head of state, make no mistake about it.

Bishop continued. "Eldon, the thing is that I believe you will need to fly down here and meet with myself and perhaps another individual. The matter at hand is not best discussed over the telephone and to be quite frank Eldon, this matter extends to your wide scope of resort and casino operations throughout the Caribbean. Do I make myself clear Mr. Davis? I do need you to fly in for a few hours."

Eldon was a bit agitated now, he answerd, "Mr. Prime Minister, you know I have very capable people who can handily address whatever situations or concerns you may have.

At this time, with my daughter being at the mercy of who knows what, it is not a time I can just jump on a plane and make my presence there. Mr. Prime Minister, I have Louis James close by in St. Vincent this week. As you well know, Louis is my Senior Vice President of Operations for Holiday Jewel Hotels and Casinos; I am certain he can address and solve any situation that may be on your plate."

Bishop cut in, “Mr. Davis, Louis and I have met, but unfortunately Mr. James doesn't seem to understand the urgency and underlying dangers involved. It is my and Secretary Rickover's opinion that you would need to come in for a short period of time.”

Eldon now thought, “Rickover,” what the hell does the US secretary of defense have anything to do with this?

Eldon knew there was a major construction project developing on the east side of the island by American contractors, but this is now a new fly in the ointment, or was Bishop just throwing out names to get him to fly down?”

Eldon replied. “Mr. Prime Minister, I will see what my schedule permits, as you can appreciate, my schedule at this time is pretty much, make as I go. I will try to clear some time for a quick flight down in the coming days. I do not usually do this sort of thing, but I will in this case. I will have one of my associates advise your office of my intended arrival date and time. It may be on very short notice.”

Bishop responded saying, “that’ll be fine Mr. Davis, but please make it soon as possible.”

The call ended.

“Felix! Get Louis James on the phone right away. I want to know what in the hell is going on.”

At this point, the phone rang again. Felix answered, “Davis residence.”

The voice on the other end said, “Felix, this is Kovacs up at the Kennedy Space Center.”

***

Chapter Eleven

Heaven is blue skies, hell is darkness and pain
Yet through the darkest hell,
Heaven's light shall shine once again.

"Hey Nick, Eldon is right here, let me get him for you."

"Eldon it's Nick up at Kennedy, he's sounding pretty excited."

Eldon took the phone from Felix, "thanks "licks" Eldon said.

"Nick! Hey, that was quick, you are calling because you have some news for me?"

Nick responded saying; "well Eldon I think I do, but the thing is, there is always something to be found on these tapes, it could be flaws in the tape itself, it could render up such things as underlying images not quite erased, even audio, extracted from prior recordings. In this instance Eldon, I used light spectrometry analysis and a spectroscopy processes. These processes reveal and show UV and infrared light wavelength activity not seen with the human eye, and although normally these light waves would have no significance whatsoever to the imagery or content of the video, in this case, however, there is something of interest."

Eldon could hardly contain himself and tears of hope and joy welled up in his eyes.

"So, Nick, what is it?

"Eldon, I'm not sure how this will configure in your mind but it certainly sends me a message. I think we have something to go on; a clue, and possibly a location, but that is something you will have to hunt down through a process of elimination or just good detective work. But Eldon, I do have something for you."

Nick sounded very encouraging, and usually with scientist, they were very skeptical about everything.

Eldon knew this very well; the scientific method demanded a certain protocol which had to be followed in order to arrive at a solution.

Theories were fine, but to find something solid and conclusive was of huge significance. So, if Nick was telling him that he had something, then by golly he did. There wasn't anything that Eldon could see on that tape other than heartache and pain, now Nick had uncovered a patch of blue sky to the darkness and gloom. Eldon listened carefully as Nick went on.

"So, here's the thing Eldon, and I'll let you think about this as I explain and see if your mind goes to the same place as mine did."

"Yeah Nick, I'm listening go on."

Nick began, "Eldon, the tape shows a pristine white environment, nothing special going on. What I did was to analyze the intensity of the color spectrum within that environment. Two things were revealed, the first; was that ever so faintly, and this could only have been revealed by computer analysis, and wavelength variation measuring equipment, every 15 seconds there is a slight increase in the intensity of white light. This slight modulation you would not have noticed at all, but my equipment's sensors can detect one millionth candlepower fluctuation, and there is in fact without a doubt an increase in intensity every fifteen seconds that lasts exactly 1.35 seconds. At first, I thought nothing of it, but it repeats every fifteen seconds, which is exactly four times each minute. This is very interesting since it is a clear indication of a pattern.

First, I thought that it might have something to do with the battery power of the camcorder; perhaps a drain in battery power as the mechanism rotating inside the electric motor drew a higher load from the battery just at certain points, causing the fluctuations in light intensity to the sensor. But then Eldon, I came across another anomaly."

Eldon was following but not quite clicking in just yet.

"So, here's the clincher Eldon. Underneath the white sheets, there are in fact, hard to see, but the evidence is there; horizontal lines. These darker line patterns on the wall, bleed through but ever so faintly." Eldon listened intently.

"Eldon, when the light intensifies every fifteen seconds for one point three five seconds, the lines register a slight tilt on the horizontal, just slight mind you but definitely confirmed to be approximately two degrees horizontally, but a definite back and forth tilting action."

Nick then paused, and waited, when suddenly Eldon cut in.

"It's wave action!" Eldon's heart was now beating out of his chest. Nick was about to fill Eldon in on what he thought both clues could point towards, but before Nick could finish, Eldon had figured it out, all of it!

"Nick, it's got to be a lighthouse with a regular fifteen-second change in light intensity and coupled with the wave action; this points to the video being made on a boat, in a marina that has a lighthouse nearby with a rotating duration of four revolutions per minute."

"Bingo!" Nick replied.

Eldon was almost jumping out of his skin. Nick had come through with flying colors!

"Nick I cannot thank you enough, you are incredible; a genius! You need to come back and work for me, you name it, whatever you want it's yours!"

Nick said, "Eldon, I am happy I can help. You know my goal is the ISS and I'm still hoping that will happen, but thank you for your generosity. I know you will prevail, you have something to go on now, it's at least a start. Let me know if I can do anything else for you, Eldon, anything."

"Thank you, Nick, thank you so so much," and with that Nick and Eldon said goodbye to one another, for now.

No sooner had Eldon finished talking to Nick, he was already on top of things with a good sense of what the upcoming steps needed to be.

"Licks, listen up."

Eldon continued to recount to Felix everything that Nick and he had just talked about and Felix too was of the same mind that this pointed in one direction only, and that was a boat, in a marina with a nearby lighthouse.

The big clue, of huge significance, was the rate of rotation that according to Nick was exactly four complete rotations per minute with the light casting change lasting exactly one point three five seconds.

Felix was smart; that is one of the reasons he was Eldon's right-hand man, confidant, and best friend.

Eldon trusted Felix and Billy for that matter with his life, and now the life of Cathy was in the hands of the three men.

They had to act fast. Felix was thinking about what Eldon had just told him.

Felix began, “Eldon, what you are saying is very interesting. I think there may, in fact, be more information we can glean from these facts.

I think we need to call Nick back and ask him to work some figures for us. So, here are the facts Eldon; you told me two very important clues.I do agree that it could only be a marina, or at the very least, someplace on the water; it’s obvious, but I believe we may have a way to determine the size of the boat as well Eldon. I will call Nick back, and ask him to run some calculations on the one point three five seconds it took for the highlight to hit the boat and pass.

Eldon, I think if he works his magic, and taking the fixed variables into consideration, the one point three five seconds of illumination will allow for the calculation and subsequent revelation of the vessel's size. Depending the on the light house's bulb rotational speed, and knowing the length of time the craft is illuminated, being one point three five seconds, we should be able to come up with the length of the craft.”

Eldon was with Felix all the way. “Yeah, I think you may have something there Felix, although I believe Nick will confirm my one point of pessimism, and that is we are missing two elements or factors of that equation.”

Felix was on the right track, but Eldon was ahead of him already.

Eldon continued. “Licks, all right its worth a try to run it by Nick again, but I think we would need to know two things to obtain the length of the craft from those variables. I'm pretty sure we would need to know the distance between the vessel and the light source and second, unless the light source is hitting and panning the craft at a direct right angle, the estimates would be inaccurate. But it's worth a shot. Nick might be able to determine the angle, as for the distance of the light source from the craft; well that is a huge unknown. Good thinking though Licks, it's definitely worth a call back to Nick."

Eldon nodded, and Licks dialed Nick's number, and pressed the speaker button. Even while Eldon was explaining what Felix had come up with, Nick was already doing the calculations on his scientific calculator.

The entire conversation took no more than a minute Eldon had his answer. Nick had already calculated some possibilities. The problem was that there were just too many possibilities. Nick worked on some assumptions. While Eldon and Licks waited, they could hear Nick mumbling to himself running the figures and scenarios though his handheld computer.

As Nick was working, he was listening and talking to Eldon and Felix.

Eldon kept talking, saying, "I would think a marina lighthouse would be positioned at the entrance. The marina would have the main walkway along the shoreline accessing the docks leading off to the slips. That would position the slips, not at right angles but along the same line as the lighthouse, therefore, the boats would be lined up with bows facing out towards the lighthouse, and that wouldn't work.

The panning of the light would take less than a second, but in the case of the video, the panning of the light source was more than that. Therefore, I am assuming the slips at this marina are at right angles to the light source."

Eldon continued. "Nick, it's all right, you could be working a thousand variables on the light source distance, it's not going to help much and we have no way of determining that piece of data. I think we have enough to go on for now.

We know we are looking for a rotating light source of four rotations each minute that is most likely at right angles to the marina. Nick, we have enough to go on, if you come up with anything I'm sure you will be calling. Thanks, and I'm glad we called back; we did get another piece of information on this callback being the likely hood of the lighthouse angle to the boat slips.

Thanks Nick, will be in touch." Eldon said.

Nick replied. "Okay Eldon, I'm here for you anytime you need me, good luck."

Eldon was more than grateful. Eldon now had six very crucial facts. The possible angle of the boat, video recorded at night, the boat was probably located in a marina; the marina was close to a lighthouse with four rotations of the bulb every sixty seconds.

Now to find the marina with a nearby lighthouse or light source meeting these conditions and configuration. Eldon felt a sense of hope forming. Felix sensed it as well. As Eldon was heading towards the door, Felix came up behind and beside him, placing his left hand on top of Eldon's right shoulder, and said, "we'll get there Eldon, we'll get there."

Just as Eldon was about to walk through the door, Billy came in, walking directly towards the two of them.

Billy could tell right away that something was up. He asked, "anything?"

Eldon and Felix replied in unison, "yeah, we have something." Eldon then looked at Billy and said, "Billy, I think we may have found a patch of blue sky in this dark bucket of pain."

Hearing those words from Eldon, Billy looked up and through the ceiling skylight, to a beam of sunlight shining through, with clenched fists, biceps bulging, crying yes, yes!

***

Chapter Twelve

A prudent question
is one half of wisdom

Sir Francis Bacon

"No I don't like it, not one bit, but for now it is what it is, and it's a situation that we can handle." Thus, spoke Vic Amber, the director of the CIA.

Just across from Wolf Trap National Park, and the Leesburg turnpike, about five miles as the crow flies from CIA headquarters in MacLean Virginia, the snow was falling this late evening. It was February. Vic Amber was at home, in his den. Vic was hosting a very rare meeting this evening in his private residence. His CIA headquarters wasn't more than a fifteen-minute drive away, but Vic felt much more comfortable in his own home.

Secured to be sure as thoroughly as the US government could provide both physically and in terms of cyber surveillance, Vic's house was cloaked to reject any electronic or satellite surveillance capabilities; it was almost as secure as was the White House except anti-aircraft defenses.

Vic still enjoyed a fine cigar from time to time, and this evening he was indulging in such a pleasure, along with a glass of port imported from Spain, he favored from time to time. Tonight, was a time and place to talk in confidence with select members of the President's cabinet.

Vic had arranged to have this exclusive meeting with his cabinet colleagues. Everyone present at the CIA director's home this evening was involved to some degree in the success of the Caribbean Initiative, and underlying "Island-Hop" covert operations.

The Caribbean Initiative was something that in itself did not pose any sort of problem or concern. On its surface, it was a clean, doable and above board undertaking that was well reported in the media receiving national news coverage and something the President was proud of in both its potential economic impact on the region and of course the further projection of American strength and influence throughout the region. All of that was fine and in good order, on the surface at least it was. The nagging little issue, which had to be dealt with, was having to introduce operation Island-Hop.

The circumstances requiring a covert operation were brought to light by Mitch Farnsworth, Secretary of State and his people in the field. Vic had to admit that Mitch had good people at State, loyal, dedicated and able to uncover secrets sewn deep into the Caribbean fabric of deceit, corruption, and to some degree a philosophically ruthless approach in getting what they wanted.

Forbes Bishop; Prime Minister of Grenada, the Caribbean Initiative, and operation Island-Hop were to be revisted in conversation tonight.

Island-Hop was the plan to make certain that Forbes Bishop stayed clean, that the corruption infiltrating his government did not jeopardize the success of the Caribbean Initiative. Island-Hop was to make certain, all of Bishop's shortcomings were to stay under wraps until at least the signing of the treaty had taken place. After that, Island-Hop would no longer be needed and disavowed.

But now a new element had recently placed a very nasty fly in this ointment, and that was the situation with Eldon Davis's Holiday Jewel Hotels and Casinos, by further pushing that fly even deeper in the ointment; was the disappearance of his daughter.

Vic was a little more tied in than his other four colleagues. Vic Amber did, in fact, have a history and understanding working relationship with Forbes Bishop going back some years. The CIA had a minor role, but a role, in securing Bishop's election results, and Bishop in return showed Amber his gratitude over the years, with the two men having become good friends.

The two other cabinet members in attendance tonight at Vic Amber's residence was the secretary of defense Howard Rickover, who had just flown in this afternoon from having met with Forbes in Grenada, and A.B. Kingsbury, director of the FBI. Cyril Burgess; NSA Director was unable to make this meeting, having pressing issues of his own ongoing in other areas, but Vic was sure to brief Cyril of whatever went down here tonight.

Vic took another sip of port and a puff from his cigar.

Mitch Farnsworth sat across from Amber, in a traditionally crafted, Miguel design club arm leather smoking chair. There was an oak side table next to Farnsworth.

He then looking at Vic Amber said, “you know Vic, it’s a good thing you invited us here tonight, because as I sit here, came to realize I am liking the aroma of your cigar. The thing is, I gave up the smoking habit a good twenty years ago, but I do think that a cigar might not be a smoking thing, I am of the opinion that I might like to try one of those.”

Amber chuckled a little and said, “well you can have one, but I may have to have Kingsbury place you under arrest, these are Cuban cigars, the best money can buy or might not buy, still illegal for us to buy them or import them onto American soil."

Kingsbury was standing in front of a wall lined with hundreds of books. This was in essence Amber's library and den combined into one.

Kingsbury said laughingly, "we all might need to get arrested if this Island-Hop doesn't go down as we plan it. Vic, I'll have one of those Cuban Montecristos as well."

Kingsbury, then out of curiosity asked, "where do you get these from anyway?"

"I have a connection with a VNN Reporter. Whenever he's sent on assignment to Havana, he arranges to have a few boxes make their way back to me, officially he doesn't buy them, he drops them off at the Swiss embassy in Havana and from there it comes to Langley in a diplomatic pouch. Anything is possible as you know." He said laughingly.

The three men smoked their cigars, while Rickover looked over at them, also chuckling to himself, then saying, "yeah, boys, let's get on with this."

Rickover was not a smoking man, nor did he like the smell of cigars much, but he was okay with it all. He had been in many an Officers' Club where the room was filled with smoke. His military days were both smoke filled and blood soaked. He now had the pleasure of being in the company of his esteemed colleagues, and he was good with it all. They were Americans, sworn to uphold the constitution and the bill of rights.

Rickover aspired to those truths and heights, a hawk to be sure when necessary but a dove in times of peace, delivering olive branches throughout the world wherever he could. He truly believed in peace through strength and lived each day in honor of those who had given the ultimate sacrifice, the veterans; the brave men and women who served with pride honor and dignity in the US armed forces.

This was Rickover, a perfect choice by President Fenton for United States Secretary of Defense.

His nomination had sailed through the congressional vetting and hearing process, was confirmed by the Congress in great confidence, and served at the pleasure of the President with impeccable regard.

Rickover continued.

"So, what have we got here gentlemen? I handed over to Forbes a cheque in the amount of five million Dollars that I believe, will hold him for a good while. The money is not the issue at this point. The funds as we all know have been properly appropriated by Congress for the establishment of the ground works and basis to enable us in moving forward with the Caribbean Initiative; this is all fine and good.

This payment of five mil, will be put to good use. I know Forbes will use this money for his people. He is in the process of modernizing the national health system and in the beginning stages of a new medical facility on the island. I believe he is staged to do good things with these funds. But that isn't my concern at the moment. I was asked to deliver this cheque to him during my visit to the island this past week, and I did so in good faith, but now I understand we have a new development with Forbes causing the creation of Island-Hop. That I believe is the reason for this meeting tonight, enlighten me if I am mistaken".

Vic Amber responded, "no you're not mistaken Howard, you are on the money, "money" being an appropriate choice of words, but yes, essentially you are right. We have an issue with Forbes that needs to be addressed, handled, taken care of, managed, you name it, call it what you will.

Here's the current situation as we see it and as reported to us by our Agents in the field. Before I get into it, I want to tell you that I advised the President the minute I received confirmation on the existence of this, and the President as we well know is fully informed. All of us in this room including Burgess who couldn't participate this evening are on the same page. I felt it best, after informing the President and following his instructions that I further create a CIA initiated action plan, as you all know, code-named: "Island-Hop."

It dovetails into the Caribbean Initiative project but to remain top-secret. The management of Island Hop will be a CIA driven effort, coordinating with your agencies as The CIA sees fit.

I first informed Howard of what the situation was, and ever since uncovering the circumstances, Howard and I have been managing best we can, but now we need to have a review of the facts, situation, and direction we are to move in. Once we have consensus from our group here tonight, then we can issue our directives to our respective agencies to see things through and make certain the situation in Grenada unfolds as we need it to."

Vic stopped speaking for a minute, took a drag from his Montecristo, looking at his colleagues, seeking signs of confirmation and approval in their eyes.

"Back last week, in the oval office, The President was very concerned about this new situation and its generation of undeniable complications. If what we are assuming to be true does, in fact, prove to be the case, and gentlemen, I regret to inform you that, it is proving to be the case, but we will expand on that later. Let's then quickly review what we have insofar as Island-Hop goes."

Vic paused for a moment, looked over to Mitch Farnsworth, nodded to him. With that, Mitch continued on, taking over the briefing from Vic.

"We have not yet informed President Fenton, this latest information and confirmation just came into my office this afternoon, and that is why we have convened this meeting tonight, to review and bring us all up to date, making sure we are on the same page with this. Burgess will be briefed once he gets back to his office in the morning. The interesting thing is, that it was with Burgess's NSA efforts, in cooperation with my people in the field that we were able to get confirmation of these activities, it was the NSA and State that brought this together just this afternoon."

Farnsworth took a puff on his cigar, raised his chin in the air, and slowly blew a smoke circle that rose and lingered for what seemed like a long time till it dissipated into thin air.

"State has a very competent Agent in the Caribbean region. Actually she is the Charge' de Affairs to the Bahamas; Kimberly Ashton.

We don't currently maintain a full-blown Embassy in Grenada, but we do have an adjunct office representing our interests there, but without a permanent residing diplomat. I first assigned Kimberly as extended Charge de Affairs to Grenada six months ago, when the Caribbean Initiative first was approved. I had anticipated a need for closer contact and cooperation, and of course increased information gathering on anything and everything to do with Grenada and its current government. That would include The Prime Minister, his cabinet and anyone of importance on the island.

Ms. Ashton has a team of six Agents assigned to her, tasked with exclusive focus on Grenada. Two Agents are I.T. experts, two are experts in banking and finance, and two others are experts in human nature, essentially, they are charged with determining who is telling the truth and who isn't.

It's a newly experimental department within the State Department, not solely based on studies in human nature, it also has elements of CIA techniques if we ever need to go there, and I'm not talking lie detector machines, but something much more intensive, I don't believe I need to elaborate.

Yes, gentlemen, this is serious business on our little island in the sun. Our main focus for the next couple of weeks is to ensure that our friend Forbes Bishop remain in power.

The signing of the treaty has been moved up and is to be signed in the coming days. The President requested the earlier signing date in order to ensure the signing treaty ceremony takes place before The Bishop government has a chance to tumble." He paused and let that sink in.

Island-Hop is to make sure it doesn't. Once the treaty is signed, as far as I am concerned, Bishop can be consumed by whatever fate awaits him. Although I believe he means well, I also am of the opinion that his desire for the greater good, has undermined his integrity in allowing for corruption to run rampant throughout his country. Not only his country but affecting neighboring islands which may factor into the destabilization of the region. Island-Hop came into existence upon the confirmation from State; s. Ashton's people in Grenada, that Forbes Bishop is an accomplice to criminal activity, at the minimum having knowledge of such activities and is receiving regular bi-monthly payments from a certain individual named Domingo Alvarez aka "Ziggy."

Alvarez is the current president of the Caribbean Hotel and Casino Workers Union, with a membership of over 45 thousand strong. Alvarez and his Union are in a position to collect tens of millions in Union dues annually. He is believed to be funding Bishop and his campaign keeping him in power. This then, in turn, enables Alvarez and his network of Union thugs to remain in power, by Forbes granting Alvarez Sanctuary in Grenada. It also provides the Union with a perceived to be pristine crime free and corruption free environment.

Alvarez and his cronies can run their empire throughout the Caribbean, bleeding hotel and resort operators of every available labor cost Dollar his Union can suck out of every operation." Mitch had everyone's full attention; this was becoming a very entangled intricate serious situation.

Mitch continued after another puff on his cigar.

"This then spawns a huge concern and problem for the fragile economy of the region.

Gentlemen, Eldon Davis's Holiday Jewel Hotels and Casinos own and operate a number of large properties throughout the Caribbean as well as internationally in Europe and Asia. HJH&C for those of us, who need a little history, has grown over the years into the international conglomerate it is today. The company's roots date back to the 1950's when Holiday Jewel Hotels was first started by Mr. Len Davis, whose son; Eldon, later assumed the reigns of his father's hotel empire, building it over the last twenty years into the combined resort and casino business it is today.

So, enough with the history. The prevailing situation with these properties is that the very existence of the hotels, vital for the economic anchor to the economy is under threat by the greed of the Caribbean Hotel and the Casino Workers Union, namely; Mr. Domingo Alvarez.

Alvarez and his cronies have now reached a point whereby the resort hotel and casino industry's viability and solvency are in question. The instability of the industry would mean the downfall and collapse of several island economies. The economic survival of the islands in the region is dependent upon tourism and the sustainability of the hotels and resorts throughout the region."

Farnsworth paused for a moment, taking note that everyone in the room was still on the same page, following the events as outlined. There seemed to be no immediate questions, so he continued.

"Now nobody in this room is in the hotel or casino business, but gentlemen, we need to be cognizant of these facts.

Eldon Barnes Davis, is the President of Davis International and I believe we are all very aware of Davis International's diversified interests extending into areas of our concerns. His subsidiary companies produce products that our government makes wide use of in surveillance technology, specifically military grade optics and electronic components essential in the building of classified satellite technology.

Therefore Mr. Davis and his company have now become a top priority for State, CIA, and DND.

It is only a matter of time, before Eldon Davis himself gets involved, which then may have repercussions reaching into our very own operations, not just his hotels and casinos.

It would be in the best interest of our national security to ensure that any financial difficulties that

Davis International may face in his Caribbean operations, because of what pressures the CHCW Union brings down on Eldon Davis, do not affect the stability of subsidiaries companies, especially his high-tech labs and production lines."

Everyone in the room now understood the severity of the situation and how a hotel and casino company's viability and solvency in the Caribbean could have repercussions on national security. This had become big; very big.

That is why we need to be on top of this, manage the situation day by day and not let things get out of hand. To top it all off; Bishop is part of the whole picture."

Another puff on the cigar, and he went on.

"Now gentlemen here's the clincher and the most important aspect of this situation. The fact is we must at all cost, ensure that Bishop stays in power for at least until the treaty is signed. That is a given. The fact is that Bishop is teetering on being toppled. As we all know, the opposition party in Grenada is not, and I stress, not at all on board with our chosen site for the new submarine base on the south shore of Grenada.

The opposition party is not for having the base built anywhere on the island; they want no part of it and will kill the project if Bishop was to be defeated.

If Bishop were to lose his post as Prime Minister through a vote of nonconfidence, the Caribbean Initiative project would be scrapped, and I don't need to tell you how vital it is for the US to have that base. To tie things together, the only reason that Bishop has not yet fallen victim to a vote of nonconfidence is that, corruption runs rampant as we know in the Caribbean and Grenada is not immune to the affliction.

Bishop has been funneling funds to some key individuals in the opposition party on a monthly basis to keep them quiet and to fend them off from calling for a no confidence action in Parliament.

People can be bought and sold; some people can be bought on a regular basis with allegiance shifting to the highest bidder. In Forbes Bishop's case, it's my opinion that he unwittingly got caught up in this somehow.

He at first meant well for his country, taking the money from Alvarez to spend on the needs of his people, but then things totally got out of hand, and now it's too late for Forbes to come clean. He is in too deep, and his coming clean would mean jail time, even in Grenada.

There you have it, and everything I have disclosed here this evening is confirmed."

Farnsworth finished and looked around at everyone.

Rickover was palming his face, exhaling into his hand, looking down at the carpet. Rickover looked over at Kingsbury; Kingsbury raised his eyebrows and said, "Wow."

Vic Amber then picked up again where Farnsworth left off.

"Yes, so I will be briefing the President on this whole thing in the morning. I know the President will be pissed to know that this has come to fruition. Now the thing about it is that he already knew there was some smoke in the air but was hoping for no fire. Unfortunately, we found and confirmed the existence of fire this afternoon. I know he is going to want us to eliminate the wind that fans these flames, but I believe we may have to let the fire burn itself out, and it may burn steadily and long after the signing of the treaty.

What we will need to make sure of in the coming days is that we are all informed, story and situation contained, treaty gets signed, and we are good to go. Afterward, if this story gets out, it will be *fait accompli*, and the United States can disavow any former knowledge of this." That is how it is to be. We all on board?" Amber asked.

"So, the last question I have is; can Bishop be trusted, be at least honest with the United States or do we have to assume he is a problem? I think we need to assume the worst."

Everyone nodded in agreement; they all knew that in politics there was no honesty to be found. In politics, there could only be win or lose, and in the end, honesty mattered not. With that, the meeting was over.

***

Chapter Thirteen

Success seems to be connected with action.
Successful people keep moving,
they make mistakes, but they don't quit.

Conrad Hilton–Founder, Hilton Hotels

It seemed to Eldon that things were picking up exponentially now. In the last few days, all of a sudden with his wife's murder and daughter's kidnapping, his world was unraveling around him. At the same time, events unfolded that had Eldon thinking somehow the glue to this madness was beginning to give way.

But then, much as he held onto a thread of hope, with broken lines becoming seemingly solid, no sooner had he grasped onto that sliver of hope, another development comes about to complicate matters more.

This all was becoming much too crazy for it to be happening randomly and out of the blue. He had just recently talked with the Grenadian Prime Minister, he had just buried his wife, his daughter kidnapped, and suddenly his presence requested in Grenada.

Agent Miller is asking him strange basic questions about his business and company; Bishop throws out the name Rickover for some unknown reason, and Eldon just answered questions that Miller already well knew, and now Eldon summoned his Senior Vice President of Caribbean Operations to his house in Pompano. He desperately tried to fit the pieces together. He had a feeling that these happenings of late would fit together in time.

Normally Eldon would never do this, but time was of the essence and it was looking like he needed to get on with it all, so he went with his gut.

Felix was on the phone to Louis James. Felix pressed the button to activate the speaker phone.

Eldon's man responsible for Holiday Jewel Hotels and Casinos operations throughout the Caribbean was someone in whom Eldon placed a great deal of trust.

Louis James, in fact, was the quintessential hospitality industry executive and with that Eldon had given Louis full autonomy in running the operations as Louis saw fit. Louis possessed the management skills, the sales and marketing background and financial savvy to keep Holiday Jewel Hotels and Casinos in the number one position in Travelers-International magazine's top resorts rating of the Caribbean for five consecutive years running.

Louis James did his job well. Eldon paid Louis James well in turn, but Eldon could see over the last three years that the bonus percentage factor payable to Louis James for achieving over and above gross operating profits was diminishing and diminishing at quite a rate.

Eldon was shrewd, making certain that Eldon attended the quarterly consolidated financial statement reviews and property performance analysis.

Every three months, Eldon would have Billy fly him over via chopper to The Bahamas where the quarterly financial review would take place for two full days at Eldon's Holiday Jewel Resort and Casino; a five hundred room mega beachside resort with the island's most elaborately manicured grounds and ultra-plush accommodations.

There on the 12th floor, Eldon would hold his top executive meeting in a private board room. In attendance, would be Louis James; VP of operations, Maggie Selwyn; VP of finance for the Caribbean sector and a number of General Managers from key resorts, usually about fifteen people in all.

Everyone in attendance had to come prepared and prepared well. There was nothing that Eldon missed; he was like a hawk when it came to financial and property quarterly performance reviews.

There were four major items that Eldon focused on. With Eldon having virtually grown up in the family hotel business, and in later years bringing Holiday Jewel Hotels and Casinos under his Davis International umbrella, there wasn't anything that Eldon didn't know or understand about the Hotel and Casino business.

Eldon focused in on, guest satisfaction index levels first. Eldon drilled it into all of his executives and managers that providing a consistent level of "service beyond expectations" at all times was the magical key ingredient to success in the hotel business.

He had once told his committee that anyone with money could build a fabulous hotel, but without paying close attention to the guest's needs and desires, that building could run empty.

The key to success was to make the guest feel like he or she was the most important person in the world; to be treated like royalty. Eldon took time at each quarterly meeting to review the guest satisfaction index for each property making certain returns on service standards, and comments were always maintained at the highest level, and all complaints and concerns were immediately answered and resolved by senior management. This to be sure, was some pretty low-level stuff for an executive quarterly financial review, but Eldon believed that without the basic foundation required to foster guest loyalty, well, in the hospitality business, without the delivery of excellent levels of hospitality his hotel rooms would soon see beds without heads. So, this was critical factor; number one.

Second, was the ability of his hotels and resorts to navigate the competition and for the sales and marketing efforts to be generating the volume of business required to remain in business.

This covered all areas in terms of advertising and promotion, sales and marketing trade shows; everything and anything to do with generating more arrivals to the islands.

The results of these efforts would be reflected on the quarterly consolidated financial statements in overall operating revenues growth. If revenues proved to be stagnant, then there was reason for concern in this second area. To date, things have been looking reasonably good.

Third on Eldon's critical list was keeping expenses in line. The most volatile type of expense in the operation of his resorts and casinos was that of employee labor cost and employee benefits. Over the years, Eldon had seen many hotel operations stumble and fall due to lack of effective labor cost control. Each property had a certain percentage threshold for labor cost Dollars. Without maintaining those labor cost percentages in line, a property could dive into the red and before you knew it, showing negative cash flow.

Eldon had noticed that although revenues were holding, recently over the last few years, labor cost was creeping higher and higher, and now with a good number of his properties becoming Unionized, he was very concerned about keeping these labor costs in line.

Already there were a few of his hotels being supported by adjacent casinos. Some of his hotels were already operating at a deficit and needed funding from the casino profits to keep the hotels open.

The critical factor in this scenario, Eldon well understood, was that without the hotels, he had no Casinos. He needed his hotels to remain viable and open, in order to pump gamblers through his Casinos on the islands, no gamblers meant no Casinos. That then translated into no resorts, and finally no Holiday Jewel Hotels and Casinos to be found anywhere in the Caribbean, and he didn't want that as his legacy.

Lastly, Eldon's concern was the local environment, by that he focused in on the local political climate; who in high places was to be trusted and who in high places needed some special attention, by that, meaning “greasing.”

The financial statements contained a line item under the Admin and General departmental expenses called “special handling fees.”

That line item reflected the amount of monies paid out monthly to local officials who needed *tip money* so to speak for the hotel and casinos to operate efficiently.

In some cases, the payouts were small. Smaller payouts to the tune of a few hundred Dollars would need to be paid for example to the shipping dock superintendent. Without greasing the palms of the dock super, Eldon's shipping containers could sit and bake in the hot Caribbean sun for days; in some cases, and never be unloaded or released from the shipping dock containment yard. This was normal, but there were other times when larger payments were required to make things happen.

Ten, twenty and sometimes thirty thousand Dollars at a time.

Every expatriate employee that Eldon's company hired and required work permits to be approved and granted by the local government, usually had a specific amount of gratuity associated as payment to certain officials to ensure the issuing of the work permit. These payments could range anywhere from ten thousand Dollars for a French Cuisine trained Sous-Chef from Paris, to work in one of the resort's gourmet restaurants to a thirty-thousand Dollar gratuity payment, *special handling fee*, for a property hotel financial controller.

Eldon recalled, he handed over one hundred thousand Dollars to the Minister of Home Affairs in the Bahamas to ensure that Louis James's work permit be granted for a two-year period. James's regional office was based out of Nassau Bahamas; located at Eldon's Holiday Jewel Resort and Casino property.

Once Eldon had successfully addressed these four areas of concern, the rest of the quarterly property reviews were pretty much routine, and he left it to the very capable and professional hands of Louis James to wrap things up on day two. Eldon usually only attended the morning sessions on the second day and was either arranging for an afternoon of diving off the reef or playing a round of golf with Felix and Billy on his adjacent Jack Nicklaus designed 18-hole golf course. The finest and most challenging course in all the Bahamas.

Felix connected the call and pressed the speaker phone button. Eldon began, “Louis, Eldon here good afternoon, how are you doing?”

Louis said, “I am well Eldon. My heartfelt condolences to you and all your family in the tragic news. I adored Linda, her magical touch on the décor and design of this hotel will be the legacy all resorts will aspire to in the islands Eldon. She was a lovely woman, and she will be missed by many. Is there any further word about your daughter, Eldon?"

Eldon appreciated Louis's emotional outreach and responded. "Thank you, Louis, your words are comforting; we are working and doing all we can in finding Cathy, no word yet. The FBI is involved as you can imagine, it's only a matter of time, and we are all counting on God's speed, and Louis, thank you for the personal thoughts attached to your card with your generous and most beautiful floral arrangement for Linda's funeral. I appreciate your heartfelt sentiments."

Eldon continued, "Louis I need to speak with you, and I need to do it in person. I want you here tomorrow morning at my residence in Pompano Beach. I am not in a position to discuss anything further over these lines, and it's not that so much, the lines I believe are well encrypted, I really do need to talk with you face to face. Can you be here in the morning?"

"Absolutely Eldon, whatever you need me to do, I will be there."

Eldon replied, "good, no need to concern yourself about a flight, I will have Billy pick you up at the resort's airfield, he will have the Canadair Jet ready for departure at 0:700 hours. Billy will chopper you into the compound here from the airport after you land. Felix will be in attendance as well, so that makes four of us for the breakfast meeting. See you tomorrow."

With that, Eldon ended his conversation with Louis.

Having graduated with honors with a degree in Hotel Management from the School of Hotel Management at Cornell University, Louis James proudly displayed his coveted degree on his office wall. Established in 1922, The School of Hotel Management at Cornell was acknowledged by all professionals in the industry as being the most prestigious learning and teaching institution in the United States for those who aspire to be hotel industry executives.

Louis James carried that flag and banner high and proud. There was a certain code of ethics etched into the fabric of the degree that demanded all graduates bestowed with this distinction and honor to bring and add excellence to the traditions, and philosophy that the hotel and lodging industry commanded at the highest level of service standards and the overall guest stay experience. Not only did Louis James bring this element of commitment to his working environment on a daily basis; but he was also the inspiration and mentor to his colleagues and employees. His employees stepped in tune, to the resort operation's culture created within Holiday Jewel Resort and Casino in the Bahamas and throughout all the properties under his purview.

Louis wasn't one hundred percent positive in what Eldon Davis was looking to speak to him about in private and at such urgency, but he did have a feeling it was to do with the upcoming Caribbean Hotel and Casino Workers Union negotiations.

Louis had already notified Eldon and made his feelings known in no uncertain terms that the upcoming Union negotiations were to be of a hostile nature, mediation Louis felt was to be of no value. Domingo Alvarez had lately become very aggressive in his dealings and approach to the entire matter.

Louis had been informed of unrest and rumblings going on within the community, not just in The Bahamas, but throughout the Caribbean, especially Puerto Rico, which was a huge employee base for the Union, and even stretching up into Bermuda.

Alvarez; Ziggy had become very troublesome, sending shock waves of labor unrest throughout the hotels and casinos germinating and fueled by gatherings at Union Hall rallies, assemblies and convocations.

Even if Eldon's concern was not this subject, it still needed addressing by Eldon. He would have to make sure it's on the agenda for tomorrow morning's breakfast meeting. It had gotten to the point where Eldon would now need to step in.

Louis had come to terms with the fact that Eldon's involvement from this point on was going to be mandatory if the situation was to be solved. It was no longer just Alvarez; now the situation called for changes in local government legislation addressing and governing Labor Union laws and the enforcement of those laws.

James called his VP of human resources and asked for a copy of the proposed new Caribbean Hotel and Casino Workers Union contract demands and proposals. He would need to make sure Eldon had a copy for himself.

There were some issues in the contract that Eldon may wish to take up with government officials. The extra copy of the contract was delivered to Louis within ten minutes. Louis was ready for tomorrow today.

***

Chapter Fourteen

Look here, look there, look everywhere
for you have not a moment to spare.

"Yes sir, Director Kingsbury, I have all my assets in the field now. We have coordinated with both State Police as well as Broward County local law enforcement. We are currently conducting a sweep of the area; we have every available Agent on this case." Agent Miller was on the secure phone with Kingsbury.

Kingsbury continued. "Agent Miller, whatever additional assets you may require, those are at your disposal. I want to make it absolutely crystal clear that the apprehension of this individual is of the highest level. Although at first blush, it may appear to be a case of kidnapping and murder, which it most certainly is, I want you to be fully aware that this case is of national security importance. As I was saying, whatever it is you may need; wherever you feel this case might take, you are authorized to do what is required.

There will be no further clearance requirements, and all law enforcement agencies have been advised of this being a level one national security protocol, to be immediately upgraded and implemented. That gives you and your assets *carte blanche* as of this minute. Do we understand one another?"

Miller was FBI Regional Division Chief for the Southeast region of the United States.

He was well equipped to address any and all matters requiring extensive investigative powers and techniques.

"All right Director," Miller answered.

"And one more thing, Chief Agent Miller; you will shortly receive a call from Ms. Kimberley Ashton, from The State Department.

State will be in need of FBI operatives in the islands; your contact will be Kimberly Ashton; Charge de Affairs. Ms. Ashton is working out of The Bahamas; you will probably hear from her or one of her people in the coming day or two. Keep me apprised of the situation. I want an update at 0:800 hours every day.

We good Agent Miller?"

"Absolutely, Director Kingsbury, I'm on it," and with that Kingsbury was out.

Miller knew his reputation was going to be on the line with the success or failure of this case. His time and dedication, and competence all rested on his ability to meet and satisfy Kingsbury's need in cracking this case on the whereabouts of the Davis girl.

Miller's time with the Bureau was all rolled up into this one final case, and Miller was not about to let this one get away. Another thing that Miller had come to realize over the past few days was that having met Eldon Davis for the very first time, well, he sort of liked the man.

He understood that it must be incredibly traumatic for a husband to lose his loving wife, especially since having learned their marriage relationship was solid with a devoted dedication to one another. Then to have his six-year-old daughter kidnapped at the same time, most men would have collapsed for days on end, leaving everything in the hands of the authorities to handle.

Not Eldon, no, Eldon needed to be on point, leading this mission. Miller knew well that whatever the FBI or other law enforcement agencies were in the process of doing, and no matter how much progress they were making, Davis would still pursue finding his daughter in his own way, with his own resources.

The cat and mouse game had begun with the disappearance of the Davis girl. The mouse had stolen the cheese, and the cat was in hot pursuit of the mouse, the problem was that the Davis cat knew not into which hole the mouse disappeared.

Miller had a gut feeling that Davis would only cooperate with Miller as long as Davis needed Miller. Otherwise, it was the Davis show, and his show alone.

Miller was willing to play along. It was after all Davis's daughter, Davis apparently has a lot of resources at hand, if Miller were in the same situation, being able to snap his fingers and have his international connections and resources at his disposal, well Miller would do the same, so he was good with it. Miller's job was to help, coordinate, pursue and try to prevent Davis from getting himself killed. Miller was going to bring on his A game in gumshoeing this case.

The Broward County Police Department had done its job well. At 4 AM the morning after the incident at the Davis house, Broward County Sheriffs had located a brown stolen van, in the parking lot of U-2-Play.

Miller hadn't yet received confirmation that the van was the one that Eldon had seen from his jet as he flew over his property that afternoon, but Miller was pretty sure it would prove to be a positive match.

DNA sampling on hair from Cathy would come in the next few hours confirming the van was, in fact, the one used in the murder and kidnapping. Also, the timing was right. The van belonged to a Wal-Mart employee who happened to work the evening shift which started at 3 PM and did not end till 11:30 PM.

The kidnapper had done his homework. The van was taken from the far side of the parking lot where Wal-Mart employees are required to park, and would not be reported as stolen until the employee's shift was over with when he would find himself without his vehicle.

Reporting the van stolen and then having it acted upon by local law enforcement would then take hours or days before it might be located, or perhaps even never located.

This would then provide ample time for the kidnapper to use the vehicle without too much of a risk factor. Miller's deductions were on the money.

This is exactly how Jason had figured things out. Jason had taken the time to case out the Wal-Mart parking lot, keying in on evening shift employees arriving to work in the afternoon. He made certain that he settled on an employee who always drove himself or herself to work; no carpoolers, in case one of them finished the shift early and needed the vehicle. He thought a Van would serve him best, offering quick access through large sliding doors.

The vehicle also had to pass for a floral delivery vehicle. Jason, had two magnetized plastic signs made saying, Martin's Flower Boutique, that he placed on either side of the vehicle making it look authentic, he had made certain that he removed those magnetic signs from either side of the van before leaving the Davis residence on Sailfish Drive.

Agent Miller's gears were turning now, “okay, so the van has been located in the U-2-Play parking lot.”

Miller called in his Agents and instructed them to obtain any video or surveillance data from surrounding stores, and businesses for evidence, especially from the U-2-Play retailer.

Miller could only hope that there may be something to go on from that. Not all parking lots had surveillance equipment or video. However the odds were good that a national chain like U-2-Play would maintain a surveillance system, chain stores were usually very cognizant of risk management factors, and one of their main concerns was leaving themselves exposed to any sort of liability issues.

That was the next step, simple and a no brainer, but it was a step that was not to be missed. Sometimes the simplest things produce unexpected outcomes; he had to look everywhere, and time was of the essence.

***

Chapter Fifteen

The evil that men do, lives after them;
The good is oft interred with their bones.

William Shakespeare – Julius Caesar

The Sharker's twin diesels pushed it along very nicely through the Gulf Stream and into Bahamian waters with an average speed of 16 knots per hour. This meant that Jason was making excellent time. His midnight departure from Gulliver's marina was projected to see him make harbor in Sandy's Point on Abaco Island between noon and 1 PM.

Jason would arrive a little early, which was a good thing as far as Jason was concerned. He could get rid of the Davis kid sooner, get her out of his hair and his evil world thereby setting him free to enjoy his eighty-thousand Dollar payday.

Manko had already contacted the harbormaster at Sandy Point Marina earlier on and obtained an ETA on Jason's arrival from the ship to shore radio. Simons was on duty today as the acting Bahamas Customs Officer.

Although Manko was the Police Chief for Abaco, Manko had no jurisdiction when it came to Bahamas Customs and Immigration. The need to fill out proper documentation and report the arrival and departure of all vessels not registered in the Bahamas was still a legal requirement.

Today, however, was going to be a little different. Jason did have an unusual package on the Sharker, a package that was to remain secret, a package that was just to be a cooler containing nothing but fish.

Simons was so used to Jason and his deep-sea fishing charter business, that the extra-large cooler was a normal item, and never something of suspicion. The cooler measured five feet by three feet by three feet. It was meant for large catches. Barracuda, grouper, tuna and wahoo, which normally occupied the cooler, but not on this day.

Jason, however, made doubly certain that the cooler's content wasn't about to come alive just when he was about to dock at Sandy Point Marina, so he gave Cathy another whiff; another dose of chloroform. This would most definitely keep her under for another few hours. He was good to go now.

The marina was within 45 minutes. He sat back in the captain's chair, looking down at Cathy on the rear deck, laying out cold comfortably in the cooler situated between the two deep-sea fish tackling chairs.

Jason being a regular at the marina, conjured up no suspicions from Harbormaster/Customs Agent; Simons.

Jason had his rented permanent slip, where Jason's Bertram; The Sharker was docked for at least half of every year for the past decade.

Manko and Jason went back a good number of years. They were well connected in their game of human trafficking.

Manko's brother-in-law; Rico would often assist Jason by personally pointing out and directing Jason to obscure pick-up locations on the deserted sections of Abaco, from where Jason would pluck his human cargo beach side, and smuggle the poor bastards close in to the Florida coastline.

Once close in to the Florida coastline, about a quarter mile or so, under cover of darkness; he would launch them to shore in a rubber inflatable with a couple of paddles and wish them good luck. After launching them off…was done and got the hell out of Dodge while under the protection of darkness. From there on end, they were left to fend for themselves, and Jason headed back to the Bahamas, always a few thousand Dollars richer.

It was a good gig, he, Manko and Rico made a good team. Jason wasn't too concerned about Manko's connections and how the refugees and asylum seekers made it to Manko's world, just so long as Jason got paid, that was good enough for him. Jason had figured that Rico had something to do with everything since all of his human cargo seemed to come from the southern Caribbean, Haiti, and Cuba mainly with a sprinkle of people from the Spice Islands, St. Vincent, the Grenadines, Grenada, Dominica, Barbuda and such.

He recalled something about Rico being from Grenada, down in the Spice Island section of the Caribbean. Some of the men he smuggled into the US were not seeking asylum at all, they were just people looking to find work under the table and make a life for themselves, illegal for sure, but it was simple to hide among the masses once they hooked up with their underground communities.

Some got into the crime syndicate, some worked for local cultural businesses that operated sweatshops, still a better living than harvesting bananas on the islands, and it put US Dollars into their pockets. It was a game of risk, but with Manko running the law on Abaco, everything seemed to be low risk with high rewards.

But Jason was still out at least forty-five minutes. The speedy Fountain party boat that had just buzzed The Sharker was Manko's eyes at sea. Manko wanted a report back to verify that Jason was on board alone, and that was confirmed by Manko’s hired scouts onboard The Fountain speed boat.

The Fountain had no problems reaching speeds of seventy to ninety miles per hour on the open water. Within ten minutes the captain from the party boat had reported in person back to Manko. The Sharker hummed along pushing through the warm Atlantic's blue-green turquoise waters.

Jason was a son of a bitch, although from time to time he managed to make an honest Dollar with his deep-sea charter parties, in his bones, he was evil through and through.

Just then a pod of speckled dolphins happened to come alongside the Sharker. The pod numbered around forty or fifty strong, some young ones as well.

The dolphins played in the waves, racing along the sides of the Sharker. Jason reached for his Beretta 38, a perfect opportunity to hone his targeting skills. Jason aimed and pulled the trigger, aiming for the lead dolphin, he shot, he missed, the dolphin was still flying in and out of the water along the starboard side of the Sharker, perfect positioning for Jason's perch.

He aimed and pulled the trigger again, clean hit right into the side of the lead dolphin's head. The unlucky dolphin stopped swimming; it was instantly dead.

Another dolphin just to the right of the lead dolphin popped up, bang! Perfect shot, another one dead.

“I’ll get you, you little fuckers,” Jason mumbled to himself. Jason was having a lot of fun killing dolphins, he was enjoying this, moving targets, “how much more fun could this be!”

Jason continued his carnage; he managed to kill eight from the pod, along with two young ones. The pod of dolphins finally figured out that they were being killed off and stopped swimming alongside. The blue-green turquoise waters just behind The Sharker was red with dolphin blood that soon blended and disappeared into the Sharker's bubbling wake.

Jason had another sip of his beer, wiped his brow with his shirt sleeve, and put his emptied-out Berretta 38 into his chairs side pocket.

"A little afternoon recreation," he thought.

The dolphin shooting gallery had broken up his boredom some, and got his blood flowing not to mention the dolphins'. It was a good diversion.

Manko and Rico were now waiting for Jason's arrival and his package. Rico Alvarez was as a dive instructor at an island resort and did some freelance dive charters, but being Domingo's brother, he was also tightly connected to the Union as Union steward for Abaco and Eleuthera Island resorts and hotels. Manko and Rico were often seen together; they had a great deal in common.

Rico was married to Manko's sister Violet, a lovely and caring woman, unfortunately, abused by Rico, but Violet knew her place. Rico was the man of the house, and her brother was the Chief of Police. Violet knew she was the woman and Rico was the man. Violet would do as she was told.

Manko had met Rico fifteen years ago back when Manko had gotten involved in the human trafficking venture. A lot of Haitians had been making their way to The Bahamas looking for work. Well, there really wasn't much work of any kind for Haitians to be had in The Bahamas, other than menial work in the hospitality business.

There was always a need for housekeepers and laundry workers. The hotels and resorts in The Bahamas welcomed the Haitians because the Haitians would take jobs for half the pay that the local Bahamians would have to be paid.

This game went on for a while until the Caribbean Hotel and Workers Union got wind of the fact that Haitians were undercutting Union workers who were being laid off by the hotels in favor of cheap Haitian labor. This word about Union dues depletion from Bahamian Hotels and Resorts filtered down to the Union boss; Domingo Alvarez in Grenada.

Alvarez got involved in fixing the problem. He arranged to promise a better life in the US for Haitians by smuggling some of them into the US through Manko's connections. The Haitians would pool their money, pay Alvarez for the smuggling service, and eventually, entire Haitian families would immigrate to the US once a Patriarch was granted a green card or citizenship.

This pattern had worked for the past ten years, and Alvarez was able to re-establish a healthy flow of Union dues, get rid of unregistered workers in the hotels and spread his tentacles of Union influence throughout the Bahamas. Domingo's assistant in this entire endeavor was his brother Rico. Rico, Domingo, and Manko became three partners in crime, with Rico taking a liking fourteen years ago, to Manko's sister Violet.

Violet had never attended school past grade five. Violet knew how to read, just enough for her to get by, and living on Abaco, there was little need to be doing much reading of any sort. She was content in her own skin, doing all of Rico's biddings. She was told that she would be in charge of looking after a house guest for the next while and she was to take good care of her. She was told it was to be a little girl, and that was all she was told. Feed, her and make sure she is kept clean and keep her out of site. Well, she could not, not keep her out of site. She was to be confined to Conch Key which was a small out island, three miles from the other side of Sandy Point off the opposite shore of Abaco Island. Conch Key was deserted save for the one small house nestled in-between the palms on top of the hill overlooking the Atlantic.

This was Manko's house, been in the family for generations, built over a hundred fifty years ago, wood and brick building mainly used as a fishing outpost. The conch beds surrounding the island were plentiful and rather than carry the conch back to Abaco and de-shell them there, it would be done on Conch Island and only the fresh conch meat taken back to market.

Rico had given her these babysitting jobs before, to look after a child or two maybe while the smuggled illegal immigrants made enough money working locally to pay Manko and Rico enough for them to continue to the US, that part of their trip was to be with Jason.

This time, however, it was to be just one little girl for Violet to look after. Violet understood and at the same time had questions and was scared, although she loved children, she knew in her heart that Manko and Rico were mixed up in something bad. But Violet did what she was told. She would look after the girl on Conch Key, but with fear in her heart. Violet made sure the small house was ready to receive a small-house guest.

Taking care of young children was nothing new to Violet, she was used to that, having taken care of plenty island children.

This was going to be different. She wasn't able to have children of her own as things turned out. Rico never forgave her for that, and Rico had fathered several kids all over the island. Bahamians were sort of famous and notorious for fathering illegitimate kids, not unusual for Bahamian men to father fifteen to twenty kids with several different women.

It looked to Violet that men from Grenada weren't much different. Violet was almost good with this; she was part of the culture and in The Bahamas, well, to be honest, all Bahamians were family. Maybe that's one of the reasons the Bahamas was also known as The Family Islands.

Violet was looking forward to caring for a little girl; she was scared somewhat in her heart of hearts because, she knew that something was not right about all this, but Violet couldn't help her emotions. Although Violet couldn't have children of her own, she had natural maternal instinct, and she was so excited to be taking care of a little one. She absolutely loved children, especially little girls.

Manko and Rico drove over to Sandy Point Marina, it was just before noon. Manko parked his Police Jeep in the shade under the palms lining the edge of the parking lot. Rico got out and opened the rear passenger door. He took out his scuba gear, dive tank, flipper, weights, mask, snorkel regulator and a spear gun. Manko helped Rico carry the gear down to Jason's slip and left it there on the dock, then went into the Harbormaster's office and shot the breeze there for a few minutes.

"Good afternoon Inspector," said Simons.

Simons doubling as Dockmaster and Bahamas Customs and Immigration Officer, (Harbormaster) was a good acquaintance of Manko's. They weren't drinking buddies as such, but they got along very well, and they were both in law enforcement and the brotherhood extended to all levels of authority. The two men had mutual respect for one another.

Rico was known all over the island as Manko's brother in law and as a diving instructor. The three men knew one another.

“Yeah mon, we're waiting for Jason to arrive, you should have heard from him by now.” Manko remarked to Simons.

“Yeah mon, he checked in a few minutes ago, he should be visible now maybe a mile or two out.”

Manko picked up Simons' binoculars and looked out into the channel. Sure enough, there was The Sharker, just ten minutes out.

“Okay, he's just a few minutes out.” Simons knew Jason well and didn't think anything unusual about Jason's arrival.

Manko went on saying, “yeah mon, Rico's boat is on the fritz, he needs to head over to Eleuthera to do a dive trip, Jason's good enough to give him a lift, once he checks in with you here. Jason my mon, he’s on his way there to Eleuthera anyway to pick up a charter group tomorrow so this will work for Rico.”

Manko lied of course, but he was good at it, and it made perfect sense.

“Okay, he's about to dock, we go give him a hand.”

Jason was aware of the plan and the way this was going to work. He was to check in with the Harbormaster and Customs at the same time, and with Rico needing a ride over to Eleuthera, this was a perfect reason for him to arrive and leave almost immediately, giving Rico the ride he needs, and for him to meet his charter booking in Eleuthera.

This was all a divergence, of course, not to raise Simons’s suspicions. Manko was to let Simons know in advance, and Manko had just finished doing that, so the game was in play.

The Sharker pulled in to slip number 11. Rico and Manko tied out The Sharker.

Usually, Simons would come out to meet the arriving vessel and fill out the paperwork on The Sharker's arrival, Captain and passenger details. But in this case, with the Chief of Police there to greet the vessel, and knowing Jason, well, those Customs formalities were not needed.

"Hello mon, you made good time, how's the package?" Manko asked, smiling, displaying his two golden shimmering incisors.

"Package is good; the package is sleeping inside the cooler," Jason responded.

"Hey man, hot today, let's get moving, check in with Simons, and we can get on our way," Rico said to Jason.

Jason jumped out onto the dock and made his way up to Simons; they shook hands; Simons filled out the paperwork and Jason returned to The Sharker.

Manko had boarded The Sharker, went downstairs to the second stateroom, and there was the cooler. He walked up to the cooler, opened the top, and there inside was Cathy Davis.

Manko's heart skipped a beat, Cathy looked somewhat flushed, her face sweating as she breathed with regular breaths. Manko could see she was fine, but Cathy had peed herself. Manko knew that Violet would be taking care of that shortly.

Manko smiled again, put the top back onto the cooler, she would stay cool, there were holes in the cooler's side close to the top near where the lid closed. Cathy would be just fine for the next few minutes until she nestled into Violet's care.

Manko came up on deck. Jason had returned already by now to The Sharker and was helping Rico load the dive equipment.

Manko then said, "The kid is good, just checked on her. Check on the kid in another ten minutes, make sure she's still out and asleep until we get her over to Violet at least," he said to Rico.

"All right mon, I will see you on the other side of the island in a half hour," and with that Manko untied The Sharker from the slip, allowing Jason to pull the boat out from the dock and head it back to sea.

The three of them, Jason, Rico, and Cathy, were heading to the bottom of Sandy Point, and up around to the eastern shore of Abaco Island, in the channel across from Conch Key.

Manko then walked back to the Harbormaster's office, and walking past the window; he waved goodbye to Simons. Simons waved back to Manko, and all was good.

On the east side of Abaco, just a ten-minute drive from Sandy Point Marina, but on the opposite side of the island, there Manko was waiting for Jason.

Of course, Jason was not heading to Eleuthera at all, he was going to Conch Island or Key as it was locally called, so Jason thought.

There was a small rickety public dock that was not in use for years now, but it was still good enough to walk out on. This was where Rico had instructed Jason to bring The Sharker and where Manko was waiting for them.

The plan was to pick up Manko, and then head on over the three miles to Conch Island, and drop off the kid. That was not going to happen, not quite yet.

It had been a few days now since Manko had the pleasure of eating his favorite lunch being "cracked conch."

Ever since Manko heard the news that Jason had killed Linda Davis in the process of nabbing the kid, Manko was not a happy man. Domingo had made it very clear to Manko, "just have him nab the kid" that's it, nothing else, and have him deliver the girl to you unharmed."

Domingo told him in person, not to fuck this up, he and Rico were counting on Manko and his boy Jason. But now, with Jason having killed the Davis woman, well...this added risk factor threw the entire hostage plan into unexpected difficulties, and it was not something Manko nor Alvarez was about to tolerate.

Jason's instructions were clear. Kidnap the girl and nothing else. With Jason not having followed strict instructions, there was now no telling what other risks Jason may have unknowingly introduced into this all, and Jason had to go.

No trace of Jason was to be found. Now Manko had to deal with this huge problem, a problem that was sure to intensify the search process. He had never met Eldon Davis, but already Manko had an uneasy feeling about it all.

Jason pulled the boat close to the dock, close enough for Manko to hop on deck. Then Manko made himself comfortable on the semi-circle vinyl seating just to the left of the Captain's chair up on the flying bridge. Rico remained on the main deck; he was going through his dive gear.

Jason pointed The Sharker due east making way for Conch Island. Jason turned on his stereo and turned up the volume. His choice of music included a variety of golden oldies. The music was nice, was a good volume level, it could be heard clearly over the hum of the diesel pushing The Sharker through the blue-green waters of the Caribbean.

Rico had finished with his dive equipment, having loaded his spear gun with the safety off.

The Sharker was well out now almost two miles off shore, and directly over a blue hole.

The Bahamas was known for several of these "blue holes," a patch of ocean floor that welled down thousands of feet, a bottomless pit of an abyss. There happened to be a blue hole, situated between the east shore of Abaco and Conch Islands.

It was also known as a good place to spot white tipped sharks, probably the most dangerous species found in Bahamian waters.

Rico had spotted a number of white tips while diving the area. This was where Manko and Rico wanted to bring Jason.

Jason was in his driver's seat, happy as can be. "The job was coming to an end, and in the next half hour or so, he would be paid the remaining fifty thousand Dollars, and be done with it all."

Jason looked ahead, eager to get to Conch Island and looking forward to his next few days.

Rico had been out on the rear deck where the dive equipment was, and had loaded the spear gun, with the safety disengaged. Rico held the spear gun and walked up the solid rear steps to the flybridge.

Jason was looking straight ahead unaware that Rico had inched his way up, now standing directly behind him.

Rico looked over at Manko, Manko with his aviator glasses nodded back at Rico. Rico reached out with the end of the spear gun and poked Jason in the back of his neck with the razor-sharp tip of the spear cutting a small slit into Jason's skin.

The pain seared into Jason's neck, causing him to suddenly reach with his right hand around to the back of his neck, and nicking his knuckles along the razor edge of the spear-tip, causing his hand to bleed like a sieve.

"What the fuck!"

Jason screamed as he reached around to the back of his neck. He then saw Rico standing behind him with the end of the spear about two inches from Jason's eye.

Terror filled Jason, his heart almost blew out of his chest.

Manko then stood up and looked at Jason saying, "Jason mon, you fucked up. What did I tell you? Take the kid and do nothing else. Jason mon, mon, mon, mon, you fucked up big. Now you gonna pay."

Jason knew it was over for him, and as a last-ditch effort, Jason reached into the captain's chair side pocket for his Beretta, found it and pulled the trigger aiming at Manko, but Jason had already emptied it into the dolphins, and the gun clicked blank.

Jason knew he was fucked. With that, Manko being a big man, six foot four inches tall, weighing well over three hundred pounds and built like a brick shithouse, pulled Jason out of the Captain's chair. Rico reached over the empty chair, pulled the throttle back and set The Sharker into the neutral position.

The 38 foot Bertram came to rest, and Rico turned the engine off.

Manko grabbed Jason by the throat and then dragged him down onto the main deck.

Rico followed them down, where Rico had two buckets of chum prepared. Rico opened up the bucket, and the smell of rotting fish guts and fish parts filled the back of the boat. He tossed the chum overboard. Within minutes, white tip sharks started arriving, after five minutes there were half a dozen white tips swimming around The Sharker.

Jason was so terrified that he emptied his bowels into his shorts. He hadn't shit himself since he had been one and a half years old, but he was doing a good job of it this afternoon under the hot Bahamian sun.

Manko one more time squeezed Jason's neck and said, “goodbye you fucker.”

With that Rico pulled the trigger launching the spear into Jason’s belly clear through Jason's stomach, with the spear tip sticking out Jason's back, not killing him; but good enough.

By now the sharks were gathering, and Jason was bleeding profusely, this was perfect, exactly what Manko wanted.

Jason's choice of music was interesting and ironically appropriate; the stereo was playing a golden oldie. It was Bobby Darin's Mac the knife, and as Bobby sang...

> “when the shark bites, with his teeth dear,
> scarlet billows start to spread…”

And with those words sung in the background, Manko and Rico reached down together, grabbing Jason as he screamed with pain from the protruding spear and the knowing terror that awaited him seconds from now in the blue hole.

They picked Jason up and tossed him over the side of The Sharker to be devoured by the white-tips. The sharks ravaged Jason’s body; his bones picked clean. The violent feeding frenzy that ensued had ripped Jason's head clear away from his spine. Jason's shark devoured body; now a broken skeleton sank to the ocean floor. His severed head sank, sitting just on the edge of the ledge to the blue hole. Just as Jason's skull was about to come to rest, a spotted dolphin swam up to Jason's head, and nudged it over and down into the abyss.

Jason's head proceeded to sink, falling deeper and deeper into the dark abyss of the blue death hole leading to hell.

Jason Garetty's evil bones were forever interred.

***

Chapter Sixteen

What can labor do for itself? This is not difficult. Labor can organize, it can
unify; it can consolidate its forces. This done, it can demand and command.

Eugene V. Debs. - Founder Industrial Labor Union of the World (1905)

The flight from Nassau Bahamas to Ft. Lauderdale International Airport on Eldon's Canadair jet was under one hour that included taxi time on the runway and Lauderdale approach. Billy Simpson was already waiting for Louis James at 6:30 this morning at Holiday Jewel Resort and Casino private airstrip. The private airstrip was a huge advantage for the Casino side of the business. Having the airstrip in close proximity to the casino and hotel meant that the "whales" who loved the Jewel Casino could avoid the hassles that came part and parcel having to deal with Customs and the throngs of tourists coming through Nassau International.

This was a very nice and convenient service provided by the Casino PR department whereby a Casino Luxury Jaguar would meet the gamblers as soon as they cleared Customs which was a very quick formality courtesy of the Bahamian Government extended specifically to guests of the Jewel Casino.

The short ride from the airfield to the Casino and Hotel was only three minutes. Louis James was dropped off by one of the hotel drivers, directly in front of the steps to the Canadair on the tarmac. Billy was there standing beside the drop down steps leading up to the plane, holding a paper cup in his hand, sipping coffee, enjoying the morning sun.

"Mr. James," Billy said. "Good morning." Louis, replied, "it's Louis Billy, Louis, and good morning to you, let's get the show on the road, shaking hands with Billy, Louis proceeded straight up the steps and inside the Canadair jet, taking a seat and buckling himself in. Billy followed, retracted the stairway and sealed the door, getting ready for takeoff. This morning there was no one at the tower, Billy was the only flight in and out till noon, and Billy's flight was unscheduled anyway.

Billy taxied the jet to the north end of the runway, rotated and speeded down runway taking off into the blue sky, heading for Ft. Lauderdale International. Having touched down in Lauderdale and cleared, Billy and Louis transferred to the Sikorsky chopper and flew on over to the helipad at 6565 Sailfish Drive. Upon landing, Louis grabbed his briefcase that was all he had with him, no overnight bag, just some documents. Louis understood this was going to be a short but very important face to face with Eldon, Felix, and Billy.

Louis had been here to the Davis estate one other time only. That was a few years back, when Eldon had first interviewed Louis for the vice president position, and two years after that initial hiring, Eldon then promoted Louis to Senior VP of Operations for Holiday Jewel Hotels and Casinos and that was for the entire Caribbean region including Bermuda. Louis looked after more than forty properties for Eldon, covering both resort hotels and casino operations.

Eldon found Louis to be very proficient. Over the years Eldon had gotten wind of the fact that competitors in the hotel and casino business were trying to lure Louis away to join their own organizations, but Eldon made sure that Louis wasn't going anywhere, other than where Eldon wanted him, and that destination was the foreseeable future with HJH&C.

By 8:30 AM Billy was just bringing the Sikorsky S76 chopper over the helipad at 6565 Sailfish Drive. The S76 was a very comfortable medium sized luxury chopper, but very agile being an all-weather suitable bird. She could attain speeds more than 160 knots per hour in the hands of the right pilot, and Billy was indeed the right pilot.

Billy landed the chopper, removed his headset, and was out the door as Louis was getting ready to exit. The two of them made their way up to Eldon's home from the helipad through the lush backyard garden along a pathway lined with towering Florida Royal Palms, creating a very picturesque setting leading to the rear patio deck. The sun was not yet high enough in the morning sky to warrant the ceiling fans above the patio, but they turned slowly providing some movement to the air and a fresh scent of hibiscus from the surrounding garden.

The gentle sound emanating from the waterfall in the adjacent pool set the atmosphere for this morning meeting of the minds. Eldon and Felix were seated around the patio table on the backyard patio as Billy and Louis walked up. Felix and Eldon stood up to greet Billy and Louis. Louis walked up to Eldon first, reaching out and extending his hand.

The two men shook hands and embraced momentarily as Louis offered once again his condolences in person, saying quietly, “Eldon, I am so sorry,” to which Eldon replied, “thank you, Louis, please have a seat,” pointing to a seat beside him, as Eldon released Louis's hand, Louis reached out over to Felix who stood beside Eldon, and said; “good to see you again Felix; I just wish it was under different circumstances."

Felix replied, "yes Louis nice seeing you again, looks to me like the island life is treating you well."

Louis replied, "Well you are right Felix, I do like island life, maybe it's the beautiful color of the water that keeps me anchored."

Eldon then spoke. "Louis, Billy is going to have to leave us for now. We have some issues of urgency that need attention and Billy will be looking into that today."

Louis replied, "well Billy great to see you again, and thanks for picking me up this morning and not scaring the crap out of me on the flight over."

Billy liked to do some acrobatics from time to time with the chopper. Being a gulf war vet Billy's chopper skills were second to none. He was already legendary in among the Davis executive team for taking five of them on a joy ride one time surprising the corporate big-wigs with a sudden barrel roll. Louis was hoping this would not be one of those flights. It wasn't, Billy was all business today and then some.

Eldon, Felix, and Billy had talked the night before, and Billy was headed out this morning to check on marinas from Miami to Stuart along the Atlantic coastline. Billy was looking for marinas with lighthouses close-by. He had done his research already and had a few locations on his hit list. Billy had the Stinger all ready and fueled. He was taking the fifty-foot Scarab out to search marinas along the Intracoastal. "Okay Louis, good to see you again, I'll be taking you back to the island when you are ready to go this evening. I will be back before sundown," Billy said.

"Good luck Billy, keep me updated," Eldon said.

"I'll be calling you and Licks as soon as I come up with something, anything." With that, Billy headed down to the Stinger docked on the Intracoastal in the back of Eldon's estate. Five minutes later they heard the Scarab's triple diesels, each generating 500 horsepower roaring to life. Billy was not about to waste any time. He headed down the Intracoastal and out the channel and out into open ocean. Instead of heading south Billy headed north, he had a hunch, and it was a good one. Billy knew of three marinas within an hour or so ride up the coastline. All three marinas had lighthouses close-by. There was lighthouse point marina just south of Deerfield Beach, Jupiter Hills Marina and Jupiter Inlet Marina; those two were also illuminated by the Jupiter lighthouse.

Billy would head up north and see what he could find out. He exited the inlet in Pompano and opened up The Stinger's three bulldogs. The Stinger sprung to life with fifteen hundred horses, jumping out of the water skimming over the waves along south Florida's coast reaching 65 knots per hour like it was on a drag strip. Billy was on a mission; he thought back to the time when he took Cathy up in the little single-prop Piper for a fun ride. Just then from his seat in the Scarab, Billy looked up towards the sky, and shouted out loud, "we're coming for you sweetheart, we're coming for you." Billy was on a mission for Eldon's darling little six-year-old co-pilot; Cathy.

◇◇◇

"You know Eldon," Louis was saying, coffee sounds good to me," as Louis reached over to the coffee pot in the center of the patio table the three of them sat around and poured himself a full cup. "Actually, this is my first cup of coffee this morning" taking a sip of the hot liquid, "yeah, that's good."

Felix looked over at Louis and said, "Louis, we understand you recently had a meeting with Prime Minister Bishop in Grenada, and that is the reason Eldon had you come in this morning."

Eldon continued on after Felix. "I was just on the phone with Forbes yesterday, and he is insisting I fly down to St. Georges in Grenada and meet with him concerning our hotel operations. I don't get it really, so I am looking to get the story straight from you this morning Louis. I will need to decide in the next day or two whether or not I will fly down to meet with Forbes Bishop" Eldon said, looking over to Louis.

Louis then started in, "Eldon, you recall I mentioned to you, a while back that we are having new labor negotiations coming up in the next few weeks."

"Yeah, sure, I know about that, so what's so urgent?" Eldon asked.

"Labor negotiations are nothing new for us. In fact, Eldon, in most cases over the past twenty or so years, the stability of employee wages locked in for a period of three to five years with incremental increases have served our industry well. It allowed our hotels and casinos to manage our labor cost budgets, thereby developing acceptable expenses regarding labor expenses and employee benefits as a certain percentage of our revenues. So, I would be the first to welcome fixed expenses with respect to labor cost Dollars." Louis stopped for a second, looking at the two of them.

Felix and Eldon listened closely to what James was explaining. They both knew well that Louis was heading somewhere with this and Louis was the type to first set the scene; this was his style.

"Go ahead Louis, we're listening," Eldon remarked.

"You well know Eldon that the payroll expense for the company is in the tens of millions which is perfectly acceptable and normal. The percentages have been in line for the most part and really the only thing we need to be vigilant about in regards to labor cost is to manage the requirement for overtime hours, company-wide, and I also include in that, sick pay and worker's compensation insurance expenses. But I believe we have a good handle on all of those specific variables; at least we have had in the past years.

It's only been in the last two years or so that things are climbing to the breaking point with the Caribbean Hotel and Casino Workers Union. Eldon, two years ago, you will recall that the CHCW Union broke its agreement with the hotels and casinos and decided to wildcat-strike a few of our properties in support of a fellowship Union; The Industrial Workers Union in The Bahamas who went out on strike; primarily the sanitation workers. With the Bahamian government not wanting to play ball, the hotel Union strike added heat to the fire and eventually the government caved granting the Industrial Union an eighteen percent increase for the first year and an additional five percent the following year. That is how that went down."

Eldon then said, "yes, I remember that. Also I recall that in order to fend off any hostilities from the Union back then, we considered it prudent to amend our own Union agreement at which time HJHC came forward with an unexpected wage increase offering the Union a four percent increase across the board to all hotel and Union members even before the Union contract was up. Yes, I know that very well. You know Louis, I was hesitant about that increase because it placed our profitability company-wide into a neutral situation. Allowing that increase as you know, pretty much negated our cash flow from positive to in some cases a negative flow in the hotel consolidated statements, which I just finished reviewing not that long ago for the last quarter. It was not a surprise to me because I was anticipating the expense. But it gives me great concern."

Eldon sat back in his chair. He looked over at Felix, nodding his head and looking back to Louis.

"Well, Eldon here's the situation, the head of the Caribbean Hotel and Casino Workers Union as you know is the one Domingo Alvarez.

I don't need to tell you; he is a ruthless and relentless bastard. Now mind you, most of his membership would disagree with me in the way I describe him, but we need make no mistake, he is militant and capable of violence. He has proven it in the past."

Eldon and Felix both nodded, now listening closely to Louis as he went on. Louis was at the top of his game. Eldon knew that very well.

"Eldon, what Alvarez, "Ziggy" is proposing in his new Union agreement proposal which I have in hand with me here, is an across the board wage increase of fifty percent. Under most circumstances, this would be a ploy and a ridiculous starting point for negotiations and could be whittled down to a reasonable increase in the four to six percent area first year with an additional two percent after that for the following three years. However, Eldon, I do not believe this is the case this time around. My meeting with Forbes Bishop last month was an eye opener. I had mentioned to you that we might have a situation with the upcoming Union negotiations this time around, but Eldon, the scenario that Forbes Bishop laid out to me was just too preposterous to believe."

Eldon and Felix listening intently, Eldon then saying, "yeah, go ahead Louis."

Louis went on, sipping from his coffee cup.

"Eldon, after having met with Forbes, I found it to be so unbelievable that I thought it best to let it lay for a few weeks to see if things would come around to reason.

So, here's what he said, Forbes told me that Alvarez came to him, and demanded that he bring me in, which I did. I flew in to meet with Forbes in his office at Government house in Grenada, and Forbes told me that if we wanted to save our skins, we; meaning us, Holiday Jewel Hotels and Casinos best sign the new Union agreement revisions or negotiations and just run with it, the new terms to remain in place. Needless to say, Eldon, I was shocked, never in my career had I been actually threatened by a head of State."

Eldon and Felix had a look of disbelief on their faces.

Louis continued on, "Forbes told me in no uncertain terms that my refusal to sign the new Union contract would bring hardship to our company and may even end in bloodshed."

Eldon suddenly jumped in his chair and jerked ahead, saying, "Forbes actually said, that unless you sign the Union agreement, there will be blood, he actually said that to you, threatening you?"

Louis responded, "as sure as I sit here in front of you, he said those exact words to my face as I sat in front of him Eldon."

Eldon responded, looking at Felix.

"Louis…! Louis, you should have called me right away after that."

Louis then said, "Eldon, I wanted to, that was my first gut reaction, but I learned over the years never to act immediately on my gut reaction, and I decided to wait for a few days.

Eldon, one of the main reasons you hired me was to look after the most crucial aspects of your company and let me deal with urgency, freeing you to handle and manage your other concerns, well I wanted to call Forbes' bluff. I couldn't just cave for him.

We are the number one hotel and casino owner operator in the entire Caribbean. He can't just kick us around as he pleases, so at first blush, I didn't believe him. But Eldon I am leaning towards believing him now. You see, the thing is, that I don't believe Forbes has much to do with things anyway. It's really Domingo Alvarez, and Alvarez has Forbes in his pocket. Alvarez is using Forbes as his pawn and getting Forbes to do his dirty work. That's how I see it."

Eldon nodded looking at Felix. Felix was listening intently and taking notes as well.

Felix then looked at Eldon and Louis, "you know Louis, I think that scenario plays out just like you say. Forbes is a gopher for Alvarez, and Alvarez wants to keep his hands clean thereby using Forbes in a diplomatic manner having Forbes Bishop speak for the entire Caribbean Hotel and Casino Workers Union, as their spokesperson thereby keeping Alvarez out of the immediate spotlight. This then allows Alvarez to work his Union members behind the scenes revving their unrest throughout the islands. Yes, Eldon, I believe Louis has drawn the right picture for us here."

Louis went on. “But Eldon, that's not half of it. You know that our hotels almost all of them are currently in a no-profit situation, mainly attributed to our already high labor cost. We have been trying to push the room rates raising the standard rack rate by 15 percent.

This has not gone well, already the tour consolidators and wholesalers are complaining that our rates are too high, and we are starting to put ourselves out of the market. Our hotels have been experiencing a downturn in occupancy, fewer rooms being occupied in our hotels mean fewer visitors coming to the island, and that translates to less airlines seats being filled.

Eldon two major air carriers that service most of the Caribbean and most of the islands where our hotels are have issued warnings to my Sales and Marketing executives along with my VP of revenue management that if this goes on, the airlines will be cutting back on the number of flights to the islands. Eldon if the airlines start pulling their flights, it will take months perhaps years to rebuild the business. Our hotel rooms will be left empty and whatever we lose will fill the cruise ships instead. That would be a killer to us. We already compete head to head with the cruise lines; any more stress on the hotels with dwindling occupancy will only result in further cutbacks.”

After listening to Louis for the past twenty or so minutes, Eldon's brain was speeding ahead at a whirlwind. Eldon had already played out the scenario in his mind, and things were starting to make sense if not quite totally formulated, but Eldon knew that in the back of his mind, events, facts, and the end-game was soon to be clearly in view. Eldon then stood up and walked out towards the edge of the patio where there was an iron railing.

He leaned back against the railing placing his hands on the top on either side of himself and addressed the issue as he saw it.

"So then, without the hotels doing well, and being full, that puts a significant strain on the revenue generated by the casinos. We need the hotels to do well. Otherwise, our casinos go under. Without tourists in the hotels, there are no players in the casinos; that is simple. As I see it, we are already funding the operational requirements of the hotels from our casino profits. Our overall viability as hotel and casino operators is still a going business and concern. Having this new Union agreement signed will mean that none of our hotel operations will be able to make any money and all of our hotels in the Caribbean will need to suck the profits away from the casinos attached to them. This then leaves our entire Caribbean operation without profitability. What does that do? What that does…is; it puts an end to my company going public.

An IPO projection just a few months ago, for HJHC was somewhere in the neighborhood of forty-eight Dollars per share, now with this looming over the company, I would be lucky to get an IPO issued at a Dollar per share.

This kills the IPO for now. But there is another thing nagging at me about this, and it's to do with Alvarez and his Union and no doubt his Union thugs, whoever they might be. So, Alvarez figures he can suck all profits away from our operations and would hold out and still operate because if I were to start closing the hotels and walking away, I would be forever be known as the killer of the hotel and resort casino industry in the Caribbean. Well, that's not going to happen. But we must be very very careful. I now see that we are in fact dealing with someone who is incredibly ruthless. You two know Alvarez's roots go back to the Union incidents in both Bermuda in 1981 and Puerto Rico in 1986."

Felix said, "yes I remember those times Eldon. Your father had just opened one of his first luxury resort properties in Bermuda the year before. I recall the huge fanfare; it was an amazing event and opening on the island. We had done well with that property over the years Eldon. But I do remember the problems in 1981."

Then Eldon to continue on, said, "Louis, you had just graduated high school back then so you wouldn't know about the problems in Bermuda, but it was the Caribbean Hotel and Casino Workers Union that brought about the problems."

'Well Eldon," Louis said, "I do in fact know about the hotel history in Bermuda, and I know all about the labor unrest problems experienced island wide, especially the hardship on the hotels as well as our's which The Bermuda Shelly Beach Resort and Spa did not escape. I read all about it Eldon. Actually, on a couple of my trips to Shelly Beach Resort the topic had come up with the General Manager of the property, we had a very enlightening conversation of those times.

Kenneth Gosling the GM there told me how the local people of the island stepped up and did the work for free that the Union members left behind. It was quite the time. The Bermuda Public Services Union had gone out on strike with ridiculous demands that the government was not about to meet at all. The initial request was almost a one hundred percent increase in wages. The Union demands were dropped by fifty percent, but even that was not going to fly.

The garbage started piling up all around the island, and after two weeks I can just imagine the stench all over the island."

Then Eldon, cut in and continued on with the history.

"That is exactly right Louis. Gosling filled you in well about those times. You know, after another week, seeing that the government was not going to budge, the CHCW Union also decided to wildcat strike, breaking their Union agreement with the hotels. This of course meant no maid service, no room service, no laundry service, no waiters, no cooks. The situation had become intolerable and topping it off, the same time the hotel workers decided to strike, so did the taxi Union, as well as the airport luggage and ground workers.

So, what you had, in essence, was a "locked down, closed-up island." For an entire week, no planes arrived or departed from the Bermuda International Airport. Tourists could not even make their way to the airport because no buses or taxis were running, and the hotels soon started running out of food and supplies.

For the first time in the history of the colony, the Government called out the Militia to maintain security island wide. Riots were threatened.

Thank God those never materialized, but the situation was becoming dire. In the end, after nine days of complete island-wide shutdown, both parties came to their senses, and the strike was settled. That was the CHCW Union in Bermuda.

But the story doesn't end there, and this is the part that really scares me. With Forbes, saying that there may be bloodshed, I tend to believe him and take him for his words, and with great concern.

Another labor dispute followed the Bermuda incident five years later in Puerto Rico; that one resulted in deaths and riots.

The "bombing" of the DuPont Plaza Hotel on December 31, 1986. Yes, that was New Year's Eve. Flammable liquids were placed throughout the casino which acted as virtual bombs. In the end, 97 people lost their lives. During the year of 1986, hotel workers had been in dispute with the government about their wages. In order to express their anger with the government, three hotel workers decided to terrorize the tourists which resulted in the tragic loss of human life.

If I didn't know any better, I would say that Alvarez was behind that entire tragic incident, and that is what scares me today. I do not want something similar happening with or to us. I will be flying down to meet with Forbes Bishop just as soon as I can get away. I know in my gut that this Alvarez will stop at nothing."

Eldon stopped talking for a minute and allowed time for those words to sink in and to sink in deep.

Alvarez and CHCW Union was now demanding, but not yet quite in command.

Eldon knew he had to make certain that Alvarez would never be in command, not of Eldon's company, not his hotels and not his casinos. Eldon would see to that.

The three men fell into silence, each one thinking their own thoughts and yet all on the same page. Just then the phone rang to break the silence.

Eldon reached for the phone and answered. It was Billy. "Eldon, I think I have it, I think I have the marina, Eldon."

Eldon then let out a huge sigh…and exhaled.

"Wow, what a turn of events."

Eldon's mind was running again a thousand miles per hour. Having gotten the gloom and doom picture from Louis regarding the problems his company was facing in the Caribbean and coming to the realization that complications were at hand which also had to be dealt with and handled, now Eldon all of a sudden finally heard some good news.

Eldon's world was turning faster every day, he had to remain focused, Cathy was out there somewhere, but Eldon felt it in his bones that he was making progress, things were happening. Even Louis's gloom and doom somehow added to things that gave Eldon reason for pause. Things seemed to be connecting; the dots were becoming visible in his mind. It was a matter now of connecting these faint, but emerging dots.

In Eldon's mind, it was just too incredible for all this to be happening at once, there was a good reason for all of these occurrences to be emerging at one time.

"Good work Billy, okay, get back here soon as you can, and we can talk about what you've come up with, but Louis is all done, and he needs to get back to the island ASAP. You'll have to fly him over to the island and get back here for sundown; we will have work to do after the sun sets today Billy."

Hearing Eldon's instructions, Billy turned the Stinger south, gunning the throttle fully forward, launching The Stinger's nose clear out of the water with a thundering sound that rocketed the ocean racer over the coastline waves heading back to Pompano. He would be there within the hour.

***

Chapter Seventeen

It's been an axiom of mine, that the little things are infinitely the most important.

Sherlock Holmes

District Director, Miller, sat in his Miami FBI office thinking about Eldon Barnes Davis. Miller had come into his office early this morning; he was on the case already at 4:30 AM. He was consumed with the FBI director having talked to Miller just a few hours ago, stressing to Miller how important this one case was considered to be, with even having prearranged State Department involvement.

This must be something of an international nature which Miller wasn't completely privy to at this point, and it bothered him. So he was anticipating what his connection to the State Department would reveal. He wondered what Ms. Kimberly Ashton would bring to the table or for that matter take from his table.

Although for the moment Miller realized his table didn't contain a whole lot to take. Miller did have one important piece of evidence that did turn up, and this was now a major break in the case. Miller recently received a videotape from Eldon. Eldon phoned Miller about the videotape, and Miller had one of his special Agents retrieve the tape from Eldon yesterday. Miller had immediately sent the tap over to the lab and forensics even before viewing it. Although the cassette had already been viewed and handled by Eldon and his people, he wanted to keep with protocol and not contaminate the evidence any more than it already was. Miller viewed the tape in the lab from a clean room video monitor. Miller had a copy of the tape made and was now once again viewing the video on his monitor in his office. Far as Miller could tell, there wasn't a great deal to go on, but he wasn't the forensics expert, he was the gumshoe man.

Eldon had not mentioned anything about the tape having been analyzed by Nick Kovacs up at Cape Kennedy, nor the discovery of encouraging possibilities. Eldon was curious if the feds would come up with anything, this was going to be a good test as to their capabilities and investigative thoroughness. Miller had another video in his possession, and that video was what he considered to be of major import. FBI Regional Director Miller was under the gun; Kingsbury was applying pressure in moving this case along.

The collaboration with local Police departments in south Florida and with Miller's Agents' efforts had been a payoff. The location of the Van and confirmation provided through DNA analysis had a positive match. The van now was being further picked apart in forensics for any clues as to the perpetrator. But there was more. A tape was obtained from the U-2 Play parking lot in Boynton Beach. The tape wasn't exactly what Miller was hoping for, but it was going to help.

Turns out that it was not a running video. The camera system mounted and located on the corner of the retail outlet building, mounted high enough to capture a wide angle of the parking area, was an interval timed capture camera and video tape system.

The video system was set to capture ten seconds of video at a frame rate of twenty-four frames per second. So, it ran for ten seconds every five minutes. This meant that the ninety-minute tape contained five thousand four hundred seconds of video portioned out into a series of five hundred forty individual ten-second video clips. Each subsequent ten-second clip being spaced apart to capture ten seconds of video at each five-minute interval. This then further calculated that each passing minute; sixty seconds contained six clips each ten-seconds long, meaning that each minute contained a half hour of coverage.

Therefore, two minutes of tape would cover an entire hour. The entire ninety-minute video cassette tape covered a period of forty-five hours. The video cassettes were not looped after each forty-five-hour cycle but kept on file for a period of one month after which time the video cassette tapes were recycled and placed back into circulation and taped over.

This provided for a reasonable effort of surveillance, warding off any pending lawsuit regarding liability issues that may arise from claims filed in regards to auto theft, negligence, and break-ins taking place in the parking area. Upon reviewing the cassette tapes on the day the murder and kidnapping took place and running the parking lot videotape, the stolen van was recorded to be in the parking lot at the 6:50 PM time stamp and marker on the video tape.

The stolen van was not yet on the videotape at the 6:45 PM time stamp and marker. However, at the 6:45 PM time stamp marker, there was a dark colored Nissan Pathfinder SUV parked directly next to where the stolen Van was now parked. Upon further viewing, the videotape shows the Nissan Pathfinder SUV showing up for the first time at the 1:35 PM time stamp marker, and continually parked up to the 6:45 PM video time stamp marker.

At the 6:50 PM time stamp marker, the Nissan SUV is no longer in the parking lot, and parked next to where the Nissan was parked is the stolen van in which Cathy Davis was kidnapped.

This was good enough for Miller to come to a tentative conclusion that the Nissan Pathfinder was the transfer vehicle. Miller was hoping for a further piece of luck, maybe capturing the individual with the Davis girl in the video, but that was not the case. The ten seconds of video for each occurrence was not long enough to have provided that activity and evidence. Miller had no choice but to pursue other clues from the video.

Miller figured that the Nissan was most likely a rental. Miller's forensics lab had confirmed his hunch that the Nissan actually was rental. The Nissan was in fact parked with the rear of the vehicle facing the parking lot; both vehicles had pulled straight in and not backed into the parking spaces. The good thing here was that at least the vehicle plates were visible; unfortunately, the quality of the video was not able to resolve the plate numbers on either vehicle. However, Miller's hunch that the Nissan might be a rental was confirmed.

Forensics was able to enhance the video clarity to at least verify that the plate was, in fact, a Florida State License plate and the most important piece of information obtained from the video, was that forensics had confirmed that on the rear window of the Nissan, there was a barcode label.

The barcode itself couldn't be read since the resolution was not clear enough even after enhancement, but it did render and verify the sticker to be a rental car barcode window sticker. Rental companies barcoded their fleet for easy tracking of vehicles exiting and entering the rental lot.

Each vehicle was scanned upon departure and arrival. Some vehicles are barcoded both front and rear windows. It was confirmed, that the Nissan was a rental. What this now meant was more good-old detective work, which would eventually lead to the agency from where the vehicle was rented.

Because of the fact that it was a Florida agency rental, that would help his hunt. Miller well knew it was now just a matter of time. Miller thought to himself, “these criminal bastards can be brave and determined, but they all slip up someplace, just need to look hard enough and be persistent, and sometimes the littlest things such as this bar code label, in this case, turns out to be the most important. Miller picked up his phone and dialed Kingsbury's private number. It was one minute before 8 AM, and it was time to call in his update and report to FBI Director Kingsbury.

Florida Atlantic University in Boca Raton Florida was not ranked as having the top political science program in the United States, but it was definitely one of the more respected schools covering the topic. It offered a Master's Degree in General Political Science and Government.

Kimberley Ashton's Alma Mater was FAU. Kimberley was a member of the faculty but only entertained lectures on a special lecture schedule that called upon her once every two months. She thoroughly did enjoy the lecture sessions; it kept her in the game and allowed her to grow in terms of maintaining a forefront in the educational process. Her skills as an orator and visiting professor were second to none. She was well respected by the Dean and her colleagues and the students absolutely loved to pick her brains. She was an expert when it came to international affairs and was fluent in French as well as Russian having majored in political science and linguistics. Kimberley enjoyed post class workshops with her students which sometimes extended late into the night as they discussed and debated the current events of the world and how nations and their leaders should act in bringing peace and prosperity, instead of war and suffering. It was a hot button topic to be sure, especially whether or not the United States should act as the Policeman of the world or if it even had the right to.

The hot topic of this morning's lecture and class had been the effectiveness of the United Nations; whether it was of any use on the world stage at all any longer or had it runs its course and purpose. The students on both sides of the issue presented their cases very well; it was going to be a significant factor in their overall marks for this semester. With Kimberley being the current Charge de Affairs to the Bahamas and extension of those duties to Grenada, she was in an enviable position to be both teaching international geopolitical studies, as well as walking the talk, and not just talking the talk.

Kimberley Ashton assumed the position and responsibility of Charge de Affairs six months ago when The Honorable Michael Lexington US Ambassador to The Bahamas took ill and was still fighting cancer at the University of Miami medical center. Secretary of State Mitch Farnsworth entrusted Kimberley to assume the US State Department's interests and responsibilities that normally ambassador Lexington and his staff in The Bahamas carried out so efficiently. Kimberley was highly regarded by Lexington, being Ashton's mentor at State for the past five years, and it was upon Lexington's personal vouching and standing up for Kimberley that Farnsworth called upon Kimberley to look after the needs of the United States in The Bahamas.

With Kimberley not having full Ambassadorial status, she was to remain Charge de Affairs until Lexington was well enough to assume his full responsibilities. Or perhaps her next step in her career was to be a full Ambassador posting, but that, of course, would be by appointment by the President of the United States and subsequent confirmation of her appointment by the United States Congress.

For now, Kimberley was very happy with her current status and eager to engage in whatever Secretary Farnsworth had carved out for her.

Within days after taking on her new long term temporary position, Farnsworth had her covering and extending her dealings and the interests of the United States with the government of Grenada.

Farnsworth briefed her on the delicacy of the situation in Grenada and how it had become apparent through CIA covert information gathering, infiltration of the island political system and activities that the current government in power headed by Forbes Bishop was unstable and teetering on an international scandal. These developing circumstances could potentially send shock waves through the Caribbean basin, the surrounding islands and worst of all embarrass the United States, staining the State Department and leaving The President with egg on his face. This at all cost was to be avoided and worked every day. Farnsworth assigned Ashton with an adjunct office in Grenada and a complement of six key State Department employees who reported directly to Ashton.

Kimberley was well aware of the sub base building project, the apparent buying of the Prime Minster placing him directly into the pocket of the Caribbean's' most powerful and widespread labor Union. She understood that Forbes Bishop was on the edge and verge of tumbling from his position and that the entire government structure was a house of cards waiting to crumble. That, of course, could not happen before the treaty was signed, and that was still a good number weeks out.

Now, Kimberley was to manage another element added to the mix, and that was to be the involvement of the FBI.

FBI director Kingsbury had his man in Florida; Agent Sam Miller, now working a case involving the murder and kidnapping of Mrs. Eldon Davis and Davis's daughter.

"This seemed a bit out of place," Kimberley thought. "But then again, Davis owned and operated a huge chunk of the resort and hotel business in the islands, and the money being funneled to Bishop, well most of it if not all of it came from the coffers of the Caribbean Hotel and Casino Workers Union. That Union was headed and run by Domingo Alvarez."

The dots were there; all Kimberley had to do was draw the lines to connect those dots. It was clear in her mind.

"Alvarez fed Bishop; Bishop made certain to keep the laws governing labor Unions in tact, and Alvarez's Union membership formed the major portion of votes at election time. The circle was complete."

Kimberley was shrewd, calculating and incredibly astute. There was no need for a clear picture to be drawn for her, she could easily figure out where all the dots were located and drew the lines required to connect those dots.

Farnsworth knew this, and so did Vic Amber. Vic's people on the island had gathered the inside info and in this case worked hand in hand with Ashton's assets. It was a rare animal to find State and CIA working hand in hand, but in this instance and with the urgency and importance unfolding daily, cooperation of the agencies was paramount.

Kimberley couldn't help it, though; something was sinister about Miller's involvement, and she was beginning to get a very very bad feeling about all of this. She gathered her thoughts and dialed Miller's number in Miami from inside her "Beemer."

Not three rings and the Regional FBI director answered; "Miller."

"Regional Director Miller, this is Kimberley Ashton with State, good afternoon."

Miller answered her very cordially. "Ah Ms. Ashton, I was expecting your call. Director Kingsbury had advised me that you would be calling. I want to assure you that we are in a position to fully cooperate with you and State, whatever you may want to coordinate with the FBI here in south Florida, I will be happy to make my priority." Miller finished saying.

"Well thank you up front for the FBI's assistance and I too along with my assets at State are counting on the expertise you and your team can provide Agent Miller. I am afraid my needs are not limited to Florida however. I don't know if Director Kingsbury briefed you on this, but my need for your services lie about two hundred miles to the east of Florida, I need your assistance over in The Bahamas."

Kimberley went on, "we do have a treaty with the Bahamas in terms of law enforcement, but it's more on a diplomatic level. The fine points are not that well defined which leaves a great deal to the interpretation of the treaty and sometimes moving about as we might please here in the US is not as easily achieved over in the islands. We have been hampered in the past on occasion and thus I will need the added weight of the FBI to be present on the island. You understand Agent Miller, us State Department types need to act in diplomatic ways which sometimes hinders our information gathering capabilities, and we need to do things very hush-hush under the table, underground, and in very clandestine ways. I need someone from the FBI who will be visible, up front and frankly, I want some FBI weight to be thrown around the island. That is what I am looking for; can you do that for me?"

Miller, thought to himself, "damn, this woman is a tough cookie."

Miller answered. "Absolutely Ms. Ashton, that's what the FBI is all about."

Kimberley replied "Good to hear Agent Miller. Then what I suggest is for our next meeting to be held over in Nassau. I will contact you within the next day or so and set up a time. One of my staff from the Embassy will pick you up at the US Customs main door... and not to worry Agent Miller, he will know who you are."

Miller replied, "Very good Ms. Ashton, I will see you then in Nassau."

Kimberley thought, "well that went all right, wonder what Miller has on his end regarding the Davis case."

Kimberley kept driving, heading down into Boca Raton. She lived over in the Bahamas where she had a residence on Cable Beach, but when she was in Florida, she stayed at the Grand Boca Raton Hotel and Club. FAU was close by, and the Grand Boca Raton Hotel and Club was a fabulous resort, yes as it turns out owned and operated by Holiday Jewel Hotels and Casinos.

Florida did not have casinos, other than those on Indian designated land, operated by the Florida

Seminole Indians. The Grand Boca Raton Hotel did just fine without a casino; it was a landmark in Boca and the number one employer and driver of the local economy.

She pulled her Beemer up to the front entrance of the hotel and valet parking took care of the rest. "Good afternoon Ms. Ashton" she was greeted by the handsome doorman Alfred, who was dressed casually but very smartly in designer threads for the warm Florida climate. Kimberley just left her car keys in the Beemer for Alfred and made her way into the main lobby. She smiled at Alfred, said good afternoon to him and continued on inside. How elegant and regal the lobby was. This Hotel and The Breakers in Palm Beach were her two favorite hotels in all of Florida. Perhaps the Breakers was her favorite on the entire east coast of the United States, but the Grand Boca was much closer to FAU and much more practical on this visit to the US. She loved staying here, although she was not royalty, the hotel was famous for treating everyone as if they were in fact royalty. It was a policy of the hotel and insisted upon by the general manager of the property. Eldon himself had instituted that level of service for his hotel managers to implement and live by.

All VIP's names and faces were to be memorized by the concierge, the bell staff and the front desk employees, and every time one of the VIPs needed service or attention by any one of those employees, the guest was always to be addressed by their surname. This policy also extended to all eight Maitre'D's and Hostesses in the gourmet restaurants throughout the property.

Addressing hotel guests by their first names was strictly prohibited and cause for immediate dismissal. Kimberley had no knowledge that that was, in fact, a policy of the hotel, but it sure was a nice touch.

As Kimberley walked past the front desk, the front desk Agent greeted Kimberley saying “good afternoon Ms. Ashton.” Kimberley smiled back at the young lady, wiggled her fingers in a small wave and proceeded to her hotel suite. She was glad she was back at the hotel. Her flight was not scheduled to depart until 8 PM this evening; she had plenty of time to enjoy the afternoon sun down at poolside. Kimberley changed into her beachwear, and was out the door within ten minutes, grabbing the Miami Trumpet on the way out; she made her way out to the pool deck and settled in on the comfortable chaise lounge.

Kimberley reached into her beach purse, found her Serengeti shades, and with her stylish sun hat sat back and picked up the Miami Trumpet. The first thing that caught her eye was the story on the front page, a follow up on the Davis murder and kidnapping written by Damon Furst in his daily column: “The Furst Report.” Kimberley couldn't resist; she wanted to just soak up some rays, go for a refreshing dip in the pool, but she decided to read Damond's column instead.

It was turning out to be an interesting day. Jimmy, the poolside waiter, brought Kimberley her usual drink poolside, an “Arnold Palmer;” ice tea with lemonade. She smiled at Jimmy as he placed her drink on the side table beside her. “Thank you Jimmy, as she accepted the bar check from Jimmy and signed for it to be charged to her room.

Taking a sip from her glass, she started in on The Furst Report. She had come to know Damond Furst over the past few years. Although Damond was known to sensationalize or even embellish the story from time to time, his basic reporting facts were for the most part true and well sourced. Damond's time with the Miami Trumpet had earned him the respect that thirty years of reporting experience gets you in the news business. Matters concerning events to do with the United States, Florida, and the Bahamas were usually addressed by Kimberley.

The US Embassy in The Bahamas did not have a specific "Press Agent," and with Kimberley being Ambassador Lexington's right hand and second in command, she usually addressed any news media issues along with the preparation of press releases, or statements and comments on events. These events in the past had covered the cooperation between the DEA, Bahamas Customs and Immigration, and The Royal Bahamas Police Force in matters of crime prevention and drug trafficking.

Over the past few years, there had been many rumors concerning human trafficking activity coming through and being expedited in the islands with the Police force "looking the other way." Damond Furst was usually the one reporter making the flight over from Miami to shove a microphone in front of Kimberley's face as she was either coming to work at the Embassy or leaving for the day.

She actually got a kick out of him from time to time and knew how to handle Damond. The two of them had developed a working relationship so to speak over the years. They were as friendly as could be with each other without actually becoming friends. As she was about to start reading Damond's column, two FBI Agents walked down onto the pool deck, Kimberley had noticed the two Agents, one man one woman, him right away and sensed they were looking for her, not anyone else.

They approached Kimberley, both wearing dark glasses, no jacket, white shirt, dress pants, the male Agent said, "my apologies for the intrusion Ms. Ashton. I am special FBI Agent Swanson," showing his badge, "and my partner special Agent Connors."

Kimberley replied asking, "what can I do for you, Agent Swanson?"

Agent Swanson then said, "The Hotel concierge directed us to the pool saying you were out here. Ms. Ashton, CIA in Langley had this package couriered to FBI regional director Miller this afternoon. Agent Miller had us deliver this package marked confidential for your eyes only, Ms. Ashton."

Kimberley accepted the package from the Agents; they thanked her and were on their way.

Kimberley was surprised and totally consumed now, thinking, "CIA, FBI, State, all rolled up into one, as well as DND the Pentagon, probably NSA as well," Kimberley thought… "Jesus, what a day!"

Damond's article was going to have to wait. Kimberley grabbed her purse, left her drink, left the newspaper where it lay, took hold of the courier package and left the pool heading to her suite. She was already reaching for an opener to break the seal on the tamper proof wrapping, not ten seconds after coming inside. She sat down on the sofa and opened the thick envelope.

Kimberley pulled the contents out of the envelope revealing several ten by eight glossy photos. One being of Eldon, another of Linda his wife, now deceased and another of the three of them together taken professionally no doubt, and another of just Eldon and Cathy, an absolutely lovely photo. Eldon sitting in a winged chair with Cathy perched like a little angel on his knee hugging Eldon's neck. Cathy truly was a beautiful little girl and her father Eldon looking so proud and protecting.

The contents of the envelope also contained a couple of pages of data and background detail about the Davis family and dates the photos were taken, along with a separate red colored tinted document.

Kimberley knew what this meant, any documents on red tinted color paper was top secret priority one and marked as such with "Top Secret" watermarked diagonally across the length of the document.

The document was from the CIA's Vic Amber copied to Mitch Farnsworth, Cyril Burgess, Kingsbury, and Rickover, and now Kimberley was enjoying the privilege of reading this herself, it was dated with yesterday's date.

No doubt Miller had received the same directive but could not talk about it during their recent phone conversation.

These document directives of top secret nature were all to be considered as sensitive and to do with national security. Upon reading and becoming aware of the contents of the document and subsequent failure to abide by the directive, or to deliberately and knowingly oppose the facts and instructions contained within the document could subject the individual to charges of treason brought against the individual by the United States of America.

Kimberley knew she was not to take this document lightly. She proceeded to read the top-secret alert. It stated in no uncertain terms that there was to be a blackout by all investigative services and this included the FBI and CIA on the Eldon Barnes Davis situation. All progress, facts, and discoveries were to remain under wraps.

The FBI had been given sole investigative dominance over the murder and kidnapping and had been totally in charge as of yesterday's, date. Local Police and Florida State Police were officially out of the picture. This was now to be exclusively an FBI, CIA, and Department of State matter.

There were to be no further independent discussions of the incident. The FBI and only the FBI were to handle any required interaction with the public or the news media. This case had been bumped up to a matter of national security until further notice. After having read the document's directive, she was now convinced; more than ever, that she was going to have a very significant role to play. Kimberley stood up and made her way over to the bar in her suite. She obtained a bottle of white Mouton Cadet from the bar fridge and poured herself a glass of wine to sip on while she read through the documents.

She couldn't help herself; she kept looking back at the ten by eight glossy of Eldon and Cathy. There was something about the photo that tugged at her heartstrings. As she stared at the photo, condensation formed on the wine goblet forming a drop that fell onto the edge of the picture. She was captivated momentarily, as she reached out with her left index finger to wipe the drop from the photo, and found herself moving over the photo onto Eldon's face, slowly moving her finger across his cheek and moving her finger ever so slowly onto his lips, as a tear formed in her eye, that clouded her vision and then with a lump forming in her throat, she said under her breath, "you poor man, you must be torn apart, let me help."

Something stirred deep inside Kimberley, never in her career had she felt like this. This was something new for Kimberley, she glanced back down at the photograph of Eldon and Cathy, both smiling back at her, and a sudden chill went down her spine. Something had awakened deep within her, and she knew it. This, indeed was a unique day in her diplomatic career and her 38 years of life.

***

Chapter Eighteen

If you are going through hell, keep going!

Winston Churchill

In February, the sun sets in Florida just after six P.M. Daylight was fading giving way to dusk as Billy flew the jet back from Nassau having taken Louis back home. Billy well knew that time was of the essence today and chose to bring the jet into Pompano saving a precious hour or so. Eldon would want to get out onto the water just as the sun was setting and the lighthouses were being turned on all along the Florida coastline.

The Sikorsky was at Pompano as well, so Billy taxied the Canadair to the end of the airfield where the chopper helipad was and flew back to Eldon's estate. It was now just after six PM and the sun had started its descent.

Felix had taken the afternoon to review Billy's notes and markings he made on the map highlighting marinas with lighthouses close by. Billy had one particular lighthouse circled which he already had checked on regarding its rate of rotation, and that was The Jupiter Island lighthouse, sitting on the north side of the Jupiter Inlet, very close to the Jupiter Inlet Marina itself.

Billy had gotten in contact with the lighthouse association that managed and maintained the lighthouse and adjacent museum. Their historical records had all sorts of information on the lighthouse and its history, as well as the data on the strength of the bulb itself and its rotation speed, which were, in fact, four rotations of the bulb every sixty seconds. This lighthouse fit the bill perfectly regarding the four rotations every minute, and this definitely warranted a return to the lighthouse tonight when it was lit and rotating. Billy had marked out other lighthouses as well two others located at marinas and a few not, but still valid since there were private docks nearby.

The thing was that it wasn't necessarily a marina location, could be just a private home on the Intracoastal Waterway with a dock catching the light of a nearby lighthouse. There were a hell of a lot more private boat docks along the Intracoastal Waterway than there were boats docked at all marinas on the east coast combined. But the odds of having a lighthouse configured in this picture pointed to a marina setting. This is where they were to look tonight.

Eldon and Felix were set and waiting for Billy, and upon Billy's arrival the three of them made their way down to The Stinger. Eldon took command. Eldon was an expert at handling The Stinger and its three five hundred horse power-house.

Every year The Stinger would see action in the Wellcraft Meteor owner's club, which usually included a run from Key West to Dry Tortugas, a fun afternoon of lobster diving and Jimmy Buffet tunes. Those days and afternoons were some of the finest memories of Linda and Cathy that Eldon ever had with his family. Those days and times were now forever gone for him and Linda, but in his power, Eldon would move a mountain if he could to make days like that fill Cathy's life once again. This trip would be somewhat different tonight. No lobsters and no parrot hats.

Billy handed out the headsets with the boom mics. These were like aircraft communications on a single engine Piper. The Stinger's engine noise when she was running full power was impossible to hear over, and headset communication apparatus was required. The Stinger was free from the dock, Eldon eased the powerful craft away from its berth, and pointed the sleek craft north on the Intracoastal, heading up towards Hillsboro inlet just a mile and a half on the Intracoastal before the exit the channel at Hillsboro and hit open ocean.

Eldon decided to head immediately up to Jupiter. It was about a 50-minute drive from Pompano Beach to Jupiter on I95, but Eldon figured he could do better time with The Stinger, zipping up the coastline with her engines wide open, maybe forty minutes or so.

Eldon cruised his way up to Hillsboro inlet, pointed the boat out towards the ocean, heading out the channel, getting past the breakers and then steered her north. He looked at his two friends, all three of them standing on the bridge, braced into the stand-up cockpit enclosures, Eldon, Billy and Felix all gave a thumbs up, and Eldon opened her up. The Stinger came to a roaring launch with her nose high, penetrating the water and pushing her fifty-foot hull through the water like it was butter on a skillet. They were on their way, to find what they were looking for and that was: answers.

Eldon was about a half mile offshore, looking at a straight run up the Florida coastline. He knew these waters well. Immediately to the right of him going east would put him onto the west shore of Grand Bahama Island, sixty miles out. He had made the trip in The Stinger several times over to The West End, Grand Bahama Bay Harbor.

Eldon owned property on Grand Bahama as well and liked showing up sometimes unannounced. A hundred and twenty miles from the West End heading farther east was Marsh Harbor on Abaco Island. Eldon enjoyed that town as well. He did not have a resort at Marsh Harbor, but he had some good friends and a former VP of finance for his hotel and casino company who retired in Marsh Harbor. Eldon had friends and acquaintances throughout the Bahamas and the Caribbean no matter where he might venture.

The Florida coastline was shining like a jewel, not unlike a long endless lit chain in the night air. They passed Hillsboro and were directly east offshore of Boca, and soon to be making their way to Palm Beach, and just fifteen minutes or so after that, they should be in sight of the Jupiter lighthouse casting its beam through the night sky.

They pressed on, their bodies consuming the gentle impact of each dip as The Stinger skimmed over the ocean swells. The night salty air smelled good, heightening their senses and keying their awareness. The seas were calm tonight; forecast was from one to three feet which were considered calm. She could handle three to five no problem and still maintain top speed. As they got closer and closer to Jupiter, the lighthouse's beam was now visible, and the closer they got, Eldon realized that this was not going to bring forth what he was looking for.

He spoke into his headset's mic. “Hey guys, I don't think this is going to be it.”

The closer they got to the lighthouse, the more Eldon doubted things. Licks picked up on it right away.

“Yeah, Eldon I see what you mean,” speaking into his mic, Billy had a disappointing look on his face, realizing he had overshot his selection of this lighthouse location.

Eldon then responded. “Yeah guys, see how the light shoots out from the bulb…it’s powerful as all hell, but much too high up.”

The closer the Stinger came to being opposite the actual lighthouse structure itself, it was plainly evident that the lighthouse's powerful beam shot clear over the top of everything within a two or three-mile radius.

The marina just off to the south of the lighthouse, tucked safely away from Atlantic storms, in the Jupiter inlet was much too close to the base of the lighthouse, and its passing beam reaching out clear over the top of the marina made no illuminating impact on the boats docked below. The light passed over them, not making any difference in illumination at all.

Eldon had turned the engines off, and they drifted in silence, thinking, disappointed, but thinking.

"The thing is, that we are in fact looking for a lighthouse, I believe that is a given. The other lighthouses that you marked on the map here Billy, well those too would be structures too high up, yes clearly visible as you saw from offshore earlier on, but much too tall, with bulbs casting their light too high and over the top of everything nearby. What we need to find are marinas that might have smaller lighthouses, marking their entrances, those would make sense, but these so far are not what we want." Felix and Billy nodded in disappointing agreement as they sat looking at the coastline.

Then Eldon said, "Okay, we are out here now, I have been around here a lot, and I know this area, the Intracoastal is loaded with marinas from Miami to Jacksonville, but I have a hunch we need to look for one in this neighborhood that matches our criteria. Let's cruise on down the Intracoastal, see what we can find, we'll make our way back to Pompano down along the Intracoastal Waterway, I don't care if it takes us till morning, we good?"

Billy and Felix answered at the same time. "Damn right I'm good," said Felix.

"Let's do it" countered Billy.

Eldon turned the ignition, and pointed The Stinger towards and in through the Jupiter Inlet, heading for the Intracoastal, south. Speed was limited to a slow 10 knots per hour in a lot of the areas, due to narrows and further limitations on speed for manatee safety zones.

The Manatee was designated an endangered species, essential to the South Florida ecosystem. Speed violations were severe penalties. Manatees had been getting cut up and sliced up more than ever by boat props, and the State Wildlife Department was trying its best to do something about protecting these docile and harmless creatures.

Eldon cruised slowly down the waterway, passing several marinas; from here to Miami there must be over two hundred marinas. Some with only fifteen or twenty slips, some with close to fifty and more. They made their way down into Juno, and there was a marina low and behold with a lighthouse marking its entrance, but the light was broken, the glass itself was cracked, but Eldon drove the Stinger up to the gas pumps anyway and parked the Stinger for a moment alongside.

The gas attendant came out, and Eldon said, "hey, how are you, nice evening."

The young lady dressed in shorts and a wearing a baseball cap, replied, "hi gentlemen, how much gas would you like, fill up?"

Eldon replied, "actually no, I'm curious about your lighthouse at the end of the dock there at the entrance to the marina. I see that it's broken, any idea how long it has been like that?"

She replied saying, "oh, it's been like that for the past month or so, the owner says he's having difficulty finding the right part for it. He says the bulb is good, but the glass housing is cracked. They don't make them any more and it has to be hand-made or something like that I hear."

Eldon then said, "Okay thanks, I'm looking for a marina that has a lighthouse something like that, that marks the entrance, would you know of any around this neighborhood?"

She answered. "You know what, I do. I work another job doing the same thing, pumping gas at the marina in Admirals Cove. It's the same owner as this place, and he marked his marina entrance there as well with a lighthouse identical to this one, but that one is working just fine, it's only about ten minutes down the Intracoastal; Gulliver's Marina."

Eldon's spirits lit up right away. "Jeez thanks a million; you have no idea how much help you have been." Then Eldon, not knowing what else to say or do, continued on saying; "look, you seem like a lovely young lady, if you are ever looking for a job I want you to call me, and I promise you I will look after you."

Eldon reached into his pocket and pulled out one of his business cards.

"What's your name sweetheart?" Eldon asked.

"My name is Pearl, sir," she replied.

Eldon then said, "and I'm sure you are a most precious pearl at that, it is a beautiful name, here is my card, and like I say…if you ever need a job, rest assured you can call me, okay?"

Pearl replied, "okie-dokie, thanks a million," and smiled.

With that Eldon fired up The Stinger and made his way out of the marina, over towards Admirals Cove. It took no longer than about six or seven minutes to get there, and right away, as soon as they made their way around the bend, Billy pointed, saying, “there…there it is.”

The three of them saw it right away. The lighthouse was at the very entrance to the marina. It was situated at the tip of the cement-surfaced dock. The lighthouse stood about fifteen feet high, tall enough to cast its light over the Intracoastal waterway, not a blinding light by any means but visible enough to mark marina entrance. Eldon turned the engines off and with the calm evening, floated in place, hardly drifting at all. Admirals Cove was a wide section of the Intracoastal with lots of boating space.

Gulliver’s marina was clearly lit and shined upon by the rotating lighthouse. They all looked at their watches.

“OK, let’s time this sucker.” Licks said.

Licks and Billy had digital watches with LED readouts. Eldon's was a Rolex GMT with a second hand, but he had a stopwatch function on The Stinger's instrumentation panel.

Eldon then, waiting for the light to rotate into direct view with The Stinger, said, “on my mark, on three.” As the bulb made its circular arch in line with the Stinger, Eldon said, “one, two three,” and on three, they started their stopwatch functions and counted in unison with each rotation, “one, two, three, and four.” Four complete rotations...exactly one minute!

“Yes! Eldon remarked, “yes, this is it, I have no doubt, it’s perfect. The lighthouse casts its shine on the boats in slips behind it, and all craft are at right angles to the light. The light is high enough to catch every boat along its length parked in here. This is it; I am certain."

Felix and Billy were in agreement.

Billy said, "this has to be it, it's got to be, and it matches up perfectly to what Nick had discovered."

Eldon added, "yeah Billy, I would say this is the place, but we can't be a hundred percent until we have some sort of confirmation. Quite honestly at this point I'm not sure how we are going to get that, unless of course, Cathy is here on one of these boats. But somehow I seriously doubt that. However; if this is indeed the marina we are looking for, then we are on track, it will only be a matter of time before we find some other clue." Eldon finished saying.

Then he said, "give me a minute, I have an idea. Licks, I want you to take over the wheel. Here's what we are going to do.

I'm going to assume this is the marina we are looking for. I am willing to make that assumption. Licks, I want you to take The Stinger into the marina and dock it alongside the temporary visitor dock. Before you pull in, I'm going to make myself scarce and go down under for the duration of the time we are there. Whoever has Cathy, and if by chance he's still here, he may recognize me. I don't want to take that chance, so take The Stinger in, dock it and see the marina attendant about renting a slip for a few days. I want us to dock The Stinger here for a while, see what we can come up with, maybe something, maybe nothing, but I want to give it a shot."

Felix was listening closely to Eldon's plan as he laid it out, both Felix and Billy nodding as Eldon talked.

"So, Licks; take the Stinger in, dock it and ask about renting a slip for a few days. If there is a slip available, reserve it starting tonight and pay for it. Then with the slip reserved, tell the attendant you'll be back later tonight, at which point Billy, I want you to stay here at the marina, while Licks and I go back to my place with The Stinger. I want Billy to stay here, and hang out for that hour or two just in case he sees something suspicious or something, anything that may point us to Cathy. Billy wouldn't be recognized, but I would be.

Billy, Licks will bring The Stinger back here, you can stay on the Stinger for the next couple of days and keep your eyes and ears open. I will drive back at the same time and pick up Licks after he leaves The Stinger with you here at the marina."

Eldon finished and asked, "so, does that sound like a plan?"

Felix and Billy both liked what Eldon had come up with.

Eldon continued on. "Okay, I'm going below to keep out of sight, for now, take her in and see if we can get this done."

Felix took over in the cockpit and gently brought The Stinger into the entrance to Gulliver's marina, alongside the visitors' dock.

The marina attendant saw the big 50 foot Wellcraft Meteor Scarab entering the marina and made his way over to the visitor dock to assist in the docking procedure and secure the lines.

"Good evening gentlemen, nice night for a ride," Jonesy said.

"Yeah, thanks for the hand," Felix replied.

Billy jumped out onto the dock and helped with the docking procedure.

"I'm looking to rent a slip for a few days, got anything available?" Felix asked.

Jonesy replied, “yes sir, it’s a buck a foot per day, that would be one of the transient slips, or if you want it for a month, it's ten bucks a foot per month.”

Felix said, “great, let’s do the paperwork, and I can take care of things right now.”

Jonesy said, “fine, follow me to the office, and I'll issue you the slip authority.”

Eldon could hear it all down in The Stinger's stateroom. “Perfect,” he thought, “just perfect.”

Felix got everything taken care of; he rented the slip initially for three days. As he was walking back to The Stinger with Jonesy, Jonesy pointed out the rental slip for The Stinger, so that was good.

Then Felix said, “my friend here Billy's had enough boating for one day, he's going to hang out in the area, make himself comfortable up there in the picnic and BBQ area till I get back.”

“Yeah, sure, no problem, but we also have a small restaurant and bar here, maybe Billy you'd like that.” Jonesy offered.

Billy replied, “maybe I would, thanks, may just take you up on that and have a cold one.”

Felix got back into The Stinger, Jonesy and Billy untied, and Felix and Eldon were heading back to Pompano.

Billy took in the sights, started memorizing the names of each boat, taking note of any special markings, lights on or off on decks.

Billy was in his “Cobra-One” mode and character, and nothing could deter him from taking everything in; the smells, the vegetation, the fencing arrangements, the entrances, and exits.

On the way, back to Pompano, Eldon remarked, “if we need to go through hell, to find Cathy, we will.”

“Got that right,” Licks said.

***

Chapter Nineteen

Hold me hostage hold me tight,
On your island, darkness will turn to light.

Rico wanted Manko to scuttle The Sharker, get rid of all evidence associated with this incident. Rico suggested to Manko that they go drop the girl off with Violet on Conch Key, wait until dark, and Rico takes Jason's boat out to the blue hole, where Manko can meet him in the Police Boston Whaler, and the two of them can send Jason's boat down after him.

That sounded like a good idea to Rico. This was what Rico proposed to Manko on their way back after dumping Jason overboard for the white tip sharks to feast upon. The sharks tore him apart live. Gruesome but clean.

Manko convinced Rico that that wasn't necessary. “Look mon; no need to get rid of a nice boat like this. Jason is gone; I'm Chief of Police around here on these islands everything is good mon, not to worry mon, not to worry,” Manko showing his bright golden incisors, smiling like he'd just landed the deal of the century.

“What we do mon, is this. We take the girl to Violet now, best before she wakes up anyway mon, we relax and stay on the island, good conch there, I want some conch mon, it’s been too long for me since I had good cracked conch mon. Now that Jason is out of the way we can relax. We wait until dark, until Sandy Point Marina closes for the night and Simons goes home. We take the boat over to the marina then and leave it there. Jason was expected back tonight anyway after his fishing charter. Not to bring the boat back may raise a concern for Simons, he's very observant you know.”

Rico was starting to see that Manko was making sense.

"The boat can stay there for weeks. Jason leaves his boat in the marina for weeks at a time and flies back to the mainland from time to time mon. Nothing unusual about that mon."

Manko was right; Simons wouldn't be expecting him to check in again since he's already checked in with Bahamas Customs procedures earlier today.

"The best part mon is that in a few weeks, you can claim the boat yourself saying you purchased the boat from Jason. Remember mon; we already told Simons your boat was under repair; you'd be needing a new boat soon, and Jason needed the money, perfect setup mon."

This was sounding better and better all the time to Rico, "and after all, Manko was the Chief, so what was he worried about anyway?"

Rico smiled at Manko, "you the mon. Mon, you my mon Manko!" Rico said smiling and reaching out to shake Manko's hand. Rico thought some more about it all and settled in on it all very comfortably, and not only that but Rico was married to Manko's sister.

Manko would make sure Rico was taken care of and kept safe. Manko on the other hand, his main concern was to keep Rico happy. Manko knew where his bread was buttered and that butter was being supplied by Domingo, Rico's brother, the last thing Manko wanted was to upset Domingo. No, that would not be good. Manko was well aware of that.

Alvarez gave Manko specific instructions regarding the contract to kidnap Cathy Davis. Manko had made it clear to Jason what needed to be done, and only that, so Manko thought.

There was to be no murdering of the Davis woman. Manko had assured and vouched for Jason to Domingo, and now Manko had to make things good with Domingo, killing Jason would get him some creds with Domingo. Rico trusted Manko, but in reality, there was no honor amongst thieves.

Rico placed The Sharker next to the rickety dock on Conch Island. They went down into the stateroom and checked on Cathy; she was still out cold. Manko picked Cathy up out of the cooler, laying her on his chest, holding her close to his body. The child was like a feather in Manko's arms. Rico tied out the boat, and the two of them walked up to the old house on the hill that overlooked the Atlantic, with an eastern view. Manko held Cathy, and she started to stir.

Manko had Rico pick up Cathy's doll, Dixie which Rico was bringing along with him. They walked up the pathway; Manko hoping Cathy would stay asleep until at least he was able to hand Cathy over to Violet. Manko knew Violet was really good with small children.

Rico walked behind Manko just two feet behind him. Cathy was being carried high up on Manko's chest, with her head resting on Manko's right shoulder. Rico walked and looked at Cathy when she opened her eyes. Rico wasn't sure what to say or do, Cathy looked directly at Rico, but that was it. She didn't cry; she didn't move. Was she not conscious?

Rico then said to Manko, “Manko mon, the girl is awake.”

Manko, patted Cathy's back lightly saying; “we're here, we're here,” and they walked into the house.

Violet jumped up out of her chair, and started exclaiming, “Jesus, my Lord, sweet Jesus, what have you done? Sweet Jesus, save my soul sweet Jesus, what have you two done!" Violet was taken aback, looking at Rico with fear in her eyes.

Rico then said, "quit your whining woman and take care of this here little one. I told you we had a girl for you to take care of, I told you."

Violet answered. "Yes, you did, you sure did Rico, but you didn't tell me that she was a white child!"

Violet took Cathy into her arms, and Cathy started crying, crying and crying, Cathy was all of a sudden shaken and terrified.

Violet walked up to Rico, holding Cathy, reached out and yanked Dixie out of Rico's hands, saying to Rico, "what trouble have you brought upon us? Are you two out of your minds? Lordy, lordy, lordy."

The two of them just stood there, with Manko now saying, "ah quit your whining Violet and just take care of the girl. Rico and me will have her away from here soon."

With that, Manko said to Rico, "okay mon, we're done here, for now, let's get back to the boat, I could use a cold beer mon."

Rico then said, "yeah, good idea," and the two of them left Violet with Cathy; now fully awake but crying still.

She was thirsty and had a very bad headache; she cried more. Violet carried her to the table and poured a cup of water, Cathy took it, drinking and crying she reached out for Dixie and hugged it. Cathy was in a world unknown to her, strangers and she cried wanting her daddy and mommy.

Violet said, "child, child child, you a pretty thing aren't ya, I'll take care of you little one, cry till you can't cry no more, then I will watch over you till your daddy and mommy come for you."

Violet was beside herself, she was very worried, but Manko and Rico, well, she had no position to question their actions. Her lot in life was to care and care she did. Violet started singing to Cathy hoping it might calm her beating heart.

"Yellow bird, high in banana tree, yellow bird, you sit all alone like me, did your lady friend, leave the nest again...... Cathy started to calm.

***

Chapter Twenty

Missions accomplished are sometimes,
looming disaster placed on temporary on hold.

The President's men met again. Rare was the occasion when five members of the President's cabinet would meet without the President in attendance. Vic Amber, CIA, Mitch Farnsworth, State, Cyril Burgess, NSA, Howard Rickover, Defense, and A.B. Kingsbury FBI, all together, all in the same private and secured room. This room was located in Vic Amber's building. It was just last week that the five of them had gotten together, now it was imperative that a follow-up meeting take place.

Kingsbury began. "Vic and I, we have issued orders to our people in the field that the situation concerning Eldon Barnes Davis, his wife's murder and missing daughter is to stay under wraps. After our meeting, here this morning, I am sure you will be issuing the same set of directives to your people as well." Kingsbury addressed the three cabinet members who were not yet in the loop, but this meeting would bring them so. Secretary of State, Mitch Farnsworth was well aware of the goings on in Grenada but had not yet made the link directly to Eldon and how Eldon's involvement might, in fact, jeopardize the Caribbean Initiative, but he will in the next few minutes, Kingsbury thought to himself.

Amber took over from Kingsbury, "we, meaning our top operatives in the CIA and FBI have been working on a scenario that we believe are the prevailing circumstances leading to the murder and kidnapping that has come upon Eldon's family. What we have done is plotted out the players. Then we built in the historical events and political climate, the forces driving the economy, and most importantly the greed factor that fuels the demands of the labor Union that supply the work force to the economy of the Caribbean, its islands, its hotels, resorts, casinos, gentlemen, in essence, its entire stabilizing economy driven by the tourist Dollar. State has estimated that the total combined gross national product of all island nations from Bermuda to Trinidad and Tobago is seventy percent derived from tourism. Our friend, Mr. Eldon Davis, holds power and property attributing at least 50 percent of that seventy percent factor. Should Mr. Davis, find that his company is not in a position to cooperate with the Caribbean Hotel and Casino Workers Union contract, well, the Union will not stand for it. We have determined in our play out scenarios that the Union will not care about keeping Holiday Jewel Hotels and Casinos solvent, they want to bleed them as much as they can.

Individual Union members pay a percentage of their hourly wages in Union dues, the higher the individual wage, the higher the overall Union dues collected each pay period, and the richer Domingo Alvarez and his cronies become. Should HJHC falter and become insolvent, the Union believes other operators will come in and pick up the droppings.

Currently, Davis' Casinos can make up for the negative cash flow generated by the hotels, to keep the hotels full, supplying the Casinos with players.

But if this new wage increase goes through that will render both the hotel and casino operations non-profitable. That would kill the flow of money to the Union, thereby ending Union member support for Bishop's government and the end of The President's plan for our new forward reaching forces in Grenada securing the entire Caribbean, gentlemen, we need that Sub base to be built in Grenada.

We believe that the Union is not beyond, and now I am talking about Domingo Alvarez, issuing the kidnapping and murder contract to bring Eldon Davis to succumb to having to sign the contract. It is our opinion that Domingo Alvarez put the order out to have the Davis girl kidnapped. We are unsure whether Linda Davis was meant to be killed, that may have been an undesirable and unfortunate complication, killing her would not aid the demands of the Union, but the kidnapping of the child is sound."

Amber went on.

"On the surface, this may, and I admit does sound like uncontrollable factors creeping into the mix complicating matters, but upon sober consideration, what this amounts to and what it requires is quite simple. We need to keep this under wraps, make sure Davis' company remains solvent for now, get that treaty signed with Grenada, that will give us clearance and legal authority to build the base, and the rest can be dealt with afterward.

The main thing is we keep the President clean. So, gentlemen, this is why we need to keep all progress and events concerning the investigation of the Davis tragedy top secret. Only the FBI and CIA are to handle the apprehension of the perpetrator, I don't want Davis poking around, I don't want him privy to any of the information we may gather or discover. I think we can all see how a man with Davis's resources will not take too long to put two and two together and come up with five; the five of us gentlemen. We cannot have him stumbling upon "island hop" I want the lid to remain tightly secured on this can."

Cyril Burgess, NSA director then spoke up. "Damn Vic…this sure is a shit can, we can't have

Davis kicking this can of shit down the road, it must be contained and sealed in this room only."

Everyone agreed.

Then Farnsworth said, "don't worry Howard, you'll have your sub base built" we'll make sure of it. We just need to put Mr. Davis on hold for a while, just long enough."

***

Chapter Twenty One

A mole in your hole ..
Is an Ace in my hole.

The super yacht Desert Seas stretching one hundred ten meters in overall length had just anchored in Nassau harbor sitting a few hundred yards next to Paradise Island. On board, the Sultan Mohammed Al Kabi was getting ready for an evening of casino enjoyment. He was a whale, and a big one. Holiday Jewel Casino was expecting his arrival having made arrangements to accommodate the Sultan. The Sultan's chopper landed on the Casino roof helipad; it was just a one minute flight from the Sultans ship to the casino rooftop helipad.

Mohammed Al Kabi liked to get on with his gambling almost immediately after his arrival in Nassau. His chopper landed and there to meet him was casino management with a special gift to meet protocol and to please the Sultan. Mohammed Al Kabi was escorted through the casino. Casino management knew well the Sultan's routine, with his favorite chosen game being black jack; he was taken to a specially prepared blackjack table, cordoned off from general gambling customers and guests. There was plenty room allowed behind the stanchions for spectators to watch, and there would be plenty. The word got around very quickly that an Arabian Sultan, whale, was present in the casino, and the curiosity spread like wildfire.

This was going to be Bernard Pinder's lucky night. The pit boss had chosen Bernard to be the Sultan's croupier "dealer." The Sultan's personal assistant accompanied Mohammed Al Kabi carrying a "chip box." This chip box contained casino chips from Holiday Jewel Casino that was the Sultan's private chip holdings. These were specially minted chips for high roller Billionaires; all chips were ten and twenty thousand Dollar denominations, and the box contained five hundred chips totaling close to ten million Dollars.

The Sultan's table contained no limitations; he could bet whatever he desired. Mohammed Al Kabi took his seat at Bernard's table. A formal introduction was made, pit boss and dealer, both actually shaking hands with the Sultan, which was in fact incredibly rare. The crowd started gathering and filling in behind the stanchions, within minutes, they were three deep, everyone stretching to see over everyone else. Al Kabi's assistant unlocked the chip box, and Mohammed obtained the first two stacks, one stack of twenty, ten thousand Dollar chips and one stack of twenty, twenty thousand Dollar chips. Bernard dealt.

Bernard had ice water running through his veins; nothing could frazzle Bernard. He had dealt sheikhs, corporate billionaires, movie stars, probably mafia types, and many international sports stars. Black Jack was the Sultan's favorite game, and he always started his evening of gambling with Black Jack, but he imposed a ten-minute time limit on each game. In ten-minutes time, Al Kabi would be done and moving on to the next game. His personal assistant kept the time watch and signaled the Sultan when it was time to move on.

The Sultan would move from Blackjack to Roulette, to Craps, gambling ten minutes at each temptation until he was done with all casino games. Afterward he would leave as quickly as he came in. Time was up at the Blackjack table; Al Kabi was down one hundred and thirty thousand Dollars. Time was up, he stood up from his seat, picked up a chip and flipped it to Bernard, out of respect Bernard did not look at the chip, he caught it in the air, nodded to the Sultan and slipped it into his pocket. Bernard's night was done. He was called in specially to deal the Sheikh and The Sheikh only.

Bernard had been working officially for only a half hour, setting up the area, cleaning the table spotless, but in this instance, he would be paid for a full shift since today was to be his day off. Bernard had been an employee of the Holiday Jewel Casino for the past three years and proven himself to be a very cool character. The US state department also thought that Bernard was a very cool character. Bernard was interviewed three and a half years ago by the US State Department for a potential position. Bernard Pinder was a Bahamian national, and a former student at the College of The Bahamas, enrolled in a political science program run by a visiting professor sponsored by the Fulbright Scholarship program that fostered foreign students in excellence in their countries of origin. Bernard's excellence and smarts had come to the attention of the visiting Fulbright professor who was very closely tied in with Kimberley Ashton at the American Embassy in Nassau.

Ambassador Lexington was looking to secure a Bahamian national to work with the State Department. State needed a trustworthy smart and savvy Bahamian who could be groomed to be a valuable asset in obtaining information on the growing and troublesome issue of Union thuggery and apparent pressures and rumblings making things difficult in keeping the peace between hotel and casino management and the Caribbean Hotel and Casino Workers Union.

Kimberley had interviewed Bernard and recommended that Lexington consider his candidacy. Lexington agreed and ever since Bernard had been a very valuable mole. Bernard's night at the casino was done, as he walked out the casino doors, he looked at his watch. It was twenty to eight, which would be plenty of time to get to the Union hall.

There was to be a rally tonight; he heard that the top brass from the Union would be there himself; Domingo Alvarez.

"Hmm, he wasn't about to miss this." Bernard got to the Union hall on Shirley Street just across from the bridges leading over to Paradise Island. As he was making his way to the Union hall, he could see there was a huge crowd already gathering outside. He could see that hc better make his way inside now if he could otherwise he would be stuck outside. The meeting and rally was to start at 8 PM but nothing ever started on time in The Bahamas, it would be another good half hour before things got under way.

This was a good thing tonight since it would give him an opportunity to find a seat inside. He walked up to the crowd and started his small talk and greetings to just about everybody as he made his way through the crowd and inside the building. People were milling around inside as well, but he could see there were only a few seats left to be had. He figured, "screw it" he'll just stand; let the ladies take the chairs.

He found himself a nice spot, inconspicuous but a good viewing and listening location close enough to the stage and podium and just next to an emergency exit door with a panic bar. "Good enough he thought." He knew pretty well everyone in the hall, after all, he grew up in Nassau; his family was from New Providence Island, a lot of his friends and neighbors were here, there were a few he did not know, not by name anyway but just a handful. He did find himself standing alone and was relieved nobody was approaching; he was happy to be left alone. He slipped his hand into his pocket and remembered the chip flipped to him by the Sultan. He pulled it out just to glance, yeah, twenty grand. A good night's work. It was only once in a blue moon that such a tip came his way. Most days he was looking at two or three hundred Dollars in tips, which was enough to live on, his pay was only Union wages, but what made it all worthwhile was that fact that he was also paid handsomely by the US Department of State. This made all the difference, and he actually loved his job and responsibilities that came with cooperating with the Americans, yes, they treated him well and valued his intelligence gathering.

He was still looking down when suddenly there was a tap tap on the microphone and a shop steward speaking into the mic "testing, testing." Bernard looked at his watch; it was just two minutes after eight. "Well this certainly was different he thought, Domingo Alvarez was always introduced by his brother Rico.

Rico would be the first one on stage the previous four times Domingo was in to talk to the Union members. Rico did not live here in New Providence but he did work as a dive instructor at a smaller resort on Abaco Island, and Rico was a Union member as well and shop steward for all Union employees on Abaco. Rico was not here; now that was strange Bernard thought. Not par for the course, something was not right about this." Also, was this meeting really going to start on time?" He thought to himself. "Great, he can get home earlier than he thought he would."

The meeting got under way a minute after the mic testing was done. The shop steward welcomed everyone and with great fanfare introduced "Domingo Alvarez," President of the Caribbean Hotel and Casino Workers Union. The crowd's buzzing settled down as Domingo walked up to the mic, tapped it a few times, thud thud thud, and started in with his greetings and acknowledging the hard work his representatives had been doing and carrying out on behalf of all Union members.

Domingo's oratory abilities were pretty good Bernard thought. He talked for a good fifteen minutes or so working up the crowd, telling the crowd how the hotels and casinos are making millions and millions on their hard-working backs, and his job was to get them more money.

This time Domingo told his membership that the Union would be asking for a 50 percent increase in wages because the Casinos could afford it and there was no way in hell that they or he was going to accept anything less. The crowd was getting into it heavily, cheering and within the next few minutes Domingo had them chanting in unison, as Domingo yelled into the mic the words; "we-want-more, we- want-more, we-want-more," and pretty soon within a few seconds the entire hall was punching the air with clenched fists in unison, punching the air and yelling. "We-want-more, we-want-more, we-want more." Bernard joined in; he punched high and yelled loud.

It was very evident to Bernard that this group could easily turn militant and violent if they were denied what they wanted. It was a very scary situation indeed. He needed to blend in; he was the mole in this hole. He would meet with Kimberley Ashton later this week. He thought it very strange that Rico Alvarez was absent from tonight's gathering, especially since

Domingo didn't provide an excuse for his brother not being in attendance, that Bernard thought was even stranger.

So, a fifty percent increase demand and now looking like the membership is wanting more, and no Rico. Kimberley would want to know this. The rally was over, and he went home to bed, twenty thousand Dollars richer tonight.

***

Chapter Twenty Two

If we work closely together today
We can manage future events in play.

Agent Miller received Kimberley's call the night before, and this morning he was boarding the FBI jet taking him over to Nassau Bahamas. He was to meet Kimberley Ashton this morning for an hour briefing at the Embassy in downtown Nassau. Miller's directive from Kingsbury arrived in his office last night and was marked “see now” for Miller. He had already left his office, and an FBI Agent brought the envelope to Miller's home in Miami.

Contained in the envelope was a red tinted document specifically spelling out the absolute requirement for a news blackout on any and all developments regarding the Davis case. Miller wasn't exactly certain why in the hell this was of such import and magnitude, but he was good at following orders.

He read the document and proceeded to burn it over the kitchen sink. Miller did have one feather in his cap this morning already. His Agents had tracked down the dark colored Nissan SUV a couple of days back. Miller caught a string of luck or so his Agents did. With the Nissan SUV being a rare vehicle supplied by rental agencies, it wasn't long before his Agents narrowed down the two agencies in south Florida that kept the Nissan SUV in their rental pool. One of the agencies was up in Tallahassee, and another location of the same company was in Jupiter.

“Fast Track SUV rental” that's all this company rented, just SUV's. His Agents were able to determine and time match the rental that fell in place exactly to the appearance of the SUV in the U-2 Play parking lot and the disappearance of the SUV from the parking lot. The SUV was returned to Fast Track SUV rental in Jupiter that evening just after seven PM. His Agents had caught a lucky break; the SUV had not had another renter and was taken in as evidence.

A sampling of fibers and hairs was conducted with DNA analysis coming back as positive on Cathy's hair. It was a match, and this was the escape vehicle they were looking for. Furthermore, the renter information was now in hand giving a name and Drivers license number on the customer. Jason Garretty.

Miller had the name, had made the perpetrator. He was most definitely making progress. This was good, all was falling in place, for now, time and time again Miller was never surprised how plain old good Police work, following up leads will in most cases take you down the road to some form of success, even if just minimal.

"Perseverance; that is the name of the game, perseverance." Miller thought.

He did face a roadblock, however, and he was now at a dead end. Problem was; that he couldn't let the media know, he couldn't place a photo for public awareness, and he couldn't put out a dragnet since there was a blackout. On top of that, he had to go on in finding this person. Jason Garretty's name could only be distributed to the FBI, and the FBI was to keep it quiet, no local law enforcement was to be involved anywhere in the US. This meant that Garretty had virtual freedom across the US. Without nationwide Police Departmental cooperation, Miller might as well have both his hands tied behind his back.

Jason Garretty had the entire continental US to escape into and the vast Caribbean just offshore. He could virtually go anywhere he pleased to at this point. However hampered Miller was with this situation, he followed orders. He did have the name though, and in Miller's mind, that alone was huge.

He buckled in, and soon his jet was in the air on its route to Nassau Bahamas. Miller was met at the US Customs gate, and whisked through, bypassing the regular clearance procedures, he was considered diplomatic personnel; coming directly through diplomatic status clearance waivers.

A young man in his late twenties who no doubt was an attaché at the State Department met him at the airport and drove him to the Embassy where he was now sitting in Kimberley Ashton's open office.

Kimberley walked in, extending her hand, Miller stood up to accept her handshake as Kimberley greeted Miller saying welcome and good morning to the FBI regional director.

"Agent Miller, thanks for coming over, it is good of you to make the time for this brief meeting, but I most definitely wanted this to take place in person. We are facing and dealing with interesting times Agent Miller." Kimberley didn't pause; she just dove right in with her preamble statement to Miller.

"The United States' interests are more defined now in this region of the world. To Americans, I am sure this nation; The Bahamas, is nothing more than a group of pretty islands with great beaches and a fun vacation playground. And to be quite honest, that is how we'd like to keep it in American's eyes. Not just the Bahamas, but as you know the Caribbean is becoming an area of greater and more importance each and every day. I'm afraid it's just not a fun playground any longer." Kimberley was relentless as she continued on, captivating Miller's attention.

"America has strategic and military interests that will strengthen our forward reaching capabilities and the islands forming a virtual barrier to the Gulf of Mexico and its vast oil fields. You know, the protection of those vital resources has raised the importance of the Caribbean to new heights. But I'm now wandering off topic a little."

Kimberley smiled at Miller, she could see he was being politely interested but was anxious to get to the real point of his visit. Kimberley in Miller's opinion was sounding like a diplomat and bearer of the stars and stripes which was all good with Miller, he sort of expected that; but it was now time for the niceties to end.

He followed with, "and how can the FBI be of assistance to you here in The Bahamas Ms. Ashton."

Kimberley didn't miss a beat, she continued..

"Our Ambassador; Ambassador Lexington as you know Agent Miller, is battling cancer and being treated in Miami. We are all hopeful his return will be soon. I am acting on Secretary Farnsworth's directive regarding The Ambassador's findings here in the islands over the last number of years.

You see, we have determined that this island is facing a potential setback in its ability to maintain a steady economic environment. For almost the past century, the hotel and casino industries have been the driving force behind the economic success of the Bahamas. But not just the Bahamas, as you well know, Bermuda, Turks and Caicos, Grand Cayman, The spice islands, Grenada, and well the list goes on Agent Miller, virtually the entire Caribbean, and for the most part, the islands' have sustained themselves with a reasonable lifestyle. Yes, there are pockets of distress, such as Haiti and a few other faltering economies. *The problem* has been creeping in over the last three years specifically, and now coming to a head within the next few days.

You see Agent Miller; there are new contract demands proposed by the Caribbean Hotel and Casino Workers Union."

Miller was now listening intently; he was finding this very fascinating and educational. He liked the way in which Ashton was able to draw a picture while providing a short history on it all. She paused for a moment. Kimberley usually had a fresh pot of coffee brought into her office which was waiting for her each morning on arrival. She walked over to the coffee, poured herself a cup, turning around to Miller, asked if he'd like a cup of fresh brew.

Miller said, "sure, that sounds lovely, just black for me thanks." Miller stood up to accept the coffee cup and saucer and remained standing leaning against his chair. Kimberley walked over to her window overlooking Nassau harbor and the cruise ships, and leaned against the window ledge, taking a sip from her cup and continuing on.

"The CHCW Union is spread right across the entire Caribbean. Sure, there are some hotels, not many that are not Unionized, but 70 percent of all hospitality and service industry workers and employees are part of this vast Union web, and that means thousands and thousands of workers in both hotels and casinos.

Our fear here at the Embassy is that the national stability of the Bahamas is under threat. We have a very well connected asset within the Union. He's an operative we've had in place for a good number of years. He currently is employed as a dealer at the Holiday Jewel Casino. We have reports from our source that give us pause Agent Miller. The Union leadership is becoming hostile and have been beating the war drums all over the Caribbean, vowing not to give in, and not willing to budge off their demand for sky-high wage increases. This of course would cripple the industry, but the leadership doesn't seem to care about that.

We don't want to see riots in the streets, and we don't want to have massive walkouts which would result in closing down the hotels and casinos. Agent Miller, our biggest fear is we don't want a repeat of what happened in Puerto Rico on December 31, 1986. That Union incident resulted in almost a hundred tourists losing their lives due to Union unrest; the casino was sabotaged, some claim there were bombs set off. Follow what I'm saying Agent Miller?"

"Wow, I sure do now Ms. Ashton."

Kimberley replied, "good, then here is what I need from the FBI. I'd like for you to assign a small detachment of Agents under my purview and directions. As you know, Director Kingsbury has stated we need to cooperate in many ways from now on, and this will be a good starting point.

Your Agents will be put up here in Nassau at the Grand Holiday Jewel; they will check in as tourists, remain under cover and only identify themselves to local law enforcement. The Royal Bahamas Police Force is on board and looking forward to any assistance and expertise that the FBI Agents can offer. Your Agents will be mainly tasked with keeping a watch on what is going on in the hotels and casinos, keeping their eyes open and ears perked. I may have other duties for them from time to time, perhaps having to send Agents to nearby islands within the Bahamas, Eleuthera, Abaco, Andros, etc.

Mainly Agent Miller, I want to be in a position to protect some of the hotel and casino executives from any harm. I know that the Union leadership is very militant in their dealings and approach with hotel and casino management, I can't imagine the types of pressures and tactics they may deploy in order to force management into succumbing to their demands. I don't want to walk into my office one morning to hear that one of the execs has been kidnapped or something."

Kimberley's eyes just went as wide as wagon wheels…what did she just say!

It hit her like a boulder rolling off the top of a mountain at a hundred miles per hour. She almost lost her balance and braced herself on the window sill. She stopped in silence, looking at Miller. She just stared at Miller.

They both sat silent for a minute. Then Miller spoke.

"Ms. Ashton, I believe your scenario was meant to be stumbled upon. It all makes sense now, totally.

It's interesting that we are on the topic of Eldon Davis, yes, the largest hotel and casino operation here in The Bahamas is Holiday Jewel. This makes perfect sense about the kidnapping of his daughter, but I have something for you, Ms. Ashton. The FBI now knows who did it.

Yes, we have a name and a face. What we don't have yet is where he is and where he is keeping the Davis girl."

Kimberley looked at Miller asking with inquisition in her voice.

"Well?"

Miller then said, "a man by the name of Jason Garretty."

Kimberley repeated the name, "Jason Garretty."

Miller was silent for a moment or two, then continued on.

"But there's not much we can do, no APB, not newspapers, no nationwide manhunts, nothing. We are at an impasse for the moment because of the blackout imposed by the FBI, CIA and State; you know exactly what I am talking about."

Kimberley replied, "Yes Agent Miller, I know exactly what you mean. There isn't much we can do about that now. Okay, it's good to know that you and your resources, Agents and efforts are paying off. You have been doing a marvelous job on this I have no doubt. I am glad we were able to meet this morning. When can you have three of your Agents assigned to my office? I will need to introduce them to RBP here in Nassau and have them cleared to carry on with whatever they need to do.

The RBP will be happy to cooperate. The last thing they want to see is trouble among the populace."

Agent Miller said, "I can have them here tomorrow Ms. Ashton. I will have their docs and background data couriered back here today for your attention via diplomatic pouch. You should have that by this evening."

"Thank you, Agent Miller, it's been my pleasure having met you, and I am looking forward to our working together closely and dealing with any future circumstances."

"Likewise Ms. Ashton" Miller said.

Kimberley showed him out, and Miller was on his way back to his office in Florida.

Kimberley walked back to her office, closed the door behind her and pulled the blinds closed. She reached into her desk drawer and took out the envelope she had received with the Davis family photos. She placed it onto her desk in front of her and drew out the ten by eight glossy of Eldon and Cathy.

She sat in silence for several minutes, looking and thinking, and after a few minutes whispered to herself, “Jason Garretty, that's who killed your wife and took Cathy, I'll make sure you know it.”

Kimberley's mind was racing, her heart pounding so hard she felt it wanting to break through her chest. Kimberley was now in very serious territory, she knew and understood well; her actions today would dictate her future, whether she survived these circumstances or whether she may lose her coveted position, career and may even be charged with treason.

Kimberley was a woman of integrity, she was not about to do what was wrong, but she was most definitely open to doing what was right. She believed in integrity, and honesty. Perhaps she was in the wrong line of work, but in her heart, she knew she was no traitor, she was doing what her instincts dictated for her to do. There was no way in hell that she was going to sit on information that would set a child free. Not now, not ever.

Kimberley did not need to decide on what she would do with this new piece of information, she already knew in her bones, in the blood that flowed through her veins, that she was going to call Eldon and give him the name of his wife's murderer and darling little girl's kidnapper. There was no question. She placed the photos back into the envelope, and back into her desk drawer, picked up the phone and dialed Louis James' number at Holiday Jewel Casino.

Louis answered, “James.”

“Good morning Mr. James, this is Kimberley Ashton at the US Embassy, how are you doing this morning Mr. James?”

Louis knew who Kimberley was; she had attended plenty of functions at the hotel, and they knew one another but strictly on a business basis.

"I am well Ms. Ashton; how can I be of service to you this morning?"

Kimberley replied, "well Mr. James, I need your boss's phone number. His private number. I have a matter of urgency I need to discuss with him."

Kimberley was emphatic and sounded very America Embassy business like. James didn't have to give out Eldon's number, but he did.

"Absolutely Ms. Ashton." He gave her Eldon's number, and that was all Kimberley wanted.

She then said, "I appreciate your cooperation Mr. James; I won't be taking up any of your time. Thank you and have a good morning."

With Eldon's number in hand, she dialed his number. Eldon answered.

"Eldon Davis."

"Good morning Mr. Davis, my name is Kimberley Ashton, I am the Charge' de Affairs with the American Embassy in The Bahamas, you and I need to meet."

Eldon was taken aback. He certainly was not expecting a call from the US Embassy in The Bahamas, but then again, stranger things have been happening lately in his world, and nothing really surprised him any longer. But the voice on the other end of the line sounded very serious; with that one simple sentence, she had his attention.

Eldon responded, "Ms. Ashton, I take it that if I ask what this is all about you will say I will find out when I get there is that right?"

"Mr. Davis, you are astute, yes, that is right. But Mr. Davis, I know you are taken up with a great deal in your life right now. I assure you, you will want to have the information I possess. I cannot stress strongly enough for you to fly here today. Do not come to the Embassy; I will meet you in your hotel."

Eldon hadn't yet agreed to fly over, and she was already telling him where she will meet him today! This was highly unusual.

"Mr. Davis, I obtained your private line number directly from Mr. James not three minutes ago, please be here by 4 PM, I will meet you in the courtyard of your hotel."

Eldon didn't have an opportunity to say no or yes, with that she ended the call." Eldon just stood in place for a minute or so, thinking… "what had just happened?"

He dialed James. "Louis, this is Eldon, what time did Ms. Ashton call you for my number?"

"Eldon, I gave her your number."

"Yeah, yeah, it's OK, I'm glad you did, what time did she call for my number?"

"Eldon not three minutes ago."

That was all that Eldon wanted to hear.

"Thanks James."

Eldon had already made plans for today to fly down to see Forbes Bishop. Forbes had called again last night and insisted Eldon fly in for an hour or so.

Felix was up at Gulliver's keeping an eye on things after having driven back up last night, and with Eldon agreeing to fly down to see Bishop, Billy came back down to prep the Canadair for the flight to Grenada. Eldon called Billy to tell him they were leaving now, change in flight plan, going to make an island hop first to Nassau for a couple of hours, then continue on down to Grenada.

***

Chapter Twenty Three

Forgiveness is the fragrance the Violet sheds
on the heels that has crushed it.

Mark Twain

Cathy still cried, and cried until as sweet Violet said, "cry till you can't cry no more, sweet child, cry till you cried all you can, and then I will hold you to comfort your heart and ease you fear." Violet looked to be gentle and kind, this little quivering bird was frightened and shaking. Violet, held Cathy until Cathy simmered down and she sniffled only, and just held onto Dixie, hugging Dixie closely and as tightly as she could and looked with big brown eyes at the strange and unfamiliar room.

Then Cathy lifted her head, twisted her neck and gazed up towards Violet. Violet comforted Cathy and she felt secure in her arms but scared in beating heart.

"Child, child," Violet said.

"You done crying now sweetheart?" Violet asked quietly, holding Cathy.

Cathy responding by not saying anything but nodding her head and sniffling, wiping her nose.

"Your mommy and daddy are coming for you soon, sweet child," she said looking down at the top of Cathy's head, softly stroking her hair.

"Don't worry baby girl; they'll be here soon," as she gently rocked Cathy back and forth.

She reached for a soft, warm moist cloth to wipe away Cathy's tears, and clean her face. She stood up holding Cathy in her arms and walked over to a large cooler that had orange juice and apple juice. Asking

Cathy "how would you like some juice sweetheart," and opened a small container and put a straw in it.

Cathy was thirsty and took the juice; she was also hungry now. She placed Cathy on the chair in front of the kitchen table, and Cathy sipped her juice while holding onto Dixie.

Violet reached into a cupboard and pulled out a plate with apple pie on it and placed it in front of Cathy with a spoon, then reached into the cooler and took out a little cup of ice cream, putting the ice cream next to the apple pie.

Cathy didn't say anything; she just began eating.

"That's good baby girl, that's good," you such a pretty girl. My name is Violet. Do you have a name sweetie-heart?"

Cathy looked down at her pie, and hugged Dixie even closer, while taking another spoonful of ice cream.

"Your doll's name is Dixie I see on her outfit, Dixie is a nice doll baby girl, she has a name; you have a name too I bet."

Violet knew Cathy's name; she was just trying to win her over a little.

Then Cathy said, "Cathy…Cathy Davis and I want to see my mommy!"

She started whimpering again lightly and dropped her spoon. Violet came around to her and held her, "Cathy baby girl, your mommy's coming soon, soon baby girl, soon."

Later that day Violet gave Cathy a bath, and she had a change of clothes for little girls that she took care of before and brought that with her.

She made sure Cathy was clean and cared for and later in the afternoon, she took Cathy outside.

The house on Conch Island was on a hilltop with palm trees on either side and a clearing in the front. The front yard sloped down to the beach but had a good view of the ocean, the blue-green waters and the beach from the hill. She took Cathy to the hillside, and they sat down. Violet brought a nice pretty colorful lollipop with her, and as the two of them sat down overlooking the ocean, Violet reached into her pocket, and pulled out the lollipop handing it over to Cathy.

Cathy looked at the lollipop, looked at Violet, Violet smiled at Cathy with big reassuring eyes, stroked Cathy's hair and said to Cathy, "you are a lovely child, you and I can be friends, you and me and Dixie, is that OK, baby girl?"

Cathy nodded her head a few times, reached up and accepted the lollipop from Violet. "That's a good girl, baby doll; that's a good girl."

The palms swayed in the Caribbean breeze, the sun shined down on their predicament, and they both wondered what tomorrow would hold.

This was going too far…whatever it was that Rico and Manko had done, Violet knew in her heart that something evil had happened. Violet knew it was not within her to ever forgive Rico for this.

She softly stroked Cathy's hair. They had become friends for now. The two of them sat there, looking out over the vast ocean holding their future.

***

Chapter Twenty Four

Living your life with honor,
Brings forth friends you didn't know you had.

Felix had settled in the night before on The Stinger. He had picked up appropriate clothing to hang out on board for the next few days. Eldon would be gone for a day or two, maybe more and for now there wasn't much else to do than stake out the marina, keep his eyes open, his ear to the ground and hope that he gets a lucky break, maybe come up with something as to the whereabouts of Cathy.

Felix couldn't act like a bull in a china shop, he had to fit in, appear to be relaxed, become part of the marina and chat up the help.

The "help" in this case was Jonesy; he seemed like a good kid. A jock, to be sure, but a kid that Felix noticed did his job and was very courteous to the marina patrons. He was a good boatman, seemed to know boats and sailors.

Felix engaged Jonesy into some small talk; Jonesy even had come over to Felix to say hi a couple of times during the day when it was quieter. Jonesy liked The Stinger; he went on about how he'd love to have one of these boats himself, but of course, that was totally out of reach on his marina gopher-wages.

Felix kept himself busy, cleaning The Stinger, but all along keeping an eye on the marina like a hawk. He was cleaning and watching, watching every move that everyone who might have been within eyesight made. He tried listening in on conversations; he'd been at this snooping and listening all afternoon but so far, nothing. He had earlier gotten the call from Eldon that he and Billy were leaving earlier than planned, needed to make a pit stop in Nassau. He told

Felix that apparently, the US Embassy had something for him, and he decided to check into whatever it was. He'd be calling Felix as soon as he had an updated available for him. Felix got himself another bucket of soapy water and got on with scrubbing the deck.

The Canadair jet took off from Pompano regional airport, flight plan filed was Pompano Nassau, private airfield at Holiday Jewel Hotel. A half hour after takeoff Billy was making his approach to the airfield. Eldon on this occasion was in the copilot seat.

Eldon liked to fly from time to time, and he brought the jet in on final and landed perfectly. Eldon had learned to fly and was cleared on the Canadair multi engine jet. Eldon didn't get a whole lot of flight time, but whenever he could, he liked to fly the plane.

Billy was teaching Eldon how to fly the Sikorsky as well, but Eldon was still in student mode in that endeavor. Another few months and Eldon should be cleared on the Sikorsky as well. Eldon brought the plane to park at the end of the runway, both he and Billy deplaned.

Billy headed up to Eldon's private suite in the hotel. Eldon had a permanent suite, a condo unit on the 12th floor overlooking Nassau Harbor. Billy could rest there, before taking off on the longer flight down to Grenada.

Eldon went directly to the courtyard. He had never had the pleasure of meeting Kimberley Ashton; this was going to be the first time, he had no idea what to expect.

He knew that Louis was acquainted with the Charge de Affairs, having hosted her and her Embassy people at a number of hotel functions. Eldon had arranged to meet Louis in the lobby and have Louis introduce him to Ms. Ashton in the courtyard.

Eldon thought it would be more in line with a proper introduction.

Eldon and Louis walked out to the courtyard. There were a few people out there enjoying beverages. Louis spotted Ms. Ashton, tapped Eldon on his arm…"there she is." And the two of them walked up toward Kimberley.

She noticed Louis right away and saw Eldon with him. She stood up, as Louis reached out to greet her.

Louis said, "Ms. Ashton, Eldon Davis."

Kimberley said, "Thank you Mr. James."

Then she looked at Eldon and said, "Mr. Davis, thank you for coming on such short notice. Is there someplace we can talk that is totally private?"

Eldon didn't know what to make of this all, but replied, "Yes there is, we can walk out to the end of the pier, that is private as we are going to find."

"I'm sure that will be fine." Kimberley replied. Eldon couldn't help himself, so he asked, "so what's this all about then Ms. Ashton?"

Kimberley looked over at Eldon as they walked, she already thought back on the emotions that overcame her when she ran her fingers over his face on the ten by eight glossy. Her feelings were confirmed; Eldon's eyes expressed caring and hurt, determination and a certain anxiety that she saw he was trying to control.

As she looked over at him, she looked directly in his eye, and softly she said, "let's wait till we get well out onto the pier Eldon, is it all right with you if I call you Eldon?"

Eldon wasn't about to say no, call me Mr. Davis, he, of course, said; "yes, absolutely."

She then said, "good, please call me Kimberley."

They walked another three minutes, reached the pier and walked out onto it. When they were out about halfway, she saw they were the only ones on the pier; they were all alone, there was a wind blowing. Their conversation would be safe.

Kimberley stopped walking, and said, “this will be fine Eldon,” she turned out towards the ocean, leaning on the railing that ran along the length of the pier, Eldon did the same, standing close beside her.

“Eldon what I am about to tell you, is confidential, you probably already figured that out I'm sure, but what makes it more so confidential is that what I am about to say, I will say now, and afterward tell you why it's confidential.”

She certainly had his attention. Eldon looked over at her, looked her straight in the eye and quietly said, “all right Kimberley, I'm listening.”

She took a deep breath, looked out over the ocean, pausing for a moment then she continued.

Eldon was standing on her right side, she turned her head to look at him, Eldon hadn't stopped looking at her, as the wind blew through her hair.

He couldn't help but feel a personal attraction to Kimberley, yes she was a very attractive woman, but Eldon was around attractive women all the time in this business, but not so much with someone of Kimberley's status. Eldon didn't walk the halls of the US government, and he found her to be intriguing and now someone apparently, whom he could trust because she apparently, had already decided to trust him, and trust him with something very sensitive.

She most definitely had his attention in more ways than one now.

Then she said: “Eldon, a man by the name of Jason Garretty killed your wife and kidnapped Cathy, we have confirmation…DNA confirmation.”

Looking at Eldon, Kimberley saw an immediate change in Eldon's face and demeanor; he all of a sudden looked stunned.

He was stunned that someone had found his daughter or maybe he was jumping to conclusions; his first reaction was; “so where is Cathy?”

Kimberley reached out and touched his arm, “no Eldon, we don't have a location, we just know that Cathy was kidnapped by this Jason Garretty, his SUV was located, and Cathy's hair sampling was verified by FBI lab a few days ago.”

“A few days ago!” Eldon exclaimed. “What's the holdup, who's in charge of this thing?” Then Eldon realized his anxiety was getting the best of him. He understood that something nefarious was up, he was getting this vital news from the US Embassy in the Bahamas, not from Agent Miller who is working the case in Florida.

Eldon was beginning to understand that maybe Kimberley was taking a chance at even telling him about this bit of new data and now, looking back at Kimberley, and seeing the desperation in her eye, yes, all of a sudden, he understood the huge chance she was taking.

“Eldon I am afraid that we are facing a huge and dangerous set of circumstances that could mean civil unrest here in the Bahamas and many other island countries.”

Eldon leaned out over the railing, looking down onto the ocean, took a deep breath and sighed, looking back at Kimberley. Eldon was coming to a conclusion he kept hidden in the back of his mind all this time. Eldon well knew that his web of influence and economic contribution to the islands, the fuel that powered this economy was in jeopardy. His empire was being threatened, and this had been coming on now for the past three years, but now it looked like it was coming to a head.

Eldon didn't want to admit it but now he was clear that the strength of the Union had reached a plateau, and in order to force his hand, the Union leadership, Alvarez had now resorted to extortion with the ransom being his daughter's safety and her life in the balance. After looking at the pieces to this puzzle and lining up all the pieces, he understood now where all the pieces belonged. In his mind, Eldon saw that the Union had arranged the kidnapping and was holding onto Cathy as their ace in the hole in forcing Eldon and Holiday Jewel Hotels and Casinos into the new Union agreement.

The local governments, in reality, had no problem with the Union agreement, if civil unrest could be avoided, the governments were all for it. As to how long the resort business could remain solvent under these new conditions, well that was another matter to be worked out even if it meant having to close properties.

These Caribbean nations did not have the foresight into the future and how events of today would play out in the months and years to come. The prevailing attitude throughout the region was "manjana, manjana" and unfortunately it permeated throughout the populace reaching into the halls of government. Most officials, virtually all, were "on the take, or in someone else's pocket, and everything could wait till tomorrow.

But Eldon couldn't, he didn't have many tomorrows left in order to find Cathy and he was not about to cave into these bastards. But not to cave in meant having to find Cathy first.

Eldon believed; when it came down to voting on the new contract, by that time his people could negotiate the terms down to something more reasonable. If the Union bosses decided not to accept the lowered terms, well it would just have to come to a vote by the membership, and in the end, everyone needed jobs and the membership would accept a more reasonable arrangement.

Eldon wasn't going to give his business away. He had considered taking his hotel and casino division public in a few months, but first, he needed to find and get Cathy back. Without her back in his arms, he'd have no choice but give the Union what they wanted, and then face losing his business, no, that was not going to happen.

Eldon wondered now, "just what in the hell did Forbes Bishop want or have to do with any of this?

Must be something he's missing, and that name he threw out a few days ago, "Rickover," well, what the fuck! Rickover was the US Secretary of Defense. Was the fucking island going to be invaded again like it had been back in 1983 by the Reagan administration?"

Eldon didn't know what to think. "Thanks to this lovely and brave woman, he had the name of his wife's killer and Cathy's abductor," but now Eldon found himself flying all over hell's half acre. Eldon needed to focus and bring this to an end and real quick.

"Eldon, I can't tell you much more, I am restricted from talking about this, but I wanted you to know the name of the person who killed your wife and took your daughter. Eldon, my hands are tied to a degree; the State Department has issued restrictions on the publication and events concerning your dilemma. The FBI is the sole law enforcement agency that can handle your case. Not the Florida Police and all news regarding the developments of your case must be disseminated by the FBI only."

Eldon just looked on out to sea, now and then glancing back at Kimberley as she told him what she knew. This moment had a very surreal feeling about it all to Eldon, but it was indeed happening.

"That is why, if you have noticed and I'm sure you have, there has been very little, virtually nothing, on the update of what happened at your place in the papers. That's because the FBI is keeping a wrap on things. I don't want to mislead you, Eldon, they are not placing a hold on the investigation, they just want to keep you out of it.

They want to keep you in the dark, the reason being; they fear you Eldon. They fear you for the havoc you could bring into the mix and cause waves, capsizing their already shaky ship in rough seas." Eldon turned to look at Kimberley, taking in every word she spoke to him. He couldn't take his eyes off her. She was the closest yet; he had come to finding Cathy, and he was becoming convinced that Kimberley would be the crucial link in all of this.

"Eldon there are things going on in the Caribbean with the State department and department of defense that have certain tie-ins to everything we have been talking about. The US is in a race to a treaty with Grenada, and I'm afraid this situation has thrown a big hammer into it all. They want you to stay out of it."

Eldon took this all in, looking back at Kimberley, saying, "They…our good ole US government, of which you are a part. Kimberley, I can see how you must be taking a huge risk meeting me here today."

Kimberley replied. "Well Eldon, most of what we have talked about you already know and knew. The only piece of information that I supplied to you is the name of the person you've been looking for and the fact that there is a blackout on updates, and the FBI has exclusive management of the case. Having given you this information alone can cause huge problems for me, but I felt it my obligation and moral responsibility as a human being to tell you.

Eldon, I couldn't have lived with myself knowing the name of your wife's killer and having to sleep with that information every night. I needed you to know, and now you do. You do with it what you see fit. I know you have resources, I know you are a man of action, and Eldon, if I can help in any other way, I will be here for you," she reached out to touch his arm again.

Eldon responded, he couldn't help himself, he stepped in towards her, put his arms around her, hugging Kimberley in very grateful manner, and said, "thank you, thank you so much for asking me to come today Kimberley," as he hugged her and spoke those words into her ear.

He then said, "Kimberley, I need to get on my way. I'm flying down to Grenada. Forbes Bishop has been on my case for the past week, and he's insisting I fly down so I told him I'd be there this afternoon." She looked at Eldon exclaiming, "really?

My area covers Grenada; The Bahamas Embassy has had its diplomatic reach extended to Grenada; I have been overseeing our ambassadorial needs there as well, since six months ago. I have operatives stationed there now."

Eldon, then said, “well then it appears we may have reason to meet again.”

She replied, “I believe you are right Mr. Davis, Eldon”, as she looked and smiled at him.

Eldon extended his hand, they shook hands and another grateful and appropriated hug, they both turned and walked back from the pier. Kimberley made her way out the lobby to the main entrance foyer. Kimberley said good night and left.

When Eldon got back to his hotel suite, the first thing he did was call Louis James. Eldon was now very cautious; he thought that his communications might be tapped into, and any direct mention of key information directly from Eldon's line may be at risk.

Eldon knew that Felix would catch on right away; there was no need to explain. Eldon got a hold of Louis and asked him to meet him in his suite on the twelfth floor. Louis knocked, Eldon opened the door, and Louis walked in. Billy was standing there beside Eldon; Louis said, “hey Billy,” Billy nodded, “hey Louis.”

Eldon then said. “Louis, don't ask me any questions just listen.

Louis listened. “I want you to call Felix's private line, I only want you to tell him this, “tell him it's you calling, he will recognize your voice, and then say, Felix, Jason Garretty, and repeat it, then hang up, okay, got it?”

“Got it Eldon.”

Then Eldon said, “do it now.” Louis did.

“That's it Louis, thanks, we will talk later,” and Eldon showed Louis out.

Then Eldon called Felix, “Licks, you got that, right?”

Licks clued in right away. “You bet I did.”

"Licks, don't ask me now how I know, will fill you in later. But Licks, I know you have a knack for getting information in the proper way, throw that piece of information around as you need to, see if you can get somewhere."

Felix replied, "wow Eldon, that's incredible, I will get on it right away."

"All right, I'll call you from Grenada when we land."

Felix ended the call, then repeated the name to himself, "Jason Garretty"…someone around here must know that prick.

Kimberley had the valet parking attendant fetch her vehicle, and she drove back to The Embassy.

The Canadair taxied out to the center of the airstrip, rotated and took off from New Providence on its way to Grenada.

Eldon sat back, thinking of where his loving little girl could be. His mind racing, "is she crying, is she hungry, is she being fed, who is taking care of his little angel? Jason Garretty, I'm going to fucking skin you alive when I find you."

Eldon looked out over the Caribbean; islands dotted the seascape below, blue-green turquoise water, lush green islands outlined by yellow sandy beaches, stretching for miles below him. Another two hours to Grenada.

Eldon lay back in his seat, closed his eyes, his mind racing now more than ever before. He had Cathy's abductor's name; he had the looming Union vote; he now believed it was the Union leadership, Alvarez who brought about his family disaster. He now had a confidante in The Bahamas Kimberley Ashton who was willing to place her career and job on the line for him, how was he ever going to make that up to her?

His hotel and casino empire was on the brink of disaster. The FBI and State Department were apparently doing everything they could to keep him out of the loop. The Bahamas was looking at civil unrest if this doesn't go through, not telling what could unravel. He was heading to Grenada, heading into some sort of unknown territory with Forbes Bishop, all along flying farther and farther away from where Cathy might be.

He placed his head back on the headrest, adjusted his seat, and tried to relax. He thought of the many times he'd sit on this plane with Linda, he missed her, wished he could reach over beside him and hold onto her hand. Eldon felt alone; he missed her so.

It didn't take long at all. Felix was surprised, Eldon was right on the money, just perfect. "Jonesy, how are you doing today?" Felix asked.

"Hey there Felix, doing good thanks, just looking after one of the charter fishing boats that came in, going to hose it down, they had some great luck out there today, but the boat came back pretty grungy, just going to wash it down from the fish blood in the back."

Felix then said, "hey Jonesy, seen "Jason around lately, was hoping he'd be back by now, was supposed to meet him here yesterday."

Jonesy replied, "Oh, you mean Mr. Garretty?" Felix could hardly control his excitement; this was it; this was it!

He continued calmly, "yeah, Garretty, we go back a ways, he was going to hook up with us here, was wondering if you heard from him lately?"

"Well, he took The Sharker out a few days ago, was going over to the Bahamas to pick up a fishing charter booking. Guess he must have picked up another trip out there, the fishing's been good lately, people bringing in all sorts of catches, marlin, wahoo, bluefin."

Felix, kept pressing, "so, he still has that same boat eh, The Sharker, what was that anyway, Egg Harbor?" Jonesy said, no it's not an "Egg" it's a 38 Bertram, real nice one too."

Felix had what he wanted, done. "Well, I'm sure he'll show up sometime, he knows where to find me."

Jonesy went about his business. Felix undid the dock lines, fired up The Stinger, and left the marina, headed back to Pompano, back to Eldon's estate.

They had what they were looking for; he would be back at Eldon's place within the next hour or so, and Eldon would be calling by then.

Felix was glad he knew how to handle The Stinger, he had a feeling he may be on the boat for a few more days. "Bahamas and Jason Garretty," he thought.

Felix, cruised down south on the Intracoastal, it was a typically nice Florida day, sunny, lots of party boats, lots of tourists; it was February.

The roads and highways were gridlocked most afternoons. Here on the Intracoastal, at least there were no crazy drivers, no traffic jams, he cruised on down, making his way back. Almost two hours had passed. Felix was waiting for Eldon's call. He should be landing anytime in Grenada by now. Felix docked The Stinger, went up to the house, got himself a Heineken, cracked it open and enjoyed a cold one out on Eldon's back patio. Felix's phone rang. It was Eldon.

"Hey Eldon," Felix answered. "Whatcha got for me Licks? Keep it simple."

"Yeah, I got it Eldon, simple. Have it all good, and a lot more, back at your place now." Felix finished saying.

That was enough for Eldon; Felix had come through again for him. Things were falling into place.

"Okay Licks, great, I'll see you later today, I have to get this meeting done with, Billy is refueling now. PMO's office is here already to pick me up. I'll see you tonight."

"God's speed Eldon, God's speed," Felix said. The call ended.

The Prime Minister's residence was on the outskirts of St. Georges, one of the most picturesque capitals in the Caribbean, a real jewel of a city. The PM's driver picked Eldon up from the airport and whisked through the traffic, with sirens on, and got to the PM's residence within minutes. Eldon was greeted by the PM's Butler at the porte-cochere, the entrance to his lavish residence, and shown through the foyer, down the hallway to a door on the left leading out to the lavish gardens.

There he was greeted by Forbes Bishop and much to Eldon's huge surprise, Vic Amber; The director of the Central Intelligence Agency and Howard Rickover; the US Defense Secretary.

This was most unusual, something totally out of the blue for Eldon, "what the hell was all this?" He wondered to himself, "soon he'd find out."

He also figured this wasn't going to last very long. These people had a way of getting to the point without much fanfare.

Bishop stood up, "Ah Mr. Davis, so good of you to come, hope your flight was uneventful, and welcome back once again to Grenada."

Eldon shook Bishop's hand and replied, "Mr. Prime Minister, yes, the flight was okay." Eldon wasn't much on gibberish, especially seeing such unexpected guests.

Bishop continued, “I believe you might know Director Amber and Secretary Rickover.”

Eldon walked in closer, “Gentlemen, good afternoon,” he reached out to shake both their hands.

They stood up and shook hands, “Mr. Davis, Mr. Davis,” both said.

Eldon was shown his seat and the four of them sat in a semi-circle around a garden table with refreshments. Eldon was too keyed up even to notice the table or refreshments.

Eldon thought to himself, “let’s get on with it, I want to get the fuck out of here!”

Bishop began, “Mr. Davis, I know you are a very intelligent man, and once again, let me express my deepest sympathy for the loss of your wife and missing daughter. I pray for her safe return into your arms.”

Somehow with Bishop saying this now to Eldon's face and the CIA director and Secretary of Defense sitting here alongside, Bishop's words of condolence no longer seemed to ring with the same tone of sincerity he felt over the phone when Bishop had called a few days before.

Amber and Rickover just sat there, Rickover however; well he did offer his condolences as well. But Amber, well he just sat in his chair.

Bishop then continued, “Director Amber and Secretary Rickover were good enough to join us this afternoon. You know Mr. Davis, the Caribbean Initiative, which President Fenton is moving forward with is going to bring much prosperity to Grenada and offer greater security to the entire Caribbean region. This is what Secretary Rickover and Director Amber are here discussing…how their assistance in seeing things through on a timely schedule will bring this project together.

Director Amber, of course, is most interested in the stability of our nation and its ongoing economic prosperity. He and his people have been a great help to Grenada, in making certain we have no undesired interference from local groups that may be opposed to this great vision of the future, for our tiny island and its people.

You must understand Mr. Davis, no matter how good one's intentions may be in securing the future of our country, there will always be opposition to anything we try in moving our destiny forward in the right direction.

Director Amber has provided my people and me with a clear path to reaching our goals. In doing so, we have now been able, and I am glad to say, move the treaty formalities forward, and in the coming days, Grenada and the United States of America will be ready to sign the Caribbean Initiative between our two nations."

Eldon sat listening, good political speech, covered all his bases, good to go for the sub base," Eldon thought, "but what was he doing here?"

Bishop went on; neither Rickover nor Amber had said a word yet. Eldon figured, "okay, its Bishop's show, so Bishop does it all."

He went on, "Mr. Davis, before the treaty is signed between our two countries, which is to take place in the coming days, Grenada will undergo a general election. The opposition party as you know is; "the opposition" party, I need not say more on that point. Mr. Davis, in the coming days, we also have the Caribbean Hotel and Casino Workers Union, and they will be presenting a new contract to its members.

All of us at this table understand the power in your hands, Mr. Davis."

That last statement, about power in Eldon's hand, on Eldon's radar, picked up the undertones of a threat, and Eldon picked up on that immediately. This was not sitting well with Eldon; he tensed up inside and waited for what was coming next.

"If for any reason, this new contract is not approved by your company, and the Union membership is not satisfied, I'm afraid that will bring an unfortunate set of circumstances with it that may see the opposition party leader sitting in this chair that I am sitting in today. Do I make myself clear Mr. Davis?"

Eldon heard Forbes Bishop loud and clear. Bishop had just set up a clear threat and extortion of his business scenario. Bishop was not kidding.

Eldon sat there motionless, leaned forward in his chair, looking Bishop in the eye and asked, "and if I decide that I want to negotiate the terms down? That Holiday Jewel Hotel and Casinos is not in a position to bleed itself dry of every penny we earn, then what?"

To Eldon's surprise, Amber spoke up to answer the question Eldon had just posed to Bishop. Eldon turned in his chair to look directly at Amber now as he spoke.

As Amber spoke up, he glanced over at Bishop nodding his head, like giving Amber the okay, and looking now at Eldon, Amber said, "Mr. Davis, you're not in a position to do that, now are you, Mr. Davis?"

Rickover turned his head and looked at Amber with a look of astonishment. Eldon caught that, and it appeared to Eldon that Rickover was caught by surprise.

Eldon was floored, but Rickover was even more floored.

"Was Amber turning on Davis, with some sort of force Rickover hadn't considered?" Eldon was thinking.

Eldon pressed on, forcing Rickover to answer for Amber.

"Secretary Rickover sir, would you mind telling me what Director Amber means?"

Amber saw that Eldon was sharper than razor wire.

Rickover was actually lost for words, but he had to come up with something; anything.

"Director Amber means Mr. Davis that we need to have that sub base built." That was a good enough answer for Amber from Rickover. But Rickover looked curiously at Amber.

Amber continued on. "We all want things to turn out right for all of us at this table Mr. Davis" Let's make sure the Union contract is not contested, and everyone goes home happy. Do I make myself clear Mr. Davis?"

Eldon's blood was starting to reach a boiling point, "these bastards arranged for the kidnapping of Cathy in order to force my hand."

Eldon knew immediately what Bishop and Amber meant very clearly, "he was in no position to refuse, agree to the Union demands and everyone goes home happy." Yes, Eldon heard that loud and clear.

Eldon had enough of this; he wanted to reach out and choke Amber and Bishop with his bare hands.

Amber could see the rage boiling over in Eldon's face. Rickover, Eldon noticed was sitting there just as stunned as ever. Eldon got up out of his seat, didn't say a word and was about to walk out, when Amber spoke up, Eldon stood looking at Amber.

"Now Mr. Davis, let me assure you, we are very aware how important this is, in fact, Mr. Davis this is a matter of national security, and with this situation rising to such a level, the United States needs to ensure that all goes well. In having said that, the United States is prepared to make up any financial losses your hotel operations may suffer for the entire duration that the new contract is in effect, you need to consider this very carefully Mr. Davis. This would go in your favor Mr. Davis, and everyone can go home happy." Amber finished saying again, driving the point home.

"We do it all the time Mr. Davis, bailout of Chrysler, GM, Banks, etc., your situation would be no different; it's a matter of National Security Mr. Davis."

Eldon's blood was now reaching even higher levels of intolerance. Now Amber was actually offering him money in exchange for Cathy, this was beyond the pale, just unbelievable. He couldn't believe how low this man could go.

Eldon looked at Amber and said, "You piece of shit." Having said that, Eldon looked around to Bishop and Rickover and then walked out and was driven back to the airport.

The whole thing took no more than fifteen minutes. Billy was surprised to see Eldon so soon; he was just now finishing the refueling process.

Eldon walked up to Billy and said, "Let's get the fuck out of here now!" Billy never heard Eldon talk like this or look so livid. Somewhere in hell, Satan wished Eldon Barnes Davis had never been born. Bishop and Amber might feel the same also. Amber looked at Rickover and said, "Well that didn't go so well, but I'm sure he'll come around." Rickover was stunned. Amber had no doubt worked his CIA bullshit in this arena as well. Rickover wasn't quite sure what it was exactly, but it wasn't something he wanted to be part of. Bishop got up from his seat, Amber and Rickover followed.

Back on the plane, Billy asked, "where to Eldon?" Eldon said, take me home Billy, take me home.

***

Chapter Twenty Five

Three things cannot stay hidden, the sun, the moon and the truth.

Buddha

Rickover was feeling very uncomfortable after the meeting with Davis. Amber and Rickover were leaving Bishop's residence and on the way out, before getting in their vehicles, Rickover stopped Amber and asked him straight. “So, Vic, what’s this you said to Davis, that he wasn't in a position to do that, what did you mean by that. So far as I can see, he can do whatever he pleases with his company. If he decides not to give into the Union, well that's his business far as I see it. He'd have to deal with that.” There was a piece of the conversation that Rickover was missing or probably not privy to.

Rickover felt uneasy about the event that just took place in Bishop's garden. Rickover understood well, that the Caribbean initiative had to move forward, and that Bishop needed to stay in power, but as far as Rickover was concerned, there was always room for negotiation, on any subject or matter, that's what partnerships and agreements were all about. Always room to give and take a little. He learned that a long time ago in the Military. Always better to negotiate yourself out of a position than to shoot your way out. That way nobody gets hurt, and everyone gets to live another day.

Amber looked over to Rickover, and said, “Howard, don't worry about things, we have the situation well in control. CIA has a handle on things; that's what we're good at, controlling the situation, setting events up to happen. Remember it was CIA who was way ahead of the game here in 1981 before the invasion you boys followed up with.

We laid the groundwork for the invasion to happen; The President would have never gone forward without the good and vital intel we provided. Not to worry Howard, I have this well in hand. You concentrate on building the sub base we need here, and I'll concentrate on working Bishop and the needs of this country. Sound fair to you? You and I have always seen eye to eye on things needing to get done. We're doers Howard, that's what we are; doers. I'll see you back in Langley I'm sure soon."

Amber got in his car and left. Rickover wasn't feeling any warm and fuzzies after that lecture. He knew there was trouble in the air. Rickover did feel good about one thing though; he felt good that he was a man of integrity. Rickover believed in doing the right thing. He never faltered.

He was the Secretary of Defense. He never faltered, and nobody had the right to talk to him the way Amber just did. Maybe The President, but certainly not Amber.

Rickover left it alone for now, but just for now. He was not a man prone to knee-jerk reactions; Rickover was calculating and strategic in methodology. His former military background and training served him well in all his ventures and was now serving The President as The President expected.

Rickover now had a very good reason "to keep his powder dry."

He turned the key in his Jeep and drove back to the temporary base command center, already under construction on Grenada's south shore.

◇◇◇

Billy landed the jet; they both transferred to the chopper and were flying back over Pompano Beach to Eldon's residence. Took only a few minutes, but Eldon was never happier to have the chopper, kept him out of traffic and home in an instant.

While Billy was bringing the chopper in, Eldon could already see Felix running towards the helipad to meet him.

Billy and Eldon got out of the bird, and Felix was already saying, “he’s in the Bahamas Eldon, I don't know where, but that's where he was last headed. It looks like he's still there, he usually does fishing charters. The kid down at Gulliver' marina filled me in about this character; he's a regular at the marina but spends a lot of time in the Bahamas running fishing charters.

So, it’s Jason Garretty, but get this, his boat is called The Sharker; it is a 38 foot Bertram. Eldon, this gives us everything we need to find this prick.”

Eldon grabbed Felix around the shoulders as the three of them walked up to the house.

“Man, you're great Licks, you really are,” pulling Felix in towards him, giving Felix a manly kiss on the top of his head.

Billy jumped in front of Felix and started walking, jumping backward in front of him, “that's great Licks, that's great man, you did so good.”

Billy started play boxing the air, pretending that he'd be getting in the fight soon, with the real guy who abducted Cathy.

The three men went up to the house. Billy went to the bar fridge and pulled out three cold bottles of Heineken. He twisted the cap off the bottles and handed them out.

Then Eldon standing there, said, “boys, we are going to The Bahamas,” they both nodded.

"Let's do it," Felix said.

"We will, but we need a game plan," Eldon; picking up where Felix left off. "

"Whatever we need to do, will become apparent when we get there. I want the three of us at the hotel in Nassau, but I want the chopper there as well as The Stinger.

Billy, you fly the chopper over to the hotel. Felix, the waters are calm tonight, I want you to take The Stinger over to Nassau and dock her at the hotel marina in my slip. I will fly the jet over in a couple of hours; I'm going to meet with Ms. Ashton again. She doesn't know it yet but she will in the next minute."

Eldon pulled out his phone and dialed Kimberley's private cell. He wasn't about to say much.

In The Bahamas, Kimberley's cell phone came to life; ringing…she picked it up and saw that it was Eldon's number on the call-display; and her heart skipped a beat, Kimberley answered, "Kimberley Ashton."

"Kimberley, Eldon. I just flew back from Grenada, and now we need to talk; I'm flying over and will be there in three hours, can you meet me in the same place?"

She knew Eldon meant the pier.

Kimberley answered, "I will see you in three hours Eldon," and the phone call ended.

"What a day, what a day," Kimberley thought, "and it's not even over!"

By the time she and Eldon were to meet, it would be close to midnight. It would be a long day for Kimberley, but she was accustomed to long days and nights. Working for the State Department definitely had its perks and benefits, but the hours were not one of them.

"Billy, I want you to rest for a while," Eldon said. "I am going to wind down a little myself, just to take a breather, I've been trying to get comfortable on the plane on the way back, but with what happened over there in Grenada, well the demons in my mind would not let me rest in peace. I only hope my baby doll Cathy is all right. Felix and Billy could see that Eldon was drained and yet they drew from him inspiration that gave the two of them the impetus to keep moving forward in the face of adversity.

Eldon was a driven man. He would not stop till his daughter was safely back in his arms; he would enter Satan's hell to fight and get her back, this they knew, there was no doubt.

Eldon said, "let's all chill for a bit, sit down guys, I'll update you on what transpired in Grenada with Bishop." The three men walked out to the patio, and relaxed, sipping on their beers. Eldon started in and explained what went down in Grenada.

It didn't take long; Eldon had the whole story told, within five minutes, his entire visit only lasted maybe fifteen. Eldon also voiced his conclusion that Amber was behind it all and mastermind.

Yes, Amber; Director of the CIA, probably sanctioned the entire thing and approved taking Cathy.

Eldon also made it clear that he didn't think Rickover was in on it. Rickover just happened to be there because he was integral to the base particulars and working with DND and the Pentagon establishing a regional command outpost in Grenada. Eldon also concluded that Amber was using Rickover as a cover or shield, the more pawns in front of you the safer you are.

In Eldon's mind, it was just Amber, Bishop, and Alvarez. Domingo Alvarez had to be in on this, but he had to sure, it could be just a CIA operation, but the CIA needed a buffer. Eldon believed that that buffer would be Alvarez, the CIA's scapegoat. The CIA could pin it all on Alvarez and his Union if it ever came out.

That was almost a certainty. It probably wasn't in the plan to kill Linda: that would have served no purpose, the abductor; Garretty, probably just found it easier to have her out of the way, but yes, Eldon was now convinced with certainty, that Amber was behind it all.

When Eldon told them how Amber offered Eldon money to make sure the contract gets signed, that was the icing on evil. Felix and Billy listened and sat in disbelief. But first was to get Cathy, find the Sharker or a trace of Garretty and that would lead them to Cathy. If the Sharker was in the Bahamas, as they thought it would be, then that would lead them to Cathy. Eldon Felix and Billy had no doubt about that. Find the Sharker, and then find Cathy. That was the plan, and Eldon knew exactly how he was going to go about it all. That is where Kimberley was going to come into play. Eldon laid it all out to Felix and Billy.

"Billy, you remember that laser microphone that our friend Nick Kovacs rigged up for us a few years back?"

"Yeah, sure do, you still have that Eldon, it's in my equipment room just over there in the guest cottage, well, it's not really an equipment room, but that's what I've been using it for the past two years."

"Okay, good, make sure you take that device with you over to the hotel in Nassau. We may need it, it's a good thing to have."

Felix said, "yeah that thing is magic, can pick up conversations a few hundred yards away from inside a room, we just point it at a window, and it picks up the subtle vibrations created on a window from voices in the room. The laser transmits the vibrations back to a decoder and presto! Can you hear me now! Yeah, bring that thing with you Billy" Felix added.

"All right, so now you both know what we are facing. Kimberley Ashton has the diplomatic authority to work her assets in the Bahamas as she pleases, and those assets are her Embassy staffers. She has close ties with DEA, and from time to time in the past, the State Department has been heavily involved in the apprehension of drug lords in the Caribbean from South America.

A lot of drugs from Columbia flowed up through the islands into The Bahamas. It was State who followed up on these smugglers.

Customs and Immigration comes under the jurisdiction of the US State Department, and with the Bahamas Customs cooperation agreement, Kimberley has virtual *carte blanche* in pursuing leads that may result in drug arrests in the Bahamas so long as she brings in and includes Bahamas customs Agents.

That is the angle we will come in with. I will ask Kimberley to conduct this search under DEA pretense, and this way she can keep Miller's FBI Agents in Nassau focused in on the goings on with the Union, and the hotel execs they are there to protect.

Kimberley filled me in on Miller and his involvement. You see, we haven't heard from Agent Miller for a long time, that's because he has nothing.

Now that it's been made clear that I am to be kept out of the loop, well, we can feed them their own medicine and keep them out of the loop as well.

I need not tell you that Embassy staffers really are "spies"; not quite everyone, but State has Embassies the world over and every Embassy gathers information on the country they're in.

The Bahamas is no different. Also because the Bahamas has an agreement with the US on drug enforcement; Kimberley can enact her powers and desires to review and ask for all customs records of all individuals coming into The Bahamas.

Everyone has to go through Customs whether you arrive by air or sea, and that includes fishing charter boats from the US. Somewhere, Garretty had to register and check in. Some marina, someplace in the Bahamas will have him registered as well as his vessel of arrival; The Sharker.

I'll get Kimberley to send out her people immediately as soon as I can talk to her. Everything we do must be kept as low profile as possible. None of this can leak out, we operate as an independent unit, and we have our ace in the hole, and that is Ms. Ashton.

She is a woman who is willing to do the right thing for the right reasons, but she must be protected, so everything we do is quietly done. Agreed?" Eldon asked.

"Agreed" Billy and Felix replied.

"Okay then, take a breather boys, I'll fly out of here in a bit, just need a few minutes to myself."

Eldon sat back and sunk into the comfortable leather backing of his easy chair, and finally got himself a few minutes of peace.

Billy went to find the laser microphone. Felix went down to The Stinger with more supplies in hand, an hour passed.

Felix had readied The Stinger, all fueled and tuned. He was ready to depart.

"Eldon, I'm good to go, I'm going to take her out and I'll see you over in Nassau. I'm thinking from here to the hotel marina in Nassau, if the wind is behind me, I should be there in five hours. So I will see you round midnight or in the morning; but I will call you as soon as soon as I'm in Nassau harbor channel and making my way over to the Jewel Marina."

Eldon stood up, walked over to Felix and hugged him, saying "god speed licks, god's speed, I will see you at the hotel"

Billy walked up to Felix, hugged him and said, "be safe my man, she should do easily 30 knots all the way over non-stop."

Felix replied, "yeah, that's about what I was figuring on, last month when I took her over, the seas were about the same, and it's a nice night, the weather forecast is for calm seas, so five or so hours should do it. See you in Nassau."

Felix and Billy and Eldon headed down to The Stinger to untie the boat and see him off. It was seven PM, the sun had just set, the sky was clear, and The Stinger roared to life as Felix opened her up. The gig was on.

Eldon said, "okay let's get the show on the road" and the two of them made their way over to the chopper, boarded and were off to Pompano airfield where Eldon would fire up the jet and fly it over to Holiday Jewel airfield in Nassau.

Billy would be on his way right away; the Sikorsky had a top speed of 155 Knots much slower than the jet, it would take Billy three times as long to arrive, but that was fine, he'd still be there in about an hour and a half. By that time, Eldon would soon be meeting with Kimberley and laying out the plan.

Billy was feeling good about everything now; now they were doing something, now the game was on. Billy would be integral; "*Cobra One*," at your service, Cathy Davis,"…Billy said under his breath as he lifted the chopper off the ground and headed out to sea.

Felix was well out in the Atlantic now. The Stinger pushed through the two-foot seas without feeling much of a bump. She was sleek and powerful. "The run across to Nassau should be pretty good tonight" Felix thought, "the only thing he would need to be careful about was crossing the gulf stream."

Normally it was not much to be concerned about, and tonight was one of those nights when concern would not enter his chosen route, but nevertheless, the gulf stream was like a river in the ocean flowing north from the Gulf up from the Florida Keys at a speed of 2.5 knots.

On a sailing craft this would have to be taken into consideration; on The Stinger, well, pushing through the waves at 40 knots per hour is not going to slow him down much, even fighting a 2.5-knot current. What it did do from time to time; was if you weren't careful and you were reckless, the current may catch you off guard if a rogue wave happened to team up with the current and hit you unexpectedly when you were in a turn. Felix was aware of this, and he took great care in how he handled The Stinger.

Moving at 40 knots per hour and being thrown off balance and suddenly not hitting the water right, could present a problem whereby the craft itself could bounce you up so high that landing back on the top of a wave, could cause some damage to the hull itself. Or if you weren't strapped in; you could go flying out of the cockpit.

Not so tonight, Felix was cognizant of all these safety issues to remember and practice. The Gulf Stream was 45 miles wide, and Felix was already half way across it. He relaxed and enjoyed the trip, but he was looking forward very much to arriving in Nassau.

Cathy was on his mind, as well as Billy and Eldon. Felix knew he would be lost without the two of them. This tragedy, as unfortunate as it was, had brought the three of them together as a unit like he could never have imagined. Truly Felix now had friends he would give his life for; he would easily without question lay down for any one of the three of them. Eldon, Billy or Cathy. Felix too, was a bachelor, as was Billy. Felix thought to himself, thinking "both him and Billy were sort of caught in the same net. Never had time for anything other than business, work and relaxing a little from time to time. Maybe after this ordeal is over and Cathy is found safe and sound, Felix might spread his wings a little and see what sort of pretty bird he could attract, maybe" Felix thought, "maybe."

He pressed on into the night air, following his compass, his electronic dashboard readout showed he was 62 kilometers into his trip and 240 kilometers from Nassau, so that was still a good four hours almost.

No problem, he'd be there by midnight. He opened up the throttle giving the engine more fuel and The Stinger lunged forward, keep her at 45knots, that's 51 miles per hour. "Good," he thought, and he pressed on.

Eldon brought the Canadair jet in so smoothly to the hotel airfield even he couldn't believe it. "Well, he was certainly getting more flight time and hours in, he did need more chopper hours though." he thought.

That was something he could leave for when his life was much less complicated. As Eldon taxied the plane, he saw out the window that Louis had arranged for a driver to meet him. Hotel Jag and driver were waiting for him. Eldon parked the jet, and the Jag pulled up beside Eldon's plane.

Eldon knew most of the employee's names in Nassau who worked at his hotel.

"Hi Morris" Eldon greeted the driver.

"Mr. Davis sir, good evening to you sir. I hope your flight was good coming in tonight, clear skies and lots of stars tonight Mr. Davis, it must be a beautiful sight at night with all those twinkling stars and just you up there Mr. Davis," Morris said.

He liked talking to the "big boss" made him feel important that he could talk like that with Mr. Davis, so friendly like.

"Morris, one of these days, I'll take you up with me, you can bring along your family if you like and we'll go for a cruise, have a look at the beauty of these islands from the air, how's that sound, Morris?"

"Sounds fine Mr. Davis, sounds just fine" as he opened the rear door for Eldon.

Within three minutes, Eldon was at the hotel main entrance. Eldon wasted no time; he was early, which gave him the chance to freshen up in his suite.

He did just that, a quick shower, fresh clothes and he felt like a new man; well sort of.

It had been a very very long day, and it still wasn't over, but the shower definitely rejuvenated him. He sat down for a bit, turned on the TV, VNN. The anchor was talking about more chaos in the world.

Eldon, thought, "yeah, it never ends does it? Chaos everywhere."

He focused on his own chaos management. Took a drink of cool water, and headed down to the pier.

It was close to the three-hour mark since he talked to Kimberley. As Eldon made his way out the garden and towards the pier, he could see Kimberley already there, standing almost directly under a pier light situated up high off the side railing. Eldon looked out at her under the light as she waited so patiently for his arrival.

He liked what he saw; he did in fact like what he saw very much. He felt a twinge of guilt and shame overcome him.

Kimberley was beautiful to be sure, but Eldon had just a few days ago buried his Linda. He didn't know really deep inside what to make of it all, he really didn't, it was just the way he felt, "good" about Kimberley, and he supposed that was all.

He kept walking, and when Kimberley saw him walking towards the pier, she started walking in his direction.

"Kimberley, thank you so much for coming to meet me again. He reached out with both his hands and she responded, extending her arms and her hands into his, "I'm sure you are surprised I called so quickly. Kimberley, I called because I have critical information that brings this all together for me. You see, I have one-half of the puzzle and Miller had come up with the other half. But without both halves, neither Miller nor I could really move on anything.

We were walking around in the dark, trying to find a corner in a circular room. But with the information you provided, being that "bastard's" name; well, I now had the other half of the puzzle and with a little digging, I matched it up with my half, and it fits perfectly."

Eldon then went on to explain how Billy and Felix were integral, and how Eldon's former employee and friend Nick Kovacs found the hidden clues in the video tape and how he and Felix and Billy found the marina. The connection is now evident; Jason is in the Bahamas, his boat should be here somewhere in these islands, or at least at one time recently having checked in with Customs.

Time, of course, is of the essence before this Jason character might leave the islands and be lost forever again. Eldon explained all this to Kimberley who listened and soaked it all in.

She was astonished, “Eldon, that is amazing forensics and detective work you and your friends have carried out, absolutely stunning!”

“That's not all of it Kimberley, not even close.” Kimberley was wide-eyed, listening intently, couldn't believe her ears as Eldon went on, telling her of his visit with Bishop, Amber, and Rickover. This information bowled her over. Eldon told her that he now believed Domingo was behind this, sanctioned by or at the least orchestrated by Amber, but Eldon needed evidence and proof before he could act on dealing with Domingo.

Kimberley couldn't believe it at first, shaking her head, all along knowing that Eldon was telling the truth.

She felt betrayed. No, she did not work for the CIA, but she did work for a government and system that she believed in, a system and way of life that she championed her entire career and now to have this happen? To hear and to realize how the CIA Director was implicated.

Then Kimberley remembered another fact that made sense to her. “CIA Director Amber had a huge estate on Grenada, had acquired it years back; it was probably worth a few million Dollars, how does one come about such wealth working for the CIA. The Director was paid well, make no mistake about that, but not that well."

It was making sense to her now. The facts that Eldon had just outlined; she had to admit was making perfect sense for the obvious scenario that could not be denied.

Her spirits were shattered; she collapsed suddenly into his arms.

Eldon held her; he understood her pain.

"Oh, my God," she said, "oh my God."

There certainly existed precedent that pointed the finger of history at CIA tactics similar to this, even worse. CIA complicit involvement in the overthrow of foreign governments, Iran-contra, Sandinistas, Gulf of Tonkin, Watergate, Laos, Papa Doc in Haiti, Bay of Pigs in Cuba, and the list goes on. Many of those CIA operations leading to and ending in bloodshed.

But Kimberley's faith in taking an oath and keeping that oath as a State Department United States of America employee meant something to her. Every time she looked at the stars and stripes, she saw in it the bravery of American soldiers who gave their lives to ensure the freedom she enjoys today. Events like this, what Eldon had just now described, brought shame to her very fiber of being American, this is what cut deep into her honor and dream to become a US Ambassador one day in her career. Eldon still held her; he felt her regaining her composure.

She looked out onto the ocean over the pier, as the moon cast its shimmering light over the Atlantic. She shivered for a moment. Kimberley straightened up, she turned around and walked away a few steps, Eldon watched her, she stopped, then turned and looked at Eldon, not three feet in front of Eldon; she had made up her mind.

Kimberley then said, "tell me what you need, tell me what you want me to do. I will help you Eldon in any way you see fit." Kimberley said those words with conviction in her voice. A decision had been made in her heart and her mind. She then continued… "these past few days have opened my eyes; I now see much farther than I ever had before."

Eldon replied, "I'm going to need a lot Kimberly, it's not going to be easy."

"No Eldon, it's not; but life is not easy, whatever you need and whatever I can give, it's yours." Kimberley said to Eldon with commitment and a feeling for his daughter with a sense of betrayal by her government laced with need for recompense in her voice.

No, it wasn't the State Department, but it was The CIA, and that meant the close inner circle to The President of the United States; President Fenton, for whom she worked. Kimberley had a different opinion today about everything concerning her job, her loyalty and her life.

She found her loyalty shifting to Eldon; she found herself now gaining strength from this man. She found herself wanting to be with him in whatever he need, and Eldon had grown to trust her beyond any doubt as she did him. The two had formed a partnership and with Billy, and Felix, that now made a team of four.

"Kimberley, it's been a very long day, but Billy and Felix will be here at the hotel soon, I want you to meet the two of them tonight. Billy and Felix have been with me for years. They both work for me Kimberley, but I tell you these two are like brothers to me. Billy is ex-military, Congressional Medal of

Honor recipient. Billy is my pilot, protector, and friend."

Kimberley then said, "you mean, Billy Simpson? I know of Billy, I was at his medal presentation at the white house just four years ago. We chatted briefly. Billy I recall was presented the Congressional Medal of Honor for his tour and bravery in Iraq. Eldon, there are only a handful of soldiers who ever rise to the level of medal of honor. There have only been six handed out for the entire gulf war. Billy Simpson is one impressive human being. I'm sure you are very happy to have Billy as a friend. I would very much look forward to seeing Billy again.

"Yeah, that's the Billy Simpson I'm talking about, he's about to land any second at the airfield; he's flying the chopper over to the island.

Felix should be here in another hour or so, he's bringing my boat in, we may have a need for that as well; I want to be prepared.

Felix and I go back many years to our university days. He's been a lifelong friend, and my business advisor, and press Agent. He's helped in allowing me to build this company into what it is today. Almost everything goes through Felix before it comes to me. You will like him; he is very efficient and one hell of a nice guy. Like I say, both like brothers to me. I don't have brothers or sisters, but Billy and Eldon the two of them are. They will be coming to my suite as soon as they arrive. Let's be there to meet them, shall we? We can then lay out the plan of action, and solidify things in the morning. But I think it would be a good thing for us to understand that we will be working as one unit, and coordinate our efforts. I have a plan in my mind for all of this already Kimberley, and I'd like to run it by everyone."

"I'm sure you do Eldon, I'm sure you do," Kimberley said. They walked back into the hotel and into the lobby. From the lobby a corridor leads down into the Casino area, and just before entering the corridor, there was an unmarked oak door to the side, with a door keypad. Eldon reached out and entered the code, and twisted the door handle, ushering Kimberley through the door and into a small foyer with an elevator. Eldon keyed in the code to the elevator, and the elevator door opened. Kimberley looked at Eldon, tilted her head in approval; they walked into the elevator that had only one button for one floor level. The elevator went to the top floor and opened into a small foyer with a door directly into Eldon's suite.

Walking through the door into the suite, Kimberley became aware of the opulence. Eldon's suite was lavish, very elegantly appointed. The living area was long, running sixty feet from end to end with four sofas, and a huge board room table and the entire length of the suite was ceiling to floor window, with a balcony that ran the length.

The suite and view were absolutely breathtaking. Eldon was about to offer Kimberley a refreshment when the knock at the door came.

Eldon said, "well that must be Billy," he went to open the door, and Billy walked through.

"Billy, I'd like you to meet Kimberley Ashton, Kimberley, Billy Simpson."

"Ms. Ashton, such a pleasure, I remember you from a few years ago, we met at the White House."

"It's Kimberley, Captain Simpson, yes I recall very well, thank you for your service Captain Simpson."

"Billy, ma'am, ah… Kimberley," as the two of them shook hands. Eldon moved over to the bar section and offered both Kimberley and Billy a drink. The three sat down on the sofa and chair. The curtains were wide open along the length of the living area.

The pier where Eldon and Kimberley had just come from was off to the left; the Atlantic Ocean stretched out into the horizon with the shimmering moonlight glistening in the darkness. Even though it was a clear night, off in the distance lightning cracked. It seemed no matter clear night or stormy night; lightning was always on the horizon over the ocean. Eldon was always fascinated by that. It was both beautiful and foreboding; that was nature, as it was meant to be. Perhaps that was life itself, beautiful at times and yet foreboding if one was not careful. Eldon thought to himself, “tomorrow would see things set into motion.”

Eldon's phone rang, it was Felix. “Eldon, I just came into Nassau, I'm in the channel, should be docked in five minutes.”

“Glad you made it safely, I had no doubt you would Felix, Ms. Ashton is here along with Billy, we were waiting for your arrival. I'll see you in a few then.”

“Be there in a bit Eldon.”

“OK Licks.” Eldon ended the call.

Felix brought The Stinger, into Nassau Harbor. He noticed a huge yacht; Desert Seas, moored just off the channel in the harbor.

“Good another whale visiting the casino.” Felix brought The Stinger close beside the Sultan's ship. There was Arabic text written under the name of the ship, “must be something to do with Allah, he thought, “God is Great” or something like that.”

Felix entered Holiday Jewel Marina. The marina deck hands were out to meet him; they well knew who The Stinger belonged to, and made certain Felix was to be serviced right away.

"Good evening Mr. Balon"

"Hi," Felix replied.

He brought The Stinger dock side, jumped off the boat, the boys handled the rest. He was out and up on his way to Eldon's suite. He had the combination, as did Billy.

Felix knocked, and Eldon opened the door. Introductions were made.

That evening and well past midnight, into the morning, Eldon laid out the plan that was to unfold the following morning. Soon afterward Billy and Felix left Eldon's suite, Eldon saw Kimberley out and escorted her to the valet parking where the attendant retrieved her Embassy issued Caddy.

As they waited for her car to be fetched, Kimberley told Eldon she would need to be in her office by 7 AM. She would get maybe five hours sleep if that. But Kimberley was okay with that; she would call Eldon as soon as she had arranged the operatives for the DEA investigation activation.

She told Eldon she should have it all done and arranged by 9 AM and be ready to go. Eldon was good with that. Kimberley's car arrived. The valet driver parked the car, driver's door open, Kimberley came around Eldon as he escorted her, and getting into her car, Eldon said, "Kimberley, I know you are going out on the limb for me, you have no idea how much I appreciate this."

Kimberley looked back at Eldon, saying, "I need to do this Eldon, I want to do this, you have me now, and soon we will have Cathy back in your arms," she reached out and as he was still leaning in towards her, with his hand holding onto the top of the open door and the other hand on the door jam, she lightly touched his face, and slowly ran her fingers over his cheek, ever so lightly near to his lips, in a very caring, loving and reassuring manner, as she had done on the ten by eight glossy photo, but this time it was not a photograph, it truly was Eldon Davis in the flesh.

She said, “sleep well; I'll be thinking of you,” then pulled her door shut, stepped on the accelerator and left the hotel.

It had been one hell of a day. Eldon went back to his suite, set his alarm for 6 AM and fell asleep finally.

***

Chapter Twenty Six

I can hear you crying, I can sense your fear
not much longer now baby doll, I am getting near.

Manko was good; Rico was good. They had just gotten rid of a problem, that being Jason. They waited till dark; it was after 11 PM now. Simons at Sandy Point Marina closed up shop and called it a night. They took The Sharer over onto the east shore of Abaco where Manko had left his vehicle. Rico made his way around the tip of Abaco Island and up into Sandy Point Marina. Entering the marina, he could see that the office was closed, nobody around, the marina was dead quiet; perfect.

He docked into Jason's slip number eleven, tied out and Manko was waiting for him at the marina gates. All, was good, the boat was back where it needed to be. Rico or Manko could take the boat out from the marina any time they needed to, on any night after 11 PM. Soon, Rico would take possession of it anyway, as the new registered owner. Manko would make sure all the paperwork would be in order for licensing the boat into Rico's name. Nothing could be simpler.

The Sharker could sit in Sandy Point marina for a few days, that was a good plan, it needed to, this was Jason's port of entry into The Bahamas. No need to mess with that. The Sharker did sit there in slip number 1. It sat there in the marina for a good number of days, Simons not even thinking about it, everything seemed perfectly normal to Simons.

Kimberley Ashton had called the operations meeting this morning. In her office was the Bahamas Customs and Immigration Chief, and five US Embassy Operatives, along with Billy Simpson who Kimberley introduced as "liaison DEA Agent" assigned to the Embassy.

Kimberley kept the Royal Bahamas Police Department out of this operation. The plan was not to mix or mingle this with any local Police or assigned FBI Agents' activities. The FBI Agents were to concentrate on Union activities at the hotels, casinos and resorts, staying ahead of any drummed up events that may lead to unrest, and shutting it down before it was to get out of hand, with the help of local Police, that's what Kimberley wanted Miller's Agents to focus on and nothing else. Eldon, Kimberley, Billy and Felix agreed that the best course of action would be to make sure Miller and his people were out of the loop, and void of any findings the four of them were able to discover.

Customs Chief Adderly was more than happy to cooperate with Kimberley, and the US Embassy. There was a great deal of mutual interest between the US and Bahamas customs. The US being a very large source of operations Dollars for his department. The DEA of the US had over the years made sure that whatever Bahamas Customs required in terms of equipment and personnel, to stop the flow of drugs was properly funded. This ensured his department had the latest detection equipment and professional know-how through training cooperation for his men and department.

With the Bahamas lying just fifty miles off shore from the US mainland, there was a tremendous amount of activity between the waters of the US and The Bahamas, not to mention air traffic.

Chief Adderly was at Kimberley's beckoning call. "Chief Adderly, I like to introduce you to Agent Simpson. Billy and Adderly shook hands.

"Agent Simpson will be the lead investigator with my people on this effort, please give him your full cooperation, you will find Agent Simpson to be most cooperative and a major asset in what we are about to do.

Chief Adderly, it has come to the attention of the US State Department that, a major drug distributor from the US has infiltrated the boundaries of these islands and is residing in hiding with the assistance of an officer from the Royal Bahamas Police Force; this fugitive is desperately trying to evade capture by the DEA. Because we no longer have a DEA detachment assigned to The Bahamas, this project has been assigned to my command and authority to be worked with Agent Simpson through the offices of my Embassy.

This operation is to remain classified, and no public knowledge or media notification is to take place. We do not wish for Mr. Garretty to be aware that we know of his presence in the islands. Also, Chief Adderly, we need to keep this very quiet. We both know the history of the Bahamas Police Force concerning the drug trade and trafficking over the past several decades, we need not get into that. We wish to apprehend him as quietly as possible, and the quieter we keep this, the sooner he will show himself, thinking there is nothing to be weary of.

We need to apprehend this person as quickly as possible before he can escape into the Caribbean and seek sanctuary in Columbia. Your customs Agents and officials have his ID and photograph that we obtained from his driver license. That is the best we can do at this time."

Adderly once again was not surprised at the involvement of a Police officer with the fugitive. Many Bahamian law enforcement officers over the years have been indicted for corruption; it was nothing new.

"So Chief Adderly, we will reconvene again same time and location in one week's time to review our progress." Kimberley finished speaking to Adderly, hoping that Adderly bought it hook line and sinker. He did.

"Ms. Ashton, I understand your concerns, and I will instruct my customs Agents to be on the lookout and to go dark on this investigation. Would you kindly give my regards to Ambassador Lexington and my best wishes for his quick recovery and return to our beautiful islands. Our thoughts are with him. The Bahamas Customs and Immigration services have always maintained a very fine relationship with Ambassador Lexington, and now with your direction, I am sure we will continue in our mutually friendly and productive relationship."

Adderly finished saying, reaching his hand out to shake Kimberley's hand as she was starting to stand up from behind her desk.

"Thank you for coming in on such short notice Chief Adderly."

Adderly looked at Billy and said, "whatever you need Agent Simpson, I'm sure we can provide. I can assign up to six customs Agents to you for direction this morning. Perhaps another four tomorrow." I will send along Bahamas Customs officials badges for your operatives Ms. Ashton, how many will you require?"

Kimberley looked at Billy; Billy said, "Chief Adderly that will be appreciated, we will require a dozen, and that is including me, that will be excellent Chief Adderly."

Adderly said, "no problem Agent Simpson, consider it done."

"The operation command center will be the Embassy; we have a situation room available for planning and data storage here. I will expect your Agents to arrive then within the hour. Please have your Agents report to room 4B upon entering the Embassy. One of our Marines on duty will show them to the situation room" Billy said.

And with that, Adderly left the Embassy.

Billy and Kimberley knew that they had just crossed one huge hurdle. Eldon had to stay out of site for now. Everyone important and some not so important on the island knew Eldon Davis, even the Chambermaids at the hotel knew Eldon; he was one to walk around trying to remember all the employees' names. Eldon thought it important that he make them feel important, even the dishwashers and the houseman. Everyone in Eldon's hotels and casinos was made to feel as important as was the guest.

Happy employees; happy guests. That's how Eldon looked at things, so Eldon could not be directly involved in this investigation on the surface. On the other hand, very few people knew that Billy even existed other than the doorman at Eldon's Hotel.

Kimberley called her State Department operatives together. The nine of them were all currently involved in other duties; but Kimberley pulled them off their current assignments and made this a priority. She introduced Billy Simpson and explained his directions were to be followed to a T. Their collective assignment was to have everyone fan out throughout the islands, as many as possible entry points, and retrieve the customs entry records from all ports of entry via water. There were over thirty, and it had to be done without delay. She explained they were working in concert with Bahamas Customs and Immigration and that they would be issued temp Customs Officer's Badges. Each one of them would have to work alongside a Bahamian Customs official; that's how it was to go down. The assignment was simple; they were looking for a major drug distributor; Jason Garretty.

Kimberley and Billy had been hard at work already this morning. They had identified all the major ports of entry along with branch ports of entry that were located in smaller marinas throughout the 700 islands that made up the Bahamas. Kimberley and Billy thought it best to start with Nassau, since they were already here, Abaco and Eleuthera, eventually going farther to Grand Bahama Island, Bimini and then south if necessary to Andros and Cat Island.

Kimberley was going to remain at the Embassy, she had other pressing work to look after, but Kimberley had done her job today. She set up the entire sting operation as Eldon, Billy and she had laid it out the night before. The operation was on the way.

Billy would make sure Felix was provided with a Customs Badge, and he would be assigned a Bahamas Customs Agent who had to tag along. That was the arrangement in joint cooperative projects. This ensured that both countries would get credit for any apprehension of drug traffickers, the confiscation of contraband and the additional funds that would pour into the agencies in keeping up the good work.

The more successful these types of operations were, the higher the budgets would be the following year. The war on drugs was a major budget expense item for the US Congress, and a large chunk of that budget was allocated to foreign assistance, meaning Adderly's department. He was very happy to give Kimberley Ashton anything and everything she needed.

The Bahamas Customs and Immigration Service's head offices were in Nassau. Here in central control, they gathered all of the ports of entry' documented data collection. These were names, dates, country of origin, type of vessel, aircraft, passport numbers as well as the frequency of visits, and a no entry list of individuals prohibited from entering The Bahamas.

As much as the central control tried to keep things up to date, it inevitably fell behind. Each one of the branches was to submit copies records compiled of all activity on a weekly basis to central command. Unfortunately, some of these outposts branches were plagued by the “manjana syndrome” some branches were pretty consistent, submitted their records weekly, some not so much, more like bi-weekly and some even just once a month.

There may have been good reason from their point of view. A few of the branch ports of entry had such little traffic that it was almost pointless to report in five or six entries a week, so they waited to send in a good number all at once. The point, however, was not only to capture all activity but to report that activity on a timely basis. Knowing and finding out that someone of dubious background had entered the Bahamas weeks ago was already too late for central command, this was information they might need to act upon immediately. So, sometimes things and people would slip through the cracks. This was not uncommon for any country, no border was a hundred percent impenetrable, but The Bahamas was more porous than most others.

Felix Balon, arrived at the US Embassy. Gunnery Sergeant Webb, of the US Marines, showed Felix to room 4B, designated as the situation room. The "Gunny" opened the door for Felix and he walked in to see Billy already drawing up plans indicating where each team of Agents were to go to gather data.

Billy was assigned a chopper provided by the Bahamas Customs and Immigration service. That was good since it would provide him with a wide reach capability. Billy had the Agents spread all throughout the Bahamas, there was to be some travel time in getting to some out islands, but most of the teams which were him; Billy, and the others made up eleven teams. Billy needed an extra badge making twelve, just in case Eldon needed to get personally involved, but that would need to be on an obscure island where nobody knew Eldon, and even that was taking a huge risk.

Felix came around the table to Billy's side. Billy was fixing the map onto the cork bulletin board. Billy had colored pins sticking in the map, each color for each team of two Agents, and to which marinas and harbors they were to visit. Billy had placed Felix's blue tagged pins into four marinas in New Providence from Hurricane Hole to Lyford Cay and a few others pinned out.

There were over thirty locations just in Nassau, Abaco and Eleuthera, and another twenty or so in Grand Bahama, Andros and Cat Island and a few more in Exuma, and the other out islands. There was a lot of territory to cover, all in all, The Bahamas covered almost fourteen thousand square kilometers; a huge section of ocean. They would need to have some luck on their side if they wanted to hit pay dirt right away.

Billy was hoping it wasn't going to be the last two places they looked, but Garretty would have had to check in at one of the ports, that was almost a certainty. Even if he hadn't checked in at this time, one of the customs Agents out there knew of him because he was a regular visitor to the Bahamas and carried on business here in his charter boat operations. So it was just going to take some good ole' find and seek.

Felix said, “hey Billy, quite the day yesterday eh? Heard from Eldon yet?”

Billy answered, “yeah, I saw him this morning before I left. He said he wasn't able to sleep much at all, and then he said something that made me think.

“What was that Billy” Felix asked.

“Well Licks, he said he was sorry that he's gotten you and me and now Kimberley mixed up in all this, he said he doesn't know how he can every make this up to us, whether we ever find Cathy or not, he said he was sorry, and that he was thinking of just giving in, and taking the money that Amber offered. That would free Cathy right away, and that would be the end of it. Each minute, each second, each minute, each hour that passed meant the candle burned quick at both ends, time was closing in on him.”

The Union contract would be presented officially in four days, if Cathy wasn't found by that time, Eldon would call Amber and tell him, he would sign the contract and Cathy would be released, or he could sign the contract now, and be done with it.”

“No, he can't sign the contract yet, he has to wait till the contract presentation date; the Union membership might want even more than what Alvarez is asking for in the contract now. The membership may press Alvarez for something even higher than the 50 percent increase. Eldon has no option; Alvarez has to hear from the Union body and that's not for another four days." Felix said.

"Yeah, he knows that, but he just wants it over with and have Cathy back in his arms."

Billy continued. "Right, but that can't happen, no matter how soon Eldon wants Cathy back he's not going to get her for another four days unless we find her before that time, and that's what we are going to do! I'll speak to Eldon this morning after I pick up my Customs Partner here. I'll tell him to meet me at Potters Cay Marina."

Then Billy said, "Licks you know The Stinger is staying where it is, I've arranged for a nice thirty foot Mako center console with two 150's from Bahamas Customs and Immigration for your use, my man." We can't take a chance on someone recognizing Eldon's boat in this operation. I've done the same; I'll be flying a Customs chopper for the next while."

"Excellent Billy, excellent," Felix said. Felix and Billy continued reviewing the plotted map marking the targeted visitation locations. Felix remarked, "whew, that's a slew of them, sooner these guys get here, sooner we can start on this."

Bernard Pinder completed his verbal report to Kimberley this morning. Kimberley was very pleased with Bernard's infiltration of the CHCW Union. Bernard was a good kid. It was a good decision by the Embassy to recruit Bernard as a National; he was becoming very proficient at his assignments.

The Embassy had spent a few thousand Dollars in sending Bernard to Croupier training in Monte Carlo. He was well trained on all Casino games in the best of the best training facilities in Europe. Bernard was very smart, he spoke three other languages, French and German, and Bernard was now learning Russian.

Kimberley knew Bernard was going to have a very bright future, especially if Bernard decided to stay with State in the capacity that he had.

This morning Bernard reported to Kimberley, what went down at the Union Hall a couple of days ago. Alvarez was there, and he had presented the proposal to the Union body in Nassau, although the Union body in Nassau alone would not make the call, their voice was very important.

The largest segment of the Union membership was in Puerto Rico, being ten times the size of the Bahamas, but the Bahamas was where Davis had his Holiday Jewel Hotels head offices, and main operation. Bernard told Kimberley that what Domingo presented was not going to be enough; the membership almost went crazy that night chanting and yelling that they wanted more.

He told Kimberley how the room went frantic until Bernard had had enough and he left. This piece of news was very significant. The Union proposal presentation was to take place in four days at which time Alvarez will most likely increase his demands. At that time and that time only, will the first opportunity to accept or reject by the Hotel and Casino Management be available. Even if Eldon wanted to accept this deal, he couldn't accept it until it was presented.

He could not sign something that wasn't in front of him, and it would be a big ceremonial event for the Union, with TV coverage and the whole nine yards. Kimberley had to get in touch with Eldon and let him know what her “mole in the hole” had just reported.

Kimberley called James Louis. Louis answered immediately. “James.”

Mr. James, this is Kimberley Ashton, would you be kind enough to let Mr. Davis know I need to see him, and that I will be at the hotel within the half hour.”

“I will Ms. Ashton, right away.” James called Eldon's line and told him the young lady was coming to see him again, he did not mention a name, Eldon knew. Eldon was surprised that Louis had caught on so quickly. Louis could be trusted, savvy and sharp. “Thanks Louis, I appreciate your discretion,” Eldon said on the phone.

Louis knew this was no rendezvous, he knew and understood this to be a very low-key and private affair, and by affair, he did not mean “affair” in the traditional sense of the word. He figured it had something to do with the upcoming Union vote and the possible unrest in Nassau; that's how he figured it to be for now.

Eldon was still fighting the demons in his head. Not knowing where Cathy was and how she was doing, what she was eating, who was it that had her confined? This was just killing Eldon. Eldon knew he had to get a grip on things; too much had gone down in the last few days, and they were making good progress, for him to start losing it now. He had better snap out of it, or he was going to lose his mind, and now Kimberley was on her way over. He took a deep breath, got himself a glass of ice water, drank it down, and that seemed to kick him out of his stupor.

Eldon hadn't even shaved yet this morning; it was already almost ten in the morning, what was he thinking! Kimberley would be over here in a half hour; he had to wake up and get with it! He quickly hopped in the shower, took a cold one, this definitely woke him up and got his blood flowing along with his brain, which had been in idle all morning long. He shaved, put on fresh clothes, low and behold; he was ready. Not five minutes later, a call from Louis, Kimberley had arrived. Eldon went down to meet her in the lobby.

As Eldon's elevator was on the way down, he suddenly recalled Kimberley's touching his face last night. That was quite the moment, yes it was. He wasn't sure what to make of it, he will just leave it alone for now, but it was in the back of his mind.

Kimberley was waiting in the lobby, and seeing Eldon come out of the elevator; she walked towards him, put her arm around his, and said: “walk with me Eldon.”

She had been to the hotel several times and knew her way around. She walked Eldon out the back and towards the beach. There down the beach about sixty yards away on the long end, she spotted an empty Tiki hut, which would be perfect she thought. Eldon walked along with her, he saw where she was headed; it would be a good spot to talk; there wasn't anyone around at all, and it was far enough back from any beach combers. The Tiki hut was up on the grassy section of the beach. Sometimes beach vendors would be in the area, but today wasn't one of those mornings.

Kimberley and Eldon reached the tiki hut. Eldon's mind had cleared up by now and was back to himself. It had been a rough night and hard morning.

Cathy was out there somewhere. He looked out onto the ocean and said, “You know she's out there somewhere, in my mind I can hear her calling my name, I can hear her calling Linda, and I can hear her crying.”

Kimberley looked desperately at Eldon saying, “I know you can, I know you can, and I cannot even imagine how hard it must be for you Eldon, but that's why I am here, I am here to help you however I can. I know that the more information we have, the more information I can get for you, from any of my sources can somehow add to finding Cathy. You have some incredibly good people who love you, Eldon, people like Billy and Felix and even Mr. James, at the hotel.

"Yeah, Louis is a good man," Eldon acknowledged.

"And Eldon, I have to tell you, I too have feelings for you, your strength and integrity and your burning desire to leave no stone unturned are qualities I find so incredibly admirable that I go to bed thinking of what you must be going through. I want to find something; anything I can do, it burns away at me each and every day. You have opened my eyes like never in my life, I see things more clearly now than ever, and that is why I am sitting here with you now. Do you hear me Eldon?"

Eldon, breathed in deeply and slowly, lifting his arms and running his fingers through his hair, with both hands over his head, letting out a big sigh.

"Kimberley, I don't know what to say, I would be lost without you, Felix and Billy. My life has taken such a sudden turn in these last few days; last two weeks that my head is spinning, my heart is broken, and yet I know that having the trust, the loyalty, and the friendship of Felix and Billy, and you Kimberley that I can go on. That is comforting and reassuring. I have to go on; my little girl is calling for me."

"And you will go on Eldon, you will, and we will with you as well."

Kimberley moved in close beside Eldon; she could see that his heart was broken and he had tears forming in his eyes as his eyes welled up, she leaned into him, and pressed her body into his side and put her arm around him.

Eldon wiped away a tear and put his arm around Kimberley saying softly to her, "thank you for saving my life" as more tears fell from his eyes.

"I didn't save your life, Eldon, you saved mine, as soon as this is over and we have Cathy, I am resigning from the State Department and going to do something I can believe in again," Kimberley pause for a few seconds, they both sat in silence, then looked at one another, Eldon nodded his head and smiled, with a knowing comfort.

Then Kimberley said, "Eldon I have some new developments for you. This morning I had a meeting with a very trusted local we have on our payroll. He's actually an employee of yours, one of your best and trusted Casino employees, Bernard Pinder."

"Yes, I know Bernard, cool character, and by that I mean he has ice in his veins, so he's a recruit for State?"

Kimberley replied, "yes, has been for a few years, we have been grooming him, and he has proven to be a very valuable asset. He has been very helpful in this Union problem. Eldon, the Union is not going to settle for a fifty percent increase.

Bernard has indicated that they are going to demand more than that across the table for everyone, and Alvarez will be revising the proposal upon presentation to Hotel Management in four days time. There isn't anything you can do, even if you wanted to until the proposal is presented for you to sign or reject. And Eldon, I know, I can imagine what's been running through your mind ever since you found out about Amber and Alvarez. You no doubt have wrestled with just agreeing to everything and seeing Cathy in your arms now, but they're not going to let you have her, not yet. So whether you or we like it or not, we have four days to wait, and Eldon four days will be plenty time to find Cathy, we have the important data now. Let's mine this data, find the boat, locate this Jason Garretty, by whatever means necessary and I do mean whatever means, and you can blow this whole thing up into their faces."

Eldon then replied, "you're right Kimberley, and that is my intention, it has always been my intention."

Eldon stood up from the curved bench around the tiki hut, and helped Kimberley up, "let's get on with it then," Eldon said.

Kimberley replied, "Felix and Billy are well into the day already and are moving on ports of entry, just like we planned it out last night. Adderly fell for the setup, hook line and sinker; it turned out to be a great idea, he even chipped in air and sea operations assets. We are using his chopper and a nice Mako. He's given us a good number of customs Agents to work with in pairs. Billy and Felix are out in the field now," Kimberley finished saying.

"Good, then Billy will be able to survey a lot of marinas from the air. Felix will be able to get close in to look for The Sharker as we discussed last night."

The two of them walked back.

"Eldon I need to get back to my office, I'll be in touch later as soon as I can. I know we will have something soon."

"I know that too Kimberley; I'll see you soon." Kimberley drove off back to the Embassy.

Eldon wasn't about to stand around and watch everyone else doing the search; he was about to get into the game as well. He could do what Billy was doing because the Sikorsky was here on the airfield, he could take the chopper out and look on his own.

Billy couldn't take the Sikorsky because he had to play the DEA Agent role, but Eldon could.

He was still a little shaky with the chopper, but it was a clear, calm day, and he needed more flying hours anyway.

He called on Louis to be his spotter. He knew Louis would be busy with hotel and casino work, especially with the upcoming Union issues, but Eldon was the boss, he'd pull Louis away from whatever he was doing and have him come along. Eldon was certain he could fly the chopper close enough in along the shorelines for Louis to pick out boat names with high powered binoculars. Eldon was back in his suite.

"Louis, drop what you are doing and meet me, dress casual, we're going for ride, I'll see you at the front lobby, we'll take a hotel car over, to the airfield that is."

Louis asked, "you mean right now?"

Eldon said, "yes, I mean right now Louis." Eldon then realized just how unusual this was, no wonder Louis was surprised, "drop what you're doing, we're going for a helicopter ride. It must have sounded insane to Louis," Eldon thought, but Louis did as Eldon asked.

Louis was waiting for Eldon in ten minutes at the front of the hotel; Louis was wearing shorts and a Hawaiian shirt, perfect Eldon thought, perfect.

Eldon, started the chopper, Louis was sitting up front with Eldon, the Sikorsky had a co-pilot seat, so Louis was there, he had the high-powered binoculars from the Sikorsky utility cabinet, and they were off.

Eldon lifted the bird, it was smooth, up a good hundred and twenty hundred feet, then, nose down, tail up and away they sped.

Eldon took the Sikorsky along the shoreline of Nassau around New Providence, out over Paradise

Island; he had instructed Louis to look for a fishing charter boat, named “The Sharker” and to look everywhere and anywhere, whenever Eldon got close enough for Louis to focus the binos onto the boats below. It would be an inboard, no outboard motors, thirty-eight foot Bertram. Louis wasn't exactly sure what was going on, he didn't ask, if Eldon wasn't going to tell him, then Louis figured Eldon didn't need him to know, and that was good enough for Louis. Louis was smart; he knew when to ask and when not to ask.

The Sikorsky had a range of 450 miles, which would be four hours at least in the air, going slowly as Eldon was, not consuming much fuel at all. Eldon would be out the full four hours, two hours out and two hours back, where ever he decided to go. Eldon took the chopper right around the island of New Providence, around the coastline, and into inlets, he hadn't realized just how many marinas there were, and not just the marinas, but the private docks with boats that looked very alike from the high up. Eldon was out there for the afternoon, He thought by now it was getting close to having to do his return run, the fuel gauge was showing just over half a tank, and remaining flying time of just over two hours, he would leave himself a little buffer of extra time and fuel. He'd been out with Louis now for two hours already, and he'd flown around New Providence, half way, now covering the other half on his way back, and this was just one island out of seven hundred.

Okay, that was a discouraging thought, most of the seven hundred islands were uninhabited anyway, and maybe just fifteen worth looking at. He wondered how Billy and Felix were making out with their coverage. Eldon kept flying; he was getting tired of the constant concentration required to fly this bird.

He'd only been out in this chopper with Billy watching his flying. He'd taken it out a half dozen times from start to finish, but always only with Billy watching and teaching.

This was a big chopper and Eldon was doing quite well he thought to himself, quite well indeed, and Billy kept this baby in top mechanical condition, Eldon was flying well, he could tell, because Louis didn't seem nervous or concerned.

"Good!" He thought, but no sign of a boat name The Sharker, not so far today.

"Time to take this baby back Louis," Eldon said, the hotel airfield was just ahead. Eldon brought it in for a smooth landing. That was his day. Nothing to cheer about. He'd have Billy refuel the chopper tonight. Eldon wanted to go out again tomorrow if the weather was good.

It wasn't to be, he heard thunderstorms in the morning, off and on all day. Eldon's chopper days were cut short for this week. They had three more days of searching left… just three.

Billy had decided to take the chopper up to Abaco Island. There his assigned Bahamas Customs partner, "Agent Albury" would make a sweep of the island, flying close in spotting for The Sharker with binoculars. It would be approximately a one-hundred mile flight; about 45 minutes up to Marsh Harbour up along the east coast of Abaco and then continuing to Coopers Town and back down along the west coast of the island's shoreline.

There would be plenty of marinas to see, maybe a good ten to check out, and larger ones. The flight there, and back plus the hovering time, they'd consume their four hours of flight time and be back in Nassau for the afternoon before it got dark, not much they could do after sunset from the air. Billy took the chopper from Nassau out over Paradise Island, he banked out over Rose Island and kept on that course since Spanish Wells on Eleuthera wasn't that far out of his way and there was a very sizable marina complex there.

Nothing at Rose Island far as Albury could see, they got to Spanish Wells on Eleuthera; there were a good number of boats at docks along South Street. Billy hovered a good while here, Albury looked and searched like a hawk but nothing. He did spot a nice cruiser, named The Shark, although Billy closed in on it, it was The Shark, not The Sharker, and besides, it was just a smaller Bayliner, not a 38 Bertram, so that was out. But Billy's heart skipped a beat when Albury said, “well I see a boat, The Shark,” but after a minute or two Billy kept on going up and over to Abaco.

From Spanish Wells to southern tip of Abaco was only just an eighteen minute flight. Billy followed the eastern coastline of Abaco Island; there were some smaller islands he saw farther off to the east. Flying the chopper over a blue hole, he saw one island to the east, with just one small house on a hill, overlooking the ocean, “must be a beautiful view from that little house surrounded by palms,” Billy thought, as they flew by.

Most of these small out islands were sought out by yachting day trippers who liked to party at secluded coves and beaches offered up by these uninhabited islands. Billy kept on going up to Coopers Town, did the survey there on a couple of marinas, nothing.

Billy saw his fuel gauge was close to halfway marker, so he turned back south down the western coast of Abaco, a few boats anchored along the beaches, he hovered in; Albury said, nothing. Albury said to Billy, "you know Agent Simpson, there's a fair sized marina, just over a ways almost at the southern tip of Abaco; Sandy Point, it's not more than ten minutes ahead."

"Okay let's check it out," Billy said.

Within a few minutes, Billy could see the marina coming into view, not a real big marina but one that accommodated larger boats, Billy brought the chopper in over the boats. Albury had the binos up to his eye; he'd been looking so much lately that his eyes were starting to water and sting; he rubbed his eyes and put the binoculars to this eyes again. "You want to get closer, Agent Simpson, closer."

Billy's heart started racing; even Billy could see from this distance that there was one vessel down there and on the stern, was a two-word name.

Agent Albury then said with excitement in his voice, "that's it, that's it!" there's a boat down there called The Sharker and Agent Simpson, it looks like a Bertram thirty-eight footer, yes, Agent Simpson, underneath the name, it says Nags Head NC. Agent Simpson, that's her, we have it!" Billy immediately sent the chopper high up, out of there and away.

Last thing he wanted to do was to bring any undue attention. There didn't seem to be anyone around this afternoon. Billy's first reaction was to stay clear, but that's not the reason they made this trip.

He had to go in. He had found the boat. He brought the chopper back in close; he looked to see if there was a clearing nearby to land, and there was, right next to the marina office. It was now 2 o'clock in the afternoon. Billy landed the chopper on the marina grounds. Billy's "Cobra persona" and mindset began to take over again, but he had to keep himself in check. There was some investigation to be carried out. He had to keep his cool.

Albury and Billy got out of the chopper. Simons thought this to be highly irregular; he didn't see too many choppers come landing here if any, especially from Customs. Simons kept a log as required, but he'd never seen a Bahamas Customs chopper here in his twenty years of working this marina.

Simons went out to meet the chopper. "Good afternoon mon," Albury said.

"Simons replied, good afternoon gentlemen, Simons."

Albury then said, this is Agent Simpson, Billy reach out, shook hands with Simons.

Albury introduced himself, "Albury."

Billy showed his badge, as did Albury. For Simons, that was unnecessary; the Customs chopper said it all.

Billy started in, "Mr. Simons, we need some information on the vessels in your marina, we're just running a lead, we have some potentials, might be nothing, but we don't want to leave any stone unturned."

"Very well, very well, Agent Simpson, you know my records are very much up to date, it's just a mid-sized marina here, we don't have too much in the way of visitors signing in from the mainland, most of them check in at their first port of call, which is up in Grand Bahama, or Bimini. We get the odd one, like Mr. Hughes in "Easy Living" and Mr. Garretty in "The Sharker" and a few others during the month. So what is it I can do for you?"

Billy then continued on, "well the thing is Mr. Simons, we need the arrival time and records and names of the owner on all the craft that entered here in the last two weeks, is that something you can help us with?"

Simons answered, “yeah mon, that's no problem come on to my office, and I will photocopy my entry logs for you for the last two weeks, has everything on there, names, times, dates, size of the boat, names of passengers, passport numbers, everything.”

Billy didn't want to raise an alarm. He actually didn't want anyone other than Simons to know they'd been here today.

“So tell me again Mr. Simons, who owns Easy Living?”

“Oh, that's the Pattersons’ boat, they retired here on Abaco a few years back. Nice folks you know, an elderly couple but they enjoy the ocean and like going out from time to time.”

Billy said, “I see, and the other gentleman, you say his name was..gar..something.”

“Oh yeah, yeah, Garretty.”

“That's right,” Billy said, “Garretty, didn't quite catch it the first time”

“Yeah,” Simons continued, “Mr. Garretty, charter boat captain he is, and good friends he is with Chief Manko here on Abaco, and Chief Manko's brother in law, Mr. Rico, as a matter of fact, Mr. Garretty's boat has been back now for a few days. I ain't seen him around lately, he must have come in after I close up at eleven. All three of them Mr. Rico and Chief Manko they were on Mr. Garretty's boat just after he arrived from Florida a while back, pretty near two weeks now. Him and Mr. Rico went over to Eleuthera there, the same day he arrived, said he was taking a charter out, but dropped Mr. Rico off. You know the marina office is closed; but people still come and go as they please you know.”

Billy thought, “Simons sure was one talkative son of a gun,” Billy didn't even have to ask any questions, Simons was just spewing information, Billy figured that’s how it was round these islands, everyone talked about everyone; “family islands” that's what the Bahamians call it.”

Albury was making notes all along, Billy was listening and committing everything Simons was saying to memory.

This was it, everything they needed, it was going to be delicate from here on in, but he had to keep pressing.

“Mr. Simons, I'm going to need to have a quick look on a few of these boats, do you know if they're unlocked?”

“Oh, nothing is ever locked here Agent Simpson; we don't have any crime or criminals in our community, it’s so peaceful and quiet, even the seagulls get bored living here.”

Simons started laughing…Billy smiled and said, “okay good; I'm just going to have a quick peek inside these two boats I'll be right back.”

Billy walked up the docks and onto The Sharker, opened the sliding door leading down into the stateroom. He saw the bed right away where Cathy was videotaped, noticing the dark horizontal lines running the width on the stateroom walls. Billy reached into his pocket and pulled out a pouch, from that he extracted several strips of sticky paper, about one foot wide and three feet long. He laid the strips down on the bed, around the walls, as many places as he could, these strips were fiber lifting strips; Billy was looking for loose strands of hair.

Eldon and Billy figured once they find the boat they will need to verify evidence that Cathy had been on board, although they had no doubt she was on The Sharker, Eldon insisted on obtaining evidence.

Billy believed he picked up enough fibers now. He even found the white sheets Garretty had laid out all over the bed. Those sheets had been just crumpled underneath the bed inside the pull-out linen drawer. He sticky stripped those as well, all the sheets he could find.

He had laid out twenty strips, he pretty much lifted the whole room, bed, bedding, walls, cabinets, counters, everything, even with just his naked eye; he could already see dark hair samplings picked up by the sticky strips. Billy had what he needed.

But something else Billy had, were names of collaborators. Police Chief Manko and Rico. That would be Rico Alvarez. It was all here. Eldon would be ecstatic.

Billy was done with the Sharker for now. He quickly went aboard "Easy Living" just to make it look good, and he walked onto four other boats pretending to be looking around, not picking on any one particular craft, but making sure Simons saw him on all boats.

Walking back to Simons, he told Simons; he wanted the names of all the owners, and where they were from, and the dates they last took their boats out, if Simons could remember or he could even ask them if he wanted to.

This was just for show. Billy didn't want to draw particular attention to The Sharker.

Then before he was done, Billy addressed Simons. "Mr. Simons, the United States of America DEA agency and The Bahamas Customs and Immigration Services is now informing you formally, that the events of this afternoon and the arrival and departure of Agent Albury and me and our visit here this afternoon is strictly confidential. No knowledge of our presence here must be made public. You are to keep this strictly confidential, as a sworn Agent of Bahamas Customs and Immigration, this is a direct order. You are not to talk about our visit today or my being on any of these boats, not to any boat owners, not to the Police, not to the Chief of Police, not to the fire department, not to the fire Chief, not to your wife, not even to your dog! Do you understand Mr. Simons?"

Simons looked at Albury and Billy wide-eyed. "Yes sir, yes sir, most definitely sir, yes sir Agent Simpson, yes sir."

"Good," Billy said, we may be back shortly, have a good day Mr. Simons.

Billy and Albury left and headed flew back to Nassau.

Billy was quite confident he had put the fear of God into Simons, and Simons was going to stay quiet. Billy could hardly wait to see Eldon, for that matter, Felix and Kimberley. Billy had a feeling that Kimberley wasn't going anywhere and that she'd be around in Eldon's life for some time to come, but it was just a feeling.

***

Chapter Twenty Seven

Be careful of your golden glitter,
It may shine upon your baby sitter.

Mitchell Farnsworth, Secretary of State, was enjoying a nice brief afternoon conversation with President Fenton. They most definitely liked each other with mutual respect. Naturally being in the same political party the two of them pretty much saw things eye to eye. Yes, they had been adversaries back not just too long ago, both having run as Presidential candidates in the last election. It was neck and neck for a while, with Farnsworth giving Fenton a real good run for his money. But when Fenton won the confidence of his party and won the party leadership, Farnsworth wasn't upset at all, because he knew Fenton and him were respectful of each other and Farnsworth gladly accepted Fenton's invitation to being his Secretary of State. The two men got along real well with President Fenton being very happy how things had progressed with Mitch running the show.

"So Mitch, my Chief of Staff advises me that everything has been arranged in Grenada to have the signing of the treaty moved up to this week as we planned right?"

"Yes Mr. President, all is good with Forbes Bishop, we are making final plans now, with a rehearsal gala garden party arranged for all dignitaries attending the signing event the following day.

This will be momentous Mr. President; all Caribbean nations will be present for this event, over twenty-five nations Mr. President. The celebrations will start the day before the official signing takes place between yourself and Forbes Bishop, and the following day will be mainly taken up with commentary from attendees.

This event, Mr. President will provide the understanding and collective cooperation economically and militarily, securing the future forward readiness and capabilities we have been looking to establish for several decades ever since we lost favor with Puerto Rico. We have been very fortunate to have Grenada step up to the plate Mr. President. Arrangements are in place for you to arrive on the island on the day of the signing event, and you will be returning to the White House the day after."

"Thank you, Mitch, glad all is in play. So, then I'll see you in Grenada, oh, and everything else is fine, is it?" Fenton asked, referring to Island Hop. Mitch knew very well what Fenton meant by "everything else."

"Oh yes, Mr. President, "everything else" is just fine Sir," Farnsworth assured Fenton.

"Thank you, Mr. President, have yourself a good day."

Farnsworth left the oval office; he was feeling good; things were moving along just fine, and soon the Caribbean Initiative would be in the bag.

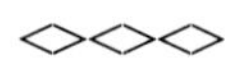

Every minute that went by was now feeling like an hour. Billy was pushing the chopper as fast as it would fly back to Nassau. There was no cell communication possible in the open ocean, and Billy did not have a satellite phone. That probably would not be a good idea anyway; it would no doubt be monitored. Not that many satellite phones out there, those were easily tracked and listened into by NSA. That was a chance Billy wouldn't take anyway. A cell phone would have been all right; he could have gotten Albury to give Kimberley a call to say they were on their way back and for her not to go anywhere. Billy kept pushing the small chopper; it topped out at 112 miles per hour. Finally, he saw Nassau coming into view.

He brought the chopper in, directly over the Embassy and landed in the courtyard. He thanked Albury for his help and told him he was free to go for the day. Albury was good with that. Billy ran into the building, through security. Kimberley had heard a chopper coming in, normally that doesn't happen at the Embassy courtyard, so she knew something was afoot.

Adrenaline pump through her hearing the chopper and her heartbeat sped up. Two minutes later, Billy was standing in front of her; she signaled to him to close the door. "I need to go through you for this Kimberley, I didn't want to waste a minute, we found The Sharker up in Abaco in Sandy Point," Billy said, could hardly contain himself.

"Fantastic, Billy; were you able to board the vessel and obtain fibers?"

That was her major concern now. Billy pulled out his pouch with the sticky strips.

"Excellent Billy, excellent. We have a lab right here in Nassau, it was established a few years ago to give us identification verification capabilities, it mainly does blood tests today, but the lab has basic DNA Mitochondrial analysis matching so long as we have control data samples, and Agent Miller copied me on that data. Billy, I can have the results in a matter of hours."

Kimberley opened a drawer in the credenza behind her desk; she pulled out an envelope; it was Cathy's DNA control data.

Billy handed the sticky strips pouch to Kimberley. She took a diplomatic pouch from off the credenza and placed both items into it. Kimberley pressed her intercom button and had the Gunnery Sergeant come to her office.

"Gunny, have this pouch taken over to US labs immediately for analysis."

"Consider it done Ma'am," the Gunny said, he took the pouch and was gone.

Billy called Eldon right away after Gunny walked out. "Eldon, we'll be right there, don't go anywhere, we have news."

Felix was sitting right in front of Eldon in Eldon's suite; they had been talking about their next moves and which marinas and areas to search the coming day.

So when Billy said; "we'll be right there," Eldon knew what that meant; Kimberley was coming with him.

Eldon thought, "Billy must have found something or a new angle; something was up because both him and Kimberley were coming over and now! "Licks, Billy and Kimberley have something. I so hate having to be so clandestine about everything; it's hindering my update abilities, but it has to be this way. I cannot be talking to Kimberley concerning any investigation related issues, it would be sure giveaway that she is collaborating with me, and that would not be good for her."

Billy and Kimberley arrived within fifteen minutes from the Embassy; walked through the door into Eldon's suite, and the first thing out of Billy's mouth was; "We have The Sharker Eldon; I found it up in Abaco at Sandy Point Marina."

Hearing those words coming out of Billy's mouth sent Eldon's spirits soaring. Kimberley was standing beside Billy, looking at Eldon and Felix, she had her fingertips flat over her mouth with her excitement, breathing in and out at a fast pace, taking in two breaths a second, "oh my God, oh my God, Eldon we almost have him." She couldn't contain her excitement for Eldon.

Billy then said, "that's not all Eldon, I was able to sticky strip the insides of the whole boat including the bed sheets that he had Cathy laying on when he made the video. Those sticky strips; containing the fiber samples; Kimberley already has them at the lab, undergoing DNA analysis.

But Eldon, I have much more, the Marina Dockmaster who also doubles as Customs officer at the marina, was spilling the beans like crazy, I hardly had to ask him anything at all. Don't ask me now how it came about but we now know this Eldon, the Chief of Police in Abaco is involved, as well as Domingo's brother Rico!"

"The Chief of Police!" Eldon eyes went wide, and Rico, well Rico I can see, being Domingo's brother, but this Manko Chief guy, well that's unreal."

"Not as unreal as you might think Eldon" Billy continued on, Rico turns out is Chief Manko's brother in law!"

Eldon then said, "Okay that's it, all comes together." Felix was just taking this all in standing there stunned. Eldon's mind was racing again, and then Kimberley spoke up.

"I should have the results on DNA hair analysis and hopefully a confirmation, before midnight Eldon; I had the samples sent over in a top priority pouch.

Our people understand that means "yesterday." Our lab people will be working overtime to get the results as fast has the lab can do it. We are fortunate that Mitochondrial DNA is obtainable from hair and a simple comparison can be done, so long as we have a control sample, and I have the data on that, Agent Miller, left that data set with me, so we should have the results back soon enough."

Eldon then said, "I don't need that damn DNA, I know Cathy was on that boat."

Felix then piped in, "what else Billy?"

Billy continued, "well, I did just as Eldon had asked me to, I didn't spook the marina attendant, I didn't let on which boat Albury and I were interested in, I walked onto all the boats and took information on all of them. I specifically asked about boats that registered with customs lately, that's when Simons; the Harbormaster started spewing on and on about The Sharker, Manko and Rico and the whole thing. I didn't pay him much attention, made it look like I wasn't interested in the Sharker much at all. What is significant however is that apparently, nobody has been around The Sharker since Jason arrived on the island, not Manko, nobody, unless of course they were there after Simons goes home, but according to Simons; Garretty hasn't been around for a couple of weeks." Billy finished saying.

"Not sure what to make of that," Eldon said, Billy continued on again. "But I made sure as hell that Simons wasn't going to say a word about my visiting him today. Simons works for Customs, and I put the fear of God into him, he's not saying a word about us being there today, you can rest assured of that." Eldon was thinking, "here, let's all sit-down, I have an idea to follow this up, it's simple, but I need Kimberley to tell me if it will work or not."

Everyone took seats around the boardroom table.

"So, first the DNA analysis; it will be good to have if for no other purpose than to verify in my own mind that Cathy was on that boat, but we all know that the facts clearly point to Alvarez. Now all the dots are connected, Garretty, Domingo, now Rico, makes perfect sense; Domingo's brother and Chief Manko fits as well, with Rico being married to his sister, and of course let us not forget our friend Vic Amber and Forbesy baby.

This then makes up the den of thieves, from the low-level charter captain to the Director of the CIA, and thus the food chain is unbroken. But once we find Cathy, and what I have in mind for Mr. Alvarez will blow this entire situation wide open, we won't be needing any DNA evidence, all of us will walk away without anyone being questioned, or even approached. But for now, and for what I have in mind, we will need the DNA evidence, at least our word that we actually have it, to hatch this idea I have.

Let me assure you, all of us, will be like kryptonite to these self-imposed supermen of democracy, and I'm talking about Amber and Bishop. I think Rickover is clean." Eldon wanted to make that clear.

Eldon went on. "We have three days before the Union contract is to be presented; we need to find Cathy before that time, we all know that, or my baby may be lost forever."

Eldon choked up for a moment, then continued, "and that's not going to happen, we are so close now, it's not something I could live with, I know that. On top of that, I understand that Forbes is having some sort of gathering for the signing of that treaty in Grenada the day after the Union contract is presented…right?"

Kimberley answered. "Yes, it's in the next few days, I was asked by Secretary Farnsworth to be in attendance for that, the whole Caribbean will be on

Grenada for that event. I'm going to need to go Eldon, or I suppose I could feign being sick,"

"No, you don't need to be sick all of a sudden, I want you there for that Kimberley. I will be there, and Billy will be there. Felix, I have something in store for you as well, but you won't be there."

Eldon now had everyone's total undivided attention.

"All right, now listen up," he paused, then said,

"Kimberley," Eldon smile at her for a second, "I don't know what I would have done without you, I really don't." He paused again for a second to let that sink in.

She reached out across the table and took a hold of his hand in hers and said, "and I'm still here Eldon, still here."

Eldon went on, "Kimberley, your relationship with Customs Chief Adderly is solid, right?"

"Totally," she replied.

"All right then, this I think is going to be quite easy. I want you to contact Chief Adderly, as soon as you get the confirmation on the DNA test results, I'm sure it will be a positive match to Cathy's control data. We should have the answer on DNA in the next few hours, right?"

"Any moment Eldon, I'm waiting for the call to come in."

"Kimberley, you've already set the scene with Adderly that we are looking to apprehend a major drug trafficker king pin, who is being aided by local law enforcement; and Adderly bought it.

So, I want you to call Adderly immediately upon confirmation of the DNA, like that you are being truthful in case we do need the DNA evidence, but we won't.

Then he'll want to know who it is, tell him its Manko, Chief of Police on Abaco and you have the evidence, as well as his accomplice Rico Alvarez, and ask him to do this now, and that is to have two units of Agents there within an hour. Have his Agents choppered in to both Rico's and Manko's residences and have him arrest them both tonight.

Then have his Agents fly Manko and Rico back to Customs clearance and interrogation facility in his compound. Tell Adderly that our Agent Mr. Simpson will meet him there and explain to Adderly we only need Manko and Rico for five minutes at the most."

Eldon looked at Billy; Billy understood perfectly.

Billy nodded and said, "yup, that's plenty of time."

"And afterward, the US DEA will release Manko and Rico into Adderly's continuing custody." Eldon finished looking around the table at everyone.

"Kimberley, do you think you can get Adderly to cooperate on this as I laid it out?"

Kimberley answered, "yes, I think so, especially if I call him now, he will see the immediate urgency of it all. It's not that often he has something like this happen on his watch."

Felix then said, "seems a lot simpler to me than I thought it would be, but yeah, it sounds doable."

Kimberley's phone rang, she answered, "thank you, and thank you for working this priority request, I won't forget it."

She looked at Eldon. "We have it," hair fibers belong to Cathy, positive match. We have it, Eldon."

"Do it now Kimberley, do it now."

Kimberley called the Embassy and obtained Adderly's number. She proceeded to call the Customs Chief. "Chief Adderly, Kimberley Ashton, my apology for calling so late, but as you can appreciate, time is of the essence. We have a positive hit on our investigation."

She went on to explain all the while looking around the table at Felix, Eldon, and Billy; they waited in silence listening to her one-sided conversation.

"Yes, Chief Adderly that is what I need, now tonight before we lose this opportunity, it must be carried out tonight before wind of this gets to both individuals, and as I say Chief Adderly, we will need Chief Manko and Mr. Alvarez for a few minutes, to ask our questions."

Chief Adderly understood. In the Bahamas, anything could be arranged, if you looked hard enough, there was a fly in everyone's jar of ointment; no one was beyond a little greasing. Kimberley would see to it with Adderly.

"All right, it's in play. Adderly is about to activate a Customs priority-one apprehension order. He told me it would take a half hour to get his people together, and if all goes well, he should have Manko and Rico apprehended late into the night, or morning hours when they are sure to be in bed. Adderly will be calling me personally when the two are under arrest and being choppered back from Abaco."

Eldon went on, "well, it's in Adderly's hands now, either way, we will find Cathy I'm sure of it now," Eldon said.

"That's just half of it" he continued.

"Once we have both in custody, I don't want to have any leaks reaching Domingo down in Grenada, and in case he does get wind of this, he will run, and he will run probably south to Columbia or disappear someplace in the Caribbean, he could disappear into thin air. We will see what Manko tells us, when we ask him, or should I say, when "Billy asks him."

Adderly arrange for two teams, two choppers each, six in each team. The four choppers lifted off from Customs Nassau International Airport at 1:35 AM, two designated for Chief Manko's residence on Don Mackay Blvd in Marsh Harbor and the other two choppers to Rico's house on Stede Bonnet Road, also in Marsh Harbor. Sandy Point Marina was a good hour's drive from Marsh Harbor. Neither Rico nor Manko was aware of the Sandy Point Marina visit by Eldon earlier in the afternoon. Distance to Marsh Harbour from Nassau International was about an hour and ten minutes flight time or a hundred eighty kilometers.

The two teams of Agents had their instructions and were ready to apprehend Manko and Rico. The choppers arrived in Marsh Harbor and swooped in for landing at both locations, time, 2:47 AM. The teams of Agents, stirred Manko out of bed, his wife was shocked; no one had ever done this before.

Manko was not amused at the intrusion but went to see what the hell all the noise was about. Manko was Chief of Police but not exactly the brightest bulb that shined on the island. Manko came out his front door to see what the commotion was all about, and much to the Chief's surprise he was being apprehended and being placed under arrest. He protested, he was the Chief of Police and all. The Customs Agents just ignored his carrying on and cuffed him.

The same thing pretty much went down at Rico's place. Rico was certainly not expecting anything like this at almost 3 AM. Both Rico and Manko were now in custody and extracted from Abaco Island, being flown to Nassau.

The chopper was noisy, whatever Manko was trying to say was totally drowned out by the chopper noise. Eventually, Manko quit his bitching and settled down to await his fate. He was a very big man, and he sweated enough to fill a bathtub on that ride back to Nassau.

Rico; he was not fairing much better. Rico had already peed himself he was so terrified. Luck was running out for him and Manko.

Adderly had shown up this morning when the choppers returned with Manko and Rico. It was now 4:20 AM, the apprehension process only took a few minutes, not much resistance at all, and the teams were out of Marsh Harbor no sooner than they got there a good clean pick.

Adderly wasn't about to disappoint Ms. Ashton; he knew where his bread was buttered and Ashton would make certain he and his division were well rewarded. One thing he would need to address which was not going to be very pleasant would be the blackout nature of this operation. He'd catch holy hell from the Chief of Police with Bahamas Royal Police Force for keeping them out of the loop. But his explanation would be simple and good. It was a cop involved in the “pick” he could not risk compromising his mission in the apprehension process. So he kept the Police out of it. Customs was called upon by DEA anyway, not the Police Department. So, Adderly was good with it all.

Adderly's Agents had Manko tied to an interrogation chair. His arms handcuffed around the back of the chair. The chair was bolted to the floor, and Manko was secured to the chair, his legs were now bound to the legs of the chair, and his head was restrained with a band around his forehead, also secured to the chair's high back, rendering him to be totally immobile.

Manko was a big man, but he didn't seem so threatening any longer. This is how Billy wanted the scene set up, and Adderly was happy to comply. Billy might not have to even raise a finger; just a nice, polite question or two and Manko would cave. Manko sat alone, breathing heavily.

The door opened, and Billy walked in. Just the sight of Billy walking in, caused Manko to suddenly jerk his body.

Billy was a master at effect. Billy was wearing a bib, and on both hands, he wore latex gloves that reached all the way up to his elbows, and in his right hand, he was holding a pair of wire cutters.

The look on Manko's face was beyond terror. So, Billy walked up to Manko and asked politely, "where is the little girl?"

Manko knew his goose was cooked. But Manko wasn't giving in that easily, he'd try at least one evasive response, "what little girl?" Manko responded.

Having heard that, Manko; denying the whereabouts of Cathy, Billy was on Manko like a lion on a warthog.

Billy lunged at Manko, and with one fell swoop shoved the open wire pincher cutter's jaws into Manko's mouth. Manko had no idea what hit him. "Cobra-One" struck with the force of a lightning bolt. Billy squeezed the wire cutter's handles tight as he could. As he squeezed, tighter and tighter, Billy could hear Cathy's voice in his head, "take me flying Billy Bob, we love you so much, Billy Bob. Cathy's voice sang out in Billy's mind, the thought of Cathy being held captive by this animal drove Billy to the brink; no mercy from "Cobra-One."

The wire cutter went deep into Manko's gums. Billy squeezed harder, squeezing the pinchers into Manko's gums feeling the blades cut deep into and clean through the root of Manko's golden shining tooth.

It took Manko by such surprise he had no time to react, Billy had cut clean through Manko's tooth at the gum, yanking it out and letting it fall to the floor.

The pain was so sudden and shocking, and excruciating; unlike anything Manko had ever experienced in his life; he blanked out, blood gushing out of his mouth and soaking his pajamas.

There was a bucket of ice water next to Billy on a table. Billy poured it over Manko's head; Manko came to.

Then Billy said, "I will ask you one more time; if the answer is the same, your other shiny tooth comes out."

Manko could hardly wait to talk; he was ready, more than ready. He would tell Billy anything, anything he wanted to know.

"Girl is on Conch Island, Rico's wife is looking after her. She's on Conch Island, please no more, please."

"Anyone else there?"

"No mon, no, just the woman and the girl please no more, I tell you anything, anything." Manko, the large man, was trembling.

Billy was in the room with Manko for no longer than fifty-five seconds, he had what he wanted.

"One more question, where is Garretty?"

"We killed him and fed him to the Sharks. He wasn't supposed to kill the Davis woman. Domingo Alvarez gave me instructions to just take the kid only, nothing else. Garretty killed the woman, so we killed him. Rico shot him with a spear, and we threw him overboard to the Sharks."

Manko was spilling everything. Billy was recording everything. Billy now had all of Manko's confession on tape.

"Where is Conch Island?" Manko came clean. Billy had what he wanted. Billy had a little blood spatter on himself, but hey, he wore a bib, plus it achieved the desired visual effect. Billy always thought ahead. He removed the bib, the gloves, placed them into the trash can, opened the door and walked out.

"Okay Chief Adderly, he's all yours, I won't be needing to see Rico, just detain him for the time being along with Manko, until you hear from me."

"You got it, Agent Simpson," Adderly said smiling. He then said to his men, "get that piece of shit out of there and take him down to the cell," same with the other prick."

Billy left. He was choppered back to the Embassy, where Kimberley was waiting for him. Upon arriving, he transferred to her car. Kimberley drove through the early morning darkness back to the hotel where Eldon and Felix were waiting.

"Cathy is on Conch Island just east of Abaco." Kimberley's tears of joy ran down her face hearing the news. Billy dialed Eldon, "be there in a minute, meet me at the chopper."

Billy was still keeping things very hush-hush and clandestine. Eldon knew things were moving. No sooner had Kimberley brought her car to a stop, Billy was already out and running to the Sikorsky. He started the big engines, Eldon and Felix were already pulling onto the airstrip in the Jag and pulling up beside the chopper; Eldon jumped out,

Kimberley was waiting for him, the blades were already turning, Eldon could hardly hear Kimberley, as she yelled to Eldon, “she's on Conch Island, just forty-five minutes away Billy says.”

Eldon couldn't help himself, he leaned into Kimberley and kissed her smack on the lips; that was enough for Kimberley, she knew, she knew, the connection had been made, and now Cathy would complete the bond.

They all boarded, Eldon had not yet closed the door, and Billy was already had the chopper up a hundred feet off the ground. They were all so excited, but nobody said a word. Billy had done an incredible thing; they had all done an incredible thing.

These next forty minutes are going to feel like forever. The Sikorsky flew fast; it was what they needed. A half hour had passed, and light was starting to show on the eastern horizon, daybreak was about to happen. Billy could now see Abaco Island on the left a few miles out and off to the right was the small island. “Conch Island”

Billy thought to himself. “Damn, I flew over that island earlier on, that's the one with the single lone house on the hilltop.”

Billy shook his head back and forth, telling Eldon about it. Billy did recall the house and the palm trees and also recalled a clearing just off to the left of the house on the hill, where he could land the helicopter. He would head for that clearing.

The Sikorsky was a modern chopper; it had some nice features, and one of the features that came with the S76 was noise suppression technology. Billy could virtually fly this baby in and land on the island almost silently. The S76 was not only a corporate favorite but also one of the preferred birds for the FBI, Coastguard and Military. Conch Island was just three minutes out. Everyone was on edge, especially Eldon. Billy brought the chopper in for a quiet, very quiet landing.

Billy had no doubt that Manko was telling the truth, after what Billy had put him through, no man was about to lie to Billy. Billy landed the Sikorsky, they all got out. The house was a good fifty yards up the hill. It's possible that whoever was inside didn't even hear them landing. No lights were on, but dawn was breaking, now with enough light to see.

Billy took point, they walked up quietly, stood at the front door for a moment, then suddenly Billy kicked in the rickety door that fell right off the hinges, causing a huge bang as it came crashing down onto the floor inside the house. It was just a one room house, it was already light inside, the windows had no curtains.

Billy could see everything inside clearly. As soon as Billy kicked in the door, screaming could be heard.

It was Violet; she screamed from fright. Eldon was right there along with Billy, both having stormed through the small doorway, running over the fallen door.

Right away, Eldon saw Violet, curled up in a bed, raising her head trying to see through her panic.

And there was Cathy, terrified from the big noise, but clutching onto her doll Dixie.

Billy and Eldon ran up to the bed, Billy standing to the side and pressing Violet down into the mattress while Eldon reached out and took his loving daughter Cathy out of Violet's arms. Cathy was startled and cried.

Eldon said, "baby doll, its daddy baby doll, its daddy."

Cathy was still in shock, but she knew it was Eldon, and she cried “daddy, daddy, daddy,” she couldn't say any other words, she just kept crying, dropping her doll Dixie and putting both her arms around Eldon's neck, clinging onto him for dear life, crying “daddy, daddy, daddy!”

“It’s okay now, baby doll, I have you, daddy has you, I missed you so much, baby doll.”

Kimberley watched as father and daughter reunited. Tears flowed down her face, her like a waterfall. It was the most beautiful thing she had ever witnessed in her life. She wiped her face from the tears of joy.

Eldon held his daughter. He looked down at Violet. Eldon didn't need to know anything about Violet; he knew enough.

Holding Cathy in his arms with Cathy hugging him around his neck, he then spoke to Violet. “My name is Eldon Davis, this is my daughter Cathy. My baby girl, was ripped from my loving family, and you somehow shared in that. I can only hope that God forgives you for it.

However I see that you have been good to my daughter and have taken care of her and comforted her during these times, for that I am grateful. I am not a man of revenge, but I do believe we need to pay for transgressions and wrongful things we cause upon others. I see you have caused no transgressions upon my daughter and perhaps you were a victim of circumstances yourself.”

Eldon saw that Violet was terrified, as she lay on the bed looking up at Eldon as Billy still held her down pressing her against the mattress. Violet was in sudden shock.

“I will leave you here alone and say no more. If you decide to stay here, there will be law enforcement

Agents to come for you. If you decide otherwise, that is your choice."

Eldon, walked out with Cathy in his arms, kissing his daughter and holding her tight in his loving arms as they all walked back to the chopper. They boarded the Sikorsky. Billy had them all safely back at the hotel with joy in their hearts.

***

Chapter Twenty Eight

Matters of the heart

Morning had broken, sunlight filled Eldon's suite. It was a great day to be alive. Cathy was sleeping in Eldon's lap. Felix, Billy, and Kimberley were all still with Eldon. They were all exhausted; it had been a harrowing last couple of days. But it was all worth it. Cathy was safe, Eldon's world had stopped spinning for a while, but now, things were much much better. Eldon looked over at Kimberley; she had fallen asleep and was still sleeping in the easy chair just across from Eldon and Cathy. Billy and Felix both went back to their rooms, but with Kimberley not having a room or suite of her own, she stayed with Eldon.

Eldon looked over at her, and then remembered kissing her before boarding the Sikorsky. He sat holding Cathy in his lap, feeling calm now, at peace with himself. His life was changing, he knew that. These past couple of weeks had brought things to light in his life that he had not seen or felt ever before. He thought of Linda, his loving wife, how incredibly loving she was, how their lives together had change them both. She was taken from him, along with his new baby she carried, and his heart sank thinking about it. He loved her so, but now she was gone, she was gone forever. Eldon knew his life needed to go on; he had Cathy to raise; he had his business to run and to save. He had incredible people in his life who counted on him and how much he counted on them was indescribable.

Billy and Felix were beyond friends. Now Kimberley had entered into his life in such an unusual way, and how thankful he was he had these incredible people in his life. But now, he had this incredible woman sleeping in his chair across from him.

This woman; Kimberley Ashton. He knew in his heart as she slept there, that never in his life would he ever find someone like her, never. Eldon admitted to himself that over the last few days, he had developed feelings for Kimberley, but events were moving much too fast for his heart to catch up with his brain. He would let things unfold as destiny demanded.

He brushed Cathy's hair as she lay sleeping, kissed the top of Cathy's head, and whispered, "everything will be good baby doll, just you wait and see, everything will be good."

***

Chapter Twenty Nine

Operation Island Hop

The morning turned into afternoon. It was Saturday morning.

In three days time, the Union contract would be presented. On the same day; there was to be a gathering of the Caribbean Nations in Grenada for the signing ceremonies in the Prime Minister's gardens. That would officially take place the following day on Tuesday. Today being Saturday, Kimberley was not needed at the Embassy, which was a blessing, because she was exhausted. Kimberley had woken up about an hour or so ago and had gone down to her car. She had an overnight bag that she kept for emergencies in case she had to fly out on Embassy business on short notice. A fresh change of clothes, toiletries etcetera.

Eldon's huge condo suite had three bedrooms and four bathrooms. Each Bedroom with its own en-suite and walk-in closets, everything you might want or expect to see and have in an ultra-luxury hotel/casino complex that hosted celebrities and Arabian Sheikhs. It was opulent to be sure, but necessary. Kimberley emerged freshen up and smiling. She walked up behind Eldon and brushed his shoulder as he was sitting, thinking. Cathy was awake and asking for Linda.

Eldon wasn't so sure how he was going to tell her. He would think about it some and see if Kimberley had any ideas. Eldon knew that Cathy was old enough to understand that sometimes people went to heaven all of a sudden. But he never really ever talked about the subject with his daughter, he will have to shortly. For now, he told Cathy that Linda had to go away.

"Baby doll, mommy, can't be here right now, but she wants you to know that she loves you very very much and she misses you so much, baby doll."

Eldon figured with time he would tell Cathy how truth is sometimes very painful, but her mommy is with God, and God loves her very much. He'd figure it out.

Eldon's hotel had everything anyone could want. Cathy was familiar with the hotel as well, not so much with the hotel itself, but more with Eldon's suite here. Cathy was also familiar with the lovely lady who would look after her when mommy and daddy were busy.

Eldon had the concierge arrange for child care services in his suite, to make sure Cathy was taken care of and entertained. Cathy would be perfectly safe and sound with hotel management. Eldon still was not finished; he was still planning and executing.

Felix and Billy were back, the time was now close to noon, and Eldon was ready to review what the three of them still had left to be done.

All was in play.

Manko and Rico were detained probably forever.

The Union could present its proposal all they wanted; Cathy had been recovered safely.

Eldon was no longer at their mercy. Amber did not know any of what had gone down. Everything so far was under wraps, along with Miller whom he never heard from any more; probably wouldn't.

The four now sat at Eldon's boardroom table.

"Kimberley, are you ready to make that call to Rickover?" Eldon asked.

"It's now or never, I have his private secured line; obtained it from the Embassy yesterday as we had planned," Kimberley replied.

Then Eldon reiterated, "now remember sweetheart, I believe Rickover is clean; I just know it. And if he isn't well, then he's going to have one hell of a problem, but I don't think we have anything to worry about, so make the call now."

Eldon nodded to her, saying, "it'll be okay, you'll see."

Kimberley dialed Howard Rickover's number, his line was secured, she was confident in that, whether her line was secured, well she no longer knew, but talking to Rickover, if he was clean, everything would work out fine. She wasn't going to place her cell on speaker, just wouldn't be appropriate, so she held the phone out from her ear as far as she could so that everyone could hear.

It rang. Two rings and Howard Rickover answered. "Rickover."

"Secretary Rickover, good afternoon Secretary, this is Kimberley Ashton, we met a number of times in Grenada, thank you for taking my call."

Rickover answered back, "Ms. Ashton, a pleasure to hear your voice, how is Ambassador Lexington doing by the way.

"We are hoping for his quick return, I have been hearing good things lately on his treatments and it shouldn't be too much longer, thank you for asking Mr. Secretary." Kimberley replied.

"And what do I owe the honor to hearing from you today Ms. Ashton.?" Rickover asked. Kimberley continued, "Secretary, what I have to tell you is of a very sensitive nature. If I wasn't certain that this line was secure, I wouldn't even be talking to you now."

This was Rickover's chance to bail or continue with the call. If he continued, she knew all was safe.

"Go ahead Ms. Ashton, I'm listening." Kimberley sighed in relief.

Okay all was good now, so she went on, Eldon nodding in silence, her giving her the thumbs up sign.

"Secretary, I am calling regarding the Eldon Davis tragedy and the fact that The Caribbean Hotel and Casino's Workers Union and Mr. Davis's hotels are to enter into an agreement that is not in the best interest of the Caribbean, its workers or its economy. We have evidentiary confirmation Mr. Secretary that Mr. Davis's wife's murder and kidnapping of his daughter was sanctioned and initiated by Domingo Alvarez the head of the Union in order to force Mr. Davis's hand in signing the Union contract." Kimberley stopped.

"Go on Ms. Davis."

The gears in Rickover's mind were now turning, and he now made the connection to what Amber was telling Davis at the meeting he, Amber and Bishop had just recently. Rickover's question to Amber was now answered, and confirmed, that being "why did you say Eldon Davis had no choice?"

Made perfect sense to Rickover now, especially, "sign the contract and "everyone goes home happy."

Rickover didn't need to hear any more; he understood what was going on perfectly.

Rickover listened to Kimberley as she went on. "Secretary Rickover I would like to play you a taped confession obtained from the Police Chief in Abaco, whom we caught in the conspiracy and kidnapping of Mr. Davis's daughter.

Chief Manko Butterfield's confession was obtained just earlier this morning; I would like to play it for you and please listen carefully where he clearly states Domingo Alvarez and his complicit involvement."

Kimberley played Manko's confession recording. Rickover didn't need the recording he already knew it was the truth, and he also knew there was going to be fireworks.

"If Amber sanctioned this, there was going to be one hell of a scandal." Rickover was a man of honor, and he knew right from wrong. Too many young men and women had given their lives on the battlefield under his command for him to dishonor their courage; to even think of doing illicit, selfish or illegalities for that matter.

Rickover responded. "I know Mr. Davis. I was in a meeting with him, Prime Minister Forbes Bishop and Vic Amber, just a few days ago.

I can imagine what Mr. Davis is going through." Rickover said.

"Well the wonderful news is that Mr. Davis's daughter has been recovered unharmed and is now safe."

"That's wonderful news Ms. Ashton, please give Mr. Davis my regards; I was very impressed with him. Now what else is it I can do for you Ms. Ashton," and he really didn't need to ask, he knew what was coming but he wanted to hear it anyway.

Kimberley continued, "Secretary Rickover, I am asking a favor from you.

I would like to ask that now knowing the criminal activities of Domingo Alvarez that you ask Admiral Huntington at the Sub Base under construction, that he issue a command to set up a perimeter around Domingo Alvarez's residence and have the Admirals men hold Mr. Alvarez until our man arrives. You might know who I am referring to Secretary, Billy Simpson, Congressional Medal of Honor recipient.

I believe you were at the presentation ceremony when the President awarded Captain Simpson the medal. Billy Simpson civilian now, of course, works for Mr. Davis and is his most trusted confidante and aide.

It was Mr. Simpson who was instrumental in the capture of Chief Manko, his accomplice, Domingo Alvarez's brother which resulted in rescuing Cathy Davis. I would like you to arrange a hold onto Mr. Alvarez and also arrange a chopper for Billy Simpson's arrival on the island Monday. I too, Mr. Secretary will be arriving on the island, for the gala ceremonial gathering at Prime Minister Bishop's Government House."

Rickover thought about this; it was out of the ordinary that was for sure, but Rickover had the power to do this. Rickover also knew Lexington very well, and Lexington had told him on several occasions that Kimberley Ashton would soon be offered her own Ambassador posting with a significant country.

She was a real jewel and someone not to lose. Fenton needed people like her in his administration, and Farnsworth would give her the first opportunity that came by.

Rickover thought about it a bit more, the line fell silent.

"All right Ms. Ashton, you have your request granted. I will have Admiral Huntington commence operations to lock down perimeter on Domingo Alvarez until Captain Simpson arrives on Monday, at which point the Navy will hand Alvarez over to Mr. Simpson, I will arrange for the chopper as well. See you when you get here, or at the Garden Gala." Rickover's call ended.

"Yes, yes!"

Kimberley exclaimed in excitement.

"You see Eldon said, "you see, I told you this would be good with him. Rickover is a man of honor; I knew it. I think he is aware of Amber's involvement as well, but I will leave that to Rickover."

Felix and Billy were sitting beside each other; they were high-fiving in the air over and over. Kimberly reached over the desk and she high fived Billy and the Felix and Eldon. They were ecstatic. This was all coming together. Eldon's plan was working. There was a risk to be sure, but the main item was complete, to rescue Cathy, this is just going to icing on the cake now. Just icing and how sweet it will be!

"Okay one more thing left on the menu, and we will be set," Eldon said to everyone, "and that is to make us and this whole ball of wax, fail-safe and bulletproof when it's all done and over with."

"Kimberley, you know what to do," Eldon said. Kimberley picked up her phone again, already had his number in her contact list and dialed.

He answered, "Damond Furst, The Furst Report."

"Damond, Kimberley Ashton."

"Yeah, I see your name popped up, what can I do for you?" Damond knew that it was always the other way around. Kimberley never called him; it was always him calling her trying to get some information. This was different, this was unique, his ears were perked.

"Damond, I have an exclusive for you, something you will want to know about and something that will blow your mind. Your readership will quadruple at the very least." Damond asked, "what is it, US Embassy being replaced by the Russian Embassy in The Bahamas?"

Damond was an ass at times; he already proved that to Felix a couple of weeks ago, asking asinine questions about Eldon, Felix had to shut him up. But he did have a readership, more than any other reporter at the Trumpet or the Beacon.

"No you Idiot," Kimberley said.

"Just listen up, I'm flying down to Grenada, on Monday morning, to take part in the ceremonies regarding the Caribbean Initiative, you're familiar with that I hope. I want you on my flight with me out of Nassau Monday morning. We leave at 8 AM it will be three hours down, and the gala takes place in the afternoon. I have a story for you; I want you to cover. Trust me; this will be a scoop."

Furst couldn't believe his ears, "okay, okay."

Kimberley continued. "I want you to catch a flight over Sunday night Damond, I want you here Monday morning, and I don't want you taking a chance on some delay out of Miami on Monday, got it? I will have made a reservation for you at the Nassau Sands Hotel, it's small but clean, on Front Street in Nassau, all right?"

Furst answered back, "okay I'll be over on Sunday and see you at the diplomatic counter on Monday morning; I'll be there."

Good" Kimberley said, and that was that.

Now they all actually had a day off, if you could call it that; Sunday. They all needed a day of rest; Sunday was a Godsend.

Sunday came and went. Eldon spent it on the beach. Eldon, Kimberley, and Cathy took The Stinger over to Rose Island just a few miles off Nassau. It was usually quiet and deserted on the north shore. It had a beautiful long beach, overhanging palms, crystal waters, lots and lots of sergeant major fish by the thousands. Cathy was having the time of her life. She was standing in waist deep water with hundreds of yellow fishes with little back strips around their bodies; it truly was magical.

Eldon and Kimberley relaxed, watching over Cathy as she played on the beach with her beach pail and shovel. It was such an idyllic day, sun beating down, palms swaying, calypso music far off in the distance, The Stinger anchored just off the beach. The three of them were able to walk right to the beach, Eldon carrying Cathy perched on his shoulders. This truly was a bit of heaven, and paradise found.

After the ordeal of the past two weeks, now having Cathy back in his arms, and well…now Kimberley was here.

"It was meant to be Eldon supposed, it was meant to be," and Eldon liked it a lot, a whole lot. He was still overcome with pain in his heart for Linda, but now there was hope in his life, and it had come about quickly.

He would need time, and Kimberley would give it, she would give him as much time as he needed, there was no rush to move forward, there was only time now to be enjoyed. Tomorrow would be another day, and with the ending of that day, if everything worked out. They would be free.

Sunday night had turned into Monday morning, and now at 7 AM, Billy and Eldon were getting the Canadair Jet ready to depart the hotel airfield. Eldon and Billy would need the jet for today's events. Their flight time to Grenada was just over three hours.

Damond Furst did as Kimberley asked and he was excited to find out what story she had in mind for him. She wasn't about to say anything. She told him Monday morning at the airport, not to pester her and just to be happy she picked him and not someone else; and she could have easily. After she had told him that, Furst settled down and kept quiet all the way to Grenada.

Eldon and Billy took off, taking the jet up to cruising altitude and settling in for the three plus hours' flight. "Will be interesting to see how Admiral Huntington deals with all this, me and Billy" Eldon thought to himself. "But knowing Rickover and his dedication to doing the right thing, events should turn out okay." Eldon well knew that complications could enter the stage at any time; he was prepared for anything at this point."

But yesterday he had a fantastic day with Cathy and Kimberley, he thought back about their time on Rose Island, it did him a world of good, as it did Kimberley and he could see that already after a couple of days, Cathy was becoming more comfortable with Kimberley, Kimberley notice that as well.

Eldon was always amazed at how resilient children could be. There would be many more days before Cathy would live normally without Linda, but Eldon was sure things would turn out all right.

For today, Eldon left Cathy in Felix's loving care till he returned later this evening. Felix was happy to babysit; he would take Cathy out for ice cream and go to play with the dolphins. Would be a fun day for Cathy, might even be a fun day for Felix.

The gala afternoon, garden party was to begin right around 2 PM. There would be a lot of people attending, that Kimberley was certain of.

Her jet touched down just before noon, and with her diplomatic clearance, she whisked right through. Kimberley did notice that she had landed later than she had expected to, almost a half hour, but the reason was evident. Kimberley's plane was required to circle Grenada international; there were just too many planes flying into this little airport on this day. Already the space on the airfield was becoming tight.

Eldon on the other hand, he had clearance to land at the military airfield already constructed next to where the sub base was being built.

Eldon arrived right on time, three hours and a bit just after leaving Nassau, so he was out of the plane by 10:18 and already talking to Admiral Huntington. Huntington wasn't absolutely certain what this was all about, but Secretary Rickover himself met Billy and Eldon's plane.

The Secretary had set this all up with the Admiral. The Admiral already had marines surrounding Domingo Alvarez's residence. Rickover recognized Billy Simpson right away from a few years back. It was good to see Billy Simpson again. Rickover absolutely doled over men like Billy; they were the epitome of American strength and honor. This just further went to lend credence to what Billy and Eldon were about to do.

Rickover understood Eldon's need in making things right, and if it wasn't for Amber's involvement, Rickover might not have agreed to this, but seeing how deep the rot had infiltrated into the Administration, well, Rickover wasn't about to stand for it. He was going to let this man Eldon Davis have his day of justice for his wife's death and kidnapping of his daughter. Rickover was going to make sure of that.

It was time to put an end to Bishop and maybe a time to rethink America's involvement in everything, but he would let things unfold as they would. There was sure to be a congressional investigation that would be spawned by the events that were about to unfold, but that was okay with Rickover; it needed to be done. Time for corruption to end was going to germinate right here and today. Rickover introduced Billy and Eldon to Admiral Huntington. Huntington hadn't met Billy in the past but knew of his record in Iraq. The Admiral thanked Billy for his service and invited Billy and Eldon to his quarters on the base.

The four walked to Huntington's command center. Billy and Eldon laid out the requirements. Huntington had been notified earlier in the day that Alvarez had wanted to leave his property this morning already. His naval commanding officer in charge of the perimeter had detained Alvarez and was holding him in custody till updated commands and instruction came in from Admiral Huntington. His commander was told to hold fast and maintain the detainee in custody. They had him just outside his house holding him in a Humvee.

“Good,” Eldon said, “that is perfect. I would like for your men to bring Mr. Alvarez here into my custody and Captain Simpson's at 14:30 hours.”

“Well I'm sure Mr. Alvarez will hold tight for the next hour and a half or so, why don't we go and have ourselves a little lunch.”

“That sounds just fine Admiral,” and they all went to have lunch served at the Admirals table in the command center. They spent time talking about the navy base, the proposed facilities, a lot of it was top secret, but there was enough to talk about. The Admiral was also very curious about Eldon's hotel empire. The Admiral had a grandson who was in the hotel business and was proud of the young man, thought Eldon could make a few suggestions. Eldon did.

Time was moving on. Kimberley had no doubt landed by now and was making her way over to the PM's residence. The invitations were sent out, Kimberley had her's and guest, it stated. Eldon didn't require an invitation, not for today.

It was now 2 PM, and most of the arriving guests had already made their way into the vast gardens of the Prime Minister's Government House residence.

Alvarez's residence was a good twenty-minute drive from the sub base construction site in Grenada. It would be 14:20 by the time the Marines returned to the base with Alvarez.

"Admiral now would be a good time to have your men bring Mr. Alvarez back to the base," Eldon said.

The Admiral contacted his commander who was waiting in the Humvee.

"Commander, bring the detainee back to the base, disengage the perimeter around the house and disperse.

"Yes Admiral, on our way."

Alvarez was not happy; he was yelling and swearing at the Marines, inside the Humvee, demanding they set him free. Half of his complaining was in English the other half in Spanish. Neither language was going to help him out.

Kimberley and Furst arrived at the porte-cochere of the PM's house. The PM's Butlers were dressed to the nines. White gloves, top hats, tailed coats, very formal. Dignitaries from the various island nations were already gathered in the garden. A lot of milling going on. Already over three hundred people in attendance.

"Kimberly how good to see you." It was CIA Director Vic Amber.

"Director Amber, how are you this afternoon?" Kimberley could hardly contain herself, but she pulled through. The disgust she had for this man was beyond her ability to describe. He was an "evil personified" through and through; she could only hope that The President would find it all out, and have him in prison. She continued with the niceties and small talk.

"Oh yes, Director Amber, Mr. Furst of the Miami Trumpet. This will be such a momentous occasion; a testament to your hard work in seeing this initiative come to fruition and many others, that I invited Mr. Furst to have exclusive coverage. You know Director Amber, Mr. Furst has the largest readership in Florida and a good part of the southern US, not to mention that his column is syndicated over fifty newspapers throughout the US. He does have millions of readers. Your name Director Amber, I am sure will be a key credit to events that are about to unfold here today and tomorrow." Kimberley finished saying.

"Well Mr. Furst, nice meeting you, I have read your column once or twice, I'm sure you will do justice to our treaty, Ms. Ashton, Mr. Furst." Amber moved on.

Kimberley had noticed that Rickover was already here, she nodded to him as he walked around. Everything was in place. Rickover confirmed that. Farnsworth was scheduled to fly in with President Fenton tomorrow for the official signing. Kimberley also noticed Cyril Burgess of the NSA, he too was already here. She wasn't on an acquaintance basis with Cyril Burgess, so she let him alone.

Kimberley mingled a little sipping on a glass of white wine, smiling as she walked. She knew a few of the local government officials, the PM's cabinet members and some of the island's dignitaries.

Prime Minister Bishop, tapped on the microphone, set up at a podium.

“Dear friends and guests,” everyone turned to see Bishop starting in on his welcome speech.

Kimberley looked at her watch; it was 2:28, Eldon and Billy would be coming in a couple of minutes. She slowly started backing away and making her way slowly not to draw attention and moved farther and farther away from the crowd.

Furst was someplace in the crowd trying to get a glimpse at Bishop. Kimberley finally eased herself out of the residence, got into her vehicle supplied by Secretary Rickover, and quietly drove off, leaving Furst behind, and heading to the airfield at the base where Eldon's jet was on the tarmac. She'd be back to the plane within ten minutes.

Alvarez was fuming mad, acting and thrashing about like a wild animal. The Marines finally restrained him. They brought Domingo back to the base. The commander placed a hood over Alvarez, as Billy had requested of Secretary Rickover. Billy saw that the hood was on Alvarez when the commander pulled him out of the Humvee and handed him over to Billy. Billy and Eldon and the Commander, forced Alvarez into the Chopper that Kimberley had arranged through Rickover, for Billy.

Alvarez was sitting in the chopper, hands behind his back cuffed, ankles cuffed. Billy rotated the chopper blades, signaled to the Marine

Commander that all was good, gave him the thumbs up and lifted off the ground.

Eldon, sitting across from Alvarez, reached out and pulled the hood off Alvarez's head. Alvarez's eyes almost popped out of his head.

Eldon asked him. "do you know who I am?"

"Yeah, you're the pig Garretty should have killed, and spat into Eldon's face."

"You had my daughter kidnapped, and my wife killed, and now you're gonna pay."

Domingo tried, but to no avail, Eldon wasn't going listen to his hollow excuses.

"I never had your lady killed Gringo; that was never supposed to go down."

Alvarez's plea fell on deaf ears.

"No maybe not, but because of you, you piece of cockroach shit, my wife is dead. We suffered greatly because of you, and people died because of you and today it's your turn. But you're going to be famous along with a whole group of your buddies."

Eldon reached into his pocket withdrawing a sealed plastic envelope. It was addressed to Damond Furst.

He then reached for the roll of duct tape in the chopper. With Alvarez having his arms behind his back and wrists handcuffed and legs shackled, he placed the envelope onto the side of Alvarez's head and wrapped the duct tape around Domingo's head securing the envelope in place.

Everything the world would need to know about Bishop, Alvarez and Amber was about to be discovered by Damond Furst of The Miami Trumpet.

Eldon had no doubt, Damond would trumpet this nationwide. Domingo looked like he was ready, and so was Eldon.

Eldon went up front to sit with Billy and buckled in. He left Alvarez sitting and bouncing around on the seat with both sides of the chopper's doors open. He left the hood off Alvarez.

Billy was now just a minute out from being over the Garden Party. He brought the chopper above the crowd and over the huge pond next to where the guests were gathered.

Bishop's microphone fell silent; he too was looking up at the chopper.

Vic Amber was stunned, his drink fell out of his hand, and his jaw dropped looking up into the clear blue Grenada sky, at the incoming helicopter.

Then coming in fast, and with Eldon being buckled in tightly; Billy said, "hold on tight, here we go."

Billy flew in close to the ground, suddenly putting the chopper into his barrel roll maneuver above The Prime Minister's garden party and directly over the shallow pond. With his hands being cuffed behind his back, and the top half of his head wrapped around with duct tape securing the envelope addressed to Furst, Alvarez came flying out of the chopper's side door.

Everyone at the Garden party shrieked, looking up seeing a person ejected from out of the helicopter.

Ladies ran screaming, people running around like ants. Alvarez fell with force into the shallow pond, splashing water over those who were still close enough.

The chopper Billy was flying was one without markings, it was anonymous. The crowd gathered back together, stunned at what just happened.

Bishop didn't know what to do; he was about to have a heart attack. Bishop had his government militia guards at his house, but they were more like ushers.

They came running and pulled Alvarez out from the pond. The Ambulance was called, but it would take a while for it to arrive. Lucky for Alvarez that Billy dumped him out over the pond. He was injured but alive; there was no need for the ambulance to rush. Furst had his story. Kimberley was certain everything would come out; Furst would see to it.

Kimberley arrived at the airfield, just as Eldon and Billy had landed the chopper. She drove straight up to Eldon's Jet; the stairs were down, and she went up into the plane.

Eldon and Billy transferred to Eldon's plane, and Billy had the Canadair's turbines turning, within a minute. Eldon and Kimberley buckled in; Billy taxied to the runway, and they were in the air not five minutes after dropping Alvarez off.

They were heading back home.

It was done, it was completed.

Eldon sat back in his seat, Kimberley sitting next to him.

When Billy reached cruising speed and altitude, Kimberley and Eldon unbuckled. She moved closer to him and snuggled up next to him.

He put his arm around her. She laid her head on his chest, reached over taking hold of his hand. Eldon bent down and kissed the top of her head, “it's over Kimberley, it's over.”

She looked up at Eldon with her big beautiful eyes, and said, “yes Eldon, it's over, but we're not, and kissed his cheek.

“We're just beginning,” she said to him. He held her tight with caring. Billy flew the jet back to Paradise.

Rickover found Amber, walked up to him and said, “Vic, what was it you were saying about you being a "doer" the other day? Looks to me like you done did yourself in.

I'd stop doing if I were you," and with that Rickover walked out and left the garden party.

"Island Hop had become a Belly Flop," Rickover thought to himself as he walked to his car chuckling.

***

Chapter Thirty

Blood Dice

Holiday Jewel Casino was hopping tonight, slots were busy, lots of players. At the blackjack tables, most of the seats were occupied, and the hotel was completely sold out.

It was February. The winter cold on the east coast of the US had the sun worshipers heading to the islands. There were even some early March Breakers.

The Sultan's yacht was still anchored in the harbor, and he was anchored to the craps table for the next few minutes till his ten-minute time limit was up.

Bernard Pinder was working the craps table. The crowd had gathered behind the Sultan filling in three; four deep, everyone was excited to see the Sultan come to play.

This game was the Sultan's least favorite game next to the big wheel.

Sultan placed his chips in front of himself into the chip trough. He pulled out two chips, put down forty grand. This was to be his first toss of the dice.

He looked around the table, found a pretty lady to blow good luck onto his dice. He shook, he tossed, and the blood dice rolled.

"Snake eyes, you lose."

The End

BLOOD DICE

Dedicated in loving memory

to

my mother and father

Izabella and Frank

I love you both forever

***

Additional books by

Frank Julius

Sequel

to

BLOOD DICE

THE RED JEWEL

THE RED JEWEL has Eldon Davis expanding his hotel and casino empire into the newly formed Russian Federation. Spurred on by the emerging democracy of the former communist regime, Eldon Davis's Holiday Jewel Hotels tackle his most challenging set of circumstances yet in operating with integrity, while having to deal with The Russian Mafia. Follow Eldon Davis as he takes on his enemies while bringing the world to Moscow through his vision, determination and ingenious solutions to crimes of the century.
A very riveting read of world-class luxury, murder, corruption, sex, violence and service beyond the guest's expectations. THE RED JEWEL tells the story of the hotel business in the new Russian frontier as you've never known it before.

MOSAIC LIFE TILES

Moving and Provocative Autobiographic Anthology :1

Mosaic Life Tiles is Frank Julius's second book.

This autobiographic book takes an inside look at the travels and life's experience in the seven countries where Frank Julius has lived.

He takes the reader on a ride that sees him escaping Communism from Hungary as a child but then going full circle in his career path that leads him to Russia, and his countless exploits along the way.

Upcoming works in the works

MOSAIC LIFE SQUARES

MOVING AND PROVOCATIVE – ANTHOLOGY: 2

Picks up where Mosaic Life Tiles ended.

Frank Julius follows up with volume 2 of life's experiences. Mosaic Life Squares takes the reader along with travels and adventures in the hospitality industry and other interesting, moving, juicy and colorful squares.